ANTHONY

That was the name the nuns gave the naked and squalling newborn child they found abandoned at their convent gate. They knew nothing of his past, of the star-crossed lovers who were his parents nor of the violent events which made him an orphan.

Playing his solitary games at the fountain in the convent courtyard, the child grew. He did not know enough of the outside world even to dream of the voyages and adventures that would be his nor of the women who would love him.

Only the statue of madonna that was left with him at the convent gate knew the story of his past, shared his thoughts and his prayers and would be witness to the extraordinary life that would come to

ANTHONY ADVERSE

Books In This Series
by Hervey Allen

Anthony Adverse Part One: The Roots of the Tree
Anthony Adverse Part Two: The Other Bronze Boy
Anthony Adverse Part Three: The Lonely Twin

Published by
WARNER BOOKS

ANTHONY ADVERSE

PART ONE

The Roots
of the Tree

Anthony Adverse

PART ONE

The Roots of the Tree

by
Hervey Allen

Decorations by
Allan McNab

WARNER BOOKS

A Warner Communications Company

ANTHONY ADVERSE

WARNER BOOKS EDITION

ISBN 0-446-81439-3

This Warner Books Edition is published by
arrangement with Holt, Rinehart and Winston

Cover art by Jim Dietz

Warner Books, Inc., 75 Rockefeller Plaza, New York, N.Y. 10019

W A Warner Communications Company

Printed in the United States of America

Not associated with Warner Press, Inc. of Anderson, Indiana

First Printing: January, 1978

10 9 8 7 6 5 4 3 2 1

"*There is something in us that can be without us, and will be after us, though indeed it hath no history of what it was before us, and cannot tell how it entered into us.*"

—Sir Thomas Browne.

To
Edna Allen Rickmers

CONTENTS

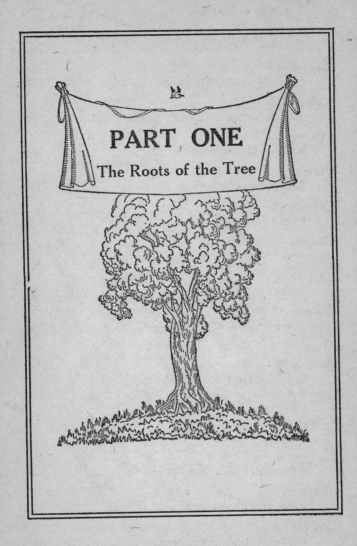

PART ONE

The Roots of the Tree

BOOK ONE

In Which the Seed Falls
in the Enchanted
Forest

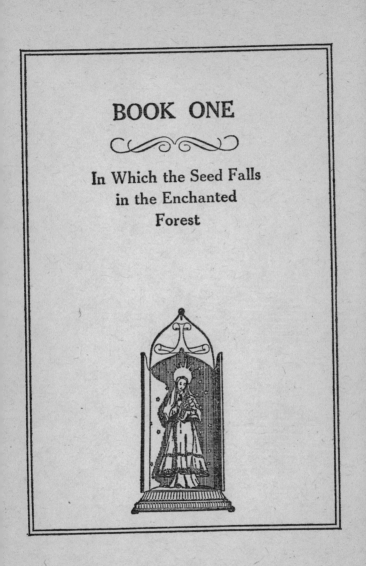

Chapter One

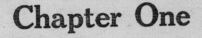

The Coach

BETWEEN the village of Aubière and Romagnat in the ancient Province of Auvergne there is an old road that comes suddenly over the top of a high hill. To stand south of this ridge looking up at the highway flowing over the skyline is to receive one of those irrefutable impressions from landscape which requires more than a philosopher to explain. In this case it is undoubtedly, for some reason, one of exalted expectation.

From the deep notch in the hillcrest where the road first appears, to the bottom of the valley below it, the fields seem to sweep down hastily for the express purpose of widening out and waiting by the way. From the low hills for a considerable distance about, the stone farm buildings all happen to face toward it, and although most of them have stood thus for centuries their expressions of curiosity remain unaltered.

Somewhat to the east the hill of Gergovia thrusts its head into the sky, and continuously stares toward the notch as if speculating whether Celtic pedlars,

Roman legionaries, Franks, crusaders, or cavaliers will raise the dust there.

In fact in whatever direction a man may look in this particular vicinity his eyes are led inevitably by the seductive tracery of the skyline to the most interesting point in all that countryside, the place where the road surmounts the hill. Almost anything might appear there suddenly against the empty sky, fix itself upon the memory, and then move on to an unknown destination.

Perhaps the high hill of Gergovia where heroic events have taken place in the remote past now misses a certain epic grandeur in the rhythms of mankind. For ages past tribes have ceased to migrate and armies to march over the highway it looks down upon. Cavalcades, or companies of pilgrims have rarely been seen upon it for some centuries now. Individual wayfaring has long been the rule. Even by the last quarter of the eighteenth century it had long been apparent what the best way of traveling the roads of this world is when one has a definite, personal object in view. Such, indeed, was then the state of society that the approach of a single individual, if he happened to belong to a certain class, might cause as much consternation to a whole countryside as the advance of a hostile army.

It was this condition of affairs, no doubt, that accounted for the alarm upon the faces of several peasants as they stood waiting uneasily in the late afternoon sunshine one spring day in the year 1775. They were gazing apprehensively at the deep notch in the hill just above them where the road, which they had been mending, surmounted the ridge. Indeed, a grinding sound of wheels from the farther side of the crest had already reached the ears of the keenest some moments before.

Presently there was the loud crack of a whip, the shouts of a postilion, and the heads of two horses made their appearance prick-eared against the sky. The off-leader, for there were evidently more horses behind, was ridden by a squat-bodied little man with abnormally short legs. A broad-brimmed felt hat with the

18

flap turned up in front served, even at considerable distance, to accentuate under its dingy green cockade an unusual breadth of countenance. The ridge at the apex is very steep. The first team had already begun to descend before immediately behind it appeared the second straining hard against the breast straps. Then the coach, a "V"-shaped body with the powdered heads of two footmen in cocked hats peering over its slightly curved roof, outlined itself sharply in the bright notch of the road and seemed for an instant to pause there.

As soon as it hove in full sight a babble of relieved exclamation arose from the group of watching peasants. It was *not* the coach of M. de Besance.

As to whose coach it might be, there was small time for speculation. The problem rapidly began to solve itself. The coach was heavy and the hill was steep. Suddenly, at a cry from the little postilion, who began to use his whip like a demon, the horses stretched themselves out. An immense cloud of dust arose and foamed about the wheels.

The black body of the coach was now seen coming down the road like a log over a waterfall. Oaths, cries, shouts from the white-faced footmen, the squall and moan of brakes, and a frantic drumming of hoofs accompanied its descent. Four horses and the carriage flashed as one object through the spray of a little stream at the foot of the hill. There was a nautical pitch as the vehicle mounted violently upon a brief length of causeway that led to the ford. But so great was the momentum which it had accumulated and the terror of the horses that the postilion was unable to check them even with the attempted assistance of the peasants.

A large hole full of water on one side of the little causeway now became horribly apparent to him. With a quick jerk on the bridle and a firm hand the clever little driver dragged his horses around it. The front wheels missed it by a fraction. But there had not been time to turn the trick entirely. For an instant the left hind wheel hung spinning. Then to the accompaniment of a shrill feminine scream from the interior of the

19

coach it sank with a sickening jar and gravelly crunch into the very centre of the pit. Nevertheless, the rear of the carriage finally rose to the level of the causeway as the horses once more struggled forward. A high water mark showed itself upon the yellow stockings of the petrified footmen. The coach lurched again violently, rocked, and stopped.

Scarcely had the coach body ceased to oscillate in its slings when from the window projected a claret-coloured face surmounted by a travel-stained wig much awry. A hand like a lion's paw flourished a gold-headed cane furiously, and from the mouth of its entirely masculine owner which vent can only be described as grim, proceeded in a series of staccato barks and lion-like roars a masterpiece of Spanish profanity. It began with God the Father and ranged through the remainder of the Trinity. It touched upon the apostles, not omitting Judas; skipped sulphurously through a score or two of saints, and ended with a few choked bellows caused by twinges of violent pain on Santiago of Compostela. During the entire period of this soul-shaking address, and for several speechless seconds after, a small, intensely black, forked beard continued to flicker like an adder's tongue through the haze of words surrounding it. Somewhat exhausted, its owner now paused.

Those who thought his vocabulary exhausted, however, were sadly mistaken.

The gentleman looking out of the coach window owned estates both in Spain and in Italy. From both he drew copious revenues not only of rents but of idiom. He was of mixed Irish, Spanish, and Tuscan ancestry, and his fluency was even thrice enhanced. He now gripped his cane more firmly and lapsed into Italian.

"You mule's bastard," roared he, twisting his head around with an obvious grin of pain to address the little man sitting astride the lead horse, "Come here, I say. Come here till I break your back. I'll . . ." The rest was cut short by a second grimace of agony and a whistling sound from the cane.

The recipient of this alluring invitation climbed down from his saddle rather slowly, but with no

20

further signs of hesitation walked imperturbably past his four quivering horses toward the door of the coach. His legs, which already appeared small when astride a horse, were now seen to be shorter than ever and crooked. Yet he moved with a certain feline motion that was somehow memorable. As he turned to face the door of the coach and removed his cocked hat, two tufts of mouse-coloured hair just over his ears, and a long, black whip thrust through his belt till it projected out of his coat tails behind, completed for the peasants, who were now crowding as close as they dared, the illusion that they were looking, not at a man, but at an animal vaguely familiar.

The door of the coach was now pushed open by the gold-headed cane revealing to those by the roadside a glimpse of the sumptuous interior of a nobleman's private carriage. Its owner had been riding with his back to the horses. As the door opened wider a long, white object projecting across the aisle toward the rear disclosed itself as a human leg disguised by a plethora of bandages and resting upon a "T"-shaped stand contrived out of a couple of varnished boards. On this couch the ill member with its swathed foot seemed to repose like a mummy. On the rear seat could be caught a glimpse of a brocaded skirt the folds of which remained motionless.

The claret-coloured face now appeared again and the cane was once more flourished as if about to descend upon the back of the unfortunate postilion waiting hat in hand just beyond its reach. But the gentleman had now reached the limit of his field of action. He was the owner of the mummified limb on the "T"-shaped stand, a fact of which he was just then agonizingly reminded, and a torrent of several languages that seemed to start at his waist literally leapt out of his mouth.

To the surprise of all but the footmen, who were thoroughly inured to such scenes, the little man in the road ventured to reply. He purred in a soft Spanish patois accompanied by gestures that provided a perfect pantomime. Due to his eloquent motions towards the peasants in the ditch and the hole in the road, it was not necessary to understand his dialect in order to follow his argument. With this the gentleman, who had meanwhile violently jerked his wig back into place, seemed inclined to agree.

Seeing how things were going, a tall fellow somewhat more intelligent than his companions now stepped forward.

"It is to be hoped that monsieur will overlook the existence of the terrible hole which has caused him such discomfort . . ."

"Overlook its existence, you scoundrel, when it nearly bumped me into purgatory!" roared the gentleman. "What do you mean?"

"Ah, if we had only known monsieur was coming this way so soon it should have been filled in before this. It is very difficult now to get these rascals to come to the corvée. We were informed you would not arrive until day after tomorrow. I can tell you, sir," continued he, turning an eye on his miserable companions which they did not seem to appreciate, "I can tell you they were just now in a fine sweat when they heard monsieur's coach ascending the hill. If it had been that of M. le Comte de Besance . . . oh, if it had been M. le Comte himself!"

"M. de Besance? Ah, then we are already upon his estates!" interrupted the gentleman in the coach. "Do you hear that, my dear?" Seemingly placated, and as if the incident were drawing to a close, he began to close the door. Noticing the crest on the outside panel for the first time, the man by the road licked his lips and hastened to correct himself.

"But yes, monseigneur," he gasped, "the Château de Besance is scarcely half an hour's drive. One goes as far as the cross-roads at Romagnat and then turns to the left by the little wood. And the road from here on monseigneur will find in excellent shape. For a week now we have laboured upon it even in wheat sowing time."

Mollified at finding himself so near the end of a long

and painful journey the gentleman's face relaxed somewhat from its unrelenting scowl. A few pale blotches began to appear through its hitherto uniform tint of scarlet. Encouraged by this the unfortunate bailiff essayed further.

"By special order we have smoothed the road from Romagnat for the illustrious guest expected at the château; but not until day after tomorrow." Here he bowed. "Yet an hour later and this accursèd hole would have been filled. A little more willingness on the part of these"—a grim smile of understanding on the face of the nobleman here transported the bailiff—"a little more skill on the part of monseigneur's coachman . . ."

Scarcely had these words left the man's mouth, however, before a hail of rocks and mud set him dodging and dancing. The small postilion who had all this time been waiting in the road hat in hand was galvanized into instant action. On all fours, he dashed about snatching up every clod and stone that came ready to his paws. The whip flickered tail-like over his back, his grey-green eyes blazed brilliantly, and he spat and squalled out a stream of curses that might have done credit to his master. One of the peasants began to mutter something about the evil eye, and all began to draw back from the coach.

"Are we all right?" shouted the master to his footmen.

"Yes, Your Excellency," they replied as if with one voice.

"Drive on then, Sancho, you devil's cat," roared the gentleman now grinning with enjoyment at the grotesque scene before him and with satisfaction at finding that neither his leg nor his coach was irreparably damaged.

But at the word "cat" the little postilion fairly bounded into the air. His hair seemed to stand on end. Those outside the coach appeared to be fascinated. They continued to stand and stare until with an impatient gesture the gentleman on the inside pulled a tasselled cord. A small bell hung in a yoke on the roof

23

tinkled musically, and the horses long accustomed to the signal moved forward.

Finding himself about to be left alone on the high-road in a hopeless minority, the postilion with a final snarl turned, picked up his hat, clapped it on his head, and in a series of panther-like leaps, for his legs were far too short to run, gained the lead horse already some yards ahead and vaulted into the saddle.

"A cat! A cat!" shrieked the peasants. The four horses broke into a trot, and the coach and its passengers rocked and rolled along the road that had been so carefully "smoothed" to the Château de Besance.

But rumour preceded it in the person of a peasant runner who took a short cut across the fields. The servants at the château were warned of the unexpectedly sudden approach of visitors. Even before the coach reached the cross-roads at Romagnat that entire village was agog. For nothing except scandal spreads so fast as an apt nickname. The two indeed are frequently related, and in this case as long as he remained in that part of Auvergne Don Luis Guzman Sotoymer y O'Connell, conde de Azuaga in Estremadura, Marquis da Vincitata in Tuscany, and Envoy Extraordinary to the Court of France from that grand duchy, was invariably associated with his feline postilion, Sancho, and referred to over the entire countryside as Monsieur le Marquis de Carabas and his cat.

Compared with the surface of the royal highway the recently smoothed road upon the estates of M. de Besance was as a calm harbour to the Bay of Biscay. Both Don Luis and his leg thus began to experience considerable benefit from the comparative ease with which the coach now rolled along. The end of a ten days' journey from Versailles was almost in sight, and the marquis began to contemplate the bandages in the vicinity of his big toe—from which only a faint, blue light now seemed to emanate—if not with entire satisfaction at least with considerable relief. As he did so his eyes happened to stray past his carefully cherished foot into the deep recess formed by the rear seat, thus

24

serving to remind him of what he was at times somewhat prone to forget.

The ample rear seat of the coach upholstered in a
smooth velvet of a light rose colour was deep enough
to form, with its painted side panels and the arched roof
above it, what seemed from the front seat, where the
marquis was now leaning back, to be a deep alcove.
Sunk in the luxurious cushions of the seat, and reclining
against the back of the coach with her head directly
under an oval window was what appeared to be the
body of a young girl scarcely eighteen years of age.
Her form was completely relaxed. Her long sensitive
hands, upon one finger of which was a wedding ring,
lay with startling and web-like whiteness against the
rose of the cushions. Two waxen arms disappeared at
the elbows into the folds of a grey silk travelling scarf
wrapped about her shoulders like a Vigée-Lebrun
drapery. She sat with one leg crossed over the other
so that her skirt, stiffly brocaded in a heavy heliotrope
and gold pattern, fell in a sharp-edged fold that might
have been moulded in porcelain to one white-slippered
foot.

Used as he was to an almost selfless yielding in his
girl-wife which constantly expressed itself in his presence in her relaxed physical attitudes, there was, as he
now looked at her across the aisle of the coach, something in her posture which caused Don Luis to glance
hastily and uneasily at her face. Her small, rather
neat head lay drooped to one side. Since Bourges,
which they had left hastily after the death of her maid
by plague, she had been unable to accomplish an
elaborate powdered coiffure. Consequently her own
hair of a pure saffron colour seldom seen in the south
of Europe, burst, rather than was combed back, into a
high Grecian knot held precariously by one gold-
knobbed pin. Across her wide, clear forehead, above
carefully pencilled and minutely pointed arcs of eyebrows, and blowing out from the temples before and
around two finely chiselled ears, sprang a delightful
hedge of ringlets and tiny silken wires. These in the rays

of the western sun, which darted now and again through the oval window behind, were touched along with a thousand dust motes that danced in the semi-darkness of the coach, into a sudden blaze and aura of golden glory. A straight nose, and a rather small, pursed mouth, whose corners were nevertheless drawn out enough to be turned down toward an obstinate little chin, completed a countenance with a bisque complexion like that of a miniature. It needed only that the eyes should be wide open and staring directly at you out of the shadows to give the impression that you were actually in the presence of some dream-like and helpless doll. But her eyes were now closed, or almost so. As her husband looked at them with their long, brown lashes disclosing only a blue polished glimmer of the pupils beneath, while the lids remained perfectly motionless, it calmly occurred to him that she might have fainted.

Yet this realization even when it became a certainty did not suggest to Don Luis any necessity for immediate action. Before everything else the marquis was a connoisseur, an appreciator of rare and accidental patterns of beauty in nature, and of their successful imitation or creation in art. The picture before him was a combination of both. The wide-flung frame of the upholstered seat, the delicate rose-leaf tint of the background, the perspective of the alcove, and the unusual arrangement of its lights and shadows were, so it happened, in exact harmony with the central and somewhat tragic figure of the portrait. There was even a high light in precisely the proper place, for a large emerald breast pin concentrated the stray beams of sunlight and deflected them in a living grey-green shaft across the folds of the girl's scarf.

Don Luis was delighted. For the time being he felt that his condescension and his trouble in marrying this young woman had been rewarded. And where had he seen that exact arrangement of head-dress and feature, accidental to be sure, but quite purely classic in effect? Ah, it was on a coin of Faustina; or was it Theodora?

Perhaps a combination of both. One's mind played tricks like that. His artistic imagination no doubt! Yes, there was something a little Byzantine here, and yet quite Grecian behind with the knot, of course. Well, he would look again in that cabinet in the Pitti next time he was in Florence. He knew the exact spot where it stood. Just next to that vile medallion by Guido. . . . But a slight trembling of his wife's eyelids reminded him that some more direct attenton to the subject of so admirable a reverie was now in order.

"Maria," said he, leaning forward and feeling along her arms as if she were a doll whose limbs might have been accidentally broken, "listen, I am speaking to you."

Recalled thus from somewhere else by a command not to be disregarded, she slowly opened her eyes, wide, and very blue, upon him. Scarcely had full consciousness returned to her look before she hastened to disengage her arms from his grasp and to whisper, "Better now. It was that last jolt. I was sure we should all be killed. I prayed to her all the way down the hill. I dreamed that I was with her now." A haze suffused itself over her eyes as if she had been looking at the little hills of a child's paradise with the morning mist still gathered upon them.

For a moment he remained silent. There was one crack, however, in his otherwise turtle-like armour. Glancing toward a statuette of the Madonna, which at his wife's entreaty had been set in a niche in the side of the coach, he crossed himself fervently. The upholstery had been cut away to allow the insertion of this figure and its little shrine, and for some time he kept his eyes fixed in its direction with an expression at once conventionally pious and fearfully sincere. Only a boyhood in Spain could have achieved it. But while it lasted and his lips moved, the girl remained still. A look of mixed jealousy and chagrin as if she were loath to share some personal possession with him hardened her eyes and brought her chin a little farther forward while his devotions went on. At last, seeing that his gaze had shifted to the window again, she ventured to ask, "What happened?"

"Nothing," said he. The coach rolled on a short distance.

Settling back he pulled up a square flap in the cushion and produced from a locker in the seat a bottle and a small, silver travelling mug. "Nothing, fortunately," he repeated, "but drink this and you will soon feel better. Shall I tell you now? It was a deep hole in the road. A few minutes later and it would have been filled. No doubt it did jar you badly sitting directly over the wheel, but the coach of monseigneur is undoubtedly a good one. We shall not be delayed."

Without spilling any of the wine which he offered her, she managed to sip it down and wipe the scarlet stain from her lips with a wisp of a handkerchief. Seeing how steady were her hands, Don Luis congratulated her and proceeded to follow up his panacea for all earthly ills, as he put the bottle back in the seat, with a little cheering chat.

"It is really too bad that both of the mishaps of the journey have fallen upon you, my dear," said he, wiping his own lips. "I could complain to M. de Besance about this last one and make it lively for those lazy peasants. He is said to prefer the high justice to the low, but it is not quite so easy in these disturbing times to take the high hand as it used to be. Hanging or driving away a tenant is not to be thought of nowadays, especially when one's luck at cards has been of the sorriest. They say some of these fellows in the country are getting impatient at sending all their rents to Versailles. The fields here look in condition though," he exclaimed, "fine, well-tilled acres!"

She nodded wearily.

"So they didn't expect us so soon," he chuckled, "otherwise that hole would not have 'existed.' Well, Sancho paid them back in their own loose dirt." He proceeded to relate the incident, at which she succeeded in smiling faintly.

"No, we are decidedly beforehand with them. If you

had not insisted on delaying at Bourges to be sure that maid would die, we might have been here two days sooner. That delay was a sheer waste of time. Oh! it has been difficult with your hair, I am sure. But do you know I admire you as you are. There is a certain classic air about you. They told me you were quite the rage at the Petit Trianon in a milkmaid's smock. It was really clever of you to manage that. To be commanded to the dairy by the queen herself, twice!"

A slight tinge of colour began to suffuse her cheeks.

"Still you should never have let them find out that you really did know how to milk," he went on. "That was a faux pas, a decidedly peculiar accomplishment for the wife of an envoy extraordinary. It is not real simplicity they want. You should have merely pretended to be learning rapidly. But to have finished milking before Madame! It was fatal! I can tell you our stock dropped after that. I felt like M. Law himself. If it had not been for my luck in the Œil-de-Bœuf and that night at de Guémené's soirée we should have been nowhere, nowhere at all. Even the mission might have failed. But when I won M. d'Orléans' new coach from him at écarté, and drove off in it with the lilies on the door! Ha! That was something, even if one's wife did know how to milk." He looked at her, stroking his beard with satisfaction.

The coach rolled on while the shadows deepened. In the depths of the seat he could not see the tears in the eyes of his young wife. The world outside glimmered before her.

A red ray of sunset dashed itself against the rose-coloured cushions and glanced into the shimmering pools of her eyes. Reflected there she saw the Palace of Love at the Petit Trianon; the torchlight on the pool before it. A dust mote became a boat gliding past in the red glow. Ghosts of music began to sound in her ears. The trees whispered outside like the park forest.

Suddenly the vision became intensely clear. Up the little steps of the temple sprang a young soldier in a white and gold uniform. He was putting roses on the

29

altar before the god of love. She leaned forward now to see his face—and found herself gazing directly into the eyes of her husband.

His lips parted slowly in a competely self-possessed smile. She gasped slightly. The vision had been so clear! She was almost afraid he must have seen it, too. But Don Luis was not given to visions. The gouty leg had unaccountably stopped pulsing and its owner now felt inclined to talk.

"M. le Comte de Besance did not come off so well in his bets with me either." His smile widened. "Five hundred louis against my living on his estates till my leg is cured! All of these fellows are so sure of their provincial springs. No one can dispute with them. It is like arguing with a country priest about a local miracle. Por Dios, how he leered over that fine hand he held. I almost believe he wanted to lose just to have me try his spa. Else how could he have played so ill? So I shall take my time here. It is due my good luck. And I like the air already. None the less that there are no handsome Irish captains of the guard to breathe it. Mark that! O'Connell was my great-grandfather's name. That is all the Irish you will get. We shall say no more about that fellow, but"—and he leaned forward clutching her knee—"*remember!*"

Having delivered this ultimatum he sat back again for some time in silence. At last one of the footmen absent-mindedly began to drum upon the roof. "Leave off that," roared his master. Outside the man snatched his hand back as if he had suddenly found it resting on a hot stove. Don Luis continued.

"You can rest here and forget all about it. They say the Château de Besance is a pleasant enough place. The last M. de Besance but one spent some time in Italy and even journeyed to see the Grand Turk. The rugs are said to be remarkable, and there are some good Venetian pieces. Besides, the place is not too large to be comfortable. I shall get you another maid, somehow, and you can indulge your cursed English taste for driving about the country."

"Scotch, you mean," the girl said softly, "my father . . ."

"It is all the same," said he, a little impatient at the interruption. "Doubtless there is a small carriage in the count's stables. But no jaunting about in peasants' carts! That was bad enough at Livorno when you were a girl. Remember!"

He had an unpleasant way of trilling the phrase in Italian, an accent that might have accompanied a sneer. She always felt it and winced. Yet seldom was he so talkative or so amiable as now. Despite an occasional sardonic fall in his tones, without which he could scarcely have expressed himself, for the first time in her married life of about a year he was verging upon the affable. Sensing the state of his feelings as well as their ephemeral nature, she decided to pick flowers while the sun shone.

"At the château—could I have a dog?" she asked. Her quick reading of the human barometer and her instant grasp of opportunity tickled his shrewd fancy. In the mood he was in he consented with an ease that astonished himself.

"At the château, yes. But it must not come into the coach. I will not be having the cushions made for royalty itself ruined."

She laughed. The very thought of a companion who could give and receive affection revived her. Leaning forward she looked out of the window and let the breeze play on her forehead. They were just approaching a village.

Presently the coach and four wheeled sharply around a well-curb at the forks of the road. A weather-beaten cross stood above the town fountain, and the usual crowd of women drawing water at that time of day put their pitchers down or slipped the bucket yokes from their shoulders at the sound of horses. Almost everyone in the village who could find an excuse to be away, and there were few who could not, stood waiting to stare curiously but silently at the coach. The only sound was the *clopping* of hoofs and the occasional snarl of the more vicious village curs carefully held back from barking. Dogs which barked at guests on the estates of M. le Comte de Besance invariably failed to return to their owners.

"To the château?" cried Sancho, drawing up and flourishing his whip.

One of the horses began to crane its neck and sniff toward the fountain. The crowd gaped and began to murmur something among themselves about a cat. "But, yes, certainly, a cat!" There seemed a humorous difference of opinion. Sancho began to jabber. The bell on the top of the coach tapped twice with unusual emphasis, and he swung the horses to the left.

"That fool!" exclaimed the marquis, "he would stop at every village well to start a brawl. An end must be put to that! If he fights with everyone who howls 'cat' after him between here and the Alps, I shall be needing a new coachman long before we get to Italy. Besides, the man does look like a cat! You can see, my love, it would never do to have a dog in the coach with Puss-in-Boots on the box, never!" Don Luis actually leaned out of the window and laughed at his own joke. In town he would never have thought of doing so. It was the first time she had ever heard him laugh heartily and something in the tone of it startled her.

They were ascending a long rise now between a pleasant park-like wood on one side and a carefully pruned vineyard on the other. A few bunches of grapes, smaller than berries as yet, showed here and there. An all but imperceptible perfume was in the air. Maria breathed deeply and lay back with her eyes closed. The scent was delightfully familiar, suggestive even in its intangibility, and she allowed herself, as she relaxed into the cushions, the unexpected boon of indulging to the full an overpowering illusion that she was returning home.

After all, perhaps the Château de Besance might have its compensations. She would play that she was coming home anyway. It would make the arrival at another strange place more bearable. The faint tinge of colour brightened in her cheeks. Even the illusion made her heart beat faster.

Her husband was looking out over the vineyards, wide and peculiarly mellow in the last, long rays of full daylight. If only that countenance with its pointed beard, the cheeks forever a dark wine colour, the hard black eyes, and the mouth like a trap,—if only *he* were not here now to spoil her dream! A small breeze blowing across the aisle of the coach fanned her cheeks and brought a more pungent whiff as of the vineyards about Livorno. Shutting her eyes tight she breathed more deeply, then she turned away from him and opened them wide.

From the little niche in the side of the coach the madonna was looking at her. The girl began to pray to her silently. The face of the Virgin was very familiar. The little statuette was the one memento which she had been allowed to keep that still reminded her of home. Her lips moved imperceptibly, her nostrils widened to the breeze, her eyes remained fixed upon the face of the statue. For a few wretched and blessed moments she was back again in her own room in her father's house.

Don Luis had no idea of what was going on in his wife's mind. He saw that she was praying and that seemed natural enough. But he did not care how, when, where, or to what a woman prayed. Just now he was nowhere in particular himself. His leg had stopped hurting and left him pleasantly vacant of mind; in an easy, almost garrulous mood. He leaned out of the window still farther and noticed they were nearly at the top of the hill. Hadn't the bailiff in charge of the peasants said the château was just over the top of the rise? The memory of that unfortunate fleeing in a hail of mud again caused Don Luis to laugh aloud.

The little postilion turned about in his saddle and looked back at his master. An amused grin spread from his whiskers along his jaws. A knowing wink passed between the master and his man. Just then the horses began to descend.

33

"What can you see ahead?" shouted the marquis.

But the reply of the postilion was lost in the sudden grinding of brakes.

Chapter Two

The Little Madonna

THE peasants working on the corvée of M. de Besance had just completed filling the hole in the causeway and were gathering up their tools to depart for a well-earned night's rest, when the sound of galloping hoofs once more fell upon their ears.

There was a short cessation of the sound. Then without any further warning a man mounted on a spirited bay horse darkened the notch at the top of the hill. Picking his way rapidly down the steep slope, he splashed at a sharp clip through the ford and cantered onto the causeway. A certain military precision lurked in the folds of a blue cloak that fell from his shoulders in trim, straight lines. As he came opposite the group of peasants he reined up his horse sharply, and at the first glance as if his judgment was seldom at a loss, picked out the bailiff in charge of the work although the man's clothes were still bespattered by the dirt with which his friend the postilion had recently favoured him. The stranger beckoned to him, but somewhat suspicious from his recent experience the man hesitated to step forward as smartly as before. Nor did two large pistols in the holsters of a military saddle, and the brass clover of a rapier scabbard projecting below the newcomer's riding cloak add to the bailiff's sense of self-possession.

"Come here," said the horseman, seeing how matters stood, in a voice that was not to be denied. With some visible hesitation the bailiff advanced.

"Have you seen a gentleman on a black gelding pass this way recently?"

"No, sir, he has not come by this road," replied the man.

The stranger's horse refreshed from its recent plunge in the ford danced about uneasily and pawed the dust. "*Ha*, Solange, you witch you, *ho*, girl!" he cried, reining her about in a semi-circle with a sure hand and bringing her back again as he called over one shoulder, "How do you know that?"

"Because, monsieur," replied his informant, "we have been working here all day and no one has passed southward except the coach of monsieur . . . pardon, I mean monseigneur, the guest of M. le Comte."

"Monseigneur!" said the stranger raising his eyebrows. "Why do you say that?"

"The crest, sir, the lilies were on the door!"

"Are you sure of it?"

"Am I likely to forget it? Dieu! am I not covered from head to foot by the filth which that devil, his cat of a postilion, threw at me. Look!" and the bailiff turned to exhibit the state of his back.

He was immediately struck by another missile, but this time of a more welcome kind. As he stooped to pick up the coin, he saw the limb of the mare suddenly gathered under her as she felt the spur. By the time he had picked up the money and bitten it, both horse and rider were fifty yards away.

"Monsieur is in a hurry," he muttered, as he pocketed the piece and prepared to go home.

It was easy enough to follow the coach. In the newly smoothed highway the broad wheel tracks of the great vehicle were as plainly to be seen as if it had just been driven over a field of virgin snow. Yet the coach itself was nowhere visible. Behind the top of a little rise above the village the stranger dismounted and made sure of this before urging his mount onto the level open ground below. He was about to gallop on when a low cloud of dust at the top of a hill across the valley caught his eye.

The coach was just emerging from a patch of woodland and going over the skyline. From where he stood he could even see someone lean from the window to speak to the postilion while the latter turned in his saddle to reply. Then the whole equipage disappeared over the ridge.

Clapping spurs to his horse the stranger galloped down the road, leaped over a low hedge, and taking an open short cut across some meadows, found himself in a trice back on the road again. The village, which he had thus avoided, lay between the highways at the "V" of the cross-roads, and he was now passing rapidly uphill with a wood on one hand and vineyards on the other. Just short of the hillcrest he again dismounted suddenly and threw the reins over the mare's neck. She stood patiently, precisely where she had been left. Muffling his cloak well about him, he strode rapidly forward a few yards, stooping low. He then left the road, and taking shelter behind a convenient shrub, looked down into the valley beyond.

Before him lay a low valley, a wide, cultivated landscape stretching away in the softly brilliant afterglow of a French sunset. In the foreground was the park of Besance. A statue gleamed here and there amid the wide-armed trees like an ivory high light. The road wound through the groves in a vague "S"-shaped curve up to the château itself, an old building with candle snuffer towers. But there was a new wing in front, with high arched renaissance windows and a row of conical trees in tubs. It was one of those minor Versailles which during the last two reigns had sprung up all over Europe. As he watched, a fountain began to play on the terrace and the downstairs windows gleamed with a saffron light as someone flitted from room to room lighting chandeliers. The coach now emerged from between a wall of hedges, made the half-circle before the entrance, and drew up before the door. In the lens-like air, as the footmen leaped to let down the steps, he could even see their brass buttons. After some little delay the coach moved out and trotted around to the rear.

A scene of considerable bustle was now revealed on the steps of the château. Four lackeys bearing a man with a white object that stuck out straight before him were swaying up the stairs, marshalled by a bustling major-domo. A woman stood waiting for them at the top while various bags and valises in charge of other servants disappeared through the door. Even at that distance he could still make out the peculiar heliotrope shade of her skirt, and that she was carrying something in her hand. "By God!" said he in English, and with an emotion so violent that it found vent in immediate action. With a determined and almost desperate gesture he plucked a handful of leaves off the bush which concealed him, and scattered them angrily.

The four men bearing their human burden now began to shuffle on the last ascent to the door. Evidently what they had in hand was no light matter. At the very top someone stumbled. The whole group began to sway perilously. Then, as the invalid's cane began to play over their heads and along their backs viciously, they fairly precipitated themselves into the gaping mouth of the door. Only the woman now remained, apparently looking out over the landscape where the shadows were beginning to gather. In the excitement attending the entrance of the baggage and the gentlemen it seemed as if she stood there forgotten.

The watcher behind the bush had never hoped for such a stroke of good fortune. She might have been looking directly at him. With a deft bound he gained a large rock that stood squarely upon the crest behind which he had been hiding. He held his cloak out wide, and tossed it. Then he began to caper and wave his hat.

For a moment the little figure on the steps stood as if transfixed. Then she too threw out her arms wildly and began to wave whatever it was she was holding in her hands. For a few seconds these mutual signals continued. Then the woman turned suddenly and hurried into the house. To the man standing on the rock it seemed as though she had taken the daylight with her.

He instantly recovered himself, however, and hurried downhill to his horse. A glow far more lasting than his exercise on the rock could have produced suffused him. He felt bursting with good nature and kindliness. Plucking some small bunches of grass he rubbed down the mare, and fondled her soft nose. The grass was next applied to a pair of long, very fine military boots. A finely worked handkerchief flicked the dust from a cocked hat whence, to judge by the shading, a braid-edging and cockade had recently been removed. The stranger as if from mere military habit then looked at the priming of his pistols, tightened the girth, and patting his horse affectionately but heartily on the flank, sprang into the saddle and trotted off at a brisk pace toward the village.

In the great hall of the Château de Besance Don Luis sat under a chandelier, propped up in a huge chair nursing his leg. The pain of having been let down upon it did not subside for some time. Immediately upon being brought in he had done full justice to the occasion, and his shattered malacca cane that lay beside him on the parqueterie was a mute witness that the man who stumbled would have good reason to recollect his misfortune. No one, indeed, had escaped wholly. Even Maria upon suddenly hastening in to help him had been ordered to let his bandages alone. He told her to go upstairs and dress for dinner, in a way which made even the servants wince. Not that the marquis had been impolite. It was merely his tone. There was a crushing viciousness in it which made his young wife's solicitude wilt like a flower caught in the cloven hoof of a bull. In her agitation she had all but fled the room, leaving the little object which she had been carrying like a favourite doll lying forgotten upon a near-by table.

The major-domo of M. de Besance was wondering

how he could fill the place of the caned lackey whose arm would be useless for a week. Well, he would have to wait upon the table himself. Monsieur was undoubtedly a hard case, and perhaps it would be better to take no chances. M. de Besance had sent strict orders for the careful entertainment of these guests. The accident was terrible! He must make amends for it. He glanced at the face of the sufferer. A restorative perhaps, something unusual. He bowed and retired, to return presently with a small, squat, greenish-black bottle.

The marquis' expression changed. He watched the cork-drawing with the eye of an expert and could find nothing at which to cavil. The man's precise mixture of art and ritual was impeccable. A divine odour as of a basket of fresh, ripe peaches left in the sun filled the room. With good care and a steady hand the butler decanted the upper inch of the liquid into a glass that had been carefully wiped, and handed it to Don Luis. The latter inhaled the bouquet and a look of understanding passed between the two men. It was an occasion.

"Of the year of Malplaquet, Your Excellency," said the man bowing.

The marquis drank slowly. Old toper as he was he was scarcely prepared for the surcharged flavour. It would have been cloying had it not been accompanied by the fiery glow that might have made a salamander start. The marquis just succeeded in not choking, and finished the glass. His eyes shone. He was surprised that such a beverage existed. It was worth having come from Paris just to sniff the bouquet. A genial glow miraculously combined with a delightful languor swam through his veins. His leg ceased to stab. When the mist of pain and the dullness of fatigue cleared from his eyes as though someone had washed a dusty window, he saw that he was seated in an apartment furnished with an exquisite but somewhat outmoded taste.

"Monsieur need not move," said the butler. He lit a fire of resinous wood which instantly began to crackle and throw lambent shadows about the brass andirons and white marble mantelpiece where two satyrs grinned at each other through a tracery of leaves and grapes.

It was not the first nobleman the old servant had treated for the gout with brandy. The great thing to do was to keep them still. "Hot water and a valet will be here instantly, Your Excellency. You shall be made comfortable." He covered the bottom of the glass again. "Supper will also be served here, and I shall have an apartment prepared for monsieur on the ground floor. The stairs are unnecessary. I did not know of His Excellency's affliction or the chamber on this floor should have been ready upon his arrival. Another accident for monsieur is unthinkable! The new room will take some few moments. After dinner it will be ready. Monsieur can retire then, if he desires, without going upstairs."

The man waited without seeming to do so for a sign of approval. Don Luis knew when he was being well served. A major-domo of the old school was rare in this degenerate reign. He raised his hand in a gesture of assent and let it fall back to the stem of his glass. The man retired. His queue, the precisely horizontal bow, and every line of his back were at once respectful and correct. As he turned to close the door silently he saw the guest of his master sitting dreamfully with his nose poised like a beak just over the rim of the glass. In his eyes there was an expression of great content.

Don Luis finished the rest of the peach brandy and sat gazing into the fire. Below the waist he seemed to have vanished. One of those rare moments of heightened consciousness and clear vision was upon him. He felt himself to be all eyes. The combination of spirits and fatigue had been precisely right. Without moving his head he permitted his glance to wander about the room. It passed with keen relish from one stately bit to another and finally came to rest on the object which his wife had left on the table. It was the little Madonna which she had carried from the coach to take to her room. In the state that he was in, his hands reached for it somewhat mechanically. For the first time he began to examine it closely, dreamfully.

It was very old, evidently the work of several dis-

tinct and widely separated historical epochs. He turned
the little shrine in which the figure stood to and fro.
The shrine itself was certainly ancient Byzantine work.
No Gothic artist could have conceived those wide, flat
arches at the top. What a vast dome had been conveyed
in-little by that curious, buttressed hood over the
Virgin's head! And that sky and those stars! Don Luis
grunted and took out a small pocket glass. The secret
of that heavenly blue must have been lost.

The figure, though small, was posed with immense
dignity against a background of night. With some fusing
of sepia, cobalt, and ebony the artist had contrived to
convey that living blue of heaven on a summer evening
which opens out through vast antres of atmosphere to
the milky shimmer of stars beyond. Spread out and
over this, like the far and near points in a crushed net,
was a galaxy of golden stars. These, as he moved them
to a better perspective, scintillated with the true zodiacal
fire. In the top of the dome he was delighted to recognize the arrangement of the constellation Virgo, and
to note, as he brought them closer again, a light dash
of silver in the rays of what would otherwise have been
too yellow a fire. The consummate brushwork of some
painter upon ceramics had wrought that. In some mysterious way the whole background had been given a
universal lustre which by reverberated reflections all
but cancelled out the shadow of the figure that stood
before it. "It was a cunning device," thought Don Luis.
He looked more closely. "By heaven, it was glaze!"

From this sea of stars the face of the Virgin swam
up to him somehow vaguely familiar. It was as if he had
seen it in life. Or, was it a kind of universal human
memory?—something learned so far back in childhood,
perhaps from the face of his mother, or before, that
it had been consciously forgotten? The expression of
the features was so deeply brooding, and yet so universal, that it had produced in him that distinct and un-
placeable sensation of having often seen them somewhere else. Those clear brows, those wide-open eyes,
the slightly distended nostrils and the archaic smile;
there was a hint of something sphinx-like, yes, distinctly

Egyptian about it. And yet the poise of the head was Greek. He was at a loss at first to place it. Now he looked more closely at the stiff, jewelled robe.

It was made of small pieces of coloured stones with a glint of a jewel-chip here and there. It was set with seed pearls about the hems, and ennobled with a gilt pattern of some papyrus-like plant. Florentine mosaic work before the grand dukes, early Medici! He could also see it was attached to the statue by minute, extended silver wires; a new coat given to her by some pious owner long ago. It rose out and away from her body, to fall lower down into a stiff, jewelled skirt such as medieval royalties once wore. He could even see behind the robe, for it stood out from her like a herald's tabard. Beneath the bodice her breasts sloped down in pointed ovals that suggested sleep, and dreaming there, in utter peace, held in the crook of her arm was the infant. He thought of Dionysius on the arm of Apollo at first. And yet, as he peered again, almost fearfully now, since the thing had become so real, there was something too intimate and tender about this child in its mother's arms to be pagan. No, it was undoubtedly the Christ-child on Mary's breast. It must have been modelled in Alexandria an age ago, the statue itself. It would have taken a Christian born a pagan to have done it, an Egyptian Greek, some artist who could combine various old gods and humanity into something new; something old but something new.

It had always been a theory of the marquis that it is in the miniature masterpieces, those which can be put into a glass cabinet, that the arts of civilization culminate. First come your gigantic architecture and your monoliths; then something more human, more livable, realism, perhaps, gradually becoming beautifully conventional; then medallions, engravings, miniatures, cameos, and statuettes. And here was a nice illustration of the thing, he liked to think. He stroked his beard.

In Byzantium this single shrine would have been part of a triptych. He could still see that the right side of it had once fitted on to something else. He put it back

43

on the table and slipped the glass into his pocket. The gilded sun-burst, that almost imperial sun-crown upon the head of the Virgin; that had Constantinople written all over it. Some devout Arian had once owned it. He leaned back and let his imagination supply the two missing panels:—God the Father most elevated in the middle, on one side of Him the dove descending out of the clouds from the Father's bosom, on the other the little shrine he held in his hands. The triptych was perfect again. How easily he had restored it! But was it necessary?

This shrine he actually held—why, it alone represented the entire Trinity and humanity, too! The cosmos for that matter; there were the stars. Had not the Holy Ghost descended upon the woman? The Son of God and man in her arms. And the Father?—why *He* was there by necessary implication, invisible as always, but the creator of all. How huge, how universal was this little symbol he could hold in one hand. For a moment he was humble before it. He came as near to worship as he could. Then his natural pride reasserted itself. His logical and theological mind laughed in his skull to think that out of that Arian triptych only this remained. How literal and how elaborate was heresy! The other panels had been unnecessary. Only the Catholic symbol was required and everything essential was there. Ah, a nice point! Something even the Jansenists could scarcely refute. A fit subject for a monograph.

And yet artistically *was* the statue perfect? Weren't those fluted mother-of-pearl inlays about her feet a little tawdry; about 1700, no doubt. But no, narrow your eyes and you could see the eternal stars mirrored in them. She was standing before the universe at the pearly gates. Seventeen centuries had contrived to make something perfect. Don Luis conferred upon them the greatest compliment of his own. Drawing a small gold box from his waistcoat he sprung back the lid, tapped his fingers lightly in a kind of salutation, and took a large pinch of snuff.

The resulting sneeze so startled a valet who had just

44

entered the room that the marquis laughed. It would never do to have all these servants afraid of him. Fear could make an antelope awkward. The marquis bade the man good evening and began to ask questions about the château. Presently the valet was at his ease and the work of revamping Don Luis proceeded comfortably enough. A small silver basin filled with hot water served to refresh him as, with the wig and cravat removed, a warm sponge was passed over his shaven head and neck. He soaked his hands in the water. A fresh, lace jabot was then wound about his neck and the frill carefully made to stand out from his shirt. A larger and more comfortable bag wig was taken out of its box and slipped onto his head. It was scarcely necessary to use the brush at all, and the bow on the queue was kept clean of powder. To Don Luis that was the test. No whisking off afterward! He preferred to beat servants rather than be beaten by them, if it came to that. A small dash of verbena on his handkerchief, and with the cushions carefully, even solicitously rearranged on the leg stand by the butler himself, the marquis felt at home, ready for dinner in fact.

The man threw a few more logs on the fire, drew up a table before Don Luis, carefully avoiding his bandaged limb, and began to lay covers for two. The napery was ivory-smooth, the candles were carefully shaded, and the plate was not only good but positively inviting. "If the chef can do the appointments justice," thought Don Luis, "I am prepared to be convinced that M. de Besance was not merely trying to cure his homesickness by a vicarious visit in my person to his ancestral halls." He preferred to remain cynical, however. Nevertheless the variety and nice arrangement of the wine glasses tended to confirm the claims of his absent host. The butler now lit a small lamp under a brazier and announced that dinner was ready when madame should be announced. "Tell her," said the marquis.

The logs crackled in the grate and in some distant part of the house a clock began to chime. The room was a large one. The table was set under the last chandelier next to the fireplace. The candlelight from the sconces and chandeliers reflected themselves and their crystals with long splashes of yellow light on the polished floor. As Maria entered the apartment from the opposite door, it seemed to her that the little table was at an immense distance. The silver and glass twinkled upon it like stars caught in a fleecy cloud, and over the edge of it, looking like the moon itself, shone the scarlet face of her husband. To a light splashing of silk she seemed to float to him over the lake of the floor in her wide panniered skirts, moving her feet invisibly like those of a swan. "Madame la Marquise." The man with the injured arm should have been at the door to announce. With some well-concealed embarrassment the butler also hastened forward to seat her.

"Bravo, my dear," said her husband, "such a toilette in so short a time is a marvel! You know the lamentable reason which keeps me from rising to the occasion." To her relief she saw him smile. She began to talk rather hastily.

"I have a maid, a woman from Fontanovo, that M. de Besance sent here some days ago. You cannot imagine how pleasant it is to hear Tuscan again. It is almost as welcome as English." She checked herself and coloured deeply. The marquis overlooked the reference to home.

"While we were in Paris I thought it best to use nothing but French, but we can now speak Italian," said he, changing into that tongue. "It is certainly charming of M. de Besance to have sent an Italian maid, probably one of his household he picked up while in Florence recently."

"She is returning to Italy and hopes to go back with us."

"Ah, that explains it then. But not altogether. Besance has been the best of fellows. Paris would have been quite a different place without him. That little journey of congratulation to the Duchess of Parma— I was able to help him with that, and we were compatible. It is not often one makes such a friend after forty. Do you suppose he would really have turned his château over to us on a bet at cards? No, he is genuinely anxious to see me cured, and his enthusiasm about the waters at Royat was really catching. I hear of many cures there, too. By the way," said he turning to the man, "Henri? Jacques?"

"Pierre, Your Excellency."

"Pierre, then. How far it is to the baths?"

"About an hour's drive, monsieur, by way of Clermont. And there is, if monsieur desires to stay overnight, an excellent inn."

The prospect seemed to cheer Don Luis greatly. Since some time before his marriage his leg had kept him little better than an invalid, and a round of high living at Paris and Versailles was not calculated to help the gout. The very thought of getting rid of his discomfort and being active again made him feel like rising from his chair then and there. Indeed, for the first time in his life the state of his health had for a year past caused him to give it some thought.

Newly married to the daughter of a Scotch merchant of Leghorn who had some vague Jacobean claim to nobility, the marquis had from the first been swept off his feet by the strange beauty of the young girl who now sat across the table from him. He had first seen her, accidentally, while settling a matter of business at her father's establishment. As he happened to be the owner of the buildings in which her father's concern did business, it was not difficult for him to find the way of gaining a swift consent to his suit. That is not to say that the marquis' method of approach was crass; on the contrary, it was adroit.

The good merchant was a widower up in years and anxious to see his only child well and securely bestowed. To that end a very considerable dowry was her portion. In fact, the old man was prepared to embarrass himself, and did so. Although Don Luis was a quarter of a century older than his bride, still in the eyes of the world, and to her father, the match had seemed a fortunate one. The marquis condescended, no doubt, but the dowry was worth stooping for, and to do him justice, in his own way Don Luis loved the girl. He held wide fiefs from both the Grand Duke of Tuscany and the Crown of Spain, and was much employed in delicate diplomatic affairs from time to time. To Maria's father in particular the marquis had seemed like a god from the machine come to snatch his daughter back to the high Olympus of court life to which in some sort she belonged. From that realm an invincible attachment to the unfortunate house of Stuart on the part of her ancestors and her father's consequent necessitous lapse into trade had effectually banished her.

The girl herself had been too young and inexperienced to realize the full implications of what her father pressed upon her in the most favourable light. Even her maid, a girl about her own age, and her one human confidante, had abetted the scheme as a wise young woman should. There had been no one else to turn to but the little Madonna. From her she received comfort but no advice. The girl's heart had continued to shiver in a premonitory way at the sight of her prospective husband. But obedience and love for her father, who she knew parted with her only because he thought he was setting her feet upon a fortunate path, sealed her lips. Yet dutiful as she was, even after her marriage there was one thing for which she could not bring herself to pray. It was for the restoration of her husband's health. The thought of physical contact, the mere touch of his hand, indeed, turned her to stone.

With Don Luis it was far, far otherwise. He had in one sense been starved for some time, and his touch was therefore too hungry to note anything but its own temperature. Yet he had deliberately starved himself. For if he was in love with his wife, he was also in love with himself, and that self was possessed of an enormous sense of the ludicrous. In the rôle of husband and lover he saw himself, not young and handsome—for he was too wise and too candid to suppose the opposite

48

of what his own mirror disclosed—but forceful; not to
be denied; a master of life upon important occasions
and possessed of some dignity withal. A man of the
world, he had no illusion about bed-time intimacies.
There was only one way to maintain a manly dignity
there. Hence he did not intend to approach his marriage
bed for the first time on crutches, with a bandaged
foot and debilitated—lights or no lights. Besides it
might be painful. The thought of it made him grin and
wince at the same time. He was anxious for an heir,
too. But so far he had deferred to circumstances.

The meal continued. The potage paysan might have
been a bit flat but the rye bread in it had been toasted
and imparted that nut-like flavour in which the marquis
delighted. A dish of trout in butter, a mushroom patty,
an endive salad with chives, together with some excellent wines from the count's cellar composed a light
meal for which Pierre apologized profusely. A fresh
cheese cool from the spring house, and a firm, white
loaf caught in a silver clamp provided with a small
steel saw in the shape of a dragon's head with teeth
amused Maria.

By the time the marquis had sampled his host's
liqueurs he was prepared to remain all summer. No
doubt the cure *would* take that long. He was tired after
Paris anyway. He rattled on about his recovery. "Have
the coach ready at nine o'clock tomorrow. Tell that
man of mine," said he to Pierre, "and don't allow him
anything but table wine tonight. I shall go to the
springs first thing in the morning. My dear, I shall
soon be well! I feel sure of it. A man you have not yet
met in fact!" He looked across the shaded candles at
his wife eagerly.

Her eyes opened wide and the colour left her cheeks.
She felt like one trying to thrust off a nightmare. Then
the vision of the figure waving to her from the rocks
came to comfort her. Watching her closely, her husband leaned back and laughed. Certain visions also
flashed across his mind. He had never seen her look so
well. It would all be well enough shortly. The child

might come in the spring, after they were in Florence. That would fill her life for her, and bind her to him. He need not worry about cavaliers after that. Not that the young Irishman at Versailles would ordinarily have caused him a second thought. A beautiful, young wife would have admirers, of course. But under the circumstances! No, it had been just as well to leave a little sooner. He was a dashing fellow and the uniform of the guard was a handsome one. It was better not to put too much strain on a young girl's sense of duty. He looked at her again. Her eyes had wandered past him and her lips were moving. Following her glance he saw that her gaze was fixed on the Madonna still standing on a near-by table. She looked up again a bit startled.

"You forgot her when you went upstairs, you know. I was examining her while you were dressing. She is quite a precious work of art. Where did you get her, by the way? Let me see her again."

She rose obediently and brought the figure in its little shrine to him. He put down his glass and took the relic in his hands.

"Where did you say you got her?"

"From my maid at home. It had been in her family for a long time. She was a Scotch girl."

"Scotch!" said he, "this at least did not come from Scotland."

"Her father was Greek or of a Greek strain at least, a Greco-Florentine. His name was Paleologus."

"What a strange combination," he smiled. "I remember her now, I think. She wanted to come along with you."

"Yes, Faith Paleologus." She turned the syllables over in her mouth as if they were somehow unpleasantly reminiscent.

"Did you ever notice this, Maria?" he asked, turning the statue sideways. Taking a knife he pointed behind the mosaic work.

It had never occurred to her to look under the Virgin's robe. She had always thought of it as part of her. Following the glittering point of the knife she now saw

50

the little silver wires holding the stiff dress out from the statue like a herald's tabard. Underneath was the figure of a naked woman with a child at her breast! Small jewelled lights glinting through the tiny bits of glass and chips of gems in her robe played upon the shadows and curves of her exquisite body. But the knife was pointing coldly at a fracture. At some remote time the statue had evidently been broken off below the knees and mended again cunningly. To the mind of the young girl, who was scarcely more than an idolator, the whole thing came as a shock. With a gasp she reached down, took the Madonna from her husband's hands, and as if the knife threatened it, caught it to her breast as though it were alive.

"Be careful," he said. But she crushed it the harder. A look of extreme happiness glimmered on her face. Then suddenly becoming aware of him again she stiffened.

"You are tired," said he, "take a good rest. I shall be leaving early tomorrow for the springs. You will have the whole day at the château to yourself. Why not arrange for a drive? That new maid can go with you." Taking her free hand he kissed it and looked up at her. The hand fell back into place. "Good night, Maria."

She recollected herself and swept him a curtsy. The shrine remained cuddled in her arms like a doll. Like a doll she carried it from the room and turning just at the door looked at him. With a little movement almost fierce in its intensity she clasped her precious thing even closer and disappeared up the stairs. "What a child she is," thought he, "what a child!" He looked around. The bell-pull on the wall was too far to reach. He struck a goblet with a knife. Pierre appeared.

"Bed," said the marquis, "and mind how you get me there!"

The man disappeared. He returned a few moments later with two sturdy assistants carrying long poles. These were lashed securely under Don Luis' chair. Placing themselves between the ends of the staffs before and behind, the men lifted the burden easily and in this improvised sedan he was carried out of the room. Pierre, holding a lighted candelabrum above his head, led the way.

The marquis smiled grimly. He saw himself proceeding down the marble hall like a Roman consul. No, it was like a bridegroom carried to his chamber with the torch before him. The fancy tickled him. There was something in the omen he liked. He seated himself upon his bed with some difficulty and began with the tenderest solicitude to unwrap the bandages from his foot. The valet with equal care aided him to remove his clothes, then the wig.

Presently a shaggy, powerful man with a closely shaved head, a thick chest, one swollen foot and large stubby hands was seen sitting on the edge of the bed. The candlelight glittered on his scalp. He slipped a long flannel sack over his head. It fell in folds about his waist. He tied on a night-cap and had a small calf-bound volume brought him as he settled himself, not without grievances, in the huge bed. The valet arranged the light. "At what hour, monsieur?" "Eight," replied the marquis in a far-away voice. The man bowed and retired. The marquis read on:

Now, my masters, you have heard a beginning of the horrific history of Pantagruel. You shall have the rest, and then you shall see how Panurge was married, and made a cuckold within a month of his wedding. How Pantagruel found out the philosopher's stone, the manner how he found it, and the way to use it. How he passed over the Caspian mountains, and how he sailed through the Atlantick sea, defeated the cannibals, and conquered the isle of Perles. How he fought against the devil, ransacked the great black chamber and threw Proserpine in the fire. How he visited the regions of the moon, and a thousand other little merriments. All veritable. These are brave things truly. Good night gentlemen. . . .

Upstairs the light from his wife's bedroom turned her window that looked toward the village into a bright yellow square.

Chapter Three

At the "Golden Sheaf"

FROM the rock on the hill where the stranger had exchanged signals with Maria to the village below it was nearly a mile. The mare at that time of the evening expected oats not far ahead and needed no urging. Indeed, as he rode into the little town of Romagnat her rider was forced to pull her up at the cross-roads with a firm rein. She stamped impatiently and pretended to shy at the grey figure of an old woman drawing water in the twilight. He heard the bucket splash in the well. It was supper time and the streets appeared deserted. Except for a few lights here and there and an occasional murmur of voices or cry of a child he might have been alone. The bucket now reappeared on the well and the woman turned toward him.

"Can you tell me, mother," said he, "where the inn is?"

"It is there, monsieur," she replied, pointing toward a dim light at the end of the street leading back in the general direction of the château, "at the lantern, where the door is opening now." Some distance up the hill a glow of firelight flooded out and vanished. "But the great hostel is at Clermont about a league from here," continued the old woman hoping for a reward.

"Thank you, I am only wanting supper." He automatically fumbled in his pocket, but then thought better of it. The less cause for being remembered the better. His disappointed informant disappeared, and he turned toward the light.

It was a dim and smoky one hung under what at first appeared to be a suspended mass of rubbish, but as he drew closer this resolved itself into a sheaf of wheat tied over a sign. *La Gerbe d'Or* could still be faintly traced in faded characters as the lantern swung gently to and fro. He stood for a moment studying the building and its surroundings carefully like an old campaigner, then he turned through a low brick archway and rode into the courtyard of the inn. The delighted whinny of the mare brought out an ostler.

"Send me your master, my lad, and be quick about it!"

The man in the door, munching a large sponge-like fragment of black bread, took a look at the long, lithe figure on the horse and disappeared. A few moments later he came back with a lantern and a round, shiny-faced little man in a white apron.

"I want a room for the night and supper," said the horseman.

"Certainly, if monsieur will descend, the request is not *very* unusual."

The face of the clown with the lantern began to prepare itself for a laugh at the stranger's expense.

"Come here, my host," said the man on the horse who did not show any intention as yet of descending. Somewhat abashed the fat man came and stood by the saddle. The horseman now leaned over and began to talk in low impressive tones. He was an adept at assuming that confidential air which by taking one into a secret both flatters and impresses. The boor with the

lantern had not been included and to the innkeeper
he represented the gaping world.

"Look, my friend," said the gentleman dismounting
and bringing an ardent and commanding countenance
close to that of the round-faced man, "I am here on
the king's business, and I do not want the world to
hear of it. Do you understand?" A small, yellow coin
with the countenance of the king upon it passed host-
ward between them. A convulsive grasp of the fingers
and a look of understanding were simultaneous. "Yes,
monsieur," whispered the fat man like a conspirator.

"Well then," said the gentleman, "can you give me
a room and serve my supper in it quickly without having
half the village in to gape at me? And how about your
wife's tongue?"

"I will serve you supper myself, monsieur, and my
poor wife's tongue has been silent these two years."
The fat man choked. The stranger laid his hand upon
his host's shoulder. "She is in heaven, my friend," said
he, "never doubt!"

"Ah, monsieur, you are very kind, but I am sure
of it. Come this way and you shall have what you
want. It shall be the private chamber upstairs. Here,
François, give me your lantern and get the other from
the settle." Unlocking a narrow door that opened into
the court the innkeeper led the way.

They ascended a circular stone stairway and came out
into a small, blunt hall. The host rattled his keys again
and presently threw open a door, standing aside for
his guest to enter. The room ran clear across the house.
On one side was a window looking out upon the court
and on the other a long, leaded casement through
which penetrated a faint glow from the street. The fat
man advanced and opening the lantern took out the
candle and kindled the fire. A bright blaze sprang up
from a pile of dry faggots revealing a low apartment
with ceiling beams, a high four-poster bed in the corner,
a table, two chests, and several chairs. On the rough
mortar wall was a black crucifix immediately over the
bed, and on the chimney a faded print of what had

once been meant for a likeness of "Louis the Well-Beloved"—some fifty years before. The host looked at his guest inquiringly.

"Excellent," said the latter.

"It was our own room before my wife died," continued the fat man lighting the sconces, "I sleep downstairs now to keep an eye on the servants. I hope monsieur will find himself comfortable. Supper will be served directly."

"The sooner the better," replied his guest. "Have that ostler bring up my saddle and bags, and see that my horse gets a full measure. No drenched chaff, mind you. A good rub-down, too. But send the man up to me."

The fat man bustled out puffing with importance. It was some time since he had had a guest who did not haggle over terms. Presently the ostler was heard ascending the stairs. His ungainly form filled the door of the room as he deposited the saddle and its heavy bags on the floor with a bump.

"Look out for the pistols, François," said the gentleman.

The man stared blankly.

"In the holsters, you know, you had better unstrap them."

The man did so, bringing them gingerly to the table and laying them down carefully. The weight of the weapons and the silver crown on the flaps filled him with awe for their possessor. The gentleman, very tall and straight, now stood before the fireplace and was holding aside his cloak to warm himself thus revealing a long rapier with a plain brass hilt. His eyes glittered with a hard steel-blue under a mass of brown curls that had escaped from the bow and queue in which he had in vain attempted to confine them. A long, straight nose with thin, quivering nostrils over a firm bow of a mouth and a stronger chin completed a countenance which with extraordinary mobility could flash from an expression of grim determination to one of extreme charm. He appeared to be about thirty years old.

"Take good care of the mare, 'Solange.' She answers to that. Fill her nose-bag full, she will not eat from a strange manger. Mind she doesn't nip you, but rub her down, and make a good deep bed."

"Yes, monsieur," said the man, "Maître Henri has already told me."

"Do it, then!" snapped out the gentleman. He snapped him a coin which fell onto the floor. The man groped for it and stood up to find himself even nearer to the stranger whose nostrils expanded. He fumbled for his cap which he had forgotten. He took it off.

"And François."

"Yes, monsieur!"

"Do not come up here again, you bring the smell of the stable with you."

"No, monsieur," said the man letting his hands fall humbly with a ponderous despair as if he had been reminded of something fatal. Suddenly a smile of vivid brightness irradiated the face of the stranger. His white teeth seemed like a flash of sunshine in the light of which the heart of the man before him became happily warm as he stood clutching his cap in one hand and the piece of silver in the other.

"François," said the gentleman continuing to smile, "would you like to earn a piece like that again tomorrow?"

"But yes, monsieur," gasped the ostler.

"Then remember this, do not say a word to anyone about my being here. Nothing, you understand?" The face suddenly became grim again, "It might be dangerous!"

"Nothing, monsieur, nothing," but now the ostler was somehow again looking at the face with a smile on it. His own expanded into a loutish grin with snagged teeth left here and there in ponderous gums. An idea slowly hatched itself. "Monsieur," said he bowing like a mountain in pain, "has never arrived. I cannot remember him—even in my prayers!"

"Precisely," said the gentleman. "Go now."

A peal of boyish laughter followed him down the

stairs. "Whew!" said the gentleman, and threw open the window that looked into the street.

It was a clear starlit night. He could see for some little distance over a tract of open country beside the hill from which he had just ridden down. Far to the right the giant, sphinx-like curve of a demi-mountain shouldered itself into the constellations. In the valley shone the brilliant windows of the château. He drew a chair up and watched. She was taking supper there now. A look of longing came over his face. Then it suddenly turned white with fury. "With him!"

He sat for a while with an exceedingly grim expression in a reverie so absorbing that he temporarily lost all count of time. Gradually, as if he were dwelling on something more pleasant in the past or some bright hope of the future, a faint smile began to play about his lips. Even with this, however, the look of determination remained. Presently his host knocked and entered bearing a tray piled high with supper. The gentleman was hungry and peculiarly sensitive to odours, and the odour which now filled the room was highly satisfactory to both his nose and his appetite.

"It is the best I could do for monsieur at short notice," said the innkeeper.

He began to lay the table. A bowl of soup, a steaming ragout of rabbit and carrots, white rolls, and a bottle of wine discovered themselves.

"Excellent!" said the stranger, as he settled himself with evident satisfaction to the repast. "Indeed, I was prepared for something worse than this." He filled his glass and after a preliminary sip tossed it off without further doubt. Nevertheless, the innkeeper continued to stand before him clasping and unclasping his hands in the folds of his white apron in considerable perturbation.

"Excellent," repeated the gentleman, polishing off the soup and sampling the ragout. The man, however, continued as before. "Well?" said the gentleman, raising his eyebrows interrogatively but with a slight tinge of annoyance. "Oh, I see," and he reached for his purse, stretching his long legs out under the table to do so.

"No, no!" said the innkeeper deprecatingly. "Monsieur mistakes me. I have no doubt of his ability to pay —when he departs. It is this. It is the law that I must report the arrival and the names of strangers who stop here together with a declaration of their business to the mayor-postmaster. They must, in fact, show their papers within twelve hours. Otherwise I shall be heavily fined." Here his hands locked themselves underneath the apron. "The times are troubled ones, you know, monsieur, the roads . . ."

"Do you take me for a brigand?" demanded the gentleman with the stern look which he was able to assume instantly. "Besides, I have not yet been here twelve hours."

"Forgive me, monsieur, but it is not so simple as that," said his host. "My brother is the mayor-postmaster. He is even now downstairs and knows that you have arrived. He has seen supper brought to your room."

The stranger paused for a moment over his ragout while the flame of the two candles on the table continued to mount steadily. There was no expression whatever on his face now. His legs continued stretched out under the table in a nonchalant manner. Suddenly he drew them up under him determinedly, and leaning forward with a quizzical grin as though he anticipated something amusing, remarked, "Show him up."

"Monsieur will not come down? My brother, the postmaster . . ."

"Postmaster be damned!" snapped the gentleman. "Who do you think *I* am?"

With a deprecatory gesture, the innkeeper disappeared. There was the sound of a short colloquy downstairs, a door opened, and two pairs of heavy feet stumbled up the stairs. The gentleman addressed himself unconcernedly to his ragout. The footfalls came down the hall and ceased. The gentleman helped himself to a particularly savoury morsel, swallowed it slowly, and looked up as if his thoughts were elsewhere.

Standing in the door, with the broad, white expanse of the innkeeper behind him, was an almost equally rotund personage with a wide, stupidly cunning face. A huge cocked hat with a moth-eaten cockade was pressed down importantly upon his brow to which it managed to impart by wrinkling the rolls of fat a portentous and official frown. There was in the man's manner a combination of obsequiousness and truculence either of which was ready to triumph over the other as events might decide. To the gentleman at the table there was no doubt as to which attitude was going to win the day, however. His spurred boot shot out swiftly from beneath the cloth. Catching a chair deftly, he kicked it precisely into the middle of the room.

"Sit down," said he.

The man advanced somewhat gingerly and sat, only to find himself looking directly into the stranger's face. Seeing the latter eyeing his hat with surprise and disapproval, after an evident inward debate, he removed it and laid it on his fat knees.

"Monsieur, the innkeeper's brother, I believe," said the stranger looking at him with the ghost of a twinkle. "No one could doubt that at least."

"And the mayor-postmaster," began the little man puffing out his cheeks.

"How am I to be sure of *that?*" asked the stranger leaning back and looking at the man grimly. "Have you your documents with you?"

The pompous look upon the face of the astonished official collapsed from his cheeks as if they had been a child's balloon pricked by a pin. He squinted anxiously from his ferret eyes and began to feel his pocket dubiously. "Not *with* me," he admitted, still fumbling. Then his hands sank back onto his hat again. The situation was unprecedented. Already he was almost convinced that he was falsely impersonating himself.

"Extraordinary!" said the gentleman regarding him doubtfully.

"But, but, I *am* the mayor, the postmaster. All the village knows it! Is it not true, Henri?" he demanded appealing desperately to his brother.

"Indeed, monsieur, it is," replied the innkeeper. "The curé lives but a few doors above and can verify it. Surely . . ."

"Well, well," replied the stranger, "I am inclined to believe you." He raised a hand to deprecate the need of the curé.

"See," cried the mayor-postmaster with a flash of inspiration on his dull face, "here is my cockade!" He shifted his hat suddenly and turned that dingy mark of office toward his doubter. "Monsieur has been looking at the wrong side! He did not see the cockade when I entered."

"Ah, that *is* different," smiled the gentleman. "Can you blame me—when I was looking at the *wrong* side?"

"Certainly not, monsieur," both voices replied together.

"In that case I shall be glad to show my own papers." He reached in his pocket and drew out a long folded sheet. "You see," continued he frowning, "I always carry my identification about me. And it would be well," he added, fixing the flustered man before him with a cold stare while rapping the knuckles of his extended hand with the edge of the document, "if you would do the same when you demand the credentials of a military gentleman."

The shot went home. With a flushed face and far from steady hand the fat man took the extended paper. He unfolded it nervously and began to read. He was almost afraid to find whom he had offended.

It was a special leave of absence issued by the Minister of War and dated from Versailles permitting M. Denis Moore, subject of His Most Christian Majesty, captain-interpreter attached to the first regiment of the royal horseguard, to travel upon private affairs in all the kingdom of France during the space of four months. Upon the expiration of leave he was to report back for duty at Versailles. The script was in the beautiful, round hand of a clerk of the war office, yet the eyes of the mayor moved over it slowly while his lips spelled out the words. At the bottom of the document, however, much to his relief, he came upon a block of good solid print. There, along with such other exalted personages as the intendants of provinces and the mayors of cities, he thought he found himself included amongst "all loyal subjects of the king" as bound to render aid, protection and assistance to the said Captain Denis Moore in all his lawful designs whatsoever. Nor as an officer of the royal household was the captain to be hindered, taxed, prevented, or delayed in his going to and fro on pain of the explicit displeasure of the king himself. "And of this ye shall take good heed."

"It is the Minister of War," said the captain, pointing to a signature whose many flourishes the poor man was in vain trying to decipher. Face to face with the signature of so great a man as the Minister of War the mayor-postmaster felt himself to be something less than dust. He also felt himself in the distinguished presence of an unusual man. Under the circumstances, it would be best to waive the usual small fee for examination. No, he would say nothing about it! He folded the paper carefully and handed it back. "Monsieur the captain will excuse the interruption I hope," he said, preparing to leave the room with evident relief.

"Without doubt," said the captain, "but sit down. I have something further to consult about with you. Come in," said he to the innkeeper, "and kindly close the door. Can we be overheard?"

"By no one!"

"You will both understand," continued the captain, "that what I am about to say to you is the king's business and goes no further than this room." He glanced significantly at both of them. While their voluble reassurances continued to flow, he again unfolded the paper.

"You will note," said he, pointing to the line upon which the phrase occurred, "that I am on 'private business.' " The mayor nodded sagely. "Now follow me"—his finger ran on down the page—"and that you are 'bound to render aid, assistance, and protection.' It is that, monsieur the mayor, which I am now about to ask of you. Draw your chairs up closer while I explain." It was not long before the three heads were so close together over the table that a fly could scarcely have crawled between them.

In a lower voice than he had been using, and with that confidential air of being about to impart a matter of capital import, the captain continued. "There arrived today at the Château de Besance a certain gentleman, the Marquis da Vincitata. He is on his way back to Genoa. He was sent last year on a special diplomatic mission by the Grand Duke of Tuscany to the court of Versailles. The matter was one of such extreme importance that you will understand I cannot possibly discuss it with you at all."

The innkeeper was already too flattered at having been made a confidant in affairs of state even to attempt to reply. His brother, however, managed to gasp out a deprecatory noise at the very idea of a complete revelation, waving his fat hand as if to brush away so ridiculous a thought. Fearful that the swelling pomposity of the mayor might become apoplectic, the captain paused for a moment before he went on.

"The marquis has certain letters in his possession." He now lowered his voice to a whisper. "I am following him. It is my mission to obtain them, and it is in this that I shall require the assistance of you both as loyal subjects, but especially of you, monsieur the mayor."

"Certainly, in any way, but . . ."

"It will be quite simple. I have already taken the first steps to ingratiate myself with the marquis' wife. She is young and pretty, and he is old." A look of extreme knowingness and worldly wisdom appeared on the faces of both worthies as they gazed with open-mouthed admiration at the captain. Scarcely able to stifle his laughter he condescended to enlighten them further. "From her I have already learned that the marquis intends to linger here for some time while taking the waters at Royat. It is my hope before the gentleman is cured to persuade the lady . . ."

"To steal the papers," mumbled the mayor.

"Exactly," said the captain, actually patting him on the arm. "I see you are able to think quickly." The combined smiles of the delighted parties now seemed to illuminate the room.

"But to do that I must have a quiet place where I can stay, reasonably close to the château, and one—mind you—where the news of my being there will not leak out. One idle word carried to the ear of the marquis and the game is up. Do you understand? One word! —and can you help me?"

Confronted by his first problem in statecraft, the mayor sat thinking ponderously. One could almost hear the wheels turn. The innkeeper finally came to his assistance by whispering something in his ear.

"Why, the very thing, why didn't *I* think of it?" cried his brother. "The farm of Jacques Honneton! He is my brother-in-law, a widower, and his place is quite close to the château."

"Not too close?" inquired the captain.

"No, no, monsieur, about a mile or so. And you can be quite comfortable there."

"I shall, of course, be glad to pay liberally," interrupted the captain, "in a case of this kind the government . . . You can see," said he turning to the innkeeper, "that under the circumstances I cannot remain *here*."

"It will all be in the family anyway," said the innkeeper.

"And," said the captain taking the words out of his host's mouth and bringing his fist down on the table, "it must stay there! Men have been broken on the wheel for a slip of the tongue in a case like this. I remember . . ."

"Never fear, my captain," cried the mayor already white to the gills. "I will take it upon myself . . ."

"Then we understand each other thoroughly I take

it, and I can leave the arrangements at the farm with you." The captain inclined his head slightly, indicating that the interview was at an end. With the air of two conspirators upon whom the burden of portentous things rested heavily, the innkeeper and his brother the mayor-postmaster left the room. The latch clicked. Snatching the napkin up hastily the captain crammed it in his mouth. For some seconds what might have been mistaken for a choking noise escaped through the folds.

Rising after a few minutes, he blew out the supper candles, noticing with an amused smile that in the midst of the conspiracy the innkeeper had forgotten to remove the tray. "How dramatic even the simplest person can become," thought he. "The man has been completely transported by his new rôle." The captain wondered whether the dramatic sense was not on the whole a weakness in human nature. It depended on who produced the play, he supposed. "Now in the army your great generals . . ." He strolled over to the window again.

The lights in the lower story of the château were being extinguished. Finally only one remained. Suddenly a single upstairs window shone out brilliantly. The captain grinned. "Separate rooms, eh! No stairs for a one-legged man. Vive the gout!" His theory about the two lighted windows at opposite ends of the château pleased him immensely. "So the marquis imagined I was calmly going to be left behind at Versailles mounting guard. It will be much easier here with him away at the springs most of the day." He looked at the lights in the upper window again. A strong tremor shook him. "Maria," he cried between his teeth, "Maria!" If he could see her tonight! No, that would be mere folly. It might spoil all. If he could only send her a message, though. God! She was going to bed alone down there less than a mile away!

He leaned half-way out of the window and for some moments continued to fill his lungs with the cool spring air that was at once refreshing and provocative. A sensuous odour of vineyards in bloom came to his nostrils as a love song might have drifted to his ears. When he drew himself back into the room again the innkeeper was removing the remains of supper.

"Pardon, monsieur," said he, "I knocked, you did not answer, and I thought you had gone downstairs."

A sudden idea flashed across the captain's mind. This man must know some people at the château. "Could you get a message to the lady at the château, my friend?" he blurted out, "tonight!"

"Not tonight, mon capitaine, it is much too late, but early tomorrow morning without doubt. The cook's sister . . ."

"I do not care how, that is for you to settle. Only of this be sure. Employ no fools. I shall pay your messenger well and the message must be delivered to the marquise, not to her husband. To the marquise herself, quietly, mind you, and without fail. I shall hold you responsible for this." He slipped a gold piece on the tray. "You can arrange the messenger's wages yourself, you know."

"It shall be done as you say, monsieur," said the innkeeper with eyes shining. "No one will ever be the wiser. We have our own ways of getting news to and fro about the château even when M. le Comte is home."

"Doubtless you have," replied the captain, looking keenly at the wine bottle.

"From the château vineyards, monsieur, but not from the count's cellars. Ma foi . . ."

"I said nothing," interrupted his guest. "But here is the message." He took a scrap of paper from his dispatch box and sat down. For a moment his crayon hung poised above it. On the whole it would be better to write nothing. He began to sketch rapidly. Presently he handed the folded paper to the landlord. "Tomorrow before breakfast, to the lady, and to no one else!"

"Without fail, monsieur." The man took up the tray and went downstairs wishing his guest a hearty good night. Arrived in the kitchen he began to set the dishes aside to be washed next morning Finally nothing remained on the tray but the folded note and the gold piece. He took them up and listened. Above his head the beams creaked reassuringly. Nevertheless, it was with some hesitation even when in his own room that he finally opened the note and spread out the paper before a dim rush light.

Before him lay no writing but a vivid little street scene sketched with an economy of line which it is safe to say was entirely wasted upon the pair of small eyes now examining it. Their owner, however, had no difficulty in recognizing instantly the peculiar gabled front of his own inn. And if there had been any doubt of it, the sheaf of wheat, the sign, and the lantern swinging beneath left nothing vague as to the place or the artist's intention. There was the brick arch, too. But with the budding critical spirit of a true connoisseur, Maître Henri noted with considerable satisfaction that the arrangement of the chimney pots was decidedly wrong. If this detail had not escaped him, it was with both surprise and indignation that he next surveyed the strange equipage which appeared to be passing before his door. It was a coach to which, with an apt stroke or two, the artist had somehow managed to give the outlines of a classical chariot. Its prancing steeds were driven by a cat. Vulcan, or some other infernal lame god with a crutch, lolled back in it. Behind him in the guise of a footman stood Mercury with a small shameless Cupid on his shoulders. The latter was shooting into the upstairs window of the inn. The arrow pointed straight toward it with a message attached.

Certainly no such vehicle had ever troubled the streets of Romagnat. Of that Maître Henri was sure. Nor did he entirely relish the half-tipsy air which the artist had managed to convey to the inn. His was a respectable place. Above all that shirt flapping from the window was a libel. The wash was always hung in the court! Bursting with indignation he hurried out to make sure, crossed the narrow street, and turned to survey the front of his establishment. The light in the captain's window was out, but certainly there was a shirt flapping there over the sill as if hung out to dry. "Morbleu! What was the place coming to?"

Chapter Four

The Enchanted Forest

THE captain was awakened next morning by his friend the innkeeper. Despite his chagrin at the shirt, which he noticed was still fluttering at the window, the good man was once more obviously in the rôle of conspirator. Nor did the fact that he came bearing a tray with a bowl of coffee and rolls prevent him from walking as though a burden of state still rested upon his shoulders. Between his half-closed eyelids Denis Moore surveyed him as he arranged the table, and permitted an inward smile to escape as an audible yawn. Finding his guest awake, the innkeeper turned and bade him good morning.

"The message was safely delivered, monsieur. The cook's sister has returned, two hours ago."

"Any reply?" yawned the captain stretching himself, but with a throb of pulses under the covers.

"No, monsieur, you said nothing about that. Did . . .?"

"I did *not* expect one."

"Oh!" said the innkeeper.

"At least not till later, you know. And what do we hear from the mayor-postmaster?"

"All has been arranged as I—as he said. There will be a room prepared for you at the farm we spoke of. You can go this morning if you like. François can drive you over in the cart with the cover. If monsieur will not mind sitting in the back, on a truss of straw, no one will see him there as he goes through the village."

"And the mare?" inquired the captain.

"She can be taken over this evening after it is dark."

The captain was visibly pleased. "I am bound to say that you have both done very well, you and your brother, the mayor-postmaster. I shall see that your services are properly mentioned in my report," he added, sitting up officially, and drawing on his shirt. "All that is needed now is a closed mouth. You can leave the rest to me."

The innkeeper bowed and puffed out his cheeks. In his mind's eye he beheld a document heavy with seals and loaded with encomiums winging its official way to Paris. What an honour for the family Gervais to be mentioned to the Minister of War! "Monsieur is indeed very kind," he murmured. With some difficulty he returned to his rôle in actual life. "Is there anything . . . is the breakfast satisfactory?"

His guest surveyed it somewhat skeptically, "A flask of whisky, perhaps." The host stared blankly. "Eau de vie, then." With incredulity upon his face the man vanished to return a few minutes later with the desired liquid. "Bon Dieu!" said he as the captain emptied a considerable portion of it into his cup and tossed it off raw. "In the morning, monsieur!"

The captain laughed. "It is a family custom, my friend. Several generations in France have not changed it. We still drink to the King of France whenever we can in Irish whisky, as my grandfather, the great O'Moore, once drank to King James." He looked at the flask wistfully. "Lacking whisky, brandy is the next best thing."

"But in the morning, monsieur!"

71

"It is a fine loyal way to begin the day. Will you join me?"

Not daring to refuse, the innkeeper gulped down a fiery potion poured out by his host, and retired gasping. "Exit," thought the captain, "I shall now be left in peace at least for some time. But what a slander on the O'Moores. Brandy before breakfast! One would think us to be Russians." Labouring under great excitement as he was, he had craved the drink.

It might be hours before he heard from the château. Hours? Days! Perhaps not at all! But he dismissed that from his mind. Underneath he could hear the morning activities of the inn already well under way. Judging by the clatter in the stable, François was currying down the mare and being nipped at for his pains. He looked out into the littered courtyard. It was a beautiful, clear day and the smoke from Maître Henri's two chimneys rose straight into the air. Then he crossed to the other window and standing back some little way so as to remain unobserved from the street, glanced toward the château. An exclamation of surprise escaped him. On the road leading to the village a cloud of dust could be seen coming his way rapidly. There was no time to lose.

He turned back into the room and from an inner flap of his saddlebag extracted a square object carefully packed in a fragment of blanket. Unwrapping this rapidly he took out a fair-sized mirror which it contained. Again hastening to the window he propped the glass on the window-sill almost at right angles to the street. Drawing up a chair some distance within the room, he seated himself, adjusted the mirror once or twice and waited.

Like many old buildings the inn did not front squarely on the road. Even the slight angle at which it was offset plus the overhang of the casement enabled the scene outside to be thrown upon the glass in a bright little miniature of that portion of the village street which the captain was most anxious to see without being seen. Despite his anxiety, the situation and his secret view amused him.

A few yards below him two women in white caps

72

could be seen gossiping and gesturing violently. Their shrill voices came in through the window. He noticed the peculiar "well-what-could-one-do-about-it" gesture of one of the women as she seemed to let the bad luck she was relating pour back onto the spine of Providence. A black goat switching a long lily stalk in its teeth wandered across the street. "What kind of omen is that?" thought the captain, who was now amused to imagine himself a crystal gazer. Undoubtedly a great deal of fate was concentrated in the mirror. He could not help feeling that way about it. Suddenly the women turned and both gazed in the same direction. There was the distant crack of a whip and a rumble. He could hear feet running to the door downstairs. A small blur appeared in the glass that grew rapidly, almost terrifyingly swiftly into a coach and four. He caught a glimpse of a squat, cat-faced postilion riding the right lead horse, and the two tall footmen behind. In the distortion of the glass there was something diabolical about them. Then horses, coach and footmen seemed to vanish uphill across the mirror into nothing. The next instant the cocked hats, white wigs and profiles of the two footmen appeared close to and on an exact level with the window. Their heads and a small part of the coach roof seemed to glide along the sill miraculously. He caught the flash of a yellow glove. There was a sharp crack, and the captain swore automatically. The mirror, shivered into a hundred jagged fragments, had tinkled musically to the floor.

He was on his knees now. He wondered if the missile had bounded back into the street. Inadvertently he had miscalculated the height of his room above the road. It had not been quite so easy to reach it as he had expected. Then he gave a relieved exclamation and rose with the desired object in his hands. In a few seconds the piece of paper was disengaged from the small stone about which it had been tightly wrapped, and opened out on the table before him. He bent over it, for the writing though clear was exceedingly minute.

He will be gone all day. This afternoon early,

73

the road to Beaumont by the mill at the first bridge. Driving. The maid can be trusted. Till then Dieu te garde—*and always*.

"And aways"—his lips moved as if in prayer and sank to the paper in Amen. All his frame flushed with happiness. He felt his throat beating in the collar that was suddenly too tight for him. No, he had never known how much he needed her. The tumult and the longing of his body surprised his mind out of thought. There could be only one meaning to the note. She had decided at last then. It had been impossible finally to bid him good-bye. Those days at Versailles had won against all her scruples at last. Or, could she only be flattered that he had followed her? But this was not the court! He ran to the window to reassure himself. No, no this was Auvergne. Miles of pastoral landscape, vineyards, fields, forests, and meadows rolled up and away to the heights of Gergovia. Sound, odour, and sight swept up to him bringing a sudden access of peace, conviction, and determination. The quest for which he had been prepared to devote his summer was about to end. He turned and threw himself upon the bed in an ecstasy that shook him. For a moment he gave himself up to a sensation of unmitigated happiness. He breathed deeply and lay still. When he arose some minutes later he noticed that he was still only in his stockings. And he had been walking about heedlessly amid the shattered fragments of the mirror that lay scattered about the floor.

In the heightened emotional state in which he found himself, the accident to the glass worried him more than he would have thought possible. An unusual sensitivity in which he became painfully aware of the strangeness of his surroundings flooded in upon him. It was like homesickness; the only remedy was to be with her wherever she was. Yet he found a positive fear of going out, of meeting strange faces, possessed him. After the moment of ecstasy he was now at the nadir of that state, and a conviction of impending tragedy overpowered him. "How could such an affair turn out well?

Suppose, yes, suppose *that* . . . what would they do then?" He reached out almost unconsciously and took a pull at the brandy. A feeling of relief and of normal assurance gradually returned. He felt better, confident. He walked about, pulled on his boots, dressed with great care, slung his rapier carefully under the arranged folds of his cloak, and tied back his hair, missing his broken glass sorely. "Damn that piece of luck!" But he would forget. He rapped on the floor and brought up the landlord.

"Monsieur must be careful or he will give himself away. Lucky that no one else heard him."

In the mood he was now in, it didn't matter. Yet he realized the man was right.

"How soon can François be ready with the wagon? I must leave for the farm as soon as possible."

"In a few minutes," replied the innkeeper. "Watch from the window. When I come out into the court without my apron all will be clear and you can come down. But do not delay, sir. People are about now all the time." The man went downstairs while the captain watched impatiently. François hitched a mule to the wagon. Presently the fat host appeared in his vest. Snatching up his holsters and saddle-bags the captain dashed downstairs and bundling his stuff hurriedly into the cart leaped in behind. It was a high, two-wheeled wagon with a kind of bulging tent over it which when drawn behind effectually concealed its burden.

"Good-bye, Maître Henri, and thank you," said the passenger to the innkeeper. "Give me your hand to clinch the bargain."

The fat man cried out at the grip he received from the gentleman under the cover. But on withdrawing his hand he found that within it which caused him to bid his guest, as he rattled out of the court, an all but affectionate farewell.

A few minutes later the captain was safely ensconced at the farm of Jacques Honneton. By his manner and the elaborate precautions in the reception of his guest, that well-to-do peasant had evidently not failed to be filled up with the importance and peculiar requirements of his charge. The mayor-postmaster must have been more than usually impressive. Best of all, the window of his room, Denis noticed, had a clear and uninterrupted view across the park and of the entire front of the château. That fact, he thought, might have strategic possibilities. He proceeded to make himself comfortable and to inquire from his new host as to the road to Beaumont.

"Là-bas, monsieur," said Honneton, pointing out a streak across the landscape that about a mile away disappeared into a dense mass of ancient greenery.

At the château that morning Maria was strangely happy. It was the first fully happy day she remembered since her marriage. Despite the cold fear which had crept along her spine the night before at supper as the marquis chatted so hopefully of his recovery—and all that it implied—the sensation of coming home, which had begun with her in the coach the afternoon before, had continued. Against the sanguine prophecy of Don Luis as to his health, she had, although she tried not to permit herself to do so, set off the glimpse of the figure waving from the rock. Without realizing that she had unconsciously leaped toward him as an alternative with all of her being, she consciously thought of the near presence of Denis as a protection. Someone to appeal to in case—in case one needed someone to whom to appeal. Then the maid was a dear, a merry and understanding person about thirty but seemingly much younger. They had already confessed their ages, while the golden childish ringlets over which the older woman leaned in unfeigned admiration were being brushed just before bed the night before.

"Ah, madame was so young—and to be married to the old monsieur, already a year!" It seemed impossible. The talk ran on in the eager Tuscan that completed for Maria the illusion that she was being put to bed again at Livorno by Faith Paleologus. Without realizing it she began to talk of her maid, her father's

76

house, of Italy, of all the old life, a forbidden subject, or practically so, for Don Luis would hear none of it.

"You are now in a new world, my dear, forget the old one," he would say, and look dubiously on the frequent letters from home. Once a month she could reply. And he must read and correct her letter when it was finally done with many sighs and not a few blots. Always it must be rewritten. "A marquise, you know, must at least be correct in her correspondence." How she hated it—and him.

Now she could talk at her ease. A flood of delightful, childish chatter was soon joined in by the maid as she brushed and brushed, and watched the bright, beautiful face tilted back at her in child-like confidence, and relief, and ease. They went to sleep whispering. At midnight Lucia found she was relating the story of her life to her mistress who was asleep. The last details of a romantic affair with the butler of M. de Besance died away with a sigh as the final candle in a corner sconce guttered and went out.

Then in the morning had come the wonderful picture from Denis. No, he had not been wrong. Of course, she understood. Perhaps without Lucia she could not have puzzled it out so quickly. And what else could she do but reply? That tallest footman had carried some notes for her before to Denis at Versailles. And Denis remembered! After all she could write a good letter; say a great deal on such a little space of paper. How surprised Don Luis would be if he read that. But heaven forbid! She could trust Lucia, though. Yes, she was sure of that. It had all taken only a few moments. And she would see him this afternoon —at that mill in the forest that Lucia knew about. What a jewel she was, and how much she knew about the château and the country around after arriving only a few days ago.

To Lucia what seemed more natural than that madame should have a cavalier. One could not expect an ogre to fill the heart of a goddess. Besides she herself must get back to Italy and it would be well to ingratiate herself with madame, to make herself indispensable. With a certain amount of knowledge one need never be discharged at all. She learned that much at Paris. One did not leave the hotel of M. de Besance with two fair-sized shoes full of gold pieces merely for dusting off the chairs. But before all she was a woman, an Italian, and the cry of youth to youth was as natural to her and as little to be cavilled at as the sunlight streaming through the window. So the drive that afternoon was arranged, and the letter, carefully wrapped about the stone, which so thoroughly shattered the captain's reflections, was dispatched.

Hence, at half past one of that beautiful spring afternoon the pony and the little landaulet painted with wreaths of roses and blue ribbons, that Mlle. de Besance now secretly pined for even in the family great coach at Versailles, was waiting at the door. Since madame herself was going to drive, the small bell on the bridle must be silenced. It would never do to have the pony shying at it, Lucia insisted. Maria pouted at this, but a knowing glance from her companion reminded her that it would never do. "No, no, it must be taken off." There was a slight delay while the offending chime was removed and then they were off, taking the great circle of the drive, the straight road through the hedges, and then a swift turn to the right and on to the road for Beaumont.

The horse was a well-behaved but eager little beast. For some time now he had been little used and he travelled the road briskly. The red tassel on the whip began to bend back into the wind and the wheels on level spaces grew dim. Maria laughed with sheer exhilaration. The sunlight drenched the rows of vines, and as if she had already extracted from it that quality that would soon be pressed out as wine, her cheeks glowed and her eyes sparkled. From the heights about looked down upon her old ruined towers, white villages, and little chapels whence the distant bells rang out now and again in what seemed like a chime to the trot and time of the horse. Always over this country of Auvergne there was the sound of bells. At that season the vines had already been tended weeks before. In the vineyards they passed through they saw no one.

Suddenly as if a cloud had passed over their heads they were in the forest. It was damp and cool. Great beeches covered with green moss on the southern side threw level arms across the road. The sound of the pony's hoofs was muffled in loam and leaves. The wheels swished through them like the prow of a boat moving rapidly through water. Their eyes grew wide in the watery, green light. The silence seemed prophetic. Bright golden patches shimmered and chequered the road ahead. Down the long, cool glades they saw the pronged antlers of the deer disappearing amid the trees and blending into the shadows of branches. It was an enchanted country. Only the forlorn and distant sound of a hunter's horn durst disturb it. No one else ever came there, no one but themselves. Then as she threw her head back to drink in the wonder of it, and to taste the essence of spring that seemed to flow from the tips of the beech buds trembling in the heat on the highest branches, her whole being for the first time partook of life to the full. She was in that hour and in that green virgin place a woman, full grown.

The old merchant's daughter was a girl, a memory moving, pathetically, only half-alive it seemed now, about a gloomy house in Livorno. Her father's voice, that careful, wise and knowing voice, was far, far off, talking to someone else that had once been she, but was so no more. And the girl-wife? Ah, Madre mia!— what had *that* man to do with *her*?

The horse sped on as if he would take her away from Don Luis forever, leaving the cold about her heart and the fear behind. A robin flicked across the road in a patch of sunlight. Against the tender green of the leaves his breast seemed to burn like scarlet. As if he had flashed a message from the heart of that enchanted forest, rushed upon her the remembrance, the knowledge, and the full conviction that she was going to meet her lover.

There could be no holding back now. Had the not followed her all the way from Paris? After the crushing of all hope by her marriage, after a year of

79

foreboding and life in death, to find this full cup of life held out to her, waiting as it were just around the next turn in the road, intoxicated her, thrilled her through every fibre and flamed up with a sudden blaze and hope of fulfilment in the very core of her being. "Yes, yes, yes—and never again no," that was what the voices amid these trees, and whispers in the night all the way from Paris—she knew it now—that was what they had all been saying.

She flicked the horse with her whip, half amazed at her own sureness and firmness of grasp. The little carriage darted along under the tunnel of great branches even faster. Lucia with surprise and fear in her eyes grasped the sides of the vehicle tighter. The road began now in a series of long even curves to descend. The speed increased. They could hear the pony breathing. A sparkle of water glittered through the leaves ahead, then some weathered stonework. They wheeled out onto an open green over which the road twisted to a high arched bridge, and drew up before a long abandoned, stone building. The singing voice of a small, rapid river talking to itself filled the air of the deserted valley in which the ruin lay.

"It is the mill, madame," said Lucia. "That way," she pointed to a squat doorway from which stairs overgrown with ferns descended to some green region below. Maria looked. A huge root writhing like a serpent had ages ago taken charge of and embraced that threshold so that nothing could now make it let go short of steel and fire. "Watch," said Maria, handing the reins to her companion who looked down at her almost enviously. A wave of colour swept over the young girl's face, tinging for a moment her neck and shoulders. Then she turned, and stepping over the threshold lightly, disappeared into the green shadows of the door.

For a moment it seemed to Maria that she was descending into darkness. The steps made a complete turn. She felt her way in the uncertain shadows. The wall grew smooth. Then, almost as soon as she became aware of the light ahead and below, her hand began to brush over the cool and lacy texture of ferns that grew ever more luxuriantly from the damp stone. When she emerged again into the daylight the whole tunnel of the ancient stairs of the mill tower was a vault of faintly vibrant green.

She now found herself almost on a level with the stream. Behind her rose the mill a whole storey to the level of the road to which it served as an embankment. Before her stretched a short natural terrace, bounded on the side of the stream by the abandoned mill race choked with water-lilies and on the other by a high bank crowned with huge trees. The place was still dewy and smelt of mallows. From the road its existence, to any casual traveller, must remain unsuspected unless he came by the stairs or cut his way through the great trees and undergrowth that now flourished on the top of the ruined dam. The miller of times past, whoever he had been, had chosen his site well.

It seemed to Maria stepping out upon the smooth, natural lawn of this sequestered coign that by some magic she had suddenly succeeded in leaving the world behind. Surely neither man nor beast came here. Those delicate white flowers, tossing themselves in hazy sprays above the grass, were meant for magic feet. The sound of the river bubbled itself monotonously into her ears She stood, she did not know how long, listening to it. The sensation of having reached a spot where time had ceased slowly grew upon her. She remembered some dim, old Scotch story of a maid who had strayed into a place like this and come back still young. But the names of the gravestones of her generation had weathered away. Then she saw him.

He had been waiting by the bank under an overhanging branch of a pine, watching her. As long as he lived he would never forget her standing there listening to the stream, gazing into another world.

There are certain expressions at times upon the faces of some women that utterly confute the doctrine of original sin but confirm predestination. Such glances of the soul are to be overtaken only when it does not know it is being watched and reveals itself unconsciously as one of the elect, sprung from love and naturally and innocently bound for it again. Whatever else circumstances may do to such a soul that has no part with evil, they can never alter the essence of its being. It remains clear as a flame does even when fed by and consuming the dreadful refuse. Such a clear glance from the depths of the young girl's being Denis Moore had just had the good fortune of seeing. It was not lost upon him. He had both sensitivity and experience enough to understand. When he stepped out from behind the branch which had concealed him, he had already abandoned utterly the very simple rôle of the hunter. It would never be sufficient merely to bring that beautiful body to the ground. Now he had seen who it was that lived within it. He must live with her, alive, all of her. That glance of hers had revealed to him a kindred thing within himself which he had forgotten. It caused him to remember the clean fire of his youth before he had begun to choke it with ashes. It was that which he desired to blend with her. Some spiritual breeze seemed to have blown the ashes away.

Perhaps on the whole it would have been better for them both if this had not been so. Better if she had found merely a cavalier waiting for her. Then they might have met, parted, and let pass. For there was one thing that the experience of the captain had not taught him. The flame kindled by the mere clashing of two bodies together is usually a flash; the fire engendered by the fusing of souls consumes the body and cannot be put out. Such things, however, are not ordered by merely worldly coincidence. They are kindled by the great urge and turn out as they may. So it was not a cavalier who stepped out into the sunlight to meet Maria, but Denis Moore stripped of all worldly regimentals, and reduced to a man quivering like a boy.

It was thus that she saw him as he was for the first time.

For a moment they stood gazing at each other. Then as if a magnet drew them together the faster they approached, they moved toward each other, cries rather than words on their lips.

"Maria!" "Denis!"—and a long silence while he

wrapped his cloak about them both. Then too overcome to speak he led her to the edge of the mill race where in the green they sat down. She bent forward and put down her face amid the cool leaves of water-lilies, bathing her forehead and cheeks with one hand, for he would not let go of the other. She had not realized what would happen in her when he actually held her in his arms. For her it was the discovery of a whole new continent of the emotions; to him a new aspect of shores that he had long thought familiar. She touched her own lips, reflected in the water, affectionately, and drank. When she looked at him again she was cool and white.

Now that she had surrendered unconditionally, womanlike, she began to plead with him and to try to make terms. So long and gallant a defence of the heart's city as hers had been, implied, she thought, that the garrison should withdraw with the honours of war. At least she had not been taken by storm. She would never admit that.

"Is it," she said leaning her head against him, "is it for always?"

"Always," he replied after her as if exchanging vows.

"And you will never leave, never go away?"

"Never!"

"You will take me away from him? Away—" Her voice trailed out.

He had not thought of that. He had not thought of her as his wife, until now. How could he? How did he know that it would turn out like this? He would have to leave France, the army. A tremendous vista of change suddenly opened up before him. Yet how could it turn out any other way if he was to be what he knew himself to be? He did not shrink from the change that yawned before him. He was not sorry that the adventure had turned into a great quest with the lady won. He was merely taken by surprise. It remained only to carry her off.

She grasped the hem of his cloak almost tearfully. "In whose arms was she folded?" He read the question in her eyes.

"Yes!" he answered pressing his lips on hers, "I swear it."

"By the Madonna?" she whispered.

"By Mary, the Mother of God, by . . ."

She put her hand over his mouth. It was enough. In her mind's eye she saw him holding his hand out over the figure in her little shrine. No oath could be holier than that. From that moment she felt herself to be his. If the holy ones had registered those other vows, how could they help hearing this? Her lips moved and the tears came into her eyes.

"Denis, Denis," she said, as if she had added him to her pantheon.

A moment of beatific oblivion enfolded them both.

Presently they were walking up and down by the little mill race talking. There was so much to tell. All the journey down from Paris. The terrible time at Bourges with the plague. The new maid at the château. How he had followed them. His "conspiracy" of the night before at the inn. She clapped her hands. And so they were safe here for a while! No one would carry the news to Don Luis. The officials, the mayor-postmaster himself— she pouted the title delightfully—were on their side. "Oh, how clever of you, Denis—and that wonderful note!"—and how she had understood it right away. "But I was *so* glad! I did not know I could be so glad to see you waving that evening." The memory of the supper that night returned and brought a cloud on her sunshine. That cloud that even now she felt was just over the horizon. She trembled, and again he must repeat his promises to take her away. "Before—before Don Luis was well!" She told him her worst fear. He comforted her and promised, delighted to find that she might still be his as he might have dreamed. Her very confusion over it exalted him.

"But when, but where shall we go?" she kept asking now.

"You must trust me, Maria, I shall find a way. It will take much planning. Your . . . the marquis has powerful friends. We must make sure. It would never do to fail."

84

"No, no!" she gasped pale at the very thought.

"But let us leave that till again, till the next time," he hastened to say. "There will be many days now to talk it all over. Let be just for now. I did not know before, could not be sure, you know, that I must plan for this."

Seeing his face become troubled, she threw herself into his arms. They would be happy now for this hour and in this place. Let all else go. What more did she need than his assurance? All would go well with them— all would go well.

The afternoon fled away before they knew it. They must tell each other of all the things they had thought and felt since they had met. When they had first begun to love. Of how wonderful it had been that evening of the fête at the Court of Love at Versailles. Of how she had known, how she had *guessed*, whom the roses were for that he had laid on the altar. How she had dared then in her own mind, but not admitted it. Of how Don Luis' suspicions had first made certain to her that "the Irish captain" was her cavalier. He had actually made her happy in her pain. She knew that now. They smiled over it together. He at Don Luis, and she at the little girl from Livorno.

How long ago it seemed. How this afternoon had changed everything. It was almost gone! The sun was behind the forest. It was getting cool. There was the voice of Lucia calling anxiously. "Madame, Maa-*dame!*" They must part. It seemed impossible. She must go back to the other world and away from him.

There was a hurried consultation. Unconsciously they talked in whispers now. Yes, she understood the arrangements of light in her window. "*One* when Don Luis was going the next morning to the springs, *two* when she could not see Denis next day. *Three* would bring him to her immediately if need be, no matter what."

"*Madame!*" there was an almost frantic note in the maid's voice now.

He made her cry out. Then she had broken away and vanished up the stairs. There was the sound of voices, a neigh from the pony, and the dwindling grit of wheels. He turned and flung himself down on the grass. When he rose again the stars had begun to shine through the branches.

He wrapped his cloak about him and took the road back through the beechwood. Despite the late twilight it was dark there and he did not arrive at the farm Honneton till quite late. When he did so a cheery fire, most unusual for that time of year, and a good supper awaited him. Afterward he went and sat in his room looking out of the window at a landscape that about ten o'clock began to grow bright under the face of a waning moon.

It was May in Auvergne. The scent of the vineyards drifted up to him as it had the night before, but this time with a seductive softness he would scarcely have thought possible. A peace greater than he had ever known filled his heart and soul. There was not a doubt in his mind or body that he had found that without which happiness would be impossible. He was glad the die was cast. Nothing could alter it now. Over the road through the notch in the hill, they would ride off together, some day, soon. He would think of that tomorrow. America, perhaps, or Ireland, he had relatives there. But tonight let there be nothing, nothing to spoil his dream.

He leaned out again into the fragrant night. The lights in the château were still burning. But none upstairs. An hour or two passed. He did not know it. Then the light in her window blazed up. Presently he could see the dot of one flame placed near the casement. He watched breathlessly. It remained, burning steadily. So it was to be tomorrow then. He got up, stumbled about headlong, found the tinder box and lit a candle. He brought it to the window and raised the flame up and down. Across the fields the candle in her window repeated the motion of his own. "Good night, good night, my lover," said the two lights. Then the candle at the château went out. He extinguished his likewise and tumbled into bed. Without knowing it he had been chilled sitting at the window—for how long? He looked at the moon. She was riding high now. The sleep of an infant engulfed him.

Don Luis had been carried to bed in the same state as the night before. The soaking in the hot water at Royat had relaxed him. And he had never seen Maria so gay as she had been tonight at supper. Almost too gay! He wondered if she could be acting, but dismissed the idea. Doubtless the château was a delight to her. She had been driving, too, and had had a good time. It was lucky Besance had sent that maid down, otherwise he would have had to drag Maria back and forth to the springs, and amuse her. Oh, yes, and there was the dog. They were going to look for that tomorrow, she said. Well, he must get better now. Two or three months the physicians insisted, and no wine. That was a long time, at best. He moved his leg impatiently and was rewarded promptly by the proper twinge. Why not begin by staying a week at the springs and get a good start? An excellent idea! He pulled the bell cord.

"Jean," said he, "pack my portmanteau tomorrow for several days' stay. Have it ready early, and tell madame I shall be gone for a week. If I need anything I can send the coach back."

The thought of not making the still painful Royat drive twice a day was an immense relief. Later on it would be easy enough. He wondered he had not thought of it immediately. He took up his book. While the two candles nodded to each other across the moonlit fields, Don Luis nodded to *Rabelais* over the counterpane.

Chapter Five

A Pastoral Interlude

EARLY the next morning after dashing a bucket of cold water over himself in the courtyard to the amazement of the stable boy, and looking after the comfort of Solange, who was now comfortably ensconced in Maître Honneton's largest stall, Denis proceeded to dress in his room with unusual care. The time he spent on shaving and the arrangement of his hair while looking at the bottom of Maître Honneton's most highly scoured milk pan would have satisfied a professional macaroni. As he was giving the ruffles of his finest shirt the final touch he had the ineffable satisfaction of seeing the coach of Monsieur le Marquis de Carabas, with Puss-in-Boots on the lead horse as usual, swing around the great drive of the château and take the road for Royat.

So the field was clear! Of course, it would be the mill again. He had forgotten to say so, he remembered now. But surely she would know. He went out and saddled Solange, in the meanwhile questioning Honneton.

"Yes, monsieur, you can reach the woods that way,"

said the farmer walking out with him to the brow of the hill on which the farm stood. He pointed to a rut across the landscape lined by old walls and hedges, more like a ditch than a highway. "It is a very ancient lane, mon capitaine, used only by the hay carts in summer-time, and not much for that now since the fields have been put to vines. You will meet no one. Nor, unless one stands on the height here, could a person see you pass. We still occasionally use it ourselves when the salt carts from Beaumont wish to dodge the gabelle, but that is only at night," and his eyes twinkled.

"Thank you, Honneton," replied Denis mounting, "you will not forget how important it is that no one . . ."

"Have no fear, monsieur. There are none but men here, except Marie, the cook, and—" he extended a sabot significantly, and laughed. The captain gave rein to his mare and disappeared a few minutes later into the mouth of the dark walls of hedge.

The lane, almost a tunnel under its sturdy hedges, extended across the landscape like a ruled line. Here and there the green way stretched before him on a straight level and he gave the mare full head. She sprang forward under him, quivering with the joy of the morning, and would have whinnied had he not checked her with his voice. "A bad habit, girl," he warned her, striking her across the neck with his glove, a punishment she danced under. On a steep slope her shoes rang on a bit of hard pavement where the turf had washed off. He saw the regular cut flagstone. A Roman road! Some of Caesar's work about Gergovia? Presently, as he had expected, the way opened out on the top of the hill into an old camp, an oblong court of green in which a few sheep were straying. Where the praetorium must have been, a young lamb was nuzzling his mother. Denis dismounted and ran up on the wall.

The old fossa was only a faint hollow now, filled with daisies, but he was much higher here than he had expected. He could look directly across to the hill of Gergovia. The roof of the château lay far below him in the trees. On the other side the beech forest began, and tumbled in waves of hills down to the river. The clear, cool, morning air, the glittering sunlight on miles of new leaves, the height, and the silence, except for a continual undercurrent of faint birdsong from the woods, flooded him with a sensation of fresh and ardent well-being, a sense of youth and of being new-born in strength that almost caused him to shout. How triumphant to be alive, to have found his mate, to be above and beyond fear! It was a sheerly masculine experience. The small fountains of life stirred within him filling his frame with premonitory thrills of the ecstasies to come. He beat his gloves on his arm till it tingled. Wrapping his cloak about him in semi-bravado he strode along the parapet like Caesar himself. Down there, down there in the forest, he was going to meet her at the old mill.

He whistled to Solange who was sniffing uneasily at the sheep. A few seconds later and the forest had engulfed them. The mystery of the place closed about him. He missed his own shadow. The hoofs of the mare fell noiselessly on the moss. He might be a ghost riding under the branches. Who knew after all the end of the errand upon which he was bound? He wondered about his own father—when and where? Presently the mare was hobbled in a glade in the forest and he was in the sunlight again on the little green by the mill. But it had been rather eery descending the old stairs, and the place was lonely, without her. He wished that she would come now. How slowly the time passed here! It was so still except for the river. Did it after all move?

When Maria came down the stairs and stepped out onto the little terrace she was terribly startled to see the white body of a young god flashing and swimming about in the mill race. For a minute her heart was in her mouth. It was as if she had surprised the youthful spirit of all these spring woods sporting in his secret pool. But the head thrust up through the lily pads was that of Denis. For a minute they both looked at each other with horrified surprise, and then burst into a laugh. The blood rushed to his face. "Wait in the tunnel," he cried. "I shall only be a moment." He could hear her laughter echoed from the fern-clad walls while he frantically slipped into his clothes. "I did not expect you so soon!" he called. "I should hope not, mon capitaine." The laughter continued. What a fool he had been, after dressing so carefully, too! Now look, there was mud on the ruffles of his shirt. And his hair!

But she loved his damp curls when she came to him at last. He could not hold her close enough. "Let me go, Denis!" she gasped at length. "You goose, I have something to tell you. Such news," she cried flinging her arms about him again, and whispering into his "driest ear." "He is going to be away for a week, for a whole week! I shall be all alone, and my own mistress at the château. It will be like a honeymoon. Let us call it that," and she clapped her hands like a child as she always did when pleased and excited. "Lucia and I have packed luncheon and brought it along. She thought of it. We might have supper here, too. He will be gone, gone all today, and tomorrow."

"And the day after that!" added Denis.

Her eyes grew large at the vista of endless happiness that was about to ensue. They began to plan out the time together, interrupting each other. He drew a little calendar in a patch of sand. Tomorrow they would drive out to a farm that Lucia knew of and get the puppy. "And the next day?" She faltered bewildered by the endless possibilities.

"We will go up on the high hill of Gergovia. It is a wonderful place that," and he began to tell her. The old story of the brave Gauls took on a new lease of life.

"And after that to the old tower on the hill I can see from the château."

"Why not?" he said. "Anywhere, anywhere with you! We can arrange it each evening and meet the next day. Only we must not be seen together anywhere. That would cause talk and might get back to the château. Remember after all a week is *not* so long."

How short, how terribly short it suddenly seemed. She had pictured him riding by the side of the little landaulet. It would have been so romantic. She could look back at him and drop her glove. He would dismount and bring it to her, and kiss her hand. The tableau enchanted her. It was not often she could imagine a scene so clearly as that. It was like something out of *Paul and Virginia*, more real than life and somehow more beautiful.

"It will be better to be very careful now, and so have many days all through the summer," he was saying.

So he was *not* planning to take her away with him soon. But why not now, this week, while Don Luis was away? They could be gone for days before he knew, she said.

"No, no, that would never do." He began to explain. "He would get the news in a few hours at most after she was missed." They must have some place to go to. He was writing a merchant at Marseilles about a ship. It would take some days, a week or so perhaps to hear. He had thought of Ireland, but America would be better on the whole. He had heard those who had campaigned there and knew the country. He began to tell her about it. By noon they were still lost in an idyll of forest life beyond the seas when Lucia called from the world above and reminded them of lunch.

She brought it down in a little basket; was charmed with monsieur, with his gift also. A brave gentleman, indeed! Her interest in the affair became quite enthusiastic. She laid the luncheon out on a white cloth under the trees and went back to keep watch. "I have mine in the cart, you know. Not many pass this way but it will be well to be with the pony. Monsieur will know what to do if I call—and madame? Ah, she is picking water-lilies!" She gathered a few, placed them in the empty lunch basket by the side of the race and departed to the world above.

They sat down under the trees and ate together. It was their first meal. In her heart she thought of it as a kind of lovers' sacrament. She said a little grace closing her eyes, while he looked on fascinated and remembered to cross himself just in time.

"Ah, it will be like this in America, will it not,

Denis? We shall eat out in the woods this way often. And you will not let the savages nor the great beasts come near me?"

He protested again and again that he would not. The tears came into his eyes as he thought of what must be ahead of her in hardships, of the long journey, the ship, a strange land, nowhere to turn, and he a poor man. For a moment his heart failed him. Could he ask that of her? She was so daintily lovely here, so fragile it seemed to him now; almost artificially beautiful with her face like a cameo against the dark convolutions of the roots in the bank before which she sat. Those little rosebuds and garlands embroidered on the clear silk of her gown, what would become of them in Canada? Could he after all? Ah, could he not!

That delightful little golden head! He was mad about that, the face that looked up at him with so much wonder and appeal, so much hope, and innocence and abandon. He must have that near him in the future, forever. The future? Why, here he was dreaming when she was near him now! Who could tell about the far-off days to come? God held them in fee. But this *now,* this was his, and she was near him. As if he were drawing her back from the shadows of the unknown and would save her from all that his mind might forebode but could not certainly form, he suddenly caught her to him. She saw that he had been weeping. An access of wonder, and unreasoning pity overcame her. She comforted him for she knew not what, for some sorrow that lay within her, too. A great tenderness engulfed them both. Of all the doors by which love enters pity is the widest. Passion, the incendiary, is always waiting close by in the disguise of an importunate beggar to glide over the threshold and set fire to the house.

The afternoon shadows slowly lengthened over the grass. The river fled away forever modulating a monotone. The dead windows of the mill with little pine trees on the sills looked out at nothing. A small bird flitted back and forth over the white table-cloth on the grass. He looked doubtfully at the two figures by the bank under the pine trees. They did not stir.

93

Finally he lit upon a thin stemmed glass and tilting back his little head drank delicately. It was a light, sweet wine but it made him a bad, bold bird. He began to scatter the fragments of Maria's cake wantonly. Finally he put his head under his wing in broad daylight and went to sleep. Under the pine branches there was nothing to show that the two who lay there were alive except the long, slow rise and fall of their breasts. The wind tangled their curls together as it would if they had both been dead. Caught in the full tide of spring they drifted closer and closer together through the long afternoon.

When Denis rode home through the starlit forest that evening it was as if he had discovered himself as an entirely new person. He was inherently one of those rare but strong and natural people in whom the realities of passion actually experienced invariably transcend expectancy. Nor was this due to a lack of imagination. It was merely that his mind could not remember with a thought vivid enough to compass the actual feel of the flesh.

For the first time as he went home that evening he began to realize that he was in a predicament. He had already been caught in the eddy of a current that flowed through him and possessed him. Once in the main stream of it he could neither control nor direct. As his imagination had been unequal to his capabilities, so his will might be found inadequate to the unexpected strain. "Might be?" He knew it would. It came upon him like fate. Yet what could he do? He could not go away now. By every tie that his heart and soul knew he was bound to her. Yes, even despite her marriage, by every tie of an honourable mind. That her father had sold her with good intentions was no reason why he should recognize the bargain. Society, the society he knew, would scoff at such scruples. Her marriage was a circumstance to be circumvented. He would do that. He would make her, so far as the world knew, honourable amends. Beyond the sea they would be man and wife. That last small remnant of his grandfather's estate and the sale of his commission would enable him to . . . oh, yes, that was all quite possible, a matter of correspondence and some little time.

Time, that was it! Could he control himself, tomorrow, or the next day? They had been so near the verge this afternoon. He knew it now. But he did not care when he was with her. He had become for a time, what? Putty in the hands of some outside force that might mould him as it desired, not as he willed. But he would summon his self-control again. He ground his teeth together and gripped the mare with his knees so that she started forward.

They came up out of the forest into the old camp again. He forced the horse onto the rampart and stood looking back. A low chattering of night birds and hooting of little owls trembled up to him through the night. The moon was just rising and a light breeze that seemed to follow the path she laid over the miles of new leaves rippled the forest like a lake. The breeze increased in intensity and pressed against him. It was warm, damp, and fragrant, moulding itself into every fold and hollow of his body. Wisps of it blew like hair across his lips and the smooth hands of the mistral caressed his cheek. He was holding her in his arms again. For an instant the spell of the afternoon recurred in full force. Every nerve of his body shuddered toward her. The past and the future were forgotten. His entire consciousness became aware of the meaning, blent with, and seemed to pass on into the languorous longing of the spring night.

When he came to again, the mare, as if she had seen a ghost, was shivering under him in the moonlight, and the last fringes of the mistral had passed over the ramparts. The wood which the wind had passed through was strangely silent. He rode home with a fear and doubt of himself knocking at his heart. Of the young man who strode so confidently along those ramparts that very morning nothing but a vague memory remained. There was only one thing that was stronger than his fear and that was his longing. When he got to his room the single candle was burning in the window at the château. He lit his own and signalled. But there was no answer. Maria had evidently gone to bed.

And, indeed, she had. Lucia had seen to it. It was only by the exertion of some tact and will power that she had prevailed on her mistress not to go down to supper in the great hall. With the quick instinct of her kind she had realized that the girl was in a state that might well attract the not unobservant eyes of Pierre. Hence the evening dress, which with great trouble and some impatience had been put on, was now with evident relief and no trouble whatever taken off. Supper was served in the room. A complete lethargy seemed now to have fallen upon Maria. She had resigned herself into the hands of Lucia as if it were a relief to have someone else make even the smallest decisions for her.

The older woman had now long passed the point where she was striving to make herself agreeable from pure self-interest. All her motherly instincts had been aroused, and it was plain from every little motion and attitude as she waited upon Maria that she was actuated by strong affection for her. Indeed, she had been completely captivated by her young mistress whom she now pitied, admired and loved with all her heart. The affair of madame had consequently taken on for Lucia a new aspect. It had became a vicarious experience of her own. She had not expected that it would be so serious and absorbing either to Maria or to herself. Denis was exactly the kind of person she would have chosen for Maria, and with the sudden turn of the affair she was at once delighted with the present and fearful for the future. Absorbed in the fate of the lovers, she scarcely paused to consider what might happen to her should a crisis of any kind occur. Her first loyalty was to her mistress, beside that any other duty as a member of the marquis' household was too pale and abstract to engage her attention. She was one of those persons whose actions are controlled purely by likes and dislikes. She loved her mistress and she disliked Don Luis.

Being of a somewhat bovine temperament herself, it was a surprise to Lucia to note the effect of an afternoon spent in the presence of her lover upon the highly strung young girl whom she was now trying in vain to soothe. That this was not the effect of surrender but of being tremendously aroused without full satisfaction, she was wise enough in the ways of her own sex to know. The result of having for the first time been stirred to the depths of her being was to Maria like the after affects of a strong and over-stimulating drug. She was now completely unnerved. Had she been a weak character she would have been hysterical. She had come away in a daze. Her body and spirit were now in an indescribable tumult. Nowhere could she find rest or satisfaction. The sense of the physical absence of her lover was devastating. At the thought of him she experienced a longing for which there seemed no adequate human control. She threw herself on her knees before the madonna, but it was in vain. The very passivity of the statue and her own attitude was an aggravation. It was now like a final twist of the rack that the thought of Don Luis intruded itself upon her mind. For the first time she fully understood what that meant. A spiritual nausea and darkness overwhelmed her. She cast herself on the bed and then leaped from it in loathing. Finally she took to walking up and down the room repeating, "Denis, Denis, where are you? Denis!"

"Hush, madame, hush, the servants will hear you." Lucia strove to engage her attention. "See, I shall put the candle in the window for him. It is a single one. You will see him tomorrow."

The girl took the candle from her and rushed to the window with it herself. She raised the light up and down several times, but there was no answer. Then she turned and burst into tears.

"Do you love him so much?" said the maid stroking her hair.

"Oh, Lucia, Lucia," cried Maria.

A few minutes later she had been put to bed and was asleep. Lucia bent over her. Except for a faint spasm now and then in the throat muscles, she was calm again, worn out. Presently she sighed and lay utterly still.

97

It was Lucia who managed next day that they should see each other only for a short time, and then not alone. In the morning she drove into the country with Maria and they returned with a puppy which was instantly taken home to the young girl's heart. It was at least a living and responsive being upon which she could pour out some of the affection that now constantly overwhelmed her. They stopped at the mill for luncheon where Denis was walking up and down distractedly. He had been there since early morning. But the good woman by the exercise of much harmless ingenuity contrived not to leave them alone. Long before sunset Denis had to watch the two women disappear along the road into the forest with Maria looking back, her scarf waving in the wind, and the small, brown face of the little dog peering over her shoulder. He was forced to admit to himself that Lucia was both right and understanding. Nevertheless, an indignation overcame him and a sick longing as they drove away and he found himself alone again without having taken Maria in his arms. Tomorrow, tomorrow, despite himself, despite Lucia, he would feel those lips on his. That hope alone made the night supportable.

Nor was he disappointed. Before noon the next day they had climbed the high hill of Gergovia and were standing alone together upon its top looking down upon all that part of Auvergne. It was the first hot day of the season and from the valleys already the warmth shimmered up to them to lose itself in the crystal heights. These in turn glowed up and away into a vault of deepest blue blown clear of clouds, quivering and sparkling.

Up here the red volcanic nature of the soil was apparent. From the rows in the vineyards below, where the grass had been stripped, emanated an almost violet hue. The domes of ancient volcanoes and little breast-like hills rolled all about them, dotted with white villages caught in a network of roads. From these came faintly but clearly the thin voices of bells. A large amphitheatre of hills covered with masses of vineyards and forest stretched southward and upward to the

Puy-de-Dôme. Even from Gergovia they looked up to see the ruined temple of the Gallic sun god overlooking his ancient domain.

The entire bowl of surrounding mountains seemed to be catching the sunlight and flinging it back at them. Over the flat meadow on the top of the shoulder, where they were now standing, and where the town of the Gauls had once stood, the bees were greedy amid the clover as if they preferred the wild, clean sweetness of the flowers in that great height to the more cloying honey of the blossoms in the valley below. Indeed, from this place still exhaled the faint memory of a fresher fragrance as if the dawn had lingered there before moving westward to the lesser steeps. But now that whole hilltop was murmurous with wings, and vibrant with a passion of light and heat.

The arms of Denis closed about the body of Maria. Had anyone looked over the slight rim of that hollow mountain meadow to the very centre of which they had wandered, so that it enclosed them with a complete circle from all but the sky, he would have seen but one figure apparently, so close were they standing. Denis bent over Maria, while her hands, as if they were tapping at the door of his heart, fumbled at his breast. They stood for an instant with the spring concentrated in them. Then he picked her up and carried her over the rim of the slope.

A jumble of huge stones, once a gate tower that had hurled back the legions of Rome, lay scattered along the brow of the hill. He picked his way amid these rapidly. Where the foundations still remained they now leaned outward, overhung with brush or vines, and sheltering a ledge-like hollow filled with last autumn's leaves. A short distance below, the shoulder of the hill fell away at a tremendous angle. It was a place where in the winter the shepherds of the neighbourhood remembered to look for lost lambs sheltering themselves from the blast. Brushing aside the long, trailing tendrils like a veil, Denis laid Maria softly in the nest of dry ferns and leaves behind them. The veil fell again. To the curious sheep cropping near by it seemed as if the man and his burden had vanished into the old wall. Soon their bells continued to sound again gently.

Only once more during that noontide were they disturbed; this time by a soft, tremulous cry.

On the meadow above, the sound of the bees' wings continued growing a little deeper in tone as the heat of the day advanced. By far the majority of these honey gatherers were of the ordinary neuter and domestic kind for whom work was an end in itself. Here and there, however, amid this host of humble workers, who took good care to avoid so dangerous a neighbourhood, cruised a large male bumble-bee like a pirate or gentle-man adventurer covered with the gold dust of the treasuries he had robbed. These for the most part seemed to have their nests or robber lairs about the tumbled stones of the old tower where a kind of white cornflower trailed through the grass.

From a fracture in the stone immediately above the little ledge where the lovers had hidden themselves a peculiarly beautiful specimen of this blossom had put forth. But a large black spider, who had also fixed on the same cranny in the rock for his abode, had fastened on this bud as a support for his web and had succeeded in dragging it to the ground. In the shadow of the rock, the flower, which could open fully only in the brightest sunshine, still lay even after the noon had passed with the small green tip of its maidenhead fastening its petals at the end of the pod.

Attracted by so lovely and virginal a store of honey, a bumble-bee lit upon this blossom and after stroking its petals for some time as if he were in love, began to tear away the small green membrane that still defended it from his assault. The petals opened slightly and began to curl. Settling back as it were upon his haunches, and raking his body back and forth over this small opening the bee finally succeeded in inserting himself into the flower. Here, as if in ecstasy, he dashed him-self about. The flower opening ever wider, trembled, and drooped upon its stem. At this moment the spider, suddenly becoming aware of what was happening, emerged from his nook and began to weave his web again across the bee.

Some hours after this lilliputian tragedy had occurred, Denis and Maria emerged from their place of concealment. All considerations except that of each for the other were now banished from their minds. The clear peace of the great height and the quiet of the late afternoon woods through which they began to descend found an answering echo in their own natures. Strangely enough it was this walk down the ancient road that approaches the plateau of Gergovia from its least precipitous side which formed for them the crowning experience of their love. The same cool mood of completion and benign contentment after having fulfilled the plan of creation that breathed from the panorama of landscape before them as the day verged toward its close, was for a few blessed moments their own. For a half mile perhaps, certainly no farther, they walked together in utter unity with each other and in complete harmony with the world without. It is this rare mood which perhaps more than any other deserves to be called "happiness." And it was this which they afterwards remembered and desired to return to and perpetuate rather than that "agony of pleasure," which, while it convulses the body, cancels the mind.

To Lucia, who had long been watching anxiously as the sun dropped toward the western hills, the lovers appeared to be subdued as they came down the forest road. It was difficult for the good woman to refrain from a smile as she noticed the subtle air of possession with which Maria now leaned against and held Denis' arm. The frantic welcome with which the young dog would have greeted her was hushed by his mistress as out of keeping with her mood and the place. Upon her face the colour now began to show.

In Denis' manner, however, there was no sign of embarrassment. Taking it as a matter of course that the maid must be in all their secrets from now on, he turned to her, and with a smile the undeniable charm of which was in itself a powerful appeal, confided Maria again to her charge.

101

"You will take good care of madame, will you not, Lucia?" he asked. Despite himself and to his surprise, his voice trembled.

"As if she were my own child! Oh, monsieur, do not doubt me," responded the woman deeply moved, "I love her, too."

"I am sure of it, sure of it," he replied, and added in a low tone, "You will trust me, also?"

She gave him a warm grasp of her hand.

Turning he clasped Maria to him murmuring, "Good-bye, good-bye." They stood together for a moment by the little carriage and would have parted with tears had not the dog in her arms insisted on trying to lick both their faces at once. His comfortable assurance that all was meant for him tipped the scales of their emotion into merriment.

"Oh, he *is* a dear, Denis, isn't he?" said she as he helped her into the cart. Under the guidance of Lucia the pony started forward. Riding for an instant on the step he had had just time enough to snatch a kiss. Maria turned and tossed something back at him. He picked it up. It was a white cornflower whose petals, although it was now nearly evening, were not yet fully blown. As he raised it to his lips there floated from it the wings of a bee.

He picked both of them up out of the grass and folded them carefully along with the petals of the flower in his pocketbook. That night when he looked out of the window in his room at the farm there were two lights burning in the upper room of the château.

Chapter Six

The Muse of Tragedy

THE marquis had returned unexpectedly. From
half-way up the heights of Gergovia Lucia had
caught sight of the great coach coming over the
ridge from Clermont. By urging the little horse it
had been possible to reach the château about half an
hour before Don Luis arrived. Maria came down to
meet Don Luis with the puppy in her arms and noted
with consternation that he was able with only a cane
to negotiate the front steps alone. She had, however,
presence of mind enough to welcome him with con-
gratulations on his improvement. To her surprise he
seemed almost childishly pleased. Even the little dog
received a reassuring pat. But that sagacious young
animal from the start evinced a very evident doubt as to
the good intentions of the man with the cane.

Sitting in the hot springs at Royat with a half dozen
other invalids, after three days the marquis had become
enormously bored. He had actually begun to miss his
young wife and to long for her company. Immensely
cheered by his remarkable progress in so short a time,

he had somewhat overrated his powers of locomotion and visualized himself as already walking about the gardens of the spa and sitting with her in the various pavilions. Not exactly a thrilling existence after Paris, he admitted, but perhaps not so completely rustic as the château. After all, Clermont was a considerable place for the provinces, and they might meet some of the local noblesse. It was not in vain that he drove in state with two footmen and a big coach. Without doubt the impression already made was a good one. With a pretty young wife by his side in a court gown of the latest mode, several doors might soon be open. Hence he had returned to fetch her back the next morning.

"A stay of a week, my dear." She could not wholly conceal her disappointment at leaving, but of course acquiesced. Under the rouge which Lucia had wisely applied she turned pale, but managed to summon a smile. Somehow she must get word tonight to Denis. Don Luis noticed her hesitation. He was somewhat nettled, but glad on the whole that she had found the château so pleasant. At the best she would have to spend considerable time there, he thought. Perhaps most of the summer. That night they packed for the stay at Royat.

Once in her room Maria could not refrain from tears. She could not see Denis at the mill tomorrow; she would be driving to Royat in that horrible coach. For a moment she had an impulse to put three candles in the window. Lucia restrained her. To do so might have fatal results. She reasoned with Maria. "There is no need to bring Monsieur Denis here tonight, madame. No danger threatens. You will return in a few days and he will still be here."

"But how will he know what has happened?" the girl cried desperately, lighting a second candle and placing it on the sill with tears in her eyes. "Ah, if it had only been one!" The answering signal seemed only to increase her woe. At last it was arranged that Lucia should carry Denis a note. She slipped out without difficulty and made her way to the farm. To Maria lying in bed listening it seemed Lucia would never return. When she did, it was with good news.

"I spoke to him through the window, madame. His light was out, but I tapped on the frame. Monsieur is so grand wrapped in a blanket! He does not even wear a night-cap." She rattled on while the girl sighed. "He will wait for you till you return again no matter how long, he said. When you do, put the candle in the window as before. Also he said, madame, that if anything went wrong to address to Maître Honneton at the farm in care of the mayor-postmaster at Romagnat. He will arrange that with the postmaster. After you fold the letter put a cross on the *outside*, too." Lucia giggled. "But do not write unless you must. No news will be good news, and he will wait." She paused.

"Was that all he said?" asked the girl after a little. "Come, Lucia, was that all?" She stamped her foot as the maid smiled provokingly.

"Lucia!"

"No, madame, that was not all. He sent you this."

It was a small chamois skin bag with a cord from it like a scapular. She went to the window and by the light of the two candles opened it with eager fingers. Inside was a gold ring worn thin.

The two women laughed and cried themselves to sleep. Lucia's merriment was taking, yet in reality she did not feel as much as she expressed. She was by no means a fool, and the possibilities of the situation were more vividly before her than she cared to indicate. Come what might, madame must be kept calm and collected. A repetition of the emotional transports of the evening before might be difficult to explain to the marquis. From her trundle bed beside her mistress, Lucia continued in a tender way to rally and to soothe Maria until the deep breathing of the girl gave place to her sleepy answers. Lucia now arose, took a candle and looked at her. The new ring was on her finger—she must remember to take *that* off!—and there was a smile on her lips which the woman, turning to the madonna, prayed might remain.

Early the next morning the dust rolled behind the

coach as it dashed along the highway toward the springs. Don Luis was buoyant but Maria had little to say. Had the marquis looked very closely he might have found that the rather ponderous wedding ring which he had conferred upon his wife in Livorno had just below it a narrow, worn, gold band. On that point alone Maria would not listen to Lucia. She had been obdurate. But Don Luis did not notice. He was not thinking just then of wedding rings.

From the brow of the hill on which the farm Honneton was situated Denis looked down gloomily. A violent thunder storm later on in the day served to relieve his feelings by expressing his mood in a larger language than he could command. That evening he sent for the mayor-postmaster and, as he expressed it, "perfected the plot." But no letter with a cross came. A week dragged by. The captain was forced to take his exercise at night. He swam at the mill. Yet to be there without her was torture.

It was now ten days since! He was about to saddle Solange and ride over to Royat for news, when the tenth night the candle, and only a single one, glowed in the window at the château. Maître Honneton was somewhat surprised to be aroused after midnight by his guest who forced him to swallow an enormous quantity of brandy. When the farmer awoke it was late in the morning and the captain had already been gone several hours.

Maria had returned and left the marquis at the springs. As early as possible without causing comment she had taken the little carriage and driven over to the mill. Denis, however, had been there a long time before. The feel of her heart throbbing against his own caused him to lean back against a tree so that he might not seem to stagger with her. The sight of his mother's ring on her finger as he kissed her hands moved him greatly.

"You will always wear it?"

"Always," she whispered. "To the grave and beyond."

"Hush! Do not say that, Maria."

She looked up at him with a trust and adoration that went to his heart. He cursed the ten days that they had been parted. Otherwise . . .

He began to tell her of his plan.

"I have been thinking while you have been away. We must lose no more time, after . . ."

"Yes?" she said.

"After what has happened." He held her closer. "I must go back to Paris, make my arrangements, which will take some days, and then come back for you."

"O Denis," she cried, "oh, you are not going away, going to leave me now! No, not for even a little while! I need you here. I must have you. I . . ." Her hands were beating at his breast again.

He explained, and even argued. "It is necessary. We shall require money. I cannot desert! I am an officer. I must sell my commission, make all our plans. We shall need money to leave France. Can't you see?"

"You can have my jewels," she said, "all but this," and she clasped the ring.

"Ah, that would not do, my little love. One may run off with a man's wife and still remain a gentleman, but one does not also make off with his jewels. Is it not so? You must come with me even in the gown which I shall give you."

"What colour will it be?" she asked, trying to laugh.

"White, like the cornflower you gave me," he said and kissed her. "But can't you see that it is as I say?"

To his surprise she could not. The very thought of his leaving reduced her to nervous despair.

"A week then," he said, "then I *must* go. Must, or the summer will be over before we know it. And we must leave from here. In the cities, as an ambassador, the marquis would have every assistance. Here, the simple officials are on my side. You see how it is? I am coming back, coming back to take you away forever." He took her again and held her close in his arms.

So they had their week. The new moon came again, and with it, for the season strode rapidly that year, not only these days but long, warm nights. Then he had ridden off for Paris and the marquis was back again at the château.

Don Luis made the trip to Royat every day now. With the rapid subsidence of all pain in his leg, he enjoyed it. For the new coach he bought some superb horses from M. de Polignac. It had provided him with as fine a turnout as the province had ever seen. So he dashed back and forth in fine style and every day or so took Maria along with him. There was little else talked about over the countryside than the Marquis de Carabas with his enchanting Puss-in-Boots for a postilion, and the adorable little wife. To the wives of the petty noblesse, and to those unfortunate great ones who could not afford to be at Versailles, the presence of Don Luis and all that was his was a positive boon. A round of suppers and small garden fêtes began. The marquis, it was whispered, was not of high birth. But after all with Puss-in-Boots in the saddle Cinderella might well ride in the coach. Undoubtedly too, her foot was small. Several eyes noted that, and not since the Chevalier de Boufflers had come that way had anyone heard such conversation as Don Luis'. What if his wife were silent? She herself was a golden little mouse.

Maria was, indeed, silent. It was now well on into July and Denis was not yet back. At last there was a letter. The arrangements at Paris had taken much longer than he supposed. He might even have to go to Havre to arrange about the ship. *"Patience, I love you. All will be well."*

The days slipped by. The motion of the rapidly driven coach began to make her seasick. Lucia began to be anxious. She questioned madame. She observed. Yes, there could be no doubt of it. There was already the difference of one eyelet in lacing. Kneeling on the floor dressing her, she clasped the girl about the knees and looking up with tears told her. Maria blanched.

But to Lucia's surprise a look of joy and triumph then irradiated her face. It was as if suddenly while looking up Maria had caught the gleam of some bright vision looking down at her. Her eyelids drooped. Behind them there stood in the green haze of an illimitable wilderness a log hut. A woman with a golden-haired child in her arms came to the door. The blood crackling in Maria's ears rang like the sound of an axe in the forest. "Denis, Denis," she whispered. She saw him coming, running toward her.

"It is our child," she cried aloud throwing up her arms, "ours!" Presently she was sitting by the window again at the château. She began to pray to the madonna to bless her baby.

Three months ago she would not have been able to meet Don Luis under such a burden of anxiety without collapsing. Despite the anxiety of Denis' continued absence and the perplexities and risks of the future, she found herself in her now fast growing maturity possessed of a fund of firmness and strength she had never known before. The delicate lines of girlhood had already begun to alter in her countenance subtly. From her eyes no longer looked a shy and virginal spirit. The glance, the widened archness of the eyes, the chin and throat, but above all the breasts began to proclaim the woman. Nor was this change entirely physical. Come what might she had determined to bear her child. Her longing for Denis had also altered. It was now more tender, deeper, but not so necessitous. Nor could even the fear of the steady recovery of her husband entirely quell the fierce joy which surged over her. At the springs, and at the evening affairs at various châteaux she began to take part in the conversation, dropping her shawl over one shoulder and letting it fall loosely as she talked, instead of holding it with one hand tightly before her bosom and answering questions respectfully as she had before.

Don Luis was delighted. Without analysing it, he noted the change with satisfaction. She was growing up. His marriage after all would hold elements of companionship to which he had scarcely dared look forward. With him she determined to be gay. And she succeeded with an ease which astonished her. He could in certain moods be fascinating. She began to understand him and to evoke them. It was Lucia who was now subdued and fearful. Only at nights a blind fear would settle upon Maria. She would think she heard her husband coming to her room. Lucia would do her best to console her. But for the most part Maria would lie at those times with her eyes wide open staring into the gloom. Here was a burden which she knew she would after all have to bear alone. Every night, and every night they looked for the candle in Denis' window. There were no more letters. It seemed aeons since she had seen him. It was beginning to be difficult now for her to recall his features when awake. In her dreams they came clearer than ever and left her weak and distrait in the morning.

Don Luis was now walking about without a cane at times, still limping, but visibly recovering mentally and physically. He would come home in the evenings, lead her out to a seat in the garden and caress her. At these times sheer terror made her passive. The strength of his hands made even his lightest touch seem threatening. "O God! If Denis would only come and take her away!"

It was well on into August when one midnight as she sat by the window while Lucia slept the candle suddenly burned again in Denis' window. A great trembling came over her. It was some time before she could kindle her own. For a minute the two lights fairly danced. He had scarcely hoped to find her awake. Then she remembered. There were to be guests at the château next day! Still trembling she lit another candle and placed it beside the first one. It was with difficulty that she refrained from lighting a third. She might bring him to her. In a few minutes he might be in her arms. She took the third taper in her hand. Then she threw it away and wakened the maid. While she dressed, Maria poured out her heart in a note to Denis.

He must meet her at the mill as soon as it was safe. She had something of all importance to tell him. But wait for the signal. She could not come to him tomorrow, would tell him why later. "Oh you are back again, back again," rang her constant refrain. The pen kept saying it over and over. She did not realize how often.

110

Lucia took the paper and disappeared. It was almost morning when she returned. The great dog at the farm had kept baying. "If monsieur had not come at last, come to meet her . . ." But Maria did not hear Lucia. She was reading Denis' letter, the long absence was explained. All was well.

The guests at the château stayed for several days. Denis had come back on a Monday. It was not until Thursday morning that Don Luis finally departed for Royat, somewhat disgruntled that Maria's headaches prevented her from going with him. She was becoming necessary to him. He would send the coach over for her next day. He even thought of deferring his own departure until then. Her solicitude that he should not miss his regular treatment at the springs secretly touched him. Well, it should not be long now. She would soon find him all that a husband ought to be. She was right about the cure. He would follow his regimen closely from now on. He would soak himself for half a day in the hot water. Sancho was surprised how alertly and easily he mounted into the coach. In his own mind Don Luis was already well. It was nearly noon when he drove off at last.

At the mill Denis waited for her from early morning, pacing up and down uneasily. "What was this 'all important thing' she had to tell him? It was?—if it was *that*—it would enormously complicate their plans."

It was the wait at some seaport that he feared. They must if possible so time their departure as to arrive when, and not before, the ship sailed. Otherwise he would have to go ahead and make arrangements. Don Luis would stir officialdom to its depths. He had the means of doing so. They must arrive ahead of the posts. Give him no time for warning. Be gone and beyond recall. The long journey made the northern ports impossible. It must be Marseilles. If she had risked all, so had he. Given up his post at Versailles, his whole past, wiped it out. All that represented it now was in his saddle-bags. Heavy enough to gall the mare. Poor lass, he would miss her. Suddenly he realized with wakeful keenness like one aroused from a dream that

111

he was leaving forever all that he knew. The thought over-powered him as if he had been suddenly told by a physician of the certainty of immediate death. It was poignant, it was undeniable. He fell into an hour of reverie listening to the stream. A foreboding note in its many voices that he had not heard before kept recurring. Then her face glimmered up from the water-lilies as it had that morning when she had stooped to drink. He stretched out his arms to the vision. It was some time before he realized that she was really standing above him looking down.

They had both imagined the transports of this re-union but it was not so. They were too near together when once more in each other's arms to strive any closer. She leaned back and looked up at him in great peace. The new strength in her face, seen now for the first time after his absence, amazed and thrilled him. Her lips began to move silently so that he leaned closer.

"Do you know what it is that I have to tell you, Denis, my Denis?"

Something of her own great tenderness as she told him overcame him, too.

Through the valley the stream rushed on as if madly prophetic in an unknown tongue. Sometimes merely colloquial, giggling, flashing into a low laugh of sheer joy, always unintelligible, this child of the mist which came apparently out of nothing, hurried headlong to the limitless sea. Beyond its gamut of musical tones that expressed so often for those who listened the moods which most moved them, moods for which there were no words, was now an undertone and now an overtone of mystery, as if in the course of geological ages the river had learned something of eternity which it was trying to reverberate amid the stones.

"Does it understand?" whispered Maria. "No," said Denis, "but we hear."

The next day she was at the springs with Don Luis again. Denis had ridden off headlong at night for Marseilles. He would be back again as soon as he could arrange a passage for America and horses for the trip down. The next time his light burned in the window she was to leave the château, come over to the farm, and they would be gone. That would give them at least six hours' start, even a full day probably. It would take the marquis some time at best to discover which way they had gone. The mayor could also be counted upon temporarily to put him on the wrong track. In the meantime the days passed swiftly. It was now the end of August.

Maria received one letter from Denis. There was a ship sailing from Marseilles for New Orleans the second Monday in September. He had arranged a cabin on board for "his wife and maid." So it was finally settled that Lucia was to go. "I shall be back on the night of the third. Watch!" Maria packed a few things in a small bag, not forgetting the little Madonna. Lucia with the aid of her mistress wrote a long letter. She would never see her parents again. Both women wept. The calendar slipped over into September.

On the first Don Luis rode horseback to the springs and felt better for it. It was with some difficulty that Maria persuaded him to allow her to follow in the coach instead of riding with him. On the second she was still trying to be gay outwardly with the wives of the invalids at the spa. On the morning of the third she sat alone in one of the pavilions half distracted with anxiety. Would they return in time to meet Denis? If not, what then?

Don Luis sat all that morning with the water above his knees. Over a small iron table set in a shallow part of the pool he and M. d'Ayen indulged in a hand of loo while the bubbles came up through their toes. The place was hot, the cards stuck to the damp table, and the game progressed slowly. The duke was a dabbler in chemistry and began to discuss the properties of the waters, the history of the baths, water clocks, time measure, classical music, and the opera of which he was a devotee. He was known as an "amiable conversationalist." Opera was a pet aversion of the marquis'.

The morning thus wore away rapidly in a spirited discussion as to whether or not opera could be regarded as a separate art. According to Don Luis opera was a mere pot-pourri of music, painting, and bad drama. The libretto was a poor fly of poetry buzzing in the transparent web of the plot. D'Ayen on the other hand maintained that, given a fine performance with great artists, all the arts employed blent into a unity of effect which in itself was unique in artistic experience. The degree of beauty, because it was compounded from so many sources, was the greatest known. Theories of aesthetics were thus involved.

M. d'Ayen had started to explain his own at great length when Lucia appeared at the railing and announced that it was long past the hour of luncheon. Madame had been waiting in the pavilion outside and was faint. The two rose from the water and hastened to dress. They were much pleased with each other. It was not to have been expected that at a place like Royat such a morning of talk could be found. They met at the door going out with mutual compliments. Maria was still seated in the pavilion some little way down the path. The duke looked at her keenly.

"Monsieur is not only to be congratulated on his present wonderful recovery but for an event of the future, I see. Allow me to anticipate the usual felicitations. There is a certain expression of the face in women, you know! I happen to be familiar with it. Tomorrow, then. We shall finish our discussion?"

"I hope so!" replied Don Luis so emphatically that the other bowed.

"Au revoir."

Don Luis turned to his wife.

That these remarks had greatly disturbed him, he could not deny. He studied her carefully as she came toward him. She flushed under his steady and appraising glance. But the marquis was not so simple as to suppose that every blush was a confession of guilt. With her heightened colour, standing in a simple gown under the shade of the trellis she appeared more beautiful to him than he had ever known her. How mature she had grown! That was all, he thought with relief, a little more mature. Doubtless d'Ayen thought himself as great an authority on women as on the opera. He

114

had felt angry with him for a moment. Yet the remark had been well meant. He now forgave him. How much—how much he wished it were *true*. Well . . .

"What were you two talking about so long?" she said. "I am nearly dead with hunger sitting here. Was it a religious discussion?"

"Hardly that, my dear," said he, "although M. d'Ayen did venture to assume the rôle of prophet and foretell a miracle. By the aid of man it may come true." He took her arm and held it closely. They walked up on the terrace together and had lunch. They were returning to the château that night.

On the way home that evening the marquis galloped on ahead of the coach like a veritable cavalier. The regimen at the springs had made him vigorous again. What with a careful diet, no liqueurs after supper, the hot water, and exercise regularly adhered to for many weeks, he was not only recovered but actually felt younger than he had for years. A good bout with the foils tomorrow would have been pleasant to anticipate. How he missed that! When he arrived home he would have his old fencing-master up from the garrison at Florence. That raising of the hilt that seemed to lower the point, the fatigued retreat, and the sudden clever rally; that was a movement worth knowing. And the fellow had other tricks in his bag that he could teach as well. Like a good pedlar he had always one more.

Don Luis galloped up to the château a mile ahead of the coach and dismounted with a spring. He hurried to his room, and calling the valet had himself shaved for the second time that day. It was already past the usual hour for dinner before his wig was properly adjusted. A white satin suit with gold frogs and lacing caused him to glitter under the chandeliers and candle-light.

To Maria, who had been awaiting him for some time, his now almost jovial presence seemed to pervade the room. She could scarcely bring herself to realize that this was to be the last meal with him. There was now an assurance and robustness in his mien and gestures, a certain sardonic vigour in his locution that made it

115

seem impossible she should ever dare to think of casting him off. Yet even as the courses proceeded she knew that Lucia was putting the last things for the journey that night in her servant's reticule. It must be small enough to go on a pillion, Denis had said. They would ride as far as Issoire tonight and take coach at three in the morning. She thought of him waiting for her now at the farm and the colour leaped to her face and her heart began to beat strangely. Ah, tomorrow, and tomorrow, and tomorrow!

Don Luis was saying something to her. She became aware now that he was also looking at her piercingly, that he must have been doing so during her entire reverie. Her heart seemed to empty itself and become dry. Far off she heard him saying: "After you have retired tonight dismiss the maid. Tell her to go to her own room and not to disturb you till morning. Do not be alarmed," he said, taking her hand which was stone cold, "you will not be sleeping alone."

The supper proceeded in silence. She ate nothing. Don Luis gradually became angry. He had expected some shrinking, perhaps. But his wife's face over the candles was now a clear, transparent white, and he found himself looking into a pair of eyes so shadowed with an agony of fear that they reminded him of a dying deer's. He had often cut their throats that way—after the chase was over. This one was. He smiled.

As she left the room, he leaned forward in his chair to watch her. She turned as usual at the door to say good night, then stood there as if in a daze. "Remember," he said in his peculiar way.

His mind flashed back to the last time he had said that to her, in the coach just before their arrival here. That young captain! The remark of M. d'Ayen recurred to him again. He started uneasily. "No, no, impossible! Nothing had occurred at Versailles!" But he sat thinking. Pierre waited silently to remove the glasses. Finally he poured out some more wine. But the marquis sat abstracted. Unconsciously he played with his coffee spoon. A certain grim tenseness began to lift the black tuft of his beard and tighten the lines of his close-shaven jaws. Finally his teeth clicked and his mouth took on the appearance of a closed trap. "Pierre," said he, turning around upon the man almost violently.

"Monsieur!" said the man startled.

"Send Sancho to me immediately. I shall be in my own room."

A few minutes later that worthy knocked at his master's door. The voice of the marquis could be heard within for some moments giving earnest and emphatic instructions. At the end of that time the servant reappeared. Holding a candle before his curious countenance, the man walked down the corridor with a light noiseless tread. As he did so his animal-like shadow sneaked after him along the wall.

Once beyond the paralysing presence of her husband, Maria's first impulse was to flee immediately. She came up the stairs on the wings of fear and sped to her room. Had the maid been there they might have left instantly and have been gone into the night. But Lucia had gone to supper. As Maria closed the door calling her, and no answer came, an access of terror and trembling overcame her and she was forced for a moment to sit down. The dim light of one candle left burning before the mirror on the dresser served only to deepen the gloom of walls and curtains, and the young girl saw her haggard face peering at her from the glass with an expression of horror. The absence of Lucia, upon whom she was so dependent, temporarily deprived Maria of will power. She felt it impossible to leave without her. At any moment Lucia might return. But the thought that at any moment Don Luis also might appear made her sick and faint. A low cry escaped her and she gasped. Her state of indecision was more than she could sustain. At last she seized the bell tassel and pulled it violently. But Lucia did not answer. A conviction of fatality amounting to despair overcame Maria. Then she rallied. Without Lucia then!

For a moment she was all activity.

She seized the candle and rushing to the window held it there waiting beat by beat of her pulses for an answering light. But there was no light whatever at the farm. Where was Denis? Not in his room! Perhaps he was already waiting at the cross-roads below the farm with the horses. Hardly yet, though. It was still early and they were not to leave the château till after midnight.

No, she knew he was not waiting at the cross-roads. That was the desperate prompting of false hope. It had all been *so* well understood. They were to go to the farm and leave from there. In no other way could the horses be so well concealed. And they were to change into new clothes there before the fire, and ride off. It was all so easy. But he had promised to answer the last light—not till later, of course. If she could only make him see now! Where was he? She waved the candle to and fro excitedly. It went out. In the darkness she stood pressing her forehead to the window. Above the edge of the hill where the farm loomed darkly came only the cold glitter of stars.

Nevertheless, she could not stay here. She lit the candle again with shaking hands. Then she hastily tore open the bag which Lucia had packed and extricating from it the statue of the Madonna and a dark riding cloak, she threw the latter over herself concealing her white dress. The bag was now nearly empty and seemed to gape at her widely. Then she tiptoed to the door, opened it gently, listened, and stepped out.

The long, gloomy corridor was empty. Except for the slight beam of light through her own keyhole and a thin radiance from either end of the hall it was almost black. At regular intervals the tall, white, locked doors of the château guest chambers glimmered duskily like the portals of so many vaults. She hesitated. To her left the corridor led to the main staircase of the château; to the right to the servants' stairs. It was from these two stairways that the light glimmered up at either end.

118

Pierre would have locked the front door by now, and the marquis' room was in that direction. She might meet him coming up! Her scalp crept at the thought. She had never been in the servants' wing, but they were probably quiet now. She might slip out that way. She might still find Lucia there. At any rate *he* was not that way. She turned to the right and crept slowly and softly down the corridor holding the small shrine in her arms like a doll. Presently she found herself by the railing of the servants' stairs. From a lamp placed on a table in the hall below a faint glow was cast upward throwing grotesque shadows. Very carefully she peeped over. The stairs were circular and it appeared to her that she was looking down a deep well with a lantern at the bottom.

She put her foot on the first tread and started to descend noiselessly. Then she was arrested in mid-air by the sound of a yawn and a scraping noise. She looked down through the banisters. Curled up in the shadow on the last step was Sancho. He was scratching himself under the arm with a peculiarly persistent motion. His head with the curious, dark grey tufts behind his ears was now and then projected into the light and she caught a green glint from his eyes. No mouse ever crept back more stealthily into the shadow than Maria. So that was why Lucia did not come! There could be no doubt about it. The man was watching. She must get back to her room instantly.

But it was not so easy to find. There were many doors down the long corridor. She started trying the handles. In her desperate haste she must have passed her own. Somehow she was too far down toward the main hall. She must go back, be methodical, and miss none. She listened for an instant. Someone was coming up the big stairs. She turned, scarcely able to stifle a scream. She saw a candleglow through the keyhole of the next room. She opened her own door, and darted in. For one second only she stood in the faint light before she closed the door softly. She even remembered not to let the latch click.

For a few instants excitement sustained her and

cleared her mind. For the first time in her life her movements became precise and of lightning rapidity. She tore the cloak off, wrapped the statue in it, thrust the bundle into the open bag, and the bag under the bed. Gathering three candlesticks from her stand and dresser she placed them in the window. She lit them from the one already kindled and threw that into the fireplace. Then she turned facing the door with her back to the wall against a long yellow curtain. Her hands were clasped behind her. For an entire minute no one came. It was that delay which at last shattered her.

Don Luis had turned into the corridor just as Maria was closing the door. Against the opposite wall he had seen a dim square of light and a shadow there like that of a cloaked woman carrying a child. It vanished like a spectre. Don Luis was carrying a candle himself. The hall beyond was dark, silent. He could not be certain. It was a very old house. He was not superstitious. But he was sufficiently startled to stop where he was for a full minute. Then he too saw the ray of light from the keyhole of his wife's room. A solution of the spectre dawned upon him. He strode forward angrily and flung open the door. . . .

While the marquis had for a moment been stayed by a shadow, Denis three leagues away at Le Crest was knocking persistently and hallooing at the door of a blacksmith who presently stuck a frowsy head through an upstairs window and inquired with sleepy insolence what was wanted. A short interchange of views on the subject of shoeing horses at night decided the point of whether the smith should come down or wait for the gentleman to come up and fetch him at the point of a pistol. Under the double impetus of threats and promised rewards the man made what he considered to be haste. Monsieur meant business, there was no doubt about it! But it was almost an hour before the fellow could blow up his fire, take the shoe off the foot which had gone lame, and fit a new one. Denis watched the man working over the cherry-coloured iron while the time passed mercilessly. In his terrible anxiety the dark shed seemed like a prison chamber and the smith some black-browed jailer who was about to put him to the question. Would he, when the iron was thrust into him, be able to remain firm? He was half dead with fatigue as it was. The smith passed close to him with the sizzling metal and he felt the heat through his sleeve and flinched. "How much pain could a man stand before he would tell?" he wondered. Tired and nervous as he was, he felt how weak he might be. He roused himself. He had almost gone to sleep. Solange had gone lame early that afternoon. He was hours late. Tossing the man a full day's wage, he spurred out of town striking sparks from the cobbles. . . .

Don Luis stepped through the door and looked at his wife standing with her back to the wall. Her attitude was so tragic, her background of the yellow curtain with the three candles burning in the window so theatrical, that he thought for a moment she was staging a scene. He drew a chair up between his knees with the back before him and sat regarding her.

"The illumination I take it is in honour of the event?" Her lips moved but no words followed. "I cannot say I ever heard so ringing a line," he sneered. "Come, come, don't you think this is rather a cold welcome for your husband? The Muse of Tragedy, the three lamps, curtain and all. Magnificent! But—considering the scene to follow—aren't you perhaps a little over-costumed? I expected to find you in bed."

Her eyes rested on him for an instant like those of an accused person seeing the state tormentor approach for the first time. He became aware that there was no art in this. He was looking at the face of terror in nature. Why was it?

"Come here!" he said softly.

She flattened herself against the wall as if waiting for him to spring. It was provocative. A gust of fury lifted him from the chair. With one stroke he ripped her gown from neck to heel. She clung desperately to the curtain. It came away, falling over both of them. The candles wavered. He had not expected her to fight him. She cried out once bitterly. He wrapped her head and arms in the curtain, and stripped her like an Indian husking maize. Then he carried her to the bed and threw her down there. She had ceased struggling now. She did not know anyone could be so strong. She felt and looked like a bird blown on to a ship by a hurricane. Her breast rose and fell quickly, but at intervals. Between breaths she lay as if dead. Only her eyelids quivered.

The last vestige of pity had vanished from the breast of Don Luis. His wig had been torn off and he happened to see himself in the glass while he was struggling with Maria. So this was the dignified approach to the marriage bed he had so fondly planned! Marriage bed? He looked at her lying under the shadow of the canopy. It was quite dark in that end of the room. He crossed to the window and taking one of the candles came back and stood beside her. Holding it above his head so that the yellow light washed over the pale body of the girl, he studied her carefully for some time. Then with a terrific imprecation he dashed the light to the floor. The two candles remaining on the sill continued to burn softly.

Presently she became aware that he was sitting on the bed beside her. She opened her eyes slightly and saw that her own hands were completely lost in his. His huge fingers curved around her arm again reminded her of the paw of some monumental lion. He was holding her hands so gently though that she almost felt sorry for him. A little harder now. She opened her eyes as the clasp became firmer and found herself looking into his very close to her face. She felt him breathe.

"His name?" said Don Luis whose grasp now began to hurt her. She looked at him again and bit her lip. Her fingers began to ache intolerably.

"*His name?*" repeated her husband.

She closed her eyes and braced herself. His hands now seemed on fire. She lost all sense of anything except the intolerable pain that began to shoot up her arms to her shoulders. Had the pain been less she might have answered, but her whole mind was now preoccupied with it. The reiterated demand of the insistent voice became only a senseless buzz. Then she fainted.

Don Luis had not meant to carry it quite as far as that. He dashed water in her face. It startled him to see the print of his own fingers on hers, which she kept contracting spasmodically. Finally he bathed them in a bowl of cold water. At that she came to, but remained in a kind of daze. She was now lying as if not only her hands but her entire body had been crushed in his grasp. Indeed, from that moment on he never saw her in any other attitude. Those masterful hands had done their work more thoroughly than he intended.

He sat down and began to ponder. A long time passed. He was annoyed with himself for having allowed his rage to reduce him to so rudimentary a procedure. He had forgotten how fragile youth was. How sensitive he had been as a boy! Pshaw! That was a long time ago now. Well, he had forgotten. He looked at her again. The cold of the hours before dawn was beginning to penetrate the chamber. He started to cover her with the counterpane, but paused. She was like the living dream, the pale counterfeit of which the sculptor occasionally detains in stone. By that body he intended to have an heir. What had happened should not swerve him from his goal. Also, it would be the most exquisite revenge possible. He would bide his time. In the meantime—this thing which she held from him? He could arrange about that! Don Luis covered her up as if putting something away for safe keeping. He sat down again and in a calm, methodical manner perfected his new plans. There was only one link still missing in a carefully welded chain. Even the pressure of his hands had not been able to forge that, as yet. But patience! There were other more subtle ways.

Toward morning she grew feverish and sat up. Her eyes did not seem to see anything in the room. She choked and clutched her throat. He began to fan her. Then he threw open the window. It was almost dawn and deathly silent. Suddenly as if a drum were beating, the sound of hoofs at a furious gallop came in a sharp staccato over the fields. "Denis, Denis!" cried Maria, and fell back on the pillow. "Ah!" said Don Luis exhaling a long breath.

Denis galloped into the courtyard of the farm, threw a blanket over his trembling horse, and rushed to his window. In the upstairs room of the château he saw two candles. They burned steadily. So all his haste had been in vain then. Something had interfered. Well, he would hear from Lucia tomorrow. There was no message yet or Honneton would have given it to him. Whatever it was he would soon know. Probably a late return from the springs had interfered. He lay back for an instant on his bed without taking off his boots and was instantly asleep. Since morning he had ridden long leagues.

Chapter Seven

The Fly Walks in

VERY early next morning the coach drew up before the door of the château and the two footmen began loading luggage. Don Luis sat in the library writing a letter of fervent appreciation to his friend the Comte de Besance. He could see the two footmen strapping on the leather trunks and putting bags in the hampers. Presently Lucia with a white, scared face ran down with something that had evidently been overlooked. It was a small, black bag which she hurriedly put in the coach. At her appearance Sancho stuck his nose in the air and began to whistle softly. She gave him a vindictive look and went back. The marquis' pen marched rapidly.

Not only have I to thank you, dear friend, for the hospitality of your delightful roof which conceals, as I have discovered, an excellent cellar, but for the restoration of my health. I am now entirely recovered. At this moment I could take a creditable part in an affair of honour, nor do I mean as a second, or with pistols.

All that you claimed for your springs here at Royat was true. Their effect upon me has been one of rejuvenation. Indeed, I am almost superstitious about them. I am forced to attribute even to their vicinity a life-invoking quality.

Our stay here would have been even longer had not my wife, whom you so much admired, unfortunately dislocated one of the small joints in her finger which will probably require the attention of a chirurgeon. One of that profession I hope will be found at the first large town on our way down.

We pass by Marseilles to Florence, but leisurely. I have purchased four magnificent horses from your neighbour M. de Polignac and we shall make as many detours as we list, thus seeing much of your beautiful country. I am in no haste. Do not, I pray you, concern yourself unduly about madame. The accident is a slight one and will soon be remedied.

He closed the letter with a host of salutations and a flourished signature, sanded it, sealed it, and rang for Pierre.

"Send this to Paris by the count's agent. I understand he leaves with the rents shortly? Good! He will travel faster than the post, I think."

"Yes, monsieur. May I say," said Pierre respectfully, "that I . . . that *we* regret monsieur is leaving so soon. He has been most generous."

"It is only on account of this accident to madame that we are hastened. Otherwise we should have stayed some days longer. You have been very attentive. I have said so in my letter to M. de Besance." Pierre looked relieved and pleased.

It was not the intention of the marquis to have any but the best rumours of his visit at the Château de Besance emanate to the world. Even the man he had caned now considered himself lucky. No one but Lucia knew anything of what had occurred through the summer or of the night before. "And I am keeping her with madame!" thought the marquis. "It will be a pity if anything leaks out." He smiled sardonically at Pierre disappearing with the letter to M. de Besance.

Don Luis opened the window and called to Sancho. Some conversation in a low tone took place between them after which the marquis handed him the gold-headed walking stick which he no longer needed, his sword, his great coat, and a small strong box to put in the coach. He then walked upstairs and saw Maria and Lucia down to the door. No words were exchanged between them. The suggestion of something doll-like had again returned to Maria. She walked like a mario-nette. Even to herself her life seemed only a semblance and her actions corresponded. They were both apa-thetic and mechanical. As she passed between the lines of bowing servants at the door many of them noted how pale she looked. The face of Lucia was more anxious than the slight sling in which her mis-tress carried one hand might seem to warrant. Don Luis saw to it that Lucia had no opportunity to ex-plain.

"Au revoir, monsieur le marquis, grand merci et bon voyage," cried the servitors, genuinely sorry at the departure of a guest who had proved so liberal. "Adieu," replied the marquis with the ghost of a smile. He helped his wife into the coach lifting her under the arms. Then he took his sword from the seat, buckled it on, and climbed in. Lucia followed. The footman folded up the little stairs. "Ready, Your Excellency?"

Don Luis grasped one side of the seat firmly and waved his hat out the window. There was a report like a pistol from the whip of Sancho. The four horses started forward so violently that the front seat upon which Don Luis had motioned the two women to seat themselves was nearly drawn out from under them. A silent "Oh" formed itself upon the lips of Maria. She caught an amused gleam in her husband's eye. "It will be hard on the harness. Fortunately it is new and strong." Lucia broke out weeping. "Leave off that!"

127

said Don Luis fingering his cane. The woman turned deathly white and swallowed her sobs.

Don Luis was like an old general who after taking all the necessary care to bring a campaign to a successful issue had been betrayed to the enemy by his adjutant. His surprise and defeat had consequently been complete. But he was also a general who never abandoned the field. Annihilation was the only way to deal with him, as it was his own method whether in advance toward or retreat from an enemy. He was now seemingly in retreat after disaster. But what might have seemed to the ordinary man an irretrievable misfortune was to him merely a blow of fate to be circumvented, or even taken advantage of in any direction that remained.

Sitting by his wife's bedside the night before, the furnace of his soul had burnt at white heat under the enormous pressure of a will that never relaxed. The result of this incandescence was a hard, clear diamond of unadulterated hate at the core of his being. Such jewels are rare as the moulds which produce them. With them a few names have been etched permanently on the window panes of the house of fame. Don Luis' diamond was for private use only.

His original purpose of enjoying Maria and of having an heir on her body remained unaltered. Indeed, it was now fixed, in the diamond, as it were. The elements of pleasure had merely been transmuted. His enjoyment would now be that of hate instead of love. This fixity of purpose had been announced to himself the night before when he had looked into the glass the second time and put his wig back into place. What had been put askew by emotional circumstance was now rearranged. The wig did not at first feel the same as before, but it looked it. No one would ever know, presently not even the man who wore it.

While adjusting his wig Don Luis had also readjusted circumstances. This he had done to his own satisfaction. Every revolution of the wheels of the coach, he imagined, was still taking him toward his goal. It remained merely to dispose of the contents of the vehicle and to ward off possible interference from the outside.

About a half mile beyond the château the coach was overtaken by Maria's little dog which had been left behind. In the extremity of the departure she had not even remembered it. Having seen its mistress enter the coach it had followed as fast as its short legs would permit. As the vehicle lumbered up a short hill, the dog appeared, barking and whining. It kept leaping for the iron step and falling off. In hopes the wheel would take care of it in a natural way, Don Luis sat for some time ignoring it. Seeing, however, that it would surely follow them through the next village, at the top of the hill he opened the door. Maria could not keep from calling it.

With a supreme effort the animal made the step and started to wriggle into the coach, wagging its tail. With tremendous force the marquis closed the door on its back. The one sharp cry that pierced the morning expressed so well for Maria her own agony that she remained passive. The coach was now moving too swiftly downhill for the footmen to leave. They expected it to stop at the bottom on account of the dog but in this they were disappointed. Sancho evidently had his instructions. Over the worst ruts and cobbles, through the long white villages, past the low, truncated hills covered with vineyards they rushed southward into the valley of the Allier. The whip cracked and the splendid horses leaped. The two men behind hung on grimly to their straps. The two women on the small front seat shot from side to side and collided with each other. Don Luis sat back in the deep, rose-coloured upholstery and hummed an air from Italian opera. As M. d'Ayen would have phrased it, from one of those "perfect scenes." Occasionally he treated himself to a pinch of Batavian snuff.

———

When Denis finally awoke the sun was high and streaming into the room. He was still staring up at the ceiling with his body flung across the bed and his booted feet on the floor just as he had gone to sleep. He found himself stiff and unrefreshed. In the hard boots in which they had been encased for nearly two days his feet were chafed and sore. It was some time before he could recollect himself. As soon as he did so he went out to find the farmer.

It was the beginning of the grape harvest and his host was at a neighbor's farm some distance away helping to tread out the first vat. It was almost an hour before he and the boy who had been sent to find him returned. Maître Honneton seemed surly at having been thus interrupted. He stood gloomily before Denis. His bare ankles where they protruded above his long sabots were dyed a rich, red purple as if he had been treading in blood.

"Monsieur sent for me?"

"The message that came this morning!" said Denis eagerly.

"Message? But there was no message, monsieur."

"What! Are you sure? Didn't the maid bring one?"

"No, monsieur, and if it was to come from the château, surely monsieur knows that the marquis and his family have left."

"Left? Gone!" cried Denis all in a breath. "Why didn't you tell me? You mean they have driven off to the springs?" His voice rose with hope as this easy solution occurred to him.

"No, no, monsieur, by the road to Issoire, very early this morning. From the vineyards we saw them pass with all the luggage strapped on. There were small trunks on the roof. It was for a journey. They are gone."

"Oh, why, why didn't you tell me?" Denis kept asking. Maître Honneton had not thought it necessary. Monsieur had left no instructions. He knew Denis was tired after so long a journey. He had heard him return late.

They walked back to the farm together while the good man's apologies continued to flow. Distracted as he was, Denis could not help but be touched by his simple solicitude. He sat down by the well-curb for a moment to gather his wits.

He was tired, desperately tired. The trip to Marseilles had nearly done him out. There had been a thousand arrangements to make; the ship, the relays of horses. They should be on their way by now. The mare's going lame yesterday had ruined it all. And that signal of two candles last night! What had that meant? To leave without a word to him—it looked bad. The disappointment and anxiety added to his fatigue made him feel sick. And he had slept all those precious hours away! God! he must do something. Not sit here like a fool. He took the mare from the stable. At any other time her gentle protest at being saddled when still footsore and weary would have touched him to the heart. Now he pulled the saddle girth tighter and swore. Honneton stood looking on blankly. He scarcely knew monsieur. "He who had been so debonair."

Denis ran to his room for his sword and pistols. He renewed the priming. One curtain he noticed was blowing out of her window at the château. It seemed to be waving him farewell. He knew he would never see this place again. He took his things out into the courtyard and mounted. Pressing a purse into the hand of the farmer, he said, "Remember, should anyone ever ask about me, you know nothing." He clasped the man's hand warmly. The sadness of all farewells came upon them both. What had he done that as the man's hand left his own Denis seemed to have lost touch with life! He felt older and alone. He rode down over the slope.

It had rained the night before and there was a pool by the gate. As the mare passed she left one footprint. The water and sand began to fill it in. Maître Honneton stood looking down at it. Presently the faint, smiling curve of the horseshoe disappeared. The man hefted the weight of the purse in his hand with satisfaction. Here was something tangible. "But how long would even that last?"

With the motion of the horse and the fresh breeze in his face Denis began to recover his powers of decision. A thought struck him. "Perhaps the marquis had remained at the château and sent the two women on ahead." If so, he had better find out. He turned the head of the mare toward the towers. Then as he came to the cross-roads where the way branched to the south he saw the broad tracks of the well-known wheels. For a moment he was at a loss. The wheel tracks drew him like a magnet. He took after the coach and hesitated no longer.

So far he had seemed in a dream. Now he was thoroughly awake. His entire nature responded to the need for action. Only in action could he find relief. Who had blundered? Had she? Lucia? What had happened? He must know! Solange felt the spurs and loped on, in the opposite direction but along the same road over which she had galloped so furiously the night before. She was still slightly lame. No matter, what was a horse to him now?

At the top of the hill he found the dog by the road. At first he thought the coach had passed over it, but as he looked down at it, shaken by a tempest of memories, something in its forlorn attitude caused him to dismount and examine the little animal. How that unresponsive thing had once welcomed him and quivered at his touch! At hers! But the coach had not passed over it. It was not crushed! Yet what an attitude, not fit to be seen! He began to kick a hole in the bank with his boot. Presently he forced himself to pick the thing up. Its back had been broken. By a blow, a cane! Whose, he thought he knew. His mind obligingly presented him with a scene. Murmuring something which choked him he covered the puppy up. The hollow bank caved in and he stamped the turf down. He was surprised to find how rage weakened him. His knees trembled as he swung into the saddle.

What a fool he had been! He cursed himself. He had been too careful. He should have taken time by the bridle and ridden off with Maria two months ago. He might have known what kind of man he was dealing with in Don Luis. Well, he knew now. Yet, would she have gone with him at first after all? Ah, the enchanted forest, the magic pool by the mill, that day on the hill! It was springtime in this volcanic country that had detained them. They had been bewitched. The thought of her in his arms swept away regrets. It was an answer even to his self-reproaches. At worst he had tried to plan too well. But what *had* happened?

He hoped to find them at Issoire but they had passed through hours before. This brought him to himself again. He must husband his own strength and that of his horse. He saw to her himself; unsaddled her, gave her a rest. He took a cup of wine and forced himself to eat. Through the afternoon he nursed the mare along with a hundred little attentions that a cavalryman knows. He walked up the hills, loosened the girth, rubbed her down, gave her a little water carefully. It was now near sunset and the wheel tracks, those broad unmistakable tracks, still led forward relentlessly. It was a problem of one tired horse and a heavy man against four tired horses and a heavy coach. At last he topped a rise from which several miles of country beyond could be seen. The mare stood with her head hanging down while Denis looked eagerly ahead. The road was empty and led straight away for some distance. Then it disappeared amid clumps of trees, the remains of a wood. Fatigue and disappointment overcame him.

It was just after sunset when the coach at Don Luis' command pulled up before an inn. It had been passing through a deserted strip of country for some time; for the last mile or so between isolated clumps of trees that were gradually closing in to form a wood. The long, rambling buildings of the inn with smoke and sparks pouring out of the chimney against the darkness of the forest beyond was the only habitation they had seen for some time. Don Luis regarded it with evident satisfaction and sent a man for the innkeeper. When that worthy appeared the marquis stepped out of the coach and proceeded to arrange matters to suit himself.

He saw Maria and Lucia upstairs into a room overlooking the courtyard. He gave it a brief inspection, and remarking that supper would follow shortly, locked the door, pocketed the key, and walked downstairs. He held a short, emphatic conversation with the innkeeper, but in a voice which was too low to be overheard by the servants or the lonely young guest in the worn garb of a curé who sat by the fire turning a capon on the spit. Greeting the curé with the respect for the Church which a Spanish upbringing made instinctive, Don Luis returned to the courtyard.

Sancho had already driven in and was preparing to feed the horses when Don Luis approached him. The master and man talked together earnestly while a number of heads appeared at various windows and loungers at the doors. The curious little man with the tail was already causing comment. Then to the surprise of the onlookers he mounted the lead horse, swung the coach in a circle, and drove off up the road toward the forest. Don Luis returned and sat down by the fire. The young priest was just taking the fowl from the spit as he entered.

"Monsieur will do me the great favor of sharing with me?" he asked. "It is a gift from one of my flock and if shared with a stranger will make a truly Christian feast." The man smiled and arranged a bowl of salad and a cup of wine invitingly. The accent of a gentleman and the face of a youthful ascetic allured Don Luis. He thought he knew the type. He would see if he had been correct—there was time yet—and he sat down. The simple feast proceeded. To Don Luis' surprise so did the conversation.

He was a young man who evidently knew something of the great world and had enjoyed it, yet he had bound himself out as a parish priest in this remote spot. Who was he? Don Luis wondered. Influence might have done better for him than this. But the priest was now talking of his parishioners, unconsciously answering the questions which the marquis could not ask. The annals of his quiet neighbourhood lived and took on a pastoral form; peasants, and his life among them, became an idyll of primitive Christianity. "Such a delightful homily," thought Don Luis, "would make the man's fortune at court, an antique style." And how the man's face lit up as he spoke of his poor. But he was not asking for money. He was pleading that men of our rank—the "our" slipped out unconsciously—should follow Christ and come down and help their brethren. "Then they would know what the love of God meant, because they would feel as Our Lord had felt in his own heart. So they would be like him."

Don Luis felt himself comfortable despite the man's earnestness. The sermon was therefore a triumph. He also caught himself thinking that he would not care to hear a rebuke from the curé's earnest lips.

"It is not liberty, about which the philosophers are all talking, that men need," the young priest was saying. "Even fraternity is not enough. That is an idea. It must be a feeling, love. Love of each for his neighbour. Love, I say, kindled by God. That will make us equal. That will raise us all at the same time into one highest rank."

"And the Church and State when we are all of the same rank—what will become of them?" asked Don Luis. He had heard of men like this. The times were uneasy. The priest's face lit with the reflected glow of the millennium. For a moment it seemed near. "The Church will then be universal and there will be no need for the State. God will be our king."

The marquis pondered and took a pinch of snuff. By God, he would have to feed the starving then! The women upstairs must be hungry. This religious glow had made him forget them. He rose and listened. From some distance up the road came the sound of a trotting horse.

"I trust I have not bored, monsieur," said the priest. "A thousand pardons. I have not meant . . ."

"Not at all," said Don Luis, "quite the contrary." He gave the man a reassuring smile. "But I have cause to think that the person approaching may be a former acquaintance of mine whom I wish to avoid. If monsieur the curé would be so kind as *not* to call attention to my presence?" The marquis quietly pushed his own plate under that of the priest, and bowed.

"Certainly," said the curé with a mild look of surprise.

Don Luis retired to a dark corner opposite the chimney and sat down. Presently a horse was heard on the cobbles. Solange stood there with her head hanging down.

Denis had seen the track of the wheels where the coach had turned in, but he had also seen them still leading beyond. So he understood they had been there and had gone. He could force himself farther but not the horse. Well, he might get another horse here and press on. At least he would ask. He must rest and eat, too. He turned in and calling for the host began to question him.

The host was a glib little man. In the story which Don Luis had paid him to tell he was quite pat. Yes, the coach and persons that monsieur described had been there that afternoon but had departed about four o'clock. It was a pity. Yes, he was sure it was as long ago as that. No, there were no horses to be had until one came to St.-Pierre—four leagues! Would monsieur care to be made comfortable for the night?

Denis was not sure about that yet, but he would take supper. After that he would see. At this last disappointment, fatigue and despair descended upon him like a pall. He had not thought they were so far ahead of him. It seemed impossible. Perhaps they had left the château earlier than he thought. He opened the door and stepped into the public room.

He was too tired even to glance about the place. He stood before the fire and warmed himself. From his dark corner Don Luis inspected him closely. He saw with great satisfaction the look of fatigue and trouble on the countenance of the young man, and the fact that he now limped slightly as if his boots chafed him. He noted his long reach as Denis dragged a chair up to the chimney, and the style of his rapier. The disarming nick on the hilt did not escape him. A handsome young dog and one sufficiently difficult to deal with, he was forced to admit. At least she had the good sense to choose a man. So this was the hero who had undertaken to provide an heir for the Marquis da Vincitata! Very quietly the possessor of that ancient title loosened his own sword in its scabbard. For something like eleven generations his family had known how, where, and when to draw. Don Luis was not going to be the exception. His cause was the best; the place was opportune.

But he was in no instant hurry. He had in fact hoped that Maria would have seen Denis from her window as he rode into the inn courtyard. In that case he had intended to tackle him on the stairs. But if that plan fell through, as it had, he intended to detain him at the inn and take his measure exactly as he was doing now. But there was something more than this. A certain element of the spider in Don Luis permitted him to enjoy vastly the opportunity of sitting back in his dark corner and watching the fly walk in. Thoroughly a Latin, he was not only an actor in, but an author-spectator of his own drama. Circumstances were now collaborating with him to his huge satisfaction.

The priest meanwhile noticed the haggard look upon the features of the newcomer. The young curé was already familiar with misery in all its various guises. He was aware that the young man across the fire from him was in great agony of soul. He longed to comfort him, but the inimical and secret presence of his recent guest effectually restrained him. Naturally sensitive, and by contact with the primal substratum of life unconsciously, if not preternaturally aware of the atmosphere attending emotion, the room to the good curé had suddenly become unbearably tense. He felt as if he were sitting waiting for an execution. So strong was this irrational feeling that he began to reason himself out of it.

Of all this Denis was totally oblivious. So far a reasonable hope had buoyed him up. But his mind and his body had now sunk temporarily into a lethargy. The comfortable warmth of the embers made his fatigue more apparent to himself, and yet relaxed him. Supper was long in coming. His eyelids began to droop despite the efforts of his will. To keep himself from being overtaken by oblivion he called for wine. There was set before him a clear glass decanter containing a liquid alleged to be burgundy. He removed the stopper and held the bottle up to the light suspiciously. Instantly he saw a red liquid sphere through which drifted, tumbling and eddying, shifting clouds of sediment. There was a certain hypnotic effect about thus gazing into those bloody depths which, tired as he was, his mind did not instantly overcome. For some seconds he continued to gaze with a blank expression. It was only for an instant or so but—

Through the wine a figure seemed to grow and advance upon him. An oval pot-shaped body began to shoot forth arms and legs that wriggled up and down the sides of the bottle. A face with a black horn below the mouth grinned at him. The grin expanded clear across the bottle in a devilishly implacable smile surrounded by familiar features. Denis turned with the speed of thought and dashed the contents of the bottle into the face of the man who had stolen upon him.

"Death for that," said the marquis. "You fool!"

For some seconds they stood facing each other. They heard the wine dripping onto the floor. The consternation on Denis' face faded into relieved joy. So they had *not* escaped him after all.

He laughed like a boy. "For *that*, monsieur? Are you sure?"

"Draw!" blazed Don Luis. His sword flashed.

As the steel flickered in the firelight there was a loud crash of crockery at the door and the falsetto voice of the innkeeper began to scream, "Not in the house, messieurs; messieurs, for the love of God, not in the house!" He ran back into the court crying for help where a babblement arose while the wreck of Denis' supper smoked on the threshold.

"For the love of God, not anywhere," cried the priest, rising up now and laying hold of Don Luis' sword arm. Thus beset and hindered, the marquis beside himself with rage stood choking. The wine trickled down his face and bubbled on his lips as he strove to speak.

"It is useless to try to interfere, father," said Denis in a calm dry tone. "You must have seen the insult which monsieur has just received from me."

"The edicts, the ordinance of 'twenty-three! Have a care, gentlemen!" cried the priest.

The marquis shook the man off with some difficulty. Had he not been a priest he would have hurled him into the fire.

"Come," said he to Denis, "we shall settle this in the court."

Protesting, the curé followed them to the door where he remained to look on with gloomy anticipation.

It had been comparatively dark in the long, low public room, but outside there still lingered the late, white European twilight. It was that hour when the sky reflects and completely suffuses the last western rays, when very small objects in nature such as men cast no shadow at all, when a certain eeriness as of the meads of the departed settles down over buildings and landscape. The sounds of life are subdued. To some melancholy temperaments it is the most tolerable hour of the day.

In this calm light the two men in their shirt sleeves stood facing each other a few paces apart on a short space of closely cropped green near the centre of the court. The litter which surrounded it marked off its limits in a roughly oval boundary. The servants and hangers-on about the inn had already crowded into the court at the cries of the landlord whose anxiety that his place would be closed for harbouring brawlers led him up until the last moment to beseech someone to interfere.

No one, however, had cared to intrude upon the two determined gentlemen who burst out of the door. The red wine upon Don Luis' face and clothes looked as if first blood had already been drawn. That more was to follow none could doubt. Doors, windows, wheelbarrows, dunghills, and other points of vantage were now at a premium.

"I think, monsieur the captain," said Don Luis in a low tone, "that under the circumstances we can omit all formalities." Denis nodded. "Since there are no seconds, do you give the word to draw. I shall simply count three and engage. The present distance is satisfactory? The end you understand?"

"Draw," said Denis.

"Monsieur the curé," cried the marquis aloud, "I call on you to witness that all is fair and understood between us here."

They fell on guard.

"One, two, three!"

Their blades rasped and hissed together. The clash of steel, the stamp of feet, and the heavy breathing of the two men filled the courtyard. There was nearly a full minute of sword play in which no very earnest attacks were made while each tried to feel out the other's school of fence.

Denis' was a simple combination of the short sword fence at which any gentleman about the court was more or less an adept, and of the onslaught and mêlée taught in barracks for the heavier military rapier. It was simple but dangerous. But there was a lack of economy in his recoveries and a waste of motion in his attacks which betrayed to the marquis that the arm behind the point which now so persistently menaced him remembered the sabre. It was upon this that he counted.

So far Don Luis had in no way betrayed himself as a subtle swordsman. To Denis' riposte and remise his counter-riposte and reprise had followed, a trifle slow Denis thought. It was that upon which *he* counted. The marquis, however, although he was no believer in the bottes secrets of the old school of fence, had learned as a boy from an ancient Spaniard, one of the last

140

of the "Captains of Complements" de la cienca de las armas, a mathematical pedant of the sword. Nor had the supple and baffling wrist movements of the Italian school been neglected by Don Luis in his later manhood in Tuscany.

Thinking it time now to bring matters to a conclusion Denis burst upon his opponent with a furious assault, hoping by sheer speed and energy to get past the guard of the "slower" man. For a moment the air about the marquis was full of the darting tongues of Denis' sword. But to the surprise of the young man, the older by slight but deft motions of his body, which Denis had never seen before, avoided the swiftest thrusts. At the last Denis was not quick enough in recovering. The blood dyed his left arm from the shoulder down. To his joy, however, Don Luis now began to give ground.

An expectant gasp went up from the lookers-on.

The marquis stepped back with a peculiar motion of the feet as if they were being planted on exact chalked circles and squares, movements that forced Denis, if he was to continue the attack, to move to one side and the other of his opponent in order to find openings for his thrusts. For with each motion of his feet the blade of the marquis assumed the exact line which at once guarded his body and advanced his point. They had moved thus with lightning rapidity to the other end of the green before Denis realized that he was being led instead of pursuing. He must change his tactics. "God!"

He was almost exhausted . . . the long ride . . .

Suddenly the marquis straightened up from the knees and leaned forward. His left hand, so far held behind him as usual, now began to move forward as he parried, as if it too would thrust Denis' blade aside. Gathered up in, and holding a heavy cuff, this was precisely what it did.

Fence with two hands, sword and dagger, had long been forgotten in France. Denis was sure his adversary was failing and could no longer keep his balance. He rallied his own last resources and changing to a kind of half sabre cut, and half rapier thrust, endeavoured to beat down this ridiculous new guard of his enemy and to strike home. The marquis lowered his hilt and retreated swiftly.

To Denis, whose eye followed rejoicing, it semed as if the marquis' point were falling. "So it was the end!"

He raised his own arm, unconsciously now that of a charging cavalryman wielding a sabre. The impulse to thrust left his brain. He thought his hand leapt forward. And so it did. But the sword fell out of it.

Passing one foot in front of the other as fast as the beat of a duck's wing, and at the same time lunging forward from the waist, the marquis had thrust Denis through the heart. Almost two hundred seconds had elapsed since he had counted "three."

Denis did not move. Two spinning black discs collapsed into whirling funnels of darkness in his eyes.

A blank silence for an instant held everyone in the courtyard. Then the young curé ran forward and turned Denis over on his back. He listened to his heart and a few seconds later looked up at the marquis with an expression in which the emotion of a woman and the indignation of a strong man struggled for mastery. From the upstairs window came a long muffled, shuddering cry. Two white, despairing hands were beating on the sill.

"Ah," said the marquis, wiping his sword, "Helen has come upon the wall to see!"

"Monsieur," said the young priest, his face turning scarlet, "God has also seen."

In the room above someone came and took the white face away from the window.

"The provocation was mortal," replied Don Luis looking at the priest as if he had suddenly remembered an unpleasant fact.

"And the sin also," said the curé, letting Denis' hand fall. Don Luis' eyes hardened.

"Monsieur, monsieur," cried the priest, rising up and facing the nobleman, " 'Thou shalt not kill!' It is you and men like you that are bringing a doom upon your-selves and your class." His face worked. "Hear me, Holy Father, I witness against this man. Hear me, ye saints . . ."

Don Luis sheathed his sword and walked away. The voice of the priest continued for some time. From the stable Solange could be heard neighing. No one had yet brought her her oats.

The courtyard had by now cleared itself as if by magic. It was some minutes before Don Luis could find the landlord, and a quarter of an hour at least before he could drive "sense" into his head. The edicts against duelling were enforced mercilessly in France. It was not the intention of Don Luis to have to fall back upon diplomatic immunity in order to avoid being hanged upside down in chains. He had other plans. He took the man roughly by the shoulder and convinced him that the less said about the matter the better. "If you want to keep your inn open, tell your people to keep their faces shut, and do likewise yourself!"

"But if there are inquiries, monsieur?"

"Refer them to the curé and hand the horse and the dead man over to him. Get him out of sight now. This is not your fault, and anyway you can do nothing about it."

The presence of the marquis' two tall footmen made this fact glaringly apparent. The innkeeper decided to make the best of a bad affair. Ten gold pieces were in his pocket; the intendant was at Clermont. Parbleu! what could a poor man do? He shrugged his shoulders.

Don Luis went upstairs. One of the footmen went out to the road and waved a lantern. Presently the jingling of harness was heard. The coach returned, made a wide circle, and drew up again before the inn.

Maria's room was almost dark. After a little Don Luis could make her out lying on the bed. Lucia crouched by her side. He called out for the man with the lantern. "We leave immediately," he said to Lucia. There was no reply. Presently the lantern came. "Take this woman and the things downstairs," he said, "and see them into the coach. Leave the lantern."

Her room seemed empty and silent now. Outside a tree stirred in the night breeze and tapped at the pane. He went to the bed and held the lantern over Maria. Looking down, he beheld her utterly bloodless face with wide, still eyes staring out of dark circles. Looking up, she saw his scarlet stained features apparently glaring out of the ceiling from a circle of light.

He set the lantern down and took her hands to raise her. Her mouth that reminded him now of his grandmother's in her coffin twitched slightly He leaned down to listen.

"I will tell you. His name is Denis," she whispered, and went limp. He carried her to the coach.

Before the inn the bulk of the coach loomed up against the feathery background of the dark forest like a hearse with plumes. About it twinkled several lanterns. The curé and the innkeeper stood by silently as Don Luis consigned his burden to Lucia and climbed in himself. The footmen began to fold up the stairs.

"Pardon, monsieur," said the footman, "but there is blood on your face."

"Get water," said Don Luis calmly. He had forgotten. "Bring a bucket." He got out again and washed himself by the road. The young priest continued to look at him, holding his lantern so as to throw the light upon him. Don Luis was annoyed.

"Have the goodness to recollect, monsieur the curé, that this is wine not blood."

"I see blood," replied the priest.

"Where?" asked Don Luis.

"On your soul, monsieur." The curé turned on his heel and went into the inn.

Despite himself Don Luis suddenly went cold. One of the horses whinnied. From the stable came the answering neigh of the lonely mare. "Drive on, Sancho, you simpleton!" cried the marquis.

"If monsieur will get into the coach?" replied the man. It was the first time he had ever known his master to be confused. "Reason enough, too," thought Sancho.

"It will be a terrible night and the horses are nearly foundered." His whip cracked viciously. "Who knows what will happen now?"

Chapter Eight

A Hole in the Wall

THE coach rolled and pitched along. The road through the forest was bad and the darkness of a moonless midnight engulfed it. The two dim driving lanterns danced and swayed across the inky landscape like fox-fires. Sancho used the whip mercilessly. At St.-Pierre early next morning two of the beasts were ready to die. A wheel was strained and had to be replaced. Don Luis was forced to pause while men, women, animals, and material, as he put it, "renewed themselves." He himself was blithe. He drove a flinty bargain with the keeper of the post relays for some heavier horses. He left his own, not without apprehension, and pressed on. He was sorry for the horses.

Don Luis could not know that Denis had severed all connections, that no one would be expecting his return. He supposed that after the death of a king's officer there would sooner or later be some hue and cry. For the purely legal offence of killing a man in a duel the marquis cared nothing. At worst he could get out of it. That Denis had first dashed wine in his face might prove fortunate in case . . . He ground his teeth at the thought of explaining away his honour. A Spaniard before a foreign tribunal! His honour required that the real cause of that duel should under no circumstances ever become known.

No, he preferred to let the innkeeper, or the curé, answer questions, should there be any to answer, and to dissever himself and all that was his utterly and forever from the man he had left lying in the courtyard of the inn. As for the child that was with Maria, he would somehow take care of *that!*

After his own child came, later, he would eventually take Maria to Spain. She should live and die secluded there. In Estremadura hidalgos did not inquire after the health or happiness of one's wife. All this might take several years. In the meantime she might see reason, reconcile herself. In the meantime he had both private and diplomatic affairs to settle before leaving Italy. He intended to arrive there ostensibly in the same condition as he had set out. He had already satisfied his honour, now he would have the use of her body. It would provide him with an heir and a means of punishing her. He might even repeat it. As he thought about it he knew now that he preferred it that way. There was a certain zest. He looked across the aisle at her where she lay in the arms of Lucia. She did not move. So these were the two women who had thought to play the fool with him. A fine clever pair! There was a little surprise coming to Lucia, too. He drooped his lids and smiled. Sancho was heading due east into the Montagnes du Forez.

If they looked for him at all it would be by the roads down the valley of the Allier or in the passes of the Cévennes. No one but a crazy man would take a great coach like this through the Montagnes du Forez. But at a little hamlet in the foothills they stopped and purchased mules from the charcoal burners. The smith spent the afternoon forging two heavy chains. At evening the long clouds draped themselves against the massif and crept down into the valley. The wolves howled. At dawn the coach started upward.

Sancho rejoiced as only a Spaniard can at finding himself on the back of a mule. The whip snapped damply in the morning mist. The coach advanced upward foot by foot. The torrent beside the road deepened into a dark gorge. Where a waterfall could be heard roaring below they hurled down the heavy luggage. The two footmen walked behind putting their shoulders to the spokes at especially bitter spots.

By noon the coach had disappeared from the plains below as if it had flown into the clouds. Indeed, for much of the time a grey mist actually wrapped it. Three weeks later it descended with chained wheels into the valley of the Rhône. Sancho licked his whiskers. He would be able to indulge in fresh fish and cream again. They galloped south along the post road, pausing only for relays, and trundled over the bridge into Avignon. Here the marquis was out of French territory in the enclave and had friends. One of the towers on the walls had for some ages past been used as a dwelling. An old washerwoman lived there. It tickled the marquis' fancy and suited his purpose. He sent Maria and Lucia to the turret room. In the evenings Lucia could walk on the ramparts. Sancho followed her. At night he slept by the stairs and watched.

The conscience of the Marquis da Vincitata was a curious blend of himself, particular circumstances, and the times. Had he been a simple-hearted or romantic person certain short cuts to an immediate oblivion for his recent and present difficulties might have been found available. They had, of course, occurred to him, but only that. He regarded such promptings as crude, open to possible embarrassments later on, and beneath him. In short, he was not a murderer by direct action. As far as a man could, he merely intended to shape events. It was here that his conscience came in.

Whether he was religious or only fundamentally superstitious might provide matter for argument. Probably he was a blend of both. At least he had been piously brought up. The words of the curé had therefore made an impression upon him which that good man would have been the last to credit. But as a matter of fact Don Luis already considered the "blood on his soul" as a burden. His code approved, but his religion disapproved. Thus he was able to balance one load exactly, but he would not add to the weight against him. Above all he was in both religion and ethics a child of his own class and the century in which he was born, that is, purely conventional. In his ideals of conduct any analysis of motive was lacking. Hence his actions were merely an application in unfailing practice of a technique acceptable to his equals in rank. In short, his conscience was a code of honour tempered by some fear of the supernatural. In this precarious balance hung the fate of the unborn child.

In fact the balance was so very delicate that the marquis had come to a temporary halt at Avignon merely to readjust the scales in which he had undertaken to weigh out his own justice. True, he had already given them every chance of tipping in the direction which he desired by throwing in the weight of the coach for good measure; by driving over as heartbreaking mountain roads as he could find. The results, however, had not been so satisfactory as he had hoped. At present it seemed as if Maria would lose her mind instead of the child. A demented wife was not in the scope of his plan. Hence, there was to be a sufficient interval of quiet.

The opportunity of torturing several wives and so of improving gradually upon the method, does not occur frequently to many men. Don Luis was neither a widower nor a Bluebeard, hence his method with his first wife was not above criticism. The numbing mental shock of having seen her lover done to death before her eyes was greater than the physical misery which the violent motion of the coach could confer. It was from mental shock that she had nearly succumbed, and it was here that her husband had miscalculated. The extreme physical exhaustion of the trip over the mountains in addition to what she had already suffered reduced her to a state of apathy in which for a time she could remember nothing at all.

This condition provided sufficient respite to allow Maria to survive. Left utterly alone, except for the constant and now tender ministrations of Lucia, she gradually regained a grasp on herself. Her memory returned, but with it came the strength to bear it. After some weeks went by she began to sit in a chair on the ramparts overlooking the placid landscape that sloped away from the walls of Avignon. The bravery of a great despair filled her, and she determined, as she sat feeling the babe stir within her, to match her own strength, her determination, and if need be her life, against the will that strove to possess her body and soul. Despite Don Luis, she would bring this child of her love into the world. Its future she must place in the hands of God. She could do no more. The statue of the Virgin came forth from the black bag again. Placing it in a little hole in the battlements where the coping had dropped away and made room for a flowering plant with long green leaves, she sat facing it, praying quietly through the long afternoons.

Every evening when the old woman returned to her tower she found the young girl sitting with sorrow and rapture in her face before the Madonna. That Maria's sorrow was a tragedy which only heaven could heal, she understood. She pitied her. She brought her small bowls of fresh goat milk, mushrooms from the pastures beyond the walls, and wild flowers for her room. Only once was this blessed solitude interrupted—by the visit of a physician at Don Luis' behest. The kindly old man would scarcely have discovered in the subsequent proceedings of his generous employer the results of medical advice.

Don Luis had been engaged for some time in working out a mate in five moves with the governor of the town who was a devotee of chess. He had also completed sundry alterations both in the body and in the chassis of the coach which were not without a certain sinister significance. The body was painted a dull black, the lilies of monseigneur were removed from the door and a blank escutcheon substituted. Heavier axles and wheels with larger hubs were prepared. The sling straps were removed, the springs reinforced, and the body of the vehicle hung from chains. Save that there were no barred gratings at the windows, from the outside the coach now resembled nothing so much as one of those vehicles in which the unfortunate objects of a lettre de cachet were transported from fortress to fortress. No one would have recognized it for the graceful equipage which had left Versailles in May.

The cat-like postilion who drove the mules with a secret and malicious joy was the only thing which remained unchanged. For Don Luis' conversations with the governor had not been entirely confined to theories of chess. About the end of October the frigate *Hermione* sailing from Marseilles with replacements for the Indies was joined by his two erstwhile footmen who had unexpectedly changed the livery of the Marquis da Vincitata for that of the King of France. Whatever stories they might have to tell of their late employer would scarcely intrigue the natives of Malabar. When the days were growing visibly much shorter the coach and its four passengers set out for the Alps. The endless wanderings of one of them were thus precariously renewed.

Had someone from a great height been able to observe the progress of the coach over the network of little roads spun like gossamer across the landscape below, he would have been convinced that the owner of the equipage was possessed of a vacillating if not a captious mind. For many weeks it appeared to advance and retreat, to seek the most unlikely of byways, to make long detours and excursions, and to pause briefly at the most remote and sequestered spots. By a series of preposterous zigzags and circumlocutions it drew slowly near to, when it did not seem to be retreating from, the pinnacles of the Maritime Alps.

The exact state of "circumstances" which Don Luis thus hoped as he told himself "to achieve" had, however, not come about. Although he had indeed weighed his fist heavily in the scale, an unexpected strength in the powers of nature implicit in the endurance of his wife had prevented him. Without imitating Nero he could not get rid of that which he hated and retain what he desired. It was now nearly the end of December. He must be in Italy early in the new year. An occasional scream from Maria which she could no longer forbear and the indignation of Lucia that fear no longer entirely controlled were also annoying him. It would not do to have scenes even in the smallest towns, and he must retain some degree of hold on the maid. The last was now most essential in any event. The delay at Avignon had been too long. He had defeated himself. As he began to enter Liguria the calendar convinced him. He gave the order and headed directly over the best roads for the pass.

Maria had long ere this lost all consciousness of place or time. She seemed to herself to be tossing endlessly on a pitiless ocean, always in misery and discomfort varied only by crests of agony and valleys of pain as the waves passed under her uneasy vessel. Lucia had woven and fitted her secretly at night with a small harness made out of the strips of a blanket. The traditions of generations of peasant women expectant of lifting and ploughing till their time was fulfilled, informed her fingers. It was this simple contrivance which had so far proved a life-saver in the midst of prolonged and premeditated shipwreck.

The coach began to mount toward the clouds again, this time on a road engineered by ancient skill. The slowness and steadiness of the first degrees of the ascent brought to Maria a freedom from pain to which she had long been a stranger. Leaning against the shoulder of Lucia she looked out of the coach window and beheld the pleasant villages of the world slumbering in the sunshine of the plains below. The fields and hills of Liguria unrolled behind them like a painted map. From the mouth of the gloomy gorge upon which they were just entering it seemed like a glimpse into that toy paradise of which she had so often dreamed.

She no longer knew where she was, or remembered what had happened. The man who sat across from her was a stranger. What a fine coat he wore! She would like some of the long lace drooping over his hands for the skirt of her doll. Her tired body seemed to be floating in air. She was a great distance from it. She was a sleepy little girl. She had been lost.

"Thank you, signore," she said suddenly, with a smile in which all her radiant beauty seemed to shine again from her face as from a revived flower, "thank you for taking me home." Then her features sank. She drooped and wilted into Lucia's arms.

So deeply was the marquis immersed in his own opaque nature that for a while he thought she had been ironical.

They had left the summer below far behind now. Through the high pass as they slowly mounted swept the white, swirling skirts of December storms. The frozen fingers of sleet trailed over them and flapped against the glass. The road grew slippery and Sancho, as if he were loath to wet his feet, went slinking through the snow leading the mules. Far above them in a coign of the cliff to which the road staggered was a mountain hamlet. Once the clouds parted and far above the village flashed amid the shining atmosphere a sheer and breathless pinnacle of glittering ice.

Inside the coach it grew bitterly cold. Even Don Luis began to regret his temerity. Travellers at this season of the year had been known to set out by this road and to fail fatally. Maria began to utter at more and more frequent intervals a sharp spasmodic cry. Her eyes were closed and she seemed to hear nothing. Lucia wrapped her as it grew ever colder in her own cloak. The marquis finally got out and walked.

It was a question now whether they would make the village ahead of them. In the gorge it would soon be dark. Even the mules seemed to understand. They strained ahead desperately. As the last sombre twilight reflected itself down upon them they began to pass through a region of vast, purgatorial rocks. Don Luis shivered and re-entered the coach. Sancho began as a last resort to ply his whip again. The now constant wailing of the woman within was answered by strange

153

voices from the winds without. Slowly the coach struggled around a huge buttress onto another incline. The light of the village came in sight. An hour later they arrived in darkness and in icy storm. A thousand feet above them the wind from Italy raved over the crest of the pass.

Roused by the yammering of Sancho, and the thuds of the marquis' stick on the door of the largest house the reluctant portal finally opened after considerable parley. Maria was carried in and laid on a bed in an inner room, a kind of cave-like place, a rear wall of which was the living stone of the mountain. Through a partition the champing and lowing of cattle could be heard in the stable beyond as Sancho made place for the mules. A few lanterns began to flit about through the storm and the women to gather as the news of the arrival and the predicament of the travellers spread from house to house. Presently an old woman with a nose like an owl's and tangled hair through which her eyes glared piercingly arrived with a large copper kettle in her hand. It was filled with snow and put on the fire to thaw and boil.

The chimney, indeed, was the one comfortable feature of the establishment. It was wide and deep and fed by great logs. Few travellers stopped here and when they did, only by necessity. There was not even a professional welcome. Don Luis was forced to content himself with some porridge, tough goat's flesh, and a stoop of vile wine. He sat in the only chair with a bare table before him and Sancho curled up at his feet. The latter was fast asleep as near the fire as he could get. His damp coat steamed while he snored with a kind of continuous purr. Outside the tumult of the wind was incredible.

The old woman with several others had gone into Maria's room with Lucia. He could hear their feet moving about in the lulls of the storm as if they were stamping upon something. Sometimes it sounded as if they were being chased by mice. Maria's cries had ceased now. Presently the pot boiled over and threatened to quench the fire. He took it off and shouted. The old woman came out again. She jabbered at him in a dialect he could not understand. Her nose seemed about to touch her chin. He laughed at her, and she cursed him. "Of what use are men!" She spat into the pot, made the sign of the cross over it, and threw in a bundle of dried leaves. Presently the pure snow-water turned a cloudy green. Taking the kettle with her, she disappeared into the room again. He grew tired waiting. If the child was born it had not cried yet. Perhaps after all . . .

He wrapped himself in his cloak and stretched out on the table with his feet to the fire and his head on a small valise. Hours passed. It was after midnight. He dozed fitfully. The table was hard. The wind gradually died away. Once he heard the women whispering together as the door opened and someone came out. They seemed to be quarrelling over what to do. Let them! He turned over. Finally he slept. Maria was lying in the next room staring up at the ceiling. The old woman was piling hot stones wrapped in cloth about her extremities. Despite these measures her feet were slowly turning cold.

Lucia had come out into the room and was sitting on the chair which the marquis had lately occupied. On her lap was a man child which she now and then held up and turned over in the warmth of the blaze. He moved feebly and breathed. A red darkness like a shadow on his face began to fade. Towards morning he gave a few feeble cries. Don Luis awoke and looked at him but said nothing. He lay for some time thinking. Lucia wrapped the child up and settled it across her knees. It was sleeping now. She herself soon fell into an exhausted slumber.

Don Luis rose quietly and went into his wife's room. He was startled to see candles burning at the foot of her bed. She lay very quiet. There could be no doubt of it. Circumstances had again defeated him.

He turned suddenly at a slight noise. The old woman was standing beside him holding out her hand.

The marquis smiled grimly. So he must pay for it, too! He began to fumble in his pocket. Then a thought

155

struck him. He reached down, and taking the wedding ring from Maria's finger dropped it into the outstretched palm of the ancient crone. There was a worn, gold band on Maria's finger underneath her ring which he had never seen before. Some childish trinket, he supposed. The iciness of his wife's hand seemed to remain in the palm of Don Luis. Even the ring had been cold.

The old crone rushed out into the morning light to look at it. A heavy snow had fallen in the night and under the first rays of the dawn there was in that high, snowy atmosphere a frosty, pale blue like the hue in the depths of a cold lake. As she held the ring up to the east its single stone seemed to have concentrated in it a spark of fire that was surrounded but not quenched by blue ice. She clutched it to her breast and trudged up the road with the dry snow blowing like dust about her. Jesu-Maria! She was rich!

Don Luis strolled over to the fire to warm his hands. Lucia was sleeping deeply, her face marked with the heavy lines of sad fatigue. Her mouth drooped. The child lay utterly still, its web-like hands to its face.

The marquis very quietly pushed two logs closer together and continued to warm himself looking down at the pair. His face retained a single inscrutable expression like a mask. Behind it he was solving what he considered to be the final problem of a disastrous episode. The two persons before him were in question. Should he drive quietly on and leave them sleeping there? Should he take them both, or take only the child? It must be baptized as soon as possible. It might not live long. He did not care to have that on his soul in addition to . . . his hands clenched uneasily.

A log burned through and fell in the fireplace behind him.

If this woman ever followed him, he would know how to take care of *her*. The story must die, be buried here with the lovely and faithless dust in the next room. He hoped the glaciers would cover it. He had seen mountain churchyards like that—the ice wall overhanging the tombs, moving slowly. His was a great and honourable name. Woe to those who hissed against

156

it! He looked at Lucia narrowly again. Well, it would be wiser to give her the opportunity to forget completely. He stirred Sancho with his foot. In the silent room they whispered together for a while.

The silence of a great height and a heavy winter morning after snowfall now wrapped the whole village. The tired women who had toiled so long and desperately the night before had gone home for a brief rest before returning. Even the cattle in the shed behind lay quiet, glad of their own warmth. Sancho had given them hay and their usual bawling was stayed. Through the partition came only occasionally the faint jingle of chains as if someone had cast down a silver coin on marble. With great stealth and skill Sancho was harnessing the mules while they ate. Presently he tiptoed into the room with a small brass receptacle filled with charcoal. He dropped a few coals into it and blew them up. Don Luis nodded approval, and raised his eyebrows inquiringly. The man nodded and left his master alone.

Unlocking the small portmanteau which had served the night before as his pillow, Don Luis drew from it an unusually long, tasselled purse. It was half full. After a little search he found a small bag and untying it proceeded without any noise to transfer from it a sufficient quantity of gold pieces to stuff the purse like a sausage. At the top he placed a tightly folded note that he scrawled, and pulled the strings tight. He now opened the portmanteau wide and placed it beside Lucia. It was too small.

He closed it again, walked out to the coach, and returned with the larger black bag which had belonged to Maria. All this stealthily. He now put the bag in the same place beside Lucia which his own had just occupied and opened it. It gaped widely. Inside were a few silver toilet articles and on the bottom Maria's black riding cloak. The toilet articles he deposited in the white heat of the fire and then stooped down to rearrange the folds of the cloak. A hard object which he felt underneath the cloth he pushed impatiently to one side. He then rose and bent over Lucia. She still

157

continued in the sleep of exhaustion. One hand clutched that part of the blanket nearest to the baby's head.

With great care Don Luis slowly withdrew the folds of the cloth from the woman's fingers and gently laid across her palm the tasselled purse. She stirred slightly while her fingers slowly closed around it. Don Luis smiled and remained standing before her for some minutes till her breathing again became regular. In the fire the backs of Maria's silver brushes began to melt. White drops of metal began to course down the faces of Cupids to mingle with small bullet-like lumps of metal that had once been festoons of grapes. They now lay in the ashes.

Very swiftly, but equally as lightly, Don Luis lifted the child from the knees of Lucia and lowered it into the bag. He closed it, and avoiding giving it the slightest jar, tiptoed to the door. He turned on the doorstep to look back. Lucia was asleep. Only the top of her high comb showed over the back of her chair. In the other room the candles still burned at the foot of Maria's bed. As he closed the door the draught blew them out. Moving silently through the deep snow he lifted the bag into the coach, climbed up, and closed himself in.

Sancho put the mules in motion. Through the silent drifts where even the iron hoofs were muffled they moved upward toward the crest of the pass. Presently the sun, which had already for some hours been looking at the plains of Tuscany, dazzled their eyes. Sancho leaned forward gazing with his hand to his forehead. The morning clouds had not yet lifted. All that was going on upon the busy plains below still remained withheld from him by their ghostly veil. To one passenger of the coach at least the future was equally mysterious. He was still riding as he had been for many months before, completely in the dark. Indeed, it was not until many hours later that the marquis was disturbed by the faint voice in the bag. Don Luis also slept soundly. The small charcoal footstove imparted a somnolent warmth to the coach. It had in fact slightly tainted the air. But it was now burnt out, and they had long left the regions of snow behind them. By the time they began to pass through the villages in the foothills the protests of the young gentleman in the bag were too strenuous to be much longer ignored.

At Aulla the marquis was forced to descend to attend to several vital necessities. They remained till next day, the marquis at the inn, and the child with a wet nurse. She found the baby nursed vigorously, tended him, and wrapped him about with long bands after the manner of her kind. Some hours of the morning were passed procuring four decent horses. The marquis had no intention of entering his own country drawn by mules. Hearing the child reported thriving, Don Luis decided to chance deferring its baptism for some hours.

Indeed, as they rapidly approached his own feudal domains his self-confidence returned apace. His bodily movements became more confident, his gestures more imperious, and he no longer worried much about his soul. As they crossed the bridge over the Arno the obsequiousness of the officer in charge of the Tuscan troops at the little guardhouse reminded Don Luis forcefully not only where, but who he was. In short the Marquis da Vincitata was himself again. The experience through which he had passed had shaken him more than he cared to admit. But for that reason his mind all the more began to thrust the memory into oblivion. Every revolution of the wheels left it further in the past.

Into the future, to which every revolution of the same wheels was also carrying him and the child, Don Luis did not need to look very far. After a few miles he would take care that their respective paths in life should never be the same again. And he would continue to see to that. Should they ever meet it would always be at right angles, and on different levels. The marquis felt sure of his own. But the probability of their meeting was, he assured himself, and for excellent reasons, extremely remote. When the cries of the baby annoyed him he closed the bag.

They turned south at Pontedera from the main route

159

to Florence and took the road to Livorno. Don Luis had two small items of business to transact there before returning to the main highway from which, he told himself, he had been turned aside after all only temporarily.

Towards nightfall of an evening unusually warm for that time of the year the coach came to a standstill on a lonely piece of road on the hills overlooking Livorno. Presently it drove on for a little and halted again. But to the eyes of its driver, who could see remarkably well in the dark, it was plain that a figure had emerged from it at the first halting place carrying something in one hand. The man with the bag turned down a quiet lane bordered by poplars and proceeded rapidly through the dusk as if the place were familiar to him. Presently he was passing along the high white wall of some ecclesiastical establishment.

The Convent of Jesus the Child was indeed familiar to Don Luis, for his family had aided greatly in its establishment. Of its present financial condition he was not aware. There was apparently no gate into the lane. The straight lines of the stone walls continued for some distance. At last he came to what was in fact merely a hole in the wall. He placed the bag upon the sill and fumbling about in the blackness finally felt a cold metal handle and pulled it. At a seemingly vast distance within arose the jangle of a small bell. He retreated some way off and stood listening in the darkness.

The child began to cry. In the tense silence of the vast twilight its feeble voice continued minute after minute in a thin wail. He was about to return and pull the bell again when the noise of a sliding shutter prevented him. A light stabbed out from the wall and across the lane. The bar of it remained for some seconds as if suspended in darkness. Then it was withdrawn as suddenly as it came. With it the cries of the child were also extinguished. For some minutes Don Luis listened intently. A bell tolled calling the nuns within to prayer. He sighed unconsciously and turned away. It was, he knew, a custom of the pious souls who

160

thus received unfortunate orphans to baptize them immediately. A great weight was now lifted from him.

He returned to Sancho in a cheerful mood. "You can light the lamps now," said he, and continued speaking, while the lanterns were being kindled, in low, familiar tones.

"Sí, sí, señor, I understand," said the curious little man coming to the door and laying his hand sympathetically on his master's arm. "Always I shall serve you." His whip cracked and they drove away.

Don Luis leaned back and closed his eyes. His hand felt the hollow in the cushions where Maria had once sat beside him. It would not be easy to break the news of the death of an only daughter to her father. "Buried in the Alps, buried do you understand?" he said, "buried!" He repeated it aloud as though rehearsing a scene in which he would soon have to take a difficult part.

Only Sancho remained. One faithful servant! But what more could a man expect of life? He shrugged his shoulders. The sound of hoofs and the grinding noise of the wheels died away in the darkness toward Livorno.

The child in the convent awoke and cried out as the bag was opened and the light dazzled it. At the sight of a raw male infant one of the nuns screamed and caught her breath.

What was to be done with it?

END OF BOOK ONE

BOOK TWO

In Which the Roots of the
Tree Are Exposed

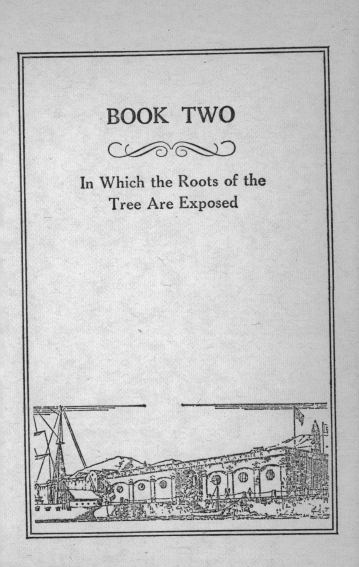

Chapter Nine

The Convent of Jesus
the Child

IN the Convent of Jesus the Child, Contessina, the lay
portress, moved about the central courtyard of the
place as quietly as her wooden pattens would permit.
She came every morning and evening to perform certain tasks for the nuns, and she was now as busy as
usual about the hour of matins. Since she was the only
able-bodied person in attendance upon ten querulous
old women and a boy infant her work was exacting
enough and would have exhausted the patience of several men.

But to the young peasant woman, who had children
of her own at home, and had no inclination to question
her lot, her acceptable labours seemed merely a form of
natural service in an immutable scheme. Her position
as "lay portress" was hereditary. It went with the land
upon which she dwelt. The convent had always been
on the little hill in the valley; her husband's broad
vineyards lay just below it, and as long as anyone
could remember there had always been a wife or
daughter from the white house in the vine-lands to

165

serve as a maid-of-all-work to the sisterhood on the hill.

Nor did it ever occur to Contessina to trouble herself that her labours were somewhat monotonous. On the contrary, she instinctively felt a decided satisfaction in their unchanging round. Change, indeed, was the last thing that anyone would immediately associate with the Convent of Jesus the Child. The very approach to it served to convey even to the most casual passer-by a sense of antiquity, security, and somnolence.

It was situated in the exact centre of a small, oval valley planted with vineyards that looked westward over the city of Livorno, the hills opening in that direction toward a wide vista of wine-coloured sea. The buildings, for there were several that rambled into a rough rectangle, were themselves built upon a little eminence in the dale, and were to be approached on all sides only by a series of deeply sunken lanes. From the high banks of these ancient, grassy tracks cropped out here and there, especially after heavy spring rains, fragments of marble masonry; the drum of an antique pillar or a mottled festoon of ivy on shattered stone.

In fact, the whole hill or mound upon which the convent stood must have been seething under its turf-covered waves and trellised terraces with the dim animal and vegetable forms of the pagan past. Perhaps there were even gods and giants, heroes and demigods with all their half-human, half-divine progeny buried there, the lost children of the ineffably beautiful and calm classic dream. If so, they remained now in a conceivably pregnant darkness, earthy spirits affecting the roots of things, while from the low tower of the convent on the hill above them fell the sound of the chapel bell tolling away by matins, angelus, and vespers the slowly passing hours of the Christian era. These had for innumerable generations been regularly marked not only by the prayers of the nuns in the chapel itself but by the bowed heads of the labourers in the vineyards below.

Yet despite the calm and serenity which undoubtedly surrounded the convent, it was still evident, to any eye

166

used to looking below the surface of things, that even here the restless forces of change had been at their usual work, albeit somewhat more calmly and with less of a tendency to become visible in violent breaks and shattered outlines than elsewhere. Here the forms of objects and the profiles of eras had quietly flowed; had simply mouldered one into the other, while to each generation that beheld only a little of this constant flux and weathering all things appeared to have remained the same.

No one except a curious and perhaps pedantic antiquary would have recognized in sections of the convent's whitewashed walls the dim entablatures of a pagan temple or have paused to wonder about certain fragments of friezes that emerged here and there into the sunlight only to disappear again behind more recently erected portions of the buildings or beneath ancient cloisters of vaulted stone. Here, as everywhere else in the vicinity, one thing melted calmly into another; only in the convent itself the process had been arrested and had congealed, if one cared to look closely.

The place where the running handwriting of time was most plainly visible and carefully preserved was in the most ancient and central courtyard or cloister. Here burst forth with a continual humorous lament, like the ironical laughter of Nature herself, a clear fountain whose source was either forgotten or unknown.

Above it rose an immense plane tree that overlooked the red tiles of the convent and all the countryside toward Livorno and the sea. Its top was the home of a flock of bronze-coloured pigeons, fed and regarded with secret superstition and reverence by the peasants for miles about. The huge, mossy roots of the tree, knotted and writhing like a cascade of gigantic serpents, overflowed the brink of the fountain, embraced the wide bowl of it, and disappeared with static, muscular convulsions into the fertile soil of the hill under the pavement.

Just at the foot of this eternal and apparently changeless tree there had stood for many ages looking down into the fountain the antique, bronze statues of the twins Castor and Pollux. In that anciently remote portion of Italy the change from paganism to Christianity had been a gradual one, and in the course of time the church had seen fit to consecrate a place which had never ceased to be venerated. The worship of the offspring of Leda and the Swan was discreetly discouraged while another legend more orthodox in its implications was fitted upon the statues. The bronze twins were said to be the youthful Saviour and his brother St. John, both in a state of boyish innocence. A church known as the Chapel of the Holy Children was constructed out of fragments of the temple and devoted to their worship. The clergy attached to it had in primitive times taken an active part in the harmless semi-pagan festivals of the neighbourhood; immersing catechumens in the fountain, and blessing the nobly responding vines.

Then, in some dim foray following the age of Charlemagne, "St. John" had been carried hence upon a galley of Byzantium into parts unknown.

The loss was a severe one. For some time the vogue of the shrine on the little hill had languished. But the ingenuity of the clergy was again equal to the occasion. The name of the chapel was now changed to that of Jesus the Child, while the illiterate memory of the countryside was encouraged to forget that the bronze boy who remained alone by the fountain had ever had a brother.

How the Chapel of Jesus the Child was afterward turned into a nunnery of perpetual adoration, how that in turn became an orphanage, and toward the end of the eighteenth century a convent school for fashionable young girls, was only the final addition of its quiet history, every chapter of which had left its mark in some indelible manner upon the venerable pile.

The tree, the fountain, and the bronze statue alone remained unchanged. Their natural and pagan outlines were quite undisguised. But the pillars of the court which had once formed the façade of the temple of Castor and Pollux were now the supports of the convent's inmost cloister.

The rest of the buildings clustered about it, a maze

of corridors and cells now for the most part long disused and in various stages of desolation and decay. The girls' school was kept in a more modern wing at the extreme end of the building, and the chapel alone was now used for worship. Even the ancient custom of a bride's strewing flowers upon the pool before the statue of Jesus the Child on the night before her marriage had been given up. The courtyard was now exclusively the abode of a number of superannuated sisters whose cells gave upon the place. And it was no wonder that Contessina, who clattered about in her wooden shoes merrily enough at home, felt constrained to walk quietly there—for upon this cloistered refuge of old age and antiquity there actually brooded a serene and immemorial quiet, a green patina of light and leafshade, a sequestered placidity that it was sacrilege to disturb.

The main impression of the place was a vision of light; a kind of trembling and watery iridescence, a flow of leaf-shadows and brilliant sunshine that filtered through the quivering leaves of the plane tree only to be reflected from the broad basin of the fountain and washed in turn along the marble walls. That, and the stream of water perpetually rushing into the fountain, lent to the whole cloister a soft, molten voice and a golden-liquid colour that endowed it with a kind of mysteriously cheerful life; with a vague and yet an essentially happy personality.

The tree, probably the last of a sacred grove, and the well or spring were long thought to have been endowed with miraculous powers. Even the conversation of the pigeons was once held to be salubrious for young married women to hear. But since the arrival of the nuns all that had been forgotten. Only the water, which came from no one knew where, continued to fall with a sleepy noise into a dateless, green, marble fountain hewn from a single vast block. The jet seemed to be wrung from the spongy mouth of a battered sea-monster whose face, scoured dim by the ages, had once stood between the bronze statues of the twins. The bronze boy who still remained was a naked child with a time-worn smile and eyes that appeared to have gone blind from contemplating for centuries the shifting changelessness of the pool.

In the very monotony of the changes which the bright fountain so constantly mirrored was a certain hypnotic fascination. All those who entered the court-yard were forced by a subtle trick of architectural perspective to look at the pool before noticing the roots of the tree. Perhaps the constant interplay of light and shadow upon the water accounted for the fixed and dreamless expression upon the face of the bronze boy, who had watched it since the gods began. Indeed, it was hard to tell, after regarding them steadily even for a few moments at a time, whether the changes in the fountain arose internally or were caused by something working upon it from without. In this its waters might be said to resemble the flowing stream of events themselves. To be sure, it shadowed forth a perpetual interplay of reflected patches of blue Etruscan sky and the verdant glooms and gleams of the plane tree soaring above. But the tree itself was obviously the prime example of still-life in eternity. And then the water, which at a first glance appeared to be stagnant in its green basin, was soon seen and heard to be flowing away at a rapid rate.

To anyone coming suddenly out of the gloom of the cloisters into the honeyed light of the courtyard the huge trunk of the tree was not at first to be discovered in the comparative darkness of its own central shadow. Raise the eyes above the line to its roots, and the tree seemed to be let down into the place; positively to be hanging in atmosphere as though aerially supported on the great fanlike vanes of its own wide-spreading foli-age, or drooping from the flaring parachute of leaves at the top. It was this effect in particular which gave to the whole courtyard that peculiar, paradoxical aspect of something immutable forever occurring without cause or reason, which is as near perhaps to a true vision of reality as the eyes of man can attain.

Most people were merely momentarily confused or idly amused by these manifestations, but during the course of centuries one or two sages and several simple-minded persons who had entered the courtyard had been suddenly shocked back into their own original and naturally mystical vision by their first glimpse of the place. All the habitual nonsense by which their minds forced them to construct a reasonable basis for reality was shattered at one blow by the amazing miracle of the hanging tree.

Yet the world remained; the fountain giggled, and the tree hung.

For a lucky moment or two only, they saw it wholly with their own eyes again. It was as if like gods, or infants, they had stumbled suddenly into a cloudy nursery where the forms of matter were toyfully assuming various astounding outlines for the amusement of the inmates.

And it was exactly in that mood or condition that a pair of eyes, hung on a convenient wall peg, were looking at the courtyard on a certain morning while Contessina walked about it quietly, hanging up some baby clothes which she had just finished washing.

––––––––––––

The pair of eyes in question were very bright ones in the head of a boy something over a year old who was hanging strapped in swaddling clothes to a backboard suspended from a peg in the wall under an arch of the cloister. He was quite used to hanging there for hours at a time. And as no one had ever paid any attention either to his cries of indignation or wails of boredom—except at precise and stated intervals when he was taken down—he had already learned the futility of protest in an indifferent universe composed apparently of vast, glimmering faces and shifting light and shade.

The world as he found it nevertheless permitted him to exist rather satisfactorily. With considerable internal discomfort at times it was true, but then he was not as yet much cursed with either memory or anticipation. And he had early discovered, was in fact fascinated by, the remarkable manifestations in the region of his eyes.

He already used those valuable organs well, that is to say, he used them both together. Through them the world was already accurately focused upon him, and he upon it; and he must, even in the course of a few hundred days since his emergence from the waters of darkness, have made many more profound inferences about it than some adult philosophers would be prepared to admit. His eyes no longer merely followed something moving or stared, they were, as often as not, directed from within and in such a manner as to indicate that he felt *he* was in the courtyard and not *it* in him. In fact, he was already quite sure of it.

It had taken several months and certain alterations in the shape of his eyes to enable him to arrive at this stupendous and not entirely logical conclusion.

The light and shade had at first been wholly in him. He was submerged in it. Then the light had brightened. As he hung on the wall and opened his eyes from the blank of infancy it was the first thing that had awakened his mind. And it had awakened it accompanied with a sense of well-being and joy. The golden trembling of the leaf-filtered light in the courtyard had washed in ripples of happiness over the closed head-of-consciousness while it had responded slowly like the submerged bud of a water-lily in a clear, sunny lake. That bud had at last come to the surface, differentiated itself from the surrounding waters, and opened its matured and sensitive flower to find what was in the light.

At first there were only shadows that moved in it like clouds over the waters of chaos. Then greyly, gigantic static outlines began to loom up in the mist. The mist itself became mottled. Patches of colours stood out; mysteriously and disappointingly disappeared. Spots of light dazzled; moved here and there like beams of a torch on a wall; vanished. Darkness resumed. He slept. Then the process would go on again—always a little farther removed; each day more distinct; not quite so deeply inside him.

And all these sights were for the most part accompanied by noises in the head, taps and thumps as shadows approached and withdrew, gurglings, chortlings, hisses, and strings of vowels. An occasional stupendous roaring or crash made him cry out. Then, lapped in his own voice, everything dissolved in sound. As he hung day after day under the arch he began to know that with the sunlight other things always happened or were part of it. These were a continuous low gurgling sound, and warmth. Sometimes the gurglings grew louder and were accompanied by certain white flutterings. This excited him pleasantly and he imitated the sound. As for all the sensations that alternately soothed or tortured him, as the wheel of life upon which he was bound and destined to be broken began to revolve, there are no names for them except legion.

Suddenly—for the instrument having prepared itself, he now blundered upon the use of it as if by accident—all this chaos was swiftly resolved. His eyes came to a focus one day as he hung on the wall. And there lay the courtyard before him, basking in the sunlight, awash with shade. The fountain glittered and the tree hung. The pigeons fluttered. Contessina, whose voice he recognized, and other forms in white moved to and fro accompanied by sound. Once having realized space, the directions of sounds next attracted his notice. Time began to glimmer upon him. Meanwhile the world beyond was every day more glittering, fresh, and beautiful. He lapsed into sleep regretfully and returned to the light with joy. He lived only in the light. Let there be light and there was light. Out of it all the forms of things had also been created from chaos for him as his own act of creation recapitulated the great original. The baby and the fountain sang together in the beautiful first morning of life.

For months this sound of pure human joy like the distant crowing of roosters had from time to time echoed from the walls of the courtyard to be re-echoed apparently by the fountain and carried off. Contessina and the nuns had unconsciously thrilled to it. It was a voice they had forgotten but still recognized. For

173

the second time since the child had come to them the great plane tree was in full leaf again.

Contessina finished tying the clothes on a line and walked over to the baby. She was passionately fond of it. She had three of her own at home but they were all dark little girls with brown eyes. The golden hair and blue-grey pupils of the man child hanging on the wall seemed to her to belong to another and better world. She made certain feminine sounds to the baby, the elliptical grammar of which conveyed to him a sense of her complete approval and a decided encouragement to continue to exist. In his own manner he replied. Contessina then walked away again.

He held out his arms to her but only tentatively. For he had already learned that affection was not always returned.

Contessina on her part was waiting for the nuns to depart to the chapel for matins. A number of the old women garbed in white with wide head-dresses were now sitting upon a marble bench in the sunlight pattering and murmuring their morning prayers with a sound as eternal as the waterspout itself.

Presently the convent bell rang. The nuns rose, formed in procession, and disappeared down a corridor in the direction of the chapel, raising a quavering morning chant. The pigeons resettled about the fountain and began to walk and talk expectantly. More and more kept coming down out of the air with the sound of tearing silk. The child cried out with delight.

Contessina now took him down from the wall, and unwrapping him from the board, carried him over to the brim of the fountain upon which she sat holding him upon her knee. He stretched and moved his limbs gratefully. The pigeons gathered about her, lit on her shoulders and covered the pavement with a plaque of iridescent bronze.

She produced a bag from her skirt and began to toss them some barley. Waves of excitement ran through the living metal. Contessina and the baby laughed. He began to seek her breasts. She opened her dress and gave him suck. The sound of falling water and the soft talk of the pigeons filled the courtyard as with one contented voice.

Contessina looked at the bronze boy on the other side of the basin under the tree and began to make a little conversational prayer to him in her heart. Her lips did not move and into her features crept the same eternal, blind expression that slept on the face of the statue.

"Dear Christ who also fed the pigeons when thou wast a boy, thou wast also once a baby, as thou art now in the chapel lying upon blessed Mary's breast, Contessina is poor and can bring to thine altar only a little wine from Jacopo's vineyards. Nevertheless, it is blessed by Father Xavier and becomes thy blood. Have mercy upon me. Accept also the milk of thy maid-servant's breast, which I share now between my own baby and this thine orphan. Remember them, thy helpless children. Remember also my old mother who Father Xavier says is still in purgatory and who suckled nine. Ah, dear Child, for thy own mother's sweet sake remember her."

Contessina's eyes filled with tears. She removed the baby from her breast, crossed herself, and dashed some water on her face.

The child was still hungry.

From the same bag in which she kept the grain for the pigeons she now brought out a little cloth package and spread it out on the rim of the fountain. The pigeons which now approached she drove away. The cloth contained some fragments of sausage boiled tender, some goat's cheese seethed with flour, mashed pieces of carrots, garlic and parsley all made into a kind of cake. She crumbled these finely, and mixing the meal with the fountain water in a clean hollow of the stone to the consistency of sticky gruel, she let it warm for a while in the sun. Then she fed it to the baby with her finger. It was a dangerous food. On it most of Caesar's veterans had been fed in infancy as a supplement to what flowed naturally from the teats of the Roman wolf.

Contessina now returned to her more usual tasks. She laid the baby on a pile of dirty clothes in the sun where he soon went to sleep. The nuns always remained out of the courtyard till about noon. Contessina pounded their linen garments with a paddle and soused them in the fountain till they were spotless. Then she laid them out in the sun to dry. By the time she came to the pile on which the baby still lay asleep she was hot and tired, and it was almost time for the old women to return.

She took the child up in her arms and went over to the fountain. Glancing hastily at the shadow on the wall-dial, to be sure she would not be disturbed, she slipped hastily into the pool with the child in her arms and sank slowly into the shell-shaped bowl. The water displaced by her body rose and overflowed. The baby gasped and clung to her. Then he relaxed and splashed comfortably as the liquid atmosphere washed delightfully over his frame. The pigeons, the woman, and the child all made similar noises. After a minute or two Contessina hastily resumed her clothes while the baby dried off in the sun. She then wrapped him in clean linen bandages, binding him to his back-board as far up as his chest. Only his arms remained free. When the nuns returned he was hanging under the arch on the wall again.

From the refectory the nuns brought him a piece of bacon on a string which they tied to his wrist. They took care of him through the afternoon until Contessina returned in the evening. She then fed him again and put him to bed.

As he grew older he began to creep about the courtyard. He played with pebbles and twigs in the sunlight. He began to stand up and dabble in the fountain. He shouted at the bronze boy across the pool. But that taciturn youth continued staring into the basin and made no reply. The days of the little boy who stood looking up at him so hopefully flowed away like the water with an unbroken joyous monotony.

Contessina would have liked to take the child home with her to the farm. As he grew older she saw that he was lonely. And she would have liked nothing better than to have had him trotting around the farmyard with her baby daughter during the afternoons. But her diffident suggestions were firmly vetoed by the mother superior.

Several curious circumstances had combined both for good and for evil to keep the boy, who had arrived so mysteriously and inopportunely, confined to the cloister. Indeed, it was largely his own doing that he finally escaped at all and acquired a worldly name.

The first thing he could distinctly remember was seeing his own face in the fountain. Someone like himself had at last come to play with him. He followed the "other boy" around and around the basin.

"Anthony," said one of the old nuns who had smiled and stopped to watch him in passing. So the boy in the fountain became "Anthony," his best, and for a while his only friend. The boy in the court watched the boy in the water and spent hours talking to him.

It was more successful than trying to talk to the bronze boy whose expression never changed. The lips of the boy in the water moved, and he laughed back at you. He was alive.

Presently when the child in the courtyard moved his own lips he said nothing aloud. "Anthony" in the pool was talking. Anthony in the court listened. And it was not long before he distinctly heard what the voice of the boy in the fountain had to say. They talked about everything. Their conversations continued for hours. They would even laugh together, a long rippling laughter.

The old nuns who sat in the court turning their breviaries or doing embroidery nudged each other and smiled. Their own conversation was always more

177

subdued than that of the water. Unconsciously, in order to be heard, they had fallen into a lower register than the constant babble of the fountain. Occasionally the pigeons and the water accidentally harmonized like a musical accompaniment.

How long these talks by the fountain with the other boy went on it would be hard to tell. At last what Anthony had always fondly wished for occurred. The bronze boy joined in, too.

It was now possible, since Anthony knew a great many words and had heard stories from both Contessina and the nuns, to continue and make variations upon the most enchanting themes. In all these "Anthony" in the pool and the "Bronze Boy" now began to take an active part.

Then there were the children of the ring who went dancing about the rim of the fountain carrying a festoon of ivy. They were somewhat confusing, because they were all the same and it made him dizzy to look at them. If he looked at them for a long while they seemed to blend into a misty ring as if they were on a wheel going at great speed. It was hard to stop them. And it was hard to play with them. For if he once began to single them out he never knew where to leave off. He kept going around and around the fountain because he could never tell with which of the marble children he had started. They worried him even in his dreams. They kept spinning and dancing around in his head till he woke up and shouted at them to stop.

Sister Agatha would come in and look at him when he shouted. She said, "Say your prayers to the Madonna." And there was some comfort in that, because *she* was always standing in exactly the same place.

He saw the Madonna when he went to bed at night. And when he woke up in the morning she was still looking at him from the little niche in the wall where she stood just at the foot of his bed. It was best to lie, he thought, so he could see her and be seen. Then he was sure just where she was when he wanted to talk to her in the dark. Perhaps she had brought him here? If not, how had he come here?

178

"Here" was the courtyard. It was bright and sunny, the centre of all things. On all sides of it extended corridors, long, dark, silent. He had once lost himself down one of these. He had been gone for a whole half-day. Contessina at last found him silent and white, shuddering in an old cell. There was a high window there and he was crouching in its shaft of sunlight. After that he knew what being "lost" meant. You were left alone with yourself in darkness. You couldn't get back to the light. And there was no Madonna to talk to in the corridors. She lived in his room, by the bed.

All the world beyond the courtyard must be made up of these endless, dark corridors and abandoned rooms. They went on and never stopped. After a while he learned that there were other courtyards. Sometimes he was taken there for a walk by the nuns.

But the other courtyards were strange. There was no bronze boy, no tree and fountain there. Only arches. Only his own courtyard was home. A universe of endless corridors leading into strange hostile courtyards surrounded him.

It was Contessina who told him about "heaven." Heaven was up there at the top of the tree where the pigeons went at night. It was in the sky into which the tree climbed. He began to lie under the tree in a bowl of its great roots near the bronze boy and look up. Sometime, he made up his mind, he would get out of the courtyard into heaven. He would climb the tree. The nuns stopped him now for fear he would fall. He began to wait until they were absent in order to try climbing.

The nuns were kindly enough. They were all fond of the child. Through the long afternoons they talked; they even played with him. They taught him his prayers. They made him clothes out of their old linen, stitched with the exquisite needlework that only they could do. He sat watching their embroidery growing on the frames. He learned to help work a little hand loom for them. They made him a doll.

But Father Xavier, the confessor of the convent, who would occasionally come into the courtyard, had taken

179

that away. He brought him a wooden horse, a ball, some coloured stones and a broken abacus instead. With these the child was rich. His life now seemed crowded. Through all his life ran the rhythm of the convent hours; the times to eat, to pray, to rise and to go to bed. It did not occur to him that this routine existence could be varied. The bell that marked the periods was as much a part of nature to him as was the rising and setting sun.

Some of the old women in the courtyard died and were buried. To Sisters Agnes, Agatha, and Ursula he clung all the closer. For the first time he became aware of mutability and a growing loneliness. The occasional visits of Father Xavier, who took a growing interest in the boy, were now attended with an excitement that the good priest took care to restrain. He pitied the child, whom he admired for his intense vigour and eager intelligence. He was at some pains to improve his speech. And he determined to speak to the mother superior about his education when the time arrived. In the meanwhile, he made friends with him. There was little difficulty about that. Even the careful Jesuit found it pleasant to be an oracle and a hero.

On the whole, however, the best times little Anthony spent were his mornings with Contessina. For several hours after matins he was left alone with her. From her came many of his rugged phrases in hill-Tuscan that so amused Father Xavier. And she seldom stopped him from doing what he pleased. "Young rabbits will play," she said.

She would let him plunge into the fountain and paddle about. The old women would never allow that. And it was pleasant especially on hot summer mornings to splash naked in the pool. In the centre it was deep enough for him to swim like a dog. Afterwards he would curl up in the roots of the tree and go to sleep in the sun. Contessina always wakened him before the nuns returned. She had long given up bathing in the pool herself. For a time he dimly remembered going into the pool in her arms. Then it seemed only one of his dreams of some vanished playmate who had haunted the fountain long ago. Soon he thought of it no more.

He was now able to climb up to the first low branch of the tree and to crawl out on it and look down into the water. From there he could see the little school of minnows in a patch of sunlight all with their heads toward the spout, breathing. He and the fish seemed to be bathed in the same golden atmosphere. It was from the limb that he talked to all of the dream playmates he had summoned from the deep.

They were as real to him now as any other people who came into the court. All he had to do was to think about them and they appeared; "Anthony" in the pool, the Bronze Boy, and the children from the stone ring who danced so gayly about. The pigeons were literally his bosom friends. They *all* came and talked with him. The dream-boy in the water would now come out of the pool. Sometimes when he himself was in the court he could see him lying out on the limb of the tree watching the minnows. The sunlight glimmered about him in the leaves. He would talk with him in a low tone of voice like the water.

"Anthony," he would call, "Anthony." And the boy in the tree would reply.

Most of these talks ranged about the wonderful fact that they both had the same name. Presently the bronze boy would join in. A story conducted in the terms of an endless conversation would go on for hours. His visions had become real. The Bronze Boy promised him that he should be able to climb the tree. At night he talked to the Madonna in his room. She remained there. Sometimes he heard her voice coming down to him through the leaves. But he could never see her. She was the image in his room.

On the whole he preferred "Anthony" in the pool to anyone else. The stone children dancing in the ring were still confusing. He marked one of them with a scratch and that stopped them dancing. Now they stood still. He had killed them himself. He looked for the boy in the pool again. Decidedly he was the best of all. He must play with someone. A year-long reverie about the boy in the pool began. It was delightful, unending. Anthony was at the same time himself and the boy in the pool.

When he was a little more than three years old his world, which had by this time become a hopeless confusion of reality and dreams, was enlarged considerably by his being taken to chapel. Father Xavier celebrated mass there. You walked down several corridors; you crossed another court, and went into the church. In some of the courts there were other things besides fountains and churches. He kept his ears open now and heard about these things surreptitiously. But he could make no pictures for the words.

Livorno? He heard often about Livorno. People went there sometimes. Livorno was in another court, then. But what was "a Livorno"? The Madonna was in the chapel, too. The same as the little Madonna in his room. He asked about her. "Yes, she was the same," they said. But larger in the chapel. She grew larger when she went there. So did Father Xavier. He was much taller in his robes, very long ones, when saying mass.

At first the child was intensely interested in the service but after a while it grew monotonous. He had no part in it, so he began to make stories in chapel, too. It was easy now, no matter where he was, to escape. All he had to do was to close his eyes and think. In the chapel he would lean against one of the stone pillars even when on his knees, and be somewhere or somebody else.

He would be the bronze boy looking at the water. He would even smile like that lonely heavenly-twin. The young lips had somehow caught the trick of the ancient, metal ones. Looking down at him, old Sister Ursula thought him rapt in childish adoration with his eyes fixed on the altar.

But to Anthony the incense was water spouting from the altar. The marble of the chancel shimmering with candles was the pool in the court, a more miraculous one. Father Xavier moving about was the shadow of the plane tree. And he, Anthony, he himself was swimming without effort in the mist. The boy in the pool would flash down amid the fishes naked as the child in bronze. How they dashed about! How cool, how beautiful it was there. Then a bell would ring and his own little miracle would be ended. He would be back in the chapel again.

It was in the mist above this miraculous pool in the chapel that he first began to see the face of the Madonna. The business of church was, he knew, in some way vaguely connected with her. Now and again during the responses he heard her name repeated. From now on she began to join the company of his dreams. She herself, of course, stood looking down at him always from her niche in his own room.

It was a small, square, whitewashed chamber. Besides a straw bed, a few clothes on pegs, and a crucifix, there was nothing there but "his Madonna." He understood that she in some peculiar way belonged to him and he to her. Before he could remember the Madonna had brought him there, Sister Ursula said. Her image dominated the place from its niche in the wall. For many years she was the last thing that glimmered in his sight as he went to sleep and the first thing he beheld when waking. All night she had been watching him, he knew. On long summer evenings when he seemed to go to bed too early her white face faded slowly into the twilight. Then the gold sun-burst above her features burned a little longer before it too went out. For a long time he said his only prayers to her. Then she became someone to talk to. He spoke to her. His lips moved slightly as though reading to himself, whispering in the dusk.

After he had once seen her in the chapel she came to join him with the water-child in the court. He saw her there now in the sunlight. The three of them began to talk to one another. The babble of the water falling into the fountain moulded itself easily in his ears into soft voices and heavenly replies. The other child lay in the arms of the great tree half lost in the gloom. The leaf shadows washed over him. Only his beautiful face stood out clearly. For many months these singular triangular conversations sufficed. The Madonna had thus more than answered Anthony's most urgent prayer. She had finally come into the courtyard herself.

No one would listen to his stories of the "other boy" without laughing, no one except Father Xavier. He seemed to take the matter seriously. He even shook his head. Finally he pointed out that the boy in the pool was only a shadow, like the dark one on the ground. Anthony had not noticed the shadow before. That followed, too! Everywhere except to bed. So it must be true about the boy in the pool. You could see for yourself.

But you did not need to see for yourself. Everything that Father Xavier said *was* true. The child parted unwillingly from his first friend. The image still came to play with him, but its face was somehow sorrowful now. That was because it knew itself to be a shadow. Now the real boy was lonely again. For a while there was no one to play with.

Then at last he found a way. He began to make "real" stories to himself about all the children of the pool. The children were imaginary, but the stories were real. After a while, if you made good stories, and did not ask Father Xavier about them, the children became real, too. If you sat very still they would even come out to play with you again.

There was no one to tell Anthony that there were any real children in the world besides himself. Everyone, of course, took it for granted that he knew. Yet how could he know? He took the world as he found it, and he had never been taken beyond the convent walls.

In absolutely forbidding Contessina or anyone else to take the child Anthony outside of the convent the mother superior had her own excellent reasons. It was not that she wished to be harsh or was narrowly bigoted; she had a duty to perform to the institution of which she was the responsible head. Both she and the boy confided to her care were, like everybody else in the world, to some extent the victims of circumstances.

Many years before Anthony had been thrust through the hole in the wall by the tender solicitude of Don Luis, the Medici had turned the little fishing village of Livorno, only a few miles below the convent, into the privileged port which has since become known to the world as "Leghorn."

The news of the "Livornina," as the grand duke's decree of free trade and religious toleration was called, penetrated into remote regions. English Catholics, Flemings fleeing from Alva, Huguenots, Turks and Jews found refuge at Livorno in great numbers. The town grew cosmopolitan and prosperous. The country around shared in the benefits. But not wholly or enthusiastically. Over the orthodox hills that looked down on the thriving seaport, where the wicked flourished according to Scripture, passed a suppressed but holy shudder.

The decree of Ferdinand was not to be gainsaid. Yet to snatch some brands from the burning of the heretical bonfire that blazed so merrily would assuredly be a work of merit.

Several pious, petty nobles of the hinterland combined in the good work urged on by the local clergy. Among them was a maternal ancestor of Don Luis. Endowments and legacies were soon forthcoming, and the ancient Chapel of Jesus the Child, which had almost languished away under an order of nuns devoted to perpetual, silent adoration, was reconstituted as an orphanage under the Sisters of Mercy. The purpose of the charitable endowment was to save souls, and the method of receiving orphans was simplicity itself.

Anyone, without let or hindrance, might leave at the hole in the convent wall provided for that purpose an otherwise unwelcome infant. They might ring the bell, also provided, and go away serene in the knowledge that the sliding panel would open and the child vanish inwards, to be baptized, nourished, and brought up in the Catholic faith.

The sisters devoted to this charity had toiled faithfully. Leghorn had become a great seaport. The bell rang more and more frequently. The numbers of the motley flock of orphans over whom the nuns watched bore ample evidence that the reasonable hope of the founders of the institution had not only been realized but greatly surpassed. Gifts consequently continued to be forthcoming, and the convent flourished according to its needs. All might have continued to go well had not the Queen of Spain insisted upon finding some spare dominions for her favourite younger son. In consequence of her maternal solicitude, one Christmas Day some fifty years before Anthony was born, the combined English and Spanish fleets had descended upon Livorno.

In the troubled times of the occupation that followed troops had been quartered in the convent. For a long time the sisters and their flock had been hopelessly scattered. When a remnant of the nuns finally returned in their old age it was to find their house dilapidated, their lands seized upon by tenacious hands, and their lambs, who might have been grateful, scattered as lost sheep.

Lawsuits had further harassed them. They lacked earthly guidance. There was nothing to do but pray. The place had been almost forgotten and the bell seldom rang. The few children who did come were hastily sent elsewhere in sheer desperation. Word of this went about the streets of the town and for some years the bell had finally ceased to ring at all. It looked as if the last of the sisterhood would soon depart in peace and poverty, when the Convent of Jesus the Child suddenly took on a new lease of life and service through the unexpected arrival of Sister Marie José.

She was not only very much younger than the other nuns, but capable, ambitious, and full of energy. What her former history had been no one at Livorno ever knew. She had been sent to rehabilitate the convent, and she prevailed against great odds. From the first by sheer force of character and circumstances she had been recognized by the remnant of the sisterhood as superior in fact. With the death of the ancient head of the house she had also become mother superior in name.

After some cogitation, her solution for the difficulties that already surrounded the convent was to avoid importing any more into it. That is to say, she tacitly abandoned the scheme of continuing it as an orphanage, which in fact no longer existed. Instead she started a convent school for prosperous young girls.

The license of the ecclesiastical authorities had not, under the circumstances, been difficult to obtain. Mother Marie José had even succeeded in awakening their languid interest. She was an educated woman herself, and she had been ably seconded in her efforts by Father Xavier, a Jesuit, who upon the suppression of his order had been removed from the court of the Duchess of Parma and had gone to reside quietly near Livorno.

Father Xavier combined simple but cultivated manners with an odour of sanctity and the smell of the lamp. He was, in short, a gentleman, a priest, and a scholar. As he had acted circumspectly, he was permitted to continue at Livorno, nominally as confessor to the convent, while his real work took him into certain cosmopolitan circles in the city that both required and appreciated diplomacy and the watchful presence of an able and educated man.

In the new school at the convent he had felt a powerful spiritual lever fall into his hands. Largely through his efforts the daughters of some of the best families of the town and neighbourhood had been obtained as pupils. Even some of the Protestant English merchants in Livorno sent their daughters to "The School on the Hill." Five new sisters had been lately received to teach. These, together with the revenues which were again ponderable, sufficed to conduct the establishment and to take care of the ancient women of the old régime who still survived but whose duties were purely nominal.

Over all this Father Xavier kept a constant and watchful eye. In most things he and Mother Marie José moved as one. But the mother superior was justly proud of the new school as her own creation and jealous of

187

its reputation. It might in a few years come to rank with those which received none but the daughters of the rich and the nobility. Such was her ambition.

It was, therefore, with no little consternation that on a certain January evening in the year 1776 she was suddenly disturbed by the unwelcome jangling of the long disused orphans' bell.

One of the nuns upon whom the habits of former years were firmly fixed had answered it automatically. A few minutes later Mother Marie José was looking down into the gaping mouth of a black bag in which lay a boy baby loudly lamenting his fate. Besides the baby and his meagre clothes, the bag contained the rich, dark riding-cloak of a lady, an ancient figurine of the Madonna and Child in a curiously worked shrine, and ten Spanish gold pieces. There was nothing else whatever.

Mother Marie José was now faced by a serious dilemma. According to the legal requirements of the founders of the convent she was bound to receive the child. On the other hand, she was now engaged in running a fashionable girls' school the reputation of which could never survive a revival of the orphanage. The two were utterly incompatible, and the baby was a boy.

It was also evident from the contents of the bag that the child was by no means a mere stray brat from the town streets. Persons of quality were somehow involved. The convent had already suffered at the hands of the civil law, and this made Mother Marie José doubly wary of a possible test case. It seemed especially suspicious that sufficient money for a year's nurture had been provided.

Besides, the statue of the Madonna that accompanied the child had thrown about him from the time of his arrival a certain glamour and protection. The pious old nuns, who secretly looked with somewhat hostile eyes upon the new school, regarded this orphan as their sacred charge from the first. If he were not received, trouble within and without the walls of the establishment might reasonably be expected to follow.

The mother superior consulted Father Xavier. A policy of caution and silence was agreed upon. The boy was duly baptized "Anthony," the saint's name day of his arrival. He was then relegated to the most sequestered parts of the building to be looked after by the old nuns skilled in the care of foundlings.

In another part of the establishment Mother Marie José and the new sisters continued to teach school without mentioning their involuntary charity. Except for Father Xavier, Contessina, and the few old sisters whose cells abutted on the courtyard, his existence remained unknown. No more unwelcome orphans came to trouble Mother Marie José. After a full year had passed from Anthony's arrival she obtained the necessary formal permission; the bell was silenced forever, and the hole in the wall bricked up. The metamorphosis of the Convent of Jesus the Child was complete. What to do about the young orphan who remained over from the old order of things was put off from time to time. The problem was not yet urgent. It seemed better and easier to let it alone.

Meanwhile the boy had begun his education.

One day Father Xavier unexpectedly came into the courtyard and took out of Anthony's hands some yarn which he had been holding up for Sister Agatha to wind.

"My son," said he, "from now on you are through with woolly things and the distaff. Come with me."

He led him down one of the long corridors and unlocked a little door at the end of it. They stepped out together into the bright sunshine of the world beyond the walls. The boy raised his little nose and sniffed the breeze. This for some reason or other caused Father Xavier to laugh.

Even here though there was nothing much to be seen of the great world outside. They had merely emerged into a deep, walled lane behind the convent. They continued down it a little way.

Overhead Anthony could see the same sky that he saw from the court. There were other trees there. He was somewhat surprised by that. So many of them! But he was still too small to see over the top of the high banks. The lane, he told himself, was merely a corridor without a roof. That was at least amusing. By and by, still chatting, they came to the door of a little house and passed through it into a marvellous room.

There was a charcoal brazier in one corner that kept the place pleasantly warm. A small window on one side looked into a court. Another court with new things in it! Birds huger than any he had ever seen were pecking about and dusting themselves. Pigeons were not to be compared with them. There were some old, high-backed, red velvet chairs against the walls. He could never admire the frayed and dusty tassels of these enough. Upon one of them he was actually permitted to sit. Father Xavier, a spare man in a tight, black gown, sat opposite him, smiling hospitably. He would answer all questions. He gave Anthony a small glass of something clear and sweet. Compared with this all else to drink was milk and water. Anthony could not find words to express himself. Finally he cried.

The narrow face of the priest worked with a surprised pity. He could, luckily for the boy, understand the fetters of the avid young mind so overwhelmed by images without words. The starved vocabulary that Anthony had picked up from Contessina and the nuns in the courtyard broke down even in this barely furnished room. The priest began to touch things and name them. They went to the window and saw "chickens." A cat Anthony knew, but not a goat. Holy Mother! what a miracle was a goat!

Here was a real interest in life for the priest. Father Xavier, whose story was a tragic one, was somewhat ennuied at his present post so different from his last, so dull. He began to freshen in the pristine glamour shed by the young mind just released in his room and beating itself about the walls like a dazzled moth going for the light. Here at least was something he could catch with his own hands and pin down, even if he had failed elsewhere. He would do it. The boy should come often. That day both his worldly and his spiritual education began. "It is fortunate," thought Father Xavier, "that they can be combined."

Father Xavier, who as a young man had once been counted one of the ablest instructors of youth in an order devoted to teaching, had long since, by his varied experience at the court of Parma and the world in general, acquired wisdom as well as knowledge. He could now look back upon his own career with discerning eyes and see what was worth dividing in order to teach, as well as how to divide it.

The suppression by the pope of the order to which he belonged had caused him to do a good deal more thinking for himself than he might otherwise have found either advisable or necessary. He was devoted to rehabilitating the Society of Jesus, but not blindly so. He, and the party to which he belonged, believed that new conditions required other methods of propaganda. Above all they desired an infusion of new blood and a number of ardent young men capable of coping with the modern world as they should find it.

In the orphan, whom adverse circumstances had so opportunely deposited in the courtyard of his convent, Father Xavier thought he saw a providential opportunity. He was not at all sure that the boy would develop into the kind of man, who, as he phrased it, would be worthy of taking up the cross. That would remain to be seen; "in the hands of God." But he might begin the good work by laying the basis of a broad and general foundation in which he determined that languages should play the principal part. Not, of course, that he meant to neglect the child's soul.

"For what," said he to Leucosta, his ancient housekeeper, whom he was wont to address for confirmation of his own opinions, "what is it at the present time we most need in the face of the breaking up of the old order? This oncoming generation is going to be confronted, mind you, Leucosta, by society in a state of flux. Why, then we need—self-realization accompanied by great self-control, a genial outward humility accompanied by a sustaining spiritual pride, and—a knowledge of the fundamental moral tenets of Christ's religion instead of a mere sentimental respect or romantic adoration for its founder."

Knowing that the father was always talkative during Sunday dinner after chapel, Leucosta, who was stone deaf, hastened to clear off the table and bring a bottle of crusty port which Mr. Udney, the English consul at Leghorn, had sent to Father Xavier. Mr. Udney was much "obleeged" to him in a certain matter. The priest sampled the wine with approval. "Fit for the orthodox," he said, and poured out a glass for the old woman as well.

Not the fecund imagination of John Knox could have surmised that Father Xavier was mentally encroaching on his vows in the direction of Leucosta.

"She looked like a mummy of the Cumaean Sibyl preserved in vinegar," said Mr. Udney to his wife, after returning from an interview with the priest preliminary to entering his young daughter Florence at the convent school. "As for the priest himself, he is the personification of geniality and wise diplomacy. My Protestant scruples were, I admit, set at rest rather too easily. I advise *you* to be watchful, however." The port had followed a month later and had something to do with mental reservations and an oath of allegiance taken to King George by an old Jacobite merchant at Leghorn. Father Xavier sipped it, reflecting.

"It will probably be a dangerous experiment and I must prepare myself to be disappointed," he said aloud. "But you agree with me, Leucosta, that it will be best to keep this boy uncontaminated by the world for some time yet. I wish a virgin field for the sowing of the seed, and the rooting up of tares is always confusing and wastes the time of the gardener. *Of course,* you will agree with me! That is the reason I keep a deaf housekeeper. You will recollect, my good woman, that one of the chief virtues of the Romans was that they consulted the Fates merely to have their own opinions decently confirmed. A deaf Sibyl is invaluable. It promotes the capacity for action, and that is the only way in which any opinion can finally be tested. In the end the Fates do answer. Thou, Leucosta, art an invaluable one."

He waved to the old crone to bring him his hat while he continued to address her.

"And what after all could we do better for the boy? A love-child, and as lusty a young pagan as I ever saw bathing in a heathen fountain. He is like the Angels that Augustine sent to Gregory. Or let us hope that he will be. Shall I turn that fine pair of arms and delicate hands over to Pietro the blacksmith as a human attachment to his bellows? No. There are more fitting ones in the village below. Or, shall I, as Monsieur Rosseau tends to advise, turn him loose into nature to become the wolf-boy of Tuscany like the little fellow in M. what's-his-name's pamphlet? No, no. One or two intellects who dwelt about this middle-sea of ours have thought of things that are worth propounding to the barbarians. And every new generation, *you* will recollect, Leucosta, is a fresh invasion of savages. Well, what can a poor teacher do then, my belle of three generations past, thou fate of all mankind? Why, I read it in thy wrinkled face. Even as all teachers have always done from the beginning of things; the best they can, under wicked and adverse circumstances. Now give me my hat, mother. That is right, brush it. The nap went years ago, but the conventions of respectability are thus observed."

And Father Xavier walked off down the closed lane to seize his young pupil by his "delicate" hand.

They slowly began to educate each other. They began first with manners and personal behaviour. One must know how to eat and drink decently. What words to say upon entering and leaving a room. When to stand up and bow, and when to sit down. There was, it appeared, a kind of being in the world called a "gentleman." Father Xavier said there were not many of them. One must learn to think and feel correctly about other people in order to become one. Manners were a sign of this. There was a certain ritual in the house for men and women as there was for *Deo* in the chapel. One must also be clean, silent, and pay attention. When you did not pay attention Father Xavier took the lobe of the ear between his sharp finger-nails and pinched. He finally left a mark there.

"Is that the mark of a gentleman?" asked Anthony looking in a small glass.

"In a way it is," said Father Xavier. "It is also *ad majoram Dei gloriam*. It would be better to have a small piece of your ear drop off than never to learn what both of them are hung on your head for. They are meant to listen with when someone wiser than yourself is talking."

In the course of several years the mark became permanent along with the lesson it conveyed.

"You see, my son, I do not talk to you very long at a time," said Father Xavier. "And when you play I do not interrupt you. You must do the same by me."

They understood each other well enough. Words began to expand into languages as the "talks" became longer. Anthony spent nearly all his afternoons at the priest's house. Languages began to expand into literature, literature into understanding and enlightenment. The old abacus had been repaired. It merged slowly from numbers into the beginning of the science of them. Along with all this went a growth of mutual respect and affection. Father Xavier had scarcely allowed for the latter. It troubled his ascetic heart sometimes as he came home to find the bright young head bent over the copying sheets or peering out of the door waiting for him to turn the corner of the walled lane by the little iron gate. Perhaps he was coming to set too much store by it. He searched his heart. No, he must not waver. Surely in this case the end *did* justify the means. If there were incidental rewards of human companionship the Lord might still call Samuel and remember Eli. "My son," he would say gently in Latin, and "Welcome to this house, father," would come the reply.

About the outside world, which he now began to apprehend lay around, but still beyond him, Anthony could never ask enough or be tired of talking. Forced to defend himself from the minutiae of every particular in the creation, Father Xavier took refuge in generalities when Anthony was six years old. He purchased a second-hand globe from some defunct scholar's library and began to talk about "the earth." Before he had even seen a field Anthony was aware of the major divisions of the planet. As long as he lived a large crack of leaking plaster extended the length of Africa from Capetown to Cairo. Soon he was reading animal fables and saints' lives in Latin and helping Father Xavier as a bare-legged little acolyte in the chapel.

The perforated incense pot which he swung there bore some resemblance to the many-nostrilled beast that spouted into the fountain in the court. At first he played he was the animal behind it throwing spray into the pool. He loved to make the smoke ripple over the smooth floor of the chancel which reflected the lights as if it were water. Then he began to learn, and to understand, what the responses meant. He began to realize someone within himself, who, as a being apart from his body, addressed words to some unseen Presence who remained a mystery. He was also taught the proper words to say to the Madonna, and he preferred always to speak to her.

For was she not visible, and real? Did she not actually live with him in his own room, not a mystery and a spirit, but close, and familiarly beloved? The thing they talked to before the altar remained unknown, a name made of three black letters in a book. But a name for which there was no image on earth, only a word. So it went for many a day with the good priest acting as father indeed. The rest of the boy's silent life was passed timelessly among the old women pacing slowly up and down the corridors with faintly rustling gowns and high, starched head-dresses. Or he was in his room, or playing in the court, or going every day down the "roofless hall" to the priest's house. Here only he expanded and lived abundantly.

How many, many times was he to recall in all the countless things that were touched upon there, and later revived in memory, Father Xavier's gentle, patient, and yet insistent voice. How many facts and fancies lived forever for him in those tones alone. Only of the reason that he must not go forth to wander and see for himself, of that alone, the priest would never treat. He must not, and that was all. Nor was this as yet a burdensome denial. The time for his release would come, he knew that. Lacking means of comparison, the boy's life seemed to him full enough.

Sweet are the uses of adversity and always unforeseen. The careful shaping which Father Xaxier had provided for the waif left in the courtyard was not to be devoted to the end by which he had justified the means. Old Leucosta, if she had not been deaf, might have told him so. The resources of the mind and soul of Father Xavier were considerable, but his foresight was by no means infallible. In the field he had so carefully fenced-in he had overlooked something. It was the giant plane tree which grew in the midst thereof, which from ancient times had overlooked both the pagan temple and the Christian convent.

––––––––––––

Half-way up, until it topped the roofs of the convent, the tree, sheltered from all winds, was a dense mass of foliage. For a long time Anthony had confined his exploits to these lower regions and pretended to himself that he was satisfied. But it was a half satisfaction only, clambering about these lower limbs. The best he could do was to lie out on the branches like his friend the dream boy and peer down into the shadows of the pool. But even this was tantalizing, for in the pool itself were to be caught now and then reflected glimpses of the open sky. Gradually as he became expert with practice, and more fearless, the boy enlarged the extent of his arboreal kingdom.

No one could find him there. Even Father Xavier had come into the court looking for him and had gone away. Anthony was at first surprised. He thought the priest would surely know. So it *was* possible to escape after all, if you desired. The sense of the possession of a secure retreat, a world all his own above the regions of the convent, aroused in the boy a feeling of independence and adventure which was the most delightful and strongest impression he had ever known. He cherished it night and day as his greatest and only private possession until it became, and remained, a passion. Behind it, gathered up now into an intensity which was equivalent to the stored force of an explosive, was a curiosity whose power could scarcely be calculated. This was impelling him farther upwards day by day.

As his skill in climbing increased, the bare, giant limbs that soared away from him to break into a second green country in the sky above appeared continually to lure him on. He thought of them for weeks. One day after matins, and an extra prayer to the Madonna in his own room, he set out after making sure that the courtyard was deserted before he crossed it. Taking off his shirt, for the day was already hot, he left the ground and swung himself like a young ape onto the lowest branch of the tree.

The first familiar stages were easily accomplished. He was soon in the great centre bole of the tree and on a level with the gutters. The leafy, sheltered area that shaded the courtyard spread out below him like a cracked, green saucer through which gleamed glints of the pool below. He was utterly alone now, dangling his feet above this flat top of polished leaves.

From here, like an inverted tripod, three great trunks split the main stem, one of which, more upright than the others, might be said to be a continuation of the tree below. It rose grandly, with here and there a few stumps of branches sheared off by the winds above the roof line, to a second and higher fork. Even beyond that it could still be traced, provided now with a more shaggy coat of shorn branches, and rising like a handle to support the dark ribs of the leafy umbrella which floated triumphantly above. Beyond that were the clouds.

The boy began to climb toward the upper fork.

197

He did not seem like a monkey now. The sense of importance of his own predicament had lent a very human caution to his movements. The slight angle of the tree helped. He hauled himself upward, placing his feet in the holes left by vanished branches and clutching the stubs and leaf clumps which remained. It was breathless. From the corner of his eyes he could see the red tile roofs glimmering below him, receding vastly at every higher step. Presently with his breast scratched and bleeding he lay panting in the last fork. The handle of the parasol now rose straight above. He looked up.

He did not dare look up or down. Should he go on, or return? After all he had come to where the tree finally forked. That was something. He might go back safely to the comfortable, sheltered life of the walls below and remain there—always—or, he might go on and see what he should see. The boy sat for some time with his head in his hands, wrestling with himself. He prayed to the Madonna again. At last he was able to look down without falling.

Along the edge of the roof trotted a cat with a dove in its mouth. "So that was where they went!" he thought. "They came and took what they wanted and went away. They climbed up as he was doing."

The cat looked over the edge of the gutter at old Sister Ursula who was tottering across the court on her cane. Through the maze of leaves below him, Anthony could hear her clicking across the flagstones. That the picture of the court was in his imagination made it the brighter. He watched the cat watching the nun. The sound of the cane passed. The cat turned, took a firmer hold of the dead bird, and trotted on over the ridge of the roof. Anthony laughed and again began to climb.

The sun beat on the back of his neck, and his chest and belly hurt him as he clasped the trunk. But it was easier than he thought. One hitch at a time, then the next. He planned each move carefully. Suddenly, before he expected it, he was safe amid the ribs of the parasol.

The pigeons, which he had often fed in the courtyard below, now began to discuss his arrival in doubtful and puzzled tones. Presently the conclave, since he remained quiet, decided in his favour. A few cautious dissenters departed. He lay resting and listening to their tones, the very language of the air.

Presently he wriggled up the last stout branches and thrust his head through the final fabric of the leaves. The spread of them just below him cut off his dizzy height from the ground. On the top of his gigantic umbrella he crooked his elbows and knees in the last branches and looked out and beyond.

At that instant his eyes were probably the only pair in Europe which beheld the world precisely as it was, a miracle of beauty beyond rapture, hung in mystery, and smiling back at the miraculous skies.

It was the colours of the world that most amazed him. He had expected to find it like the pictures in books, white and grey. In a state of pleasant rest after the exhausting climb he hung there in the boughs for a brief period of ecstasy, the greatest he was ever to know; time suspended, and all expectations surpassed.

Gradually he became conscious of himself again as the cool wind played on his face and rocked him. He began to fit pieces of things together.

The view coalesced surprisingly well. He could understand most of it in the large; the sun flashing enormously on the sea to the west; the dim blue outline that was an island; the far wavering coasts hemmed with white where they met the sea; the white roads all tumbling down to the town below. He could never see enough of it! He longed to be able to fly; to swoop down and examine things intimately like the pigeons; to cross over that blue line where the water met the sky.

Already his mood of complete happiness had vanished. A cosmic curiosity overwhelmed him and made him unhappy. He was like a starving man with food dangled before his eyes. He reached out as if to clutch all that lay below. The small pattern of his own hand blotted out half the view. He almost lost his balance, and burst into tears.

That night he was back in his room again, worn out with fatigue and excitement, but no longer a child. Like the cats he would keep this means of escape to himself. Some day, soon, he would get out and keep going, always. He would see it all. He would take no one with him, no one!

The face of the Madonna glimmered from the wall. After the great height and uncertainty it was pleasant to be back with her again. She had brought him here, they said. He began to ponder and altered his plan. He would take her along when he went away. It would be better not to be entirely alone. There should be someone to talk to. He began to tell her about the world beyond, softly, so only she could hear. It was a relief thus to share his secret. He slept.

Once having discovered the way to such a vantage point Anthony returned again and again. To the visits to Father Xavier's room, to the hours of reading and talking with the priest, there were now added long periods of observation in the treetop. The tree was used to supplement and as a check upon the more formal instruction received in the realms below. But from the day he first climbed it the dream companions in the courtyard below betook themselves into the limbo of memory. The boy by the spout retired with an archaic smile into the bronze; the dancing children in stone remained as if frozen forever by the chill world of reality.

Had the Madonna not remained constantly in his room it is possible that she too might have followed the others into the land whence only the burning wand of passion or fever could afterward summon them. She stood fixed there, however, day and night. Unforgettable, immovable, part of the living furniture of his existence. For he was taught and commanded to speak with her; to bring his troubles before her as a good and helpful act. In the life about him he saw others doing likewise and heard her name spoken by living

200

lips. The Madonna was not like the others of his dreams. His dream of her was accepted by other people as a reality. It seemed to be the same as reality. The Madonna had the advantage of still possessing a cult. That of the bronze boy and his brother had disappeared from the memory of men ages before. So the Madonna remained.

With Anthony she had already become a habit of thought. There were paths in his brain which belonged to her. Strapping her carefully on his back, he took her with him one day to the top of the tree as if to tempt her with the kingdoms of the world. Her silence in regard to them when he went to sleep that night was a distinct disappointment.

As time went on he began, as he lay in the treetop day after day, to learn much of the life of the neighbourhood. The houses and the people that lived in them, the horses, asses, and oxen that plied in and out to Livorno or from village to village became known to him. The very creaking of the carts as they passed by took on an individuality. It was in this way that he became aware of the presence of other real children in the convent besides himself as one morning he watched a small fleet of carriages bringing the pupils to Mother Marie José's school.

A small crowd of them emerged about the same time along the road from the town just before the convent bell rang, he observed. Once in the lane by the convent wall he could not see what became of them. Before long he became familiar, nevertheless, with the passengers of every carriage. Every morning they were always the same. It was seldom that he missed watching at that time.

So far he had kept his vantage point an utter secret. The joy of sole possession, the example of the cats, and an instinctive feeling of defensive reticence combined to seal his lips. Yet above all things he longed to speak with these other children who were now, he knew, so close to him. Even to ask about them would, he also knew, serve to betray himself. But he pondered the problem, nevertheless, day by day. He had almost

201

come to a dangerous conclusion about the matter. He was going to wave to them from the tree, when with the approach of summer the school stopped.

For a long, dreary time Anthony considered himself to have been left alone. He moped. Why did they not come back? It was often upon the tip of his tongue to ask. He began to approach it obliquely with Father Xavier, plying him with questions about the world without which seemed to the priest to be surprisingly knowing ones. But the boy dared not come to the point and would fall into silence and sulk.

Father Xavier felt that the time had come to settle something about Anthony. He had his own plans. He would have liked to prepare the boy for entrance to a seminary near Rome. He must begin by taking him about with him outside. There was something about the cast of the boy's mind which he did not altogether like. His avid questionings and the things which moved him most reminded the priest too frequently of the idle curiosity of the age without the walls. He had tried to protect his charge from this in a way, and yet perhaps he had also been to blame for awakening it. Under the circumstances though . . . He spoke to Mother Marie José about it. She agreed with him.

By all means the boy should be given his first sight of life beyond the walls in the company of his ghostly tutor. How better could it first be brought home to him? In fact she had almost forgotten about Anthony. She was very busy about several things. It might be better, too, to wait until the pupils for the coming term were secured before parading the unwelcome presence of this orphan about the town. Undoubtedly, that would be talked about. She sent for Anthony. In her formal presence the boy froze within himself. Her voice from long hours of instruction was unintentionally harsh. Anthony remained silent. She could find nothing in him of the qualities Father Xavier had enlarged upon. The misplaced enthusiasm of the childless priest, she thought. This could wait. Anthony was remanded to the courtyard. Indeed he fled there in relief. He climbed the tree and Father Xavier could not find him.

Another summer slipped by punctuated only by escape into the cool heights of the boughs, the droning of the pigeons and of Father Xavier.

Chapter Ten

The Chick Emerges

IT WAS a great day for Anthony when in the late autumn he once more saw the dust of the approaching vehicles and the children returned. Reality was once more brought home to him. There were several new girls. One, who arrived nearly always a little late in a cart behind a lazy, fat pony, especially delighted him. She was about his own size and her wriggles were noteworthy. He could not quite make out her features. The cart always disappeared when he was just about to catch a full glimpse of her face into the lane behind the wall. It was impossible to look closer for the edge of the roof cut off his view. He tried to imagine her into the court but she had no face. Somehow, too, he had lost the trick of evoking vivid dreams. The reality was now so much plainer. The glimpses of her enchanting arrivals and departures grew more and more tantalizing. See her face, speak to her, he must.

He began to investigate the plan of the corridors beyond the huge, half-vacant wing of the convent that he already knew. He soon discovered an important fact. While the children were present, all the nuns in the other part of the building were absent from their rooms. This gave him courage. He began to explore more thoroughly.

On the third day, he found the corridor that led to the door. Breathless and on tiptoe, more frightened even than when he had climbed the tree, he ventured to the threshold and looked out. The world lay before him on its own level. All he had to do was to put his feet upon it and walk out. He did so cautiously, then brazenly. As the shadow of the roof passed from his head and the full sunlight burst upon him, he ceased from half-crouching and stood up manfully. At last, and forever, he knew himself to be free. The spell of the place had been broken conclusively. No one had led him. He had found the way out himself.

Even now, however, he still found himself in a lane with the convent on one side and a high wall on the other. In both directions it made a slight curve and he could not see beyond. He turned to the right and started to walk. He passed a place in the wall of the convent that was filled up with new bricks of a brighter colour than the rest, a blind window. Then the trees started to meet overhead and became vaguely familiar. Suddenly he found himself before the door of the priest's house. "Come in," said Father Xavier's voice.

Anthony walked in and sat down. He felt weak with apprehension. It was some minutes before he could bring himself to believe that the priest had not noticed the unusual direction of his approach. Not to have been found out upon this occasion gave him a confidence which he never lost. That afternoon Father Xavier began to talk to Anthony about his future. To the priest's suggestion of the seminary the boy made no comment. He sat silent, puzzling over the direction of the lane. "In a few years if you are attentive and do well, you can go to Rome," Father Xavier was saying. Anthony was wondering where the lane led when you turned the other way. The next day he found out for himself.

It was lucky, thought Anthony, that the little girl

whose face he could not see always came late. He watched her one morning from the tree approaching after all the others had arrived. The pony took considerable persuading. The boy slithered to the ground and darting through the corridors ran out and placed himself in an offset of the wall until she drove up. A half-grown Italian lad held the reins. Anthony was dressed in nothing but a long, ragged cassock that flapped about his bare feet. It had once belonged to Father Xavier and the row of rusty buttons ran from the neck to the ground. The boy had a good view of the little girl. Under a mop of brown hair, she had a fair, chubby face and blue eyes. Anthony lounged close to the wall and said nothing. Neither the little girl nor her driver paid any attention to him beyond giving him a glance. The sight of acolytes lounging about near chapels was not novel to them. The little girl took her satchel and went into school. Beyond making a face at Anthony when he drove away even the driver ignored him.

Morning after morning, whenever circumstances would permit him to leave the court without being noticed, and regardless of the weather, Anthony continued to wait by the same nook in the wall. Some time during the second week he was rewarded by a smile. A little later he ventured to hold the pony while she left the cart, and to strike up a friendship with the lad who drove her. Anthony was now rewarded with a "good morning" to which after some days he ventured to reply. Secretly, to both children, the sound of their own voices thus exchanged was thrilling, but especially to Anthony. The little girl was proud that he came to hold her pony. No one did so for the other girls. Knowing that she would be teased about it if she said anything, she held her tongue.

From Angelo the driver, Anthony gradually learned all there was to know about his "puella." The older boy laughed at his queer jargon of convent Latin and Italian, correcting him loftily. Anthony had the good sense to be humble before this older boy and thus lived in his good graces. He, Angelo, worked for

Meester Udney, the English consul at Livorno. *Mees* Florence was the consul's daughter. The Udneys had two great houses and were very rich. All of the Inglesi were rich. Most of them were heretics. Angelo crossed himself. He lived in great fear of the evil eye. It was from the villa that they drove every day, only sometimes in town. The pony was slow, and they had permission from the mother superior to be late—when necessary. It was always necessary. Angelo grinned. Miss Florence, it appeared, usually had her own way.

One morning Anthony presented her with some pigeon eggs in a little nest of woven leaves which he had made. The gift was acceptable. About Totnes she had once hunted for birds' eggs with her cousins. Here at Livorno it was not permitted. She was the consul's daughter! The eggs were adorable. In return she brought Anthony a pair of shoes. They were too short for him but he cut out the toes and after that refrained from meeting her in entirely bare feet.

He told her about the pigeons and how he had first seen her from the tree where the birds lived. The restraint gradually wore off from their brief morning talks. Every day they had some childish news to exchange, usually about animals. Anthony about his pigeons and the cats; the girl about her pets at home. Before the term was over it was arranged between them that Anthony should come to see her rabbits. There were also several puppies that had become the heroes of an animal epic recounted from day to day.

Angelo demurred to this plan at first. Anthony would have to ride to the villa in the pony cart. It appeared slightly irregular. Orders had been given by Mr. Udney that no one should be given rides in the cart. Miss Florence stamped her foot, however, and argued her case. After several days of appeal, cajolery, and threats Angelo succumbed. Anthony was to lie in the back of the cart with a wrap thrown over him. How he was to return did not concern either himself or the other conspirators—as yet.

One afternoon he borrowed Father Xavier's hat and whisking himself to the end of the lane stood waiting patiently till the rumble of the departing carriages ceased. Some minutes later the pony cart with Angelo and Florence passed by slowly as had been arranged. Climbing into it hastily, Anthony wriggled under the rug in the back, and they were off.

It was a marvellous sensation bumping along by the efforts of someone else. Miss Florence was bubbling with suppressed excitement and laughter. Angelo put the pony through what paces it might be said to have had. He succeeded at least in making it wheeze. It is doubtful if Elijah enjoyed the triumph of his chariot journey to Heaven as keenly as did Anthony his trip in the pony cart to the modest villa of Mr. Udney. Both were a transit to paradise. But to be able to peep out from the blanket and to see the scenes which he had so often observed from the tree actually passing before his eyes, to catch a glimpse now and then of a laughing face, a real one, smiling down at him—what were the rewards of a mere prophet compared to all this? Besides, the speed, particularly downhill, was prodigious. He could scarcely believe he was not dreaming when he closed his eyes under the blanket. The very pain of the bumps gave him pleasure. They were so reassuring. Presently they turned into an avenue lined with poplars. Anthony was commanded to cover up and keep still. After some delay, strange voices, and the smell of a strange place, Angelo uncovered him and the boy found himself in the stable yard of the villa. He was being shown the horses, huge beasts he thought, when Florence came out and joined him. She had changed out of her school dress and was in a long, blue frock with ribbons. She was more beautiful than anything Anthony had ever seen. Miss Florence was a very small girl but she was not too young to enjoy being admired even by a ragged acolyte. After giving him more than sufficient time to recover his breath, they went to see her rabbit hutch.

Confronted by such an ideal beast as a rabbit for the first time; actually permitted to hold one in his hands, Anthony was reduced to tears. He could not help himself. It was too much.

"They *are* lovely," whispered Florence. "I like the white ones best."

He nodded sympathetically, wiping his eyes on Father Xavier's best hat. They both agreed that the tweaking nose of the largest rabbit was a miracle of rare device. From the rabbits they passed out into the rear courtyard which, it appeared, was the abode of the pups.

By this time Anthony had forgotten his entire past, and the future did not yet exist. Lost solely in each other, and in the animal riot about their feet, the sylvan voices of the two children laughing uncontrollably at the comical pranks of dogdom floated into the library window to the ears of Mrs. Udney. She crossed the room to look out, stood for a minute amazed, and then turned her head to say in a half whisper, "Come here, Henry." Mr. Udney—who was perusing a document the last line of which averred, "your petitioner will ever pray"—was glad to be recalled to life. He dropped the paper on the floor and joined his wife. It was a singular scene upon which they now looked down.

Standing in the middle of the yard was their daughter Florence with her frock in the most admired disorder. She was looking up with an expression of extreme happiness into the face of a figure whose grotesqueness passed belief.

Presented to the view of Mr. and Mrs. Udney was the back of a huge triangular priest's hat clapped upon the invisible head of a young body in a long, black, clerical gown that fell in one sheer line from neck to bare, brown calves. One point of the hat, which was worn at the angle of a shed roof, was exactly between a pair of shoulder blades that appeared through the gown as did two elbows from their ragged sleeves. The effect upon the spectator was that of having been suddenly presented with the eye of Don Quixote, or, that Lazarus had taken orders. While the Udneys gasped, the laughter in the court continued till the stable arches rang.

The laughter was the least bit hysterical now. Mrs.

Udney giggled. "My dear," said she, "where do you suppose she found him?" "I'll be demned!" said Mr. Udney, changing the sound of one vowel out of deference to his spouse. "Let us have them up." He cleared his throat in a preparatory manner—"Florence!" Laughter in the court ceased. The children felt they were seen. Anthony felt an impulse to run, mastered it, and turned toward the direction of the voice. "Take off your hat," whispered the little girl, "it's mother." The boy removed his hat with an unavoidable flourish owing to its size and tucked it like a picture frame under his arm. He looked up.

The removal of the hat did not disclose an ecclesiastical gnome but the fair face of an English boy rather deeply tanned, yet still unmistakable, under delicate ringlets of yellow hair. His features were more than usually aquiline. There was a firm little jaw, a broad brow, and grey-blue eyes. If anything, the face was perhaps a little too thin. But this not unpleasant hint of keenness was tempered by far-looking eyes and half-parted lips into the expression of one not fully awakened yet from a remembered dream. The head sat upon a firm neck, while the narrow-waisted black gown with its long row of buttons made the boy look taller than he actually was. In the afternoon's sunlight he seemed to radiate a certain indescribable lustre like the leaves of a fresh plant after rain. Mrs. Udney, who had no son as yet, felt her bodice move. Her husband laughed unconsciously. "Upon my word!" he said. "Florence," he called, "bring up your prince of the church for tea." He turned away from the window chuckling.

"How do you suppose a face like that got to Italy?" he asked his wife. "Leghorn is a peculiar place. King George seems to have lost a subject somehow." The consul in him felt a dim impulse to inquire—at which Mr. Udney smiled. His wife remained by the window. Their cogitations upon different lines were now interrupted by the arrival of one Signore Terrini, a dandified young painter, whose tailor aped English styles in an Italian way.

210

Florence took Anthony by the hand not engaged with the hat and led him up to the library. The boy could not forget that room; the long white curtains rippling in and out through the shaft of sunlight, the warm, brown rows of calf-bound volumes, Mr. Udney's desk heaped with papers, the ink, sand, and black seals. The smell of sealing wax forever after served to summon it to view. There was Mrs. Udney in a soft, white, low-bosomed dress, seated by the tea table, the silver, the sound of low, happy voices within, that of poplar trees without. That such places existed, he had no inkling. He had never seen a lady. He stood entranced and showed it.

They were talking Italian to the artist to whom Anthony was now introduced. Mrs. Udney took the boy by both hands, looked in his face, and declared he was an angel. He blushed, but liked it. Florence was enormously proud of her acquisition who was soon seated on a chaise longue eating a raspberry tart and drinking weak tea, neither of which delights he had ever tasted before. A mist came over his eyes. He experienced the sensation of being at home.

Terrini leaned forward. He would give anything to catch that expression for a copy of the young St. John he was doing. The face of the original he worked from was blurred. The slight plumpness of the lower part of the fingers and back of the hands—one should remember that in portraits of little boys. The children of merchants were the artist's chief subject and stock in trade. What a model! One could repeat it indefinitely. He began to ask Anthony about himself.

Miss Florence broke in and was permitted to help explain. She did so with giggles which were contagious. The atmosphere grew even easier. They were gay at no one's expense. Soon Anthony was talking about himself. His queer jargon of obsolete Tuscan interspersed with learned and stilted phrases from Latin and French amazed and secretly convulsed them. In this lingo the brief annals of his quiet existence were soon told. Mr. Udney became interested and led Anthony about the room talking to him. The avid mind and the starved curiosity of the boy were at once apparent to him. The audience looked on quietly, amazed at the lad's exclamations over the ordinary furniture of domestic life and his familiarity with classics. A lecture on the use of the library globes, which Mr. Udney's encouragement drew forth, was inimitable. The gentleman was "demned" again.

From the standpoint of the British consul the whole exhibition was a confirmation of his own opinion as to the wrong-headed education provided by the Romish clergy. Probably his own daughter was having much the same kind of stuff driven into her head by the nuns. It was a sore point between him and his wife. To be sure, there was no other school, but . . . He would have enlarged on the subject to her had it not been for the presence of the Italian artist who was, of course, of the "opposite persuasion." Besides it occurred to him again, as he looked at Anthony sidewise, that the boy *did* look English. His own son, if he ever had one, might look like that, he flattered himself.

Mrs. Udney, on the other hand, was quietly scheming behind the teacups to have Anthony remain for the night. Instinctively she wanted him in the house. By these vague prejudices and emotions passing unrecorded through the hearts and brains of strangers the future of the boy was irrevocably shaped.

Mrs. Udney advanced her proposition only tentatively, but she was heartily seconded by Florence. To her surprise, her husband seemed amused and easily consented. Even Signore Terrini entered into the spirit of the occasion, as he always made a point of doing, and sketched Anthony with his hat on while Mr. Udney wrote a note. A charming sketch of Florence followed as a slight hint of what might be done. This with a magnificent flourish the artist signed "Terrini, Livorno, 1785," and handed to Mrs. Udney. As for Anthony, he was invited forthwith to late dinner which proved to be the climax of a clearly miraculous day.

Mother Marie José was considerably disturbed when she was informed about an hour before vespers that Anthony was missing. It annoyed her to find that old Sister Agatha was more worried about the child than the consequences which might follow his disappearance. The woman was too venerable, weak, and frightened to be disciplined any longer. The mother superior blamed herself for not having acted promptly upon Father Xavier's recommendation of some months before. After another thorough search of the convent she sent for the priest. They agreed that if Anthony did not appear shortly, inquiry should be made next day leading to his return. There was a difference of opinion between them as to how he should then be disposed of. Father Xavier was for continuing his instructions at the convent until he could send him to Rome. Mother Marie was for placing him with some honest tradesman as an apprentice.

In the continued presence of Anthony at the convent she saw many and increasing difficulties. Above all she hoped that he might now return without having caused any talk. Her school was in too flourishing a condition to be blown upon by gossip. She recollected that the boy was now ten years old and this worried her. On the other hand, she was infinitely indebted to Father Xavier. Without him she could scarcely have obtained her more fashionable hopefuls. The priest's securing of the English consul's daughter had been especially satisfactory. The patronage of the English element in the town was essential.

It was with some reluctance, therefore, after carefully weighing the matter, that she finally consented to the priest's plea, and then only with the understanding that he would make himself responsible for the boy's whereabouts and good behaviour if he continued to remain at the convent. Father Xavier was surprised to find how relieved and happy he was at this outcome. He had become more interested in the child than he had realized.

Such was the state of affairs when Mr. Udney's groom arrived with a note for the mother superior. The

213

messenger desired an answer. Mother Marie turned pale. The note was the confirmation of her worst fears. In her agitation she saw the work of a decade about to tumble about her ears.

. . . Kindly carry my compliments to Father Xavier and inform him that his hat has been very much admired here . . .

Mr. Udney had not quite been able to restrain himself.

Mother Marie did not understand. She was scandalized she should be asked to "convey compliments" from one man to another. At the thought of the ragged orphan riding "concealed in a carriage" with the daughter of one of her most valued patrons the roots of her hair crept. It outraged every convention of a hard training and an unimaginative soul. She forgot the children were very small. Mr. Udney's "explanation" had only made matters worse. She changed her mind on the instant. Anthony would have to go.

Father Xavier had never seen her so vehement. He was secretly somewhat afraid of Mother Marie. It would never do to oppose her now. He could see that. If he was going to do anything for the boy, prevent him from being turned into a peasant or a carpenter, for instance, he would have to act promptly. He would have to act that night! So he agreed with the mother superior.

"And this note?" she groaned.

"Allow me to carry the answer myself," he suggested. "I shall call on Mr. Udney immediately—to get my hat."

"Your hat!" cried she indignantly.

"But I shall also take the opportunity," continued Father Xavier, "of explaining matters there. I can do so I am sure. Also," he hurried on, seeing her look of doubt still lingering, "when I return I shall have disposed of your orphan. I am well known to Signore Udney, you know." He spread his hands out appealingly, and with a hint of caution. "You will be well advised I think if you leave the matter to me." She nodded. "It is a lonely life we lead, sometimes, my sister, is it not? We orphans, you know," he said as he passed out. She nodded again. "Yes, sometimes," he heard her reply in a low voice. "Do as you wish with him." But he did not hear that. He had gone.

She sat in a mist of recollection longer than she knew. For the first time in ten years they waited for her at vespers. Before she rose from her knees she had changed her mind again. Father Xavier should keep his pupil.

The priest in the meanwhile in his best gown but hatless was being driven to Mr. Udney's. He arrived there when they were half through dinner to be welcomed warmly by all including Anthony whose cup was now running over with happiness.

"I have come for my hat and for the young rascal who took it," Father Xavier declared as he sat down.

"In the meantime let this refurbish you internally as well," said Mr. Udney loading his plate. He was fond of the priest who did not insist on his cloth. "A wise and kindly man," thought the Englishman cutting him a choice slice of mutton. They had in fact been able to help each other on several occasions. It was not the first time Mr. Udney had carved for the priest. Over the wine—while Mrs. Udney, Signore Terrini and the children gathered about her spinet in the next room—Father Xavier related all that he knew of the story of Anthony to Mr. Udney . . .

"And so, my good friend," he ended,—the genuine eloquence of affection having already lent wings to his plea,—"I would I could say my co-religionist, I want your assistance in this matter, just as you lately were in want of mine." Mr. Udney held up his hand.

"Have you any plans?" he asked.

"There is the Casa da Bonnyfeather. I had thought of that." Mr. Udney smiled at the priest's evident familiarity with lay affairs in the town.

"Yes, I could help you there. Old Bonnyfeather is, or was a Jacobite, yet in his trading here, and everywhere, he needs his British protection. You see I made certain concessions about his oath of allegiance.

Nothing really irregular, you know," he added hastily. The priest smiled.

"I also made certain concessions."

"Ah, he is of your persuasion then. You are his confessor?" Mr. Udney did not press that point. The father sipped his port.

"In other words, if both of us should call on him, say, tomorrow," continued Mr. Udney, "he might find room in his establishment for a promising orphan. It would be difficult to resist both the temporal and ecclesiastical authorities combined. Would it not, father?"

"Impossible, I think," smiled the priest. "But why not tonight?"

"Why not?" echoed his host. "Mr. Bonnyfeather will not be busy."

They came out and sat in the hall looking into the big room. Mrs. Udney was touching the keys while Signore Terrini twittered through an aria in an affected tenor. The children were sitting close together, Anthony's bare toes gleaming out of his shoes. They seemed to be reflecting the warmth of his expression of happiness. Suddenly they started to dance. Mrs. Udney had caught sight of her audience in the hall and cutting off Signor Terrini rather mercilessly, had broken into the stirring strains of "Malbrouk s'en va-t-en guerre." The notes rang and the face of the boy became exalted. Mrs. Udney managed to beckon to her husband who came near. A smile passed between them quietly as they looked at the rapt face of Anthony. "Does he really stay tonight, then?" she asked. "Yes," said he stooping lower, watching her hands flutter over the keyboard. "Father Xavier and I are making final arrangements for him, I trust. Mr. Bonnyfeather!"

"Good," said she. "Splendid! I knew you would do something."

He rejoined Father Xavier in the hall.

Presently the sound of wheels was heard above the tune. The music ceased and Anthony returned to this world to find a strange little girl seated beside him.

216

Mrs. Udney rose and took the children to their rooms.

Between the cool, lavender-scented sheets, a totally new experience for Anthony, his body seemed to be floating in the smooth water of the pool. From somewhere down the hall came the silvery voice of a little girl wishing him good night. As he sank deeper into the complete rest of tired happiness, he looked in vain for the face of the Madonna over the foot of his bed. Presently a soft glow suffusing the white wall of his chamber, and the habit of his mind combined to place her there where she belonged. He began his prayer. His lips moved making a sound like the trees outside, and like that dying away into the peace of the night.

Father Xavier and Mr. Udney trotted rapidly down the winding road to Livorno. The moon was rising. The water and air about it became visible and blent together in a pervading white shimmer. In this the whiter buildings of the town and the long harbour mole seemed to swim. The coloured lights of the shipping were caught like fireflies in a dark web of tangled rigging and masts. The streets were silent, but from a Maltese ketch some distance out came the ecstatic agony of a pulsing stringed instrument punctuated by the beating of feet on deck. An occasional weird cry arose. In the light warm air the music was alternately loud and soft.

"The boy is in good hands tonight at least," said Father Xavier softly. "I wish . . ."

"It is curious," remarked Mr. Udney, "that no men are too savage to be affected by moonlight. It is the same to us all. Like imagination it presents a familiar world in a new light." Mr. Udney was privately given to this kind of semi-profundity. He hoped Father Xavier would be impressed.

"I am wondering," said the latter, "how Mr. Bonnyfeather will take the proposal of receiving so young a lad into his establishment. Since the death of his daughter . . ."

"Tush, man! That was a decade or so ago, wasn't it? Never fear. Secretly he may be glad to have this boy. A Scot, though, would never say so, you know."

They drew up before a long building whose arches looped along the water front, and were soon knocking loudly at a high double gate. The echo boomed through the emptiness beyond. In the sombre archway a streak of lantern light suddenly flowed under the gate.

"Wha be ye poondin' at sic a rate oot there?" grumbled a voice to itself while a chain rattled. A small grille opened and a head in a red night-cap peered through.

"It's Mr. Udney, Sandy," said that gentleman reassuringly. "And Father Xavier," he added as the lantern was flashed on them both suspiciously.

"Losh, mon, come in, come in!" replied the voice as the bolts were shot back. "To think I hae kepit the Breetish consul, and the faither durlen withoot. Mind ye dinna trrip ower the besom the noo."

Mr. Udney chuckled as their footfalls wakened the stones of the court.

Mr. Bonnyfeather was at home.

Chapter Eleven

Between Two Worlds

ANTHONY was driven back to the convent the next morning in the cart with Florence. He was received in tears by Sister Agatha. There was a message for him to report to the mother superior. She had already relented and had made up her mind to give the boy only a sharp lesson and allow him to continue with Father Xavier. That the priest had already made other arrangements for bestowing the lad, she did not yet know.

His room and the court seemed warm and pleasantly familiar to Anthony. It was home after all. He was glad to see the Madonna, but it was with a sinking sensation in the pit of his stomach that he threaded the maze of long corridors leading to the mother superior's room. One was not summoned there for trifles. Already the outside world seemed distant and ineffectual. His feet raised stony echoes that might call a dangerous attention to himself. He began to walk on tiptoe.

Mother Marie José's cheek band had been illy

laundered. It was rough and chafed her under the chin. She had removed it and was changing her head-dress when Anthony appeared silently and unexpectedly at the door. Looking in, the boy saw a perfectly smooth-shaven head shining like a skull, a face unexpectedly broad with two glittering, brown eyes staring out of it, and a birthmark that flowed down over the woman's chin into the breast of her black gown. Between the chin and the eyes the face seemed terribly vacant by contrast. It was an almost supernatural countenance. A comet seemed passing beneath two burning stars. Intense fear and horror contorted the face of the boy. Mother Marie José gave a faint scream and snatched at her head-dress which covered the secret of her life. From its broad, linen band only her fine wide forehead and her statuesque profile now showed. She had indeed taken the veil again, but from her eyes there still darted an intensely feminine fire. She approached Anthony deliberately and laid hold of his arm.

"Never tell what you saw," she said through her teeth. The grasp tightened. "Do you understand, you boy!" She began to shake him. Her face drew nearer. With a sudden desperate jerk he tore his arm free and dashed down the corridor. He flashed headlong into his room and stood there while a mixture of rage, fear, indignation, and surprise clutched his throat in dry, hard sobs. Presently he saw the calm face of the Madonna through his tears. He snatched her to him from her niche and peeped out of the door. Old Sister Agatha had gone from the court. He took the statue, and climbed with it into the tree, and hid himself.

Mother Marie José was also trembling with conflicting emotion in which anger and fear predominated. She rang her bell and sent urgently for Father Xavier. She spoke to him imperatively when he appeared. Her one idea now was to get Anthony away.

"I am sorry he has been impudent to you," he replied.

She accepted his unconscious explanation eagerly.

"Take him to your house until you have made your

arrangements for him. I will not permit him to stay here. It is impossible. Not an hour. I . . ."

"Recollect yourself, madam," said the priest.

She saw she had gone too far. "Do as I ask you then," she said beseechingly. "I will send his belongings and a certificate of character to you shortly, but get him beyond these walls."

The priest looked at her sorrowfully and turned away. No matter what had occurred, he thought her haste petulant to say the least. He was surprised that she should show such feeling. One never knew what a woman would do. He had intended to take Anthony to town tomorrow. So it must be today, then! His heart sank. He tried to shut the image of the child out of his mind. It would never do to torture himself for a whole day longer. Now, it must be now.

Anthony was not in his room. Father Xavier bundled a few of the child's pitiful belongings into a pillow case. A broken wooden horse smote his eyes dim. He turned to the door and called.

The boy did not answer at first. Then he saw that Father Xavier was weeping. "I am here, father," he called. His bright hair and face peered out of the leaves half-way up the tree.

"Come down, my son, I have something to tell you that you must hear." He kept trying to smile. The boy climbed down and approached him bravely.

"You are to come with me," said Father Xavier, and took him by the hand. They went down the lane to the house together silently. Anthony was still holding fast to the statue of the Madonna.

The priest had intended to keep the lad with him all afternoon. He had carefully prepared in his own mind the things which he most wished to impress upon Anthony, a last and memorable lesson as it were, and he had also counted upon explaining some of the things which would be required of the boy in the strange, new world where he would shortly find himself. Faced by the actual fact of parting, and shaken by the unexpected violence of Mother Marie José, the heart and nerves of the man had combined to drive

221

his excellent little homily from his head. A genuine ascetic, Father Xavier was also shocked to find himself yearning over this orphan whom chance had thrown in his way as if he had been a child of his own flesh. "The flesh is indeed weak," he told himself. Affection shown at leave-taking would be weakening with himself. To save himself from that, he knew that he might become stern. He did not want to do that. He could not be sure of himself either way. Plainly it would never do to prolong things. He had intended to send out for a decent suit for the boy. Well, he would have to go in his ragged cassock now. The priest walked up and down keeping his face from Anthony. "How long would the Mother Superior take with her certificate and the other things? One might think a prince was departing with paraphernalia. Did she know she was torturing him?" Presently the portress came with a black, mildewed bag.

"Is that all?" said Father Xavier.

"There was a statue of the Madonna in his room which is also his. It is to go too, the mother superior said," replied the woman. "Here is the certificate. You will please be sure to have this receipt signed for all of his things, father. I was told to be sure not to forget to tell you that."

The priest nodded, and pointed to the Madonna lying on the chair. "All here," he said. The good Contessina turned to go. Anthony was sitting by the window watching the chickens. Suddenly he found himself in the woman's arms. She was crying over him, hugging him.

"The saints be with you, my bright little pigeon. May you fly far. Mary go with you!—my God! Good-bye, good-bye!" Then she was gone. A natural phenomenon had dimmed the scene from Father Xavier's eyes. Pretending not to notice, he busied himself by putting the Madonna into the bag. He now closed it and looked up. Anthony was standing with a blank face.

"I am going away?" he asked.

"Yes."

"Now?"

The priest nodded slowly.

"Because of what I have done?"

"No," said the man in spite of himself.

"Tell me, then!" cried the boy. A sudden hope leaped into his eyes. "Is it to Signore Udney? Ma donna there is not like . . ."

"Like whom?"

The boy faltered. "Thou knowest," he said finally.

"Come," said Father Xavier. "I shall tell you as we go." He took the bag from the table and led the boy from the room. As they passed down the lane a certain bricked-up window in the wall gaped at them like a mouth that had been stopped with clay.

It was a good two miles to Livorno, a hot day, and a dusty road. The stones of the highway hurt the feet of the boy used only to the smooth courts of the convent. He limped, but he listened so intently to what Father Xavier was telling him that he scarcely had time to notice his feet.

The priest's voice was once more calm. In affectionate tones he was creating for Anthony a new vista in life. "Apprenticed"—Father Xavier had to explain what that meant. Yes, he had arranged it all the night before. "While I was sleeping at Signore Udney's," thought Anthony. He looked back. Nothing was to be seen now of the convent except its red roofs and the pigeons circling about the top of his tree. They swooped down and disappeared. Contessina was feeding them then. So, they could get along without him! He pondered the fact. "But I shall come several times a week, my son," the father's voice was saying, "to continue your instruction—for at least a while." The man sighed. "Then, who knows?" Anthony looked up as the tones faltered again. "Often?" he asked. The priest nodded with a determined look. The boy smiled. "I am glad," he said.

They walked on in silence. Anthony did not look back again. It was a relief when he felt the warm, smooth flagstones of the approach to the Porta Pisa under his feet. There was a throng of country carts lined up there from which two Austrian soldiers in glistening, white uniforms, with muskets slung behind them, were collecting small copper coins. Anthony stared. They passed by the striped sentry boxes with the grand ducal arms, and turned toward the water front. The whirl and colour of a seaport dizened itself into his eyes. For a moment it threatened to engulf him.

He had never imagined there were so many people in the world, or so many tongues. Along the rivers of the streets poured in both directions a mass of vehicles; wheelbarrows piloted by whistling, bawling porters; creaking oxcarts. Donkeys with huge barrels slung on either side crowded pedestrians to the wall and swept all before them triumphantly. Army wagons like canal boats on wheels, laden with wine and forage for the garrison, jolted down the Castello Vecchio. They often seemed to dam up the whole street. As they turned the corner of the Piazza d'Arme a flood of low-hung drays piled with bales, or loaded with live cattle and poultry swept past them, whips cracking.

Father Xavier and Anthony stood back against the wall to avoid the whisking tails of horses and mules that slithered by with ears laid back. The dust rolled, streaked with pencilled sunlight at the cross streets. Porters jostled them, and merchants in laced coats laughed. Anthony could scarcely repress an impulse to take refuge in the dark, cool alleyways, or to dart into one of the many courtyards filled with bright, fluttering clothes. At times he seemed lost in a forest of legs, knee breeches, and flapping trousers of British tars. Above his head their black glazed hats sailed past, a yard of ribbon fluttering behind. He tripped over a beggar who cursed him horribly. The stench of everything-at-once overpowered him, and clutched at his throat. Suddenly they turned a corner and came out on the long cobble-paved water front of the minor, inner port or Darsena.

As long as he lived Anthony never forgot that moment. There was a vividness about it which was, at the time, more than he could appreciate. For the first time the lenses of his senses now came to a completely clear and perfectly blent focus. Into the still bare, and somewhat misty room of his mind burst the glorious, light-flooded vision of reality. There was not still-life only as heretofore. On this crowded water front there was motion and song. He lifted his head to drink it all in. He felt his heritage as one of the swarm fully conferred upon him. The vision beyond and the beholder for the first time lost themselves in each other and became one.

For years it was impossible, except at rare moments, or by the aid of closed eyelids to separate them again. That, as he came to know afterwards, was both the reward and the stumbling-block of a good mind in a healthy body.

But this first impression of Livorno was his awakening. As he thought of it years later, it seemed to him that at the convent his vision of life had taken place mysteriously in the camera obscura of a child's mind. Indeed, as he looked back, there was even a kind of charm about it, a rather dark, melancholy tinge with bright tufts of colour standing out beautifully. Looking at a street scene reflected in a black, polished stone in a jeweller's window at Paris many years afterward, he was forcibly reminded again of his days at the convent. Things grew and disappeared in the black mirror in a vista without reason. They moved by a totally disconnected motion with a volition all their own. One could be a polytheist in a world like that. It was lovely, dimly god-like and beautiful, but entirely unreal.

The one exception to this had been his first vision from the treetop.

Now—now as he stood at the street corner just where the land met the sea—life became more than a mere proper focus of several clear lenses. It seemed as if the windows of his soul had suddenly been thrown wide open. He felt the air, he heard a clangour, the light streamed in and flooded the room. Whimsical circumstance decreed that all this wealth of the senses, the very odour of it, should forever be carried for him in a Fortunatus purse of orange peel.

For in the quay opposite, a felucca from Sardinia was unloading. Piles of oranges lay heaped upon its deck. Some had been crushed beneath the feet of the crew and the air reeked with them. Father Xavier held up his hand and a dark sailor in a red jacket tossed him a yellow globe. As the two stood at the corner sharing it, Anthony's eyes continued to wander along the water front.

Landwise stretched an apparently endless row of long, white buildings facing the harbour. Between them and the quays was a broad, cobble-paved way crawling with jolting, roaring drays, piled with sea stores and merchandise. On the water side sharp bows, gilded figureheads, and bowsprits pierced and overhung the roadway, while a geometrical forest of dark masts, spars, and cordage swept clear around and bordered the inner port. Amid this, like snowdrifts caught here and there in the boughs of a leafless wood, hung drying sails. The sun twinkled at a thousand points on polished brass. It seemed to Anthony that each ship was alive, looking at him narrowly out of its eyelike hawseholes. Farther off was the flashing water beyond the molo, or outer harbour, with a glimpse of the white tower on the breakwater and the dark purple of the sea beyond.

Father Xavier also stood looking at it. While he finished his half of the orange he unconsciously permitted himself a few moments of purely sensuous enjoyment by beholding the view as if through the boy's eyes. The spell was broken as a ship's bell suddenly clanged out. The strokes were instantly taken up and swept the harbour front in a gust of molten sound. The priest threw his orange away, picked up the bag, and grasping Anthony by the hand continued along the narrow sidewalk.

It was somewhat difficult now to make way there. The sound of the ship's bells had been the signal releasing a throng of clerks and apprentices. They poured out of a hundred doors and gates laughing, bawling out, and chaffing one another. Besides that, certain Italian urchins of the crowd began to attach themselves to Father Xavier and his charge. In the tall, thin-

waisted priest with the huge hat who carried a peculiar
black bag, in the tow-headed acolyte whose ragged
cassock flapped about his bare calves there was something rare and too earnest, an air of visitors from another world bound upon some destiny that smacked of
strangeness and drama. Despite all they could do to
hurry on, a small procession began to form behind the
backs of Father Xavier and Anthony. It grew like a
snowball, but moved like a queue to the accompaniment of whistles and catcalls. At last they began to
pass under the cool arcade of a long, low building
whose arches looped for some distance along the
water front.

Just above the head of Anthony large, oval windows
heavily barred peered out from under a heavy parapet
like a row of eyes under the shaded brim of a monstrous
hat. Under the arches these eyes seemed to be staring
through gigantic spectacles. The total expression of the
house was one of annoyed surprise. Since it had commenced life as a nobleman's palace and ended as a
warehouse, there was some reason for that. Indeed,
what had once been known as the Palazzo Gobo now
bore shamefacedly along its entire forehead, as if
it had been caught in the act and branded, a scarlet
legend that could be read afar from the decks of ships,
CASA DA BONNYFEATHER. Yet an air of ill-used magnificence still continued to haunt it doubtfully as if
loath to depart. It succeeded in concealing itself somehow and eluded the passers-by in the deep grooves and
convolutions of the rusticated marble front.

Before the central bronze gates of this peculiar
edifice, upon which some vestiges of gilding could still
be traced, Father Xavier and his charge came to a
sudden halt. The crowd of youngsters following became expectantly silent but finally hooted when after
some time no one came. In the meanwhile Anthony
peered through the grille.

Beyond the dark, tunnelled archway of the entrance,
he could see a sun-flooded courtyard. There was a
dilapidated fountain in pie-crust style, and behind
that a broad flight of steps led up rather too grandly

to a great double door only one leaf of which was open. As he leaned forward to peer in, someone from behind tweaked his cassock violently. It ripped up the back exuberantly. There was a shout of delight. Another urchin laid hold of him.

"Cosa volete, birbante?" yelled Father Xavier shaking the culprit.

Matters were obviously approaching a crisis when one of the crowd shouted that the facchino was coming, and a Swiss porter opened the gate. Holding his torn skirt about him, Anthony stepped through after Father Xavier.

He was not quite quick enough, however. There was a sudden rush behind him and his cassock was this time ripped clear off his back and whisked away. A shower of rubbish followed him as the gate clanged. He ran a little distance down the archway and stood shivering. Father Xavier's face was still red, but both he and the porter now started to laugh heartily.

It was thus, naked as when he was born, that Anthony first found shelter in the Casa da Bonnyfeather.

Chapter Twelve

Casa da Bonnyfeather

THEY turned to the left through a door half-way
down the vaulted tunnel of the entrance and found
themselves in a vestibule provided with black
marble benches. It had evidently once been the guard-
room of the palace. Against the wall there was a rack
for halberds now occupied by a couple of mops and
a frayed broom. Anthony found the benches too cold
to sit upon. He stood disconsolately in the middle of
the apartment with mosaic dolphins sporting about
his cold feet. The porter departed to inform the Capo
della Casa of unexpected guests. Father Xavier reflected with some alarm that the present costume of
his charge was not that proper to the introduction of
an apprentice to his master. Suddenly he remembered
something, and with great eagerness opened the bag.

From it he extracted a lady's riding cloak moth-eaten
along the folds. He shook it dubiously. Several small
spiders scampered away and the dried petals of a white
flower lilted to the floor. It would have to do—under
the circumstances. He dropped it over the boy's shoul-

229

ders who gathered it about him eagerly, holding it with crossed hands. Presently the porter returned and beckoned to Father Xavier to follow him. The priest told Anthony to wait.

To Anthony standing alone in the centre of the vestibule, it seemed as if he had been left in a limbo between two worlds. The chill of the stone made his feet ache and crept up his spine like a cold iron. Somewhere, in another world, he could hear a clock ticking. It went on and on. Presently he could stand it no longer. The old silk cloak rustled eerily when he moved, and smelt mouldy. He followed where the others had led, mounted several steps, and stepped through a doorway.

At the end of what seemed to be a vast apartment, Father Xavier was talking to an elderly gentleman in black who was seated behind a desk in a high-backed chair. Anthony remembered now that Father Xavier had told him to wait. He therefore stopped and gathered the old cloak about him holding it close at the breast. He was afraid to go back now. If he moved they might see him.

What daunted the boy most was the fact that the portion of the room where the two men were talking was raised several feet above the rest of the apartment like the quarter-deck of a ship. It even had a rail across it. Before the old gentleman, who wore an immense old-fashioned wig, was a large bronze inkstand full of quills. From the railing to Anthony stretched a long aisle lined on either side by a perspective of empty desks piled high with ledgers and copy books. The clerks had all left. In either wall a row of big oval windows admitted bars of sunlight. Father Xavier and the gentleman continued talking. They were talking in English. Anthony knew that. He heard his own name several times. It grew tiresome. He looked up.

In an oval panel in the ceiling a number of people in cloudy costumes were gathered banqueting about a huge man with a beard. Anthony was particularly intrigued by a slim figure with wings on his heels. "How convenient," the boy thought, "but how small the wings are!" He pondered with his chin in the air.

"You will understand, then, what has happened," Father Xavier was saying. "The mother superior was most insistent. I had not intended to bring the boy to you until tomorrow, as we had arranged, but under the circumstances—" He spread out his hands in a comprehensive gesture. "Were it not for her request I should not bother you about signing this receipt. There is nothing in the bag of any value I am quite sure except the ten gold pieces. We have never quite fathomed this case, apparently one of desertion by people of means. The boy has some of the earmarks of gentle blood. For that reason, in view of possible influential complications later on, it seems best to be able to show that not only did the convent care for the orphan as its foundation on the old status required, but restored him to the world with the best of prospects —I am sure!—and with every item of his property intact. Bag and baggage complete for his earthly journey, you see."

"But a not too extensive wardrobe as I gather," interpolated the gentleman smiling quizzically.

"My dear Mr. Bonnyfeather," replied Father Xavier, "you will not only gain merit for having sheltered the orphan, but for clothing the naked as well. A rare opportunity, I assure you. Now, as to the receipt? Shall I get the bag first?"

"Tut, *tut*, man, of course I'll sign it. You act as if you suspected me of thinking you had spent the money for drink on the way down." Mr. Bonnyfeather leaned forward to dip his pen, but never touched it. His fingers remained extended pointing at the door. A look of astonished recognition and extreme fear worked in his countenance.

"Who . . . who is that?" he finally rasped.

Father Xavier turned hastily and saw Anthony contemplating the ceiling with a seraphic look.

"Why, that is the young gentleman of whom we have just been speaking," exclaimed the priest. "He seems to be admiring your frescoes. I told him to wait in the vestibule!"

"The benches are hard there," observed Mr. Bonnyfeather, regaining his self-control with an obvious effort, "we save them for our minor creditors." He laughed half-heartedly. "The truth is," he hurried on in an uncontrollable and unusual burst of confidence, "the truth is, standing there with his face just in that position he reminded me forcibly just now of—my daughter." The phrase passed his lips for the first time in ten years. It aroused a thousand silent echoes of emotion in the merchant's empty heart. He wiped his forehead. The priest remained silent for some time.

"Perhaps you will speak with the boy now?" he said at last. Mr. Bonnyfeather nodded.

"Come here, Anthony," said Father Xavier a little sternly. The boy advanced slowly holding his cape about him. Mr. Bonnyfeather's mind flashed back to a night ten years before. In the chair now occupied by the priest sat a bulky nobleman with a florid face and black-pointed beard. "Buried in the Alps," he was saying, "both of them. Buried! Do you understand?" The black beard punctuated the remark emphatically. Through the haze of this vision, as if in warm denial, the bright, serious face of the boy intervened. The priest was speaking again.

"Shake hands with your benefactor, my son. You are fortunate in having so kindly and sheltering an arm extended to you." Father Xavier was in reality congratulating himself on a good piece of work. Mr. Bonnyfeather now recollected himself and took the small palm extended to him out of the folds of the faded cloak with a kindly pressure. The boy's face still troubled him. He cleared his throat.

"Do you think you will like it here, my boy?"

"I cannot tell yet, signore," replied Anthony gravely.

"That is right," said the merchant evidently gratified. "Be frank and we shall have no difficulty in getting along. *Hummmm!* I shall arrange for some other— for some clothes for you directly." Anthony coloured.

"Thank you," he said.

As if the matter were concluded satisfactorily, Mr. Bonnyfeather now reached down, carefully read, and signed the receipt. "The indentures will be ready tomorrow, father. You can stop in for them then or the next time you come to town. It will be best I think to have our own notary. No one outside need then know that the convent has had anything to do with this case. You yourself can witness the mother superior's signature."

The priest bowed in assent. "May I," said he, "attempt to thank you again? To me it is more than . . ."

Mr. Bonnyfeather held up his hand and rose from his chair.

They walked down the room together, Anthony trailing behind. "That is the bag," said the priest as they came into the vestibule. "Not a very heavy one, I see," replied Mr. Bonnyfeather. "It is hard to tell what there might be in it, though." The old man's eyes twinkled. A small lock of grey hair had escaped from under his wig on one side. It conferred upon his rather austere and regular face a decided touch of benignity. "Will you be staying for supper with us?" The priest shook his head. "No, it is time to go—now." A misty look came into his eyes.

"I shall be back to continue your lessons, you know," he said to Anthony trying to be casual, and added softly, "my son." The boy flung up his arms. Father Xavier stopped short for an instant, hesitated, then seized his hat and almost fled through the door. Mr. Bonnyfeather whose heart had for a long time kept the same beat as the clock which regulated his establishment felt a slight internal pause in time as he looked at Anthony.

"Come," he said, "let us have a look at your new home." They walked down the archway together into the courtyard.

Seated before the fountain with her back toward them while she was milking a goat, was the largest woman in Italy. She had flaming hair, and from where they were standing her figure appeared to be that of a huge pear with a ripe cherry on top of the pear. A small keg under her seemed to provide ridiculous support, and for every quiver of her frame as she milked, the goat bobbed its tufted tail. Anthony laughed till he had to clutch at his cape to keep it from falling off. At this sound the pear rose from the bucket, and pivoting on what appeared to be two mast stumps ending in dumplings, took hold of a green petticoat and quivered a curtsy to Mr. Bonnyfeather.

"Angela," said he, "this is Master Anthony, the new apprentice. Will you look after him in the kitchen till after supper? I may change my mind about his sleeping in the clerk's dormitory. You might lend him some of your son's clothes, temporarily. He has suffered a mishap."

The face of the woman of a fine olive complexion beamed broadly upon the small figure before her.

"Benvenuto, signore," she said. "I shall attend to your clothes, sir, as soon as I milk. Saints! The goat has gone!"

She started after the animal much in the manner of a mountain pursuing a flea, but holding up her skirt. The goat had taken refuge in some defunct garden-beds, the graceful stone outlines of which on either side of the court now enclosed nothing but heaps of rubbish. As the mountain approached, the flea merely hopped away and the process repeated itself. Finally it shifted to the other flower-bed.

Mr. Bonnyfeather, although he had emitted no unseemly noises, was in no shape to aid even had he been so inclined. He was, however, still able to nod to Anthony who now joined in the hunt. The mountain was thus aided in its pursuit of the flea by a small, flapping blackbird with white, gawky legs. Mr. Bonnyfeather could no longer restrain his guffaws. Anthony now approached. The goat lowered its horns, and the boy flapped his cloak. At this ill omen, Capricorna departed nimbly up a staircase to the flat roof. Its bearded, female countenance appeared shortly afterward peering solemnly over the low parapet.

"M-a-a-a-a, my friends."

The challenge was accepted and the chase moved

heavenward. The small boy preceded the huge woman up the narrow staircase toward the roof. Suddenly, the goat appeared at the top. Her pursuers paused thoughtfull in mid-air, but not for long. Gathering her feet under her like a bird in flight, the goat descended upon those below in the manner of an ancient battering ram. Two sounds marked the whizzing return of her body to the earth below; a small puff when it hit Anthony, and a grunt like a startled cow when Anthony hit Angela. The goat passed over them. They both rolled to the bottom of the stairs where they were met by Mr. Bonnyfeather who was trying to laugh and cry at the same time.

For a few breathless moments the mountain appeared to be in travail. Then it wheezed, groaned, arose, and departed to the kitchen feeling itself below the timber line for broken bones. An enormous clattering of pots and pans later ensued.

Anthony had luckily been saved serious injury by being driven into a soft place on the mountain. Nevertheless, he was in a miserable enough state. Mr. Bonnyfeather carried his limp form into the house and sat down with him by a table near the door. The boy's face was chalky and his white eyelids trembled. He gasped occasionally and there was blood on his lips.

"Welcome, indeed!" thought Mr. Bonnyfeather, "puir little laddie!" He sat for a minute wondering what he could do.

"Faith, Faith," he called at last. There was no answer. "Drat the woman, she'll be oot wi the clarks, brisket bonny, nae doot." His indignation rose with his anxiety. The whole establishment had availed themselves of his permission to go to a carnival performance. Gianfaldoni was to dance. Only the cook, who had no interest in that art any longer, remained in the courtyard. Mr. Bonnyfeather reflected with some bitterness that even Faith Paleologus, his trusted housekeeper of a decade of more, would desert him to see a mere ballerino. Alone with the hurt child in his arms in a huge, dusty, old ballroom seething with mouldy frescoes and hung with cobwebbed chandeliers, he felt as if fate had played him a scurvy trick.

It was in this baroque scene of departed grandeur that the merchant habitually ate and entertained visiting ship captains. As he looked about it now in the fast-fading light, the moth-eaten splendours of the high-roofed and too ample apartment seemed to be mocking his loneliness. There was not a human sound in the generally thronged courtyard. An occasional suppressed bleat from the goat only served to lend a slightly demoniac quality to the unusual quiet. It was suddenly borne in upon Mr. Bonnyfeather sitting in the silence and the twilight that every living thing had deserted him—that life would leave him alone thus a helpless and childless old man. He looked down at the pallid face of the boy and sighed.

It was some thirty years now since he had held a child in his arms who resembled this one. The similarity of their features was undoubted. It troubled him. It stirred, and not vaguely, a sorrow so deep as to be tearless, a grief lapped as it were in deep, damp stone, but one from which great pressure or a sudden shattering blow might still extort drops of moisture. It was in this deep vein that he was now penetrated. It came upon him that even the cloak looked familiar. But all women's cloaks look the same. Pooh! He was a foolish old man alone in the dark, aegri somnia. Stop dreaming! He must do something for this child who was ill, who had been flung as it seemed into his arms by the Church—and that devil of a goat, Auld Hornie himself.

Well, he *would* do something about it. He *was* lonely. He could cheat the devil at least. As if he had come to a sudden and irrevocable resolution Mr. Bonnyfeather rose determinately and laid Anthony on the big oak table putting an old leather cushion under his head. The boy stirred weakly, and half opening his eyes closed them again with a shiver.

The great ballroom of the Palazzo Gobo had once extended the entire length of the lower floor, but in its second incarnation as the Casa da Bonnyfeather this painted scene of much ancient, ceremonious gayety had been divided like Gaul. Stone partitions had been thrown across either end and the space behind them divided in turn into several smaller rooms. Of the two new apartments, thus laid off at either end of the old, one was occupied by the cook with a numerous family, and the other by Mr. Bonnyfeather himself.

It was toward his own particular section of the building that the merchant now made his way. Taking a large bunch of keys from his bulging pockets, he unlocked the door in the partition.

Before him was a long hall floored with a carpet of deep pile upon which his feet fell noiselessly. In the daytime this corridor was lighted from above by a skylight. That, however, was only a glimmer now above his head where a few stars appeared as if peering through a hole in the roof. All that part of the building would now have been entirely dark had it not been for a subdued radiance that escaped from a small Chinese lamp on a gilt stand at the extreme end of the hall.

Set beside the wide, white door of Mr. Bonnyfeather's room, the gilded and carved lintel of which it invested with important shadows, the light of this oriental lantern seemed to percolate its jade screen statically as if determined to tinge even the shadows upon which it now shone with its own quiet serenity. Behind the partition he had reared, and amid these shadows, the merchant had attempted to build for himself a refuge from the world. Once over the threshold of these precincts, Mr. Bonnyfeather shook off the rather staid man of business that the world knew and became a mere man. He unbent and moved now, not only more at ease, but more gracefully, as if he had cast off the habits of half a lifetime and returned to those of his youth.

Besides his own room at the end of the corridor, there were two others on each side of it as he passed down. The two on the left were empty and had been so for years. One had belonged to his wife who had died in childbirth, and the other to the daughter she had borne. The rooms on the right, which looked into the

237

court, were those of Faith Paleologus, the housekeeper, and Sandy McNab, the chief clerk.

On this evening, while the living were absent, as he stepped into the corridor the place seemed to Mr. Bonnyfeather unbearably quiet. The sense of loneliness which he had experienced so vividly a few moments earlier was now reinforced and increased severalfold, and this time with a kind of stealthy eeriness inherent in the close quarters and the silent carpet underfoot.

As he passed the long-locked doors on his left, there arose in him a strong impression that the rooms behind them were still occupied. The memory of voices, footfalls, and faces once familiar to them surged up in him toward reality again. They suddenly threatened to force conviction upon him. They succeeded. A blind terror overcame him and stopped him sweating before the last door on the left. His keys tinkled in his hands. He had heard a sound in there! Had he? He listened intently again. A minute passed. "Maria?" he called.

At the sound of his own voice his self-possession flooded back. Nevertheless, to reassure himself, he tried the handle of the door immediately across the hall on the right. It was that of his housekeeper. It too was locked. He had hoped after all she might be in. He mumbled something and stood baffled. "Drat that woman! Cauld she no trust the maister wi his ain linen!" The dialect rasped in his head when he grew excited. He had intended to put the boy in there for a while.

But how long it had been since there were any sounds of life in the room across the hall! If he *was* going to hear things there—they had better be real ones. Besides, that child was still lying out in the big room ill in the dark. Well, he *could* do it. Open Maria's room alone? But who was there to open it with him, now? No one. He would put somebody alive in there. It needed the familiar face of that young stranger. Something gay there, laughter, life! And he would do it before Faith returned.

He strode into his own room and dashed a shower

of sparks into the tinder box. Presently a number of candles were blazing, all that he had. He felt reassured. Their sudden cheerfulness seemed to beam approval on his plan. Taking a candelabrum with no less than six tapers in it, he came back into the hall again, set it down on the floor, and with determined fingers thrust a rusty key into the lock of his daughter's room. He winced as the ward rasped, but steeled himself. He turned the knob boldly, thrust back the door on its faintly complaining hinges, and faced the past.

It was not so poignant as he had expected. Through a window set high in the wall at the other end came lively noises from the street beyond. A horse trotted by. The empty bed under an empty niche in one corner of the wall had dust upon it. That was all. There was a dressing table with a cloth hung over its mirror. He removed the cloth and set the candle before the glass as rapidly as possible. The room seemed to glare then. Some faded, girlish dresses hanging in an open wardrobe he did not try to look at. He dusted the bed off, returned to his room, and came back with covers taken from his own couch. These he disposed rapidly in a comfortable way putting the pillow at the foot of the bed. Then he took a candle and went for Anthony.

The boy had opened his eyes and was trying to remember where he was. His belly and his ribs hurt him. He felt sick. The effort of recollection was just now too much. Presently there was a gleam of light on the ceiling. He looked up dizzily and saw the outline of a chariot drawn by plunging horses disappearing into a dark bank of clouds. The face of the driver had dropped out of the plaster. Then he saw the old merchant leaning over him and felt himself being gathered into the man's arms. He remembered now. But where was he being taken? If Father Xavier were only here! "Father," he called. He felt the man who carried him tremble.

As he neared the door with the boy in his arms, Mr. Bonnyfeather saw a lantern crossing the court. Suddenly its owner tripped over something and began to swear. The language was Protestant and from north of the Tweed. Ignoring all intercessors, the man, who was now trying to relight his lantern, addressed himself exclusively to God Almighty.

"Come in, Sandy mon, I want ye," said Mr. Bonnyfeather. "It's argint," he called as he passed through the door with Anthony. A few seconds later, the boy was lying on the bed which had been prepared for him. Sandy McNab's florid countenance was soon staring in at the proceedings of Mr. Bonnyfeather with astonishment.

"I'll no deny that it gave me a jert to see the licht from her door the noo. I couldna faddom it. Mon, yon laddie looks forfairn!" he exclaimed as his eyes fell on Anthony.

"You'd no be feelin' so gawsy yoursel' if you'd had the hourns of a gait aneath your breastie, atwell," replied Mr. Bonnyfeather.

"Whaws bairn is he?" asked Sandy, ignoring the rebuke implied in the merchant's tone of voice. "I dinna ken thot—aiblins," replied the merchant. "He's the new apprentice." Mr. McNab whistled and grinned. "Haud your fissle," said the merchant with some heat, "rin and fetch me a ship's doctor. The first ye can find aboot the dock. Dinna ye see the laddie's in a vera bad wa'?"

"Ye maun busk him," countered the irrepressible McNab.

Mr. Bonnyfeather arose. "Will ye stand there and bleeze the nicht awa'?" he asked icily.

"Barlafumble!" cried Sandy. "I'll no try to arglebargle wi ye aughtlins. Ye ken I'm too auld-farrant for thot. But it's een blank—new to a blinkie o' a clark like mysel' to find the maistre o' this establishment singin' balow-baloo to a bit breekless apprentice. It gars me a' mixty-maxty. You're a' the guid mon agin."

"Bletheration!" said his master laughing in spite of himself. That was exactly what the man at the door had hoped for. It was unusual for Mr. Bonnyfeather to become excited. It was several years now since the chief clerk had seen the merchant's high cheek bones with that faint flush on them and his eyes shining.

Something more important than appeared on the surface was toward, he thought. Besides, in this room! He noticed Mr. Bonnyfeather's hands trembled. He needed company. That was evident. The boy on the bed began to gasp.

"Mind yoursel' he's aboot to bock!" cried Sandy. Lacking anything better he snatched off his hat into which Anthony "bocked." "Puir bairn, you maun be corn't wi crappit head. You're donzie, but wha will reimbarse me for your clappin' my headpiece like a coggie. Dinna coghle ower it so. I'm na feelin' sae cantie and chancy mysel'. Coomin' ower the coort, ye ken, I trippet ower yon clatch of a bag and was like to clout oot me brain pan. Wha would ken a dorlach cauld cleek-it a mon by the foot?"

Mr. McNab took his hat to the window gingerly, opened the window, and somewhat regretfully threw out the hat. "I hope they keep to the crown o' the causey oot there in the nicht," he opined. "And noo I'll rin for the physeecian." Glancing at his master with more anxiety than at the boy, he sauntered out, indicating the offending bag with his foot. Mr. Bonnyfeather nodded helplessly. For the second time that day, he wanted to laugh and cry at the same time. He placed the bag on the dresser and sat down close by the bedside. The silence of the house was once more audible.

Anthony alternately dozed and awoke fitfully. When he opened his eyes now, he semed to be back in his room at the convent. The place had somehow altered. There was a very bright light. The window had shifted its place and altered its shape. The niche in the wall was there, but the statue had vanished from it. That troubled him. He closed his eyes once more and tried to collect himself. When he opened them again they inevitably fell on the vacant niche. The process repeated itself and grew irritating. He muttered about it to himself; talked as though in his sleep. Mr. Bonnyfeather leaned over him rearranging the covers. He wished McNab would come back with the doctor, or that Faith would return. The boy seemed out of his head. What was all this talk about the Madonna? It was some little time before the merchant could make out that "the Madonna" was missing from her niche. Then he remembered the receipt he had signed that afternoon. Perhaps the thing was in the bag. He also remembered vaguely that there had once been a saint's image or something in the niche when it was in her room.

There was some difficulty with the bag. It seemed reluctant to open after Sandy had tripped over it. The old catch was bent. The boy cried out something and Mr. Bonnyfeather's hand slipped. Inadvertently he ripped the old leather while tugging at it. The bag fell open and gaped like a mouth that had nothing more to say. Out of it Mr. Bonnyfeather extracted a long red purse like a tongue—and the Madonna. The sunburst on her head had been bent a little. He straightened it gingerly and put the statue in the niche where the boy evidently wanted it. Somehow it too seemed vaguely familiar. He tried to remember. But all Madonnas were alike, more or less. Yet she did seem to belong there, to fit nicely. It was as if she had been there before.

The boy's eyes opened again and now found what they had sought. An expression like that of a little girl whose lost doll had been found just at bedtime flitted over his face. His eyes caressed the statue and closed happily. He began to breathe more easily. Some colour crept into his cheeks as he slept.

After a while Mr. Bonnyfeather ventured to wipe the blood from Anthony's mouth. He saw now that it had come from a small cut in the boy's lip. He sat by the bed and waited. An hour slipped by. As he gazed steadily at the lad's quiet face, the conviction of his first impression of it again attained the feeling of certainty. He felt as though he were being haunted. Below the nostrils the resemblance certainly weakened. There was a firmer and broader chin. He placed his hands across the boy's mouth so as to shield it from his view. Instantly from the pillow the face of his daughter looked up at him. The merchant sat down overcome. His head dropped forward into his hands.

His thoughts were still in a whirl when McNab came back with a ship's surgeon. Searching along the dock, it had taken him some time to find one. The doctor was an orderly soul and it irked him to find the patient's head placed at the foot of the bed. He forthwith shifted Anthony about and Mr. Bonnyfeather was forced to see the boy's face just where he had tried to avoid placing it. The doctor's examination disclosed no broken bones. He removed the old cloak, and despite the fact that Anthony cried out, went over him thoroughly. Lacking his instruments for bleeding, the surgeon prescribed rest. He departed with the chief clerk after having received one of the gold pieces from the purse that had come in the bag. It was a large fee. Mr. McNab began to recollect audibly that his hat recently sacrificed in the same good cause was of the best quality. Mr. Bonnyfeather, however, was obtuse. In a short while he was left alone again.

This time the face of the boy was exactly where that of the last occupant of the bed had been. In the mind of the man watching, the two faces were already confused or combined. It was hard to tell which. Only his reason refused to consent. He began to go over word by word the nocturnal interview with Don Luis of ten years before. The words, the very gestures of the marquis, precise, formal, not to be evaded, came back now across the warmth of his new yearning like a wind from glacial peaks. He heard the heavy wheels of the coach rolling away again into the night leaving him standing dazed. "Buried in the Alps."

His own wife had died in childbed, too. It had been like that with Maria! If only her child had lived! Whether it had been a boy or girl he did not know. Don Luis had done all the talking. Futile to ask! The man seemed to be in a white rage that night about something. Not a word for Maria. Only the cold facts, and a final farewell. Disappointment, no doubt. Well, he could understand that. Don Luis had never married again either. Gone to Spain. Nothing had passed between him and the marquis afterwards—nothing but the rent. Ought he to write now? About what? A facial resemblance? Certainly not like Don Luis. Mr. Bonny-feather thought of something and started. Impossible!

Impossible any way you looked at it. Why, he would have to begin by doubting the marquis' word. What a letter that would be. And what a reply! He winced.

He must collect himself. The events of the past few hours were not sufficient to explain the state in which he now found himself. He should not have stayed here alone looking at the boy's face, nor should he have opened her room. That was a mistake after all. If the housekeeper had only not been out. "Damn the woman, would she never come home!" It must be nearly midnight. He drew out his watch. In doing so he became aware that someone was standing in the doorway. He turned about swiftly, terribly startled in spite of himself.

Chapter Thirteen

The Evidence of Things Unseen

A COUNTENANCE so regular and aquiline as to suggest a bird of prey in forward flight was looking into the chamber where Mr. Bonnyfeather sat grasping his watch convulsively. The face was so pallid and so deep-set in a round straw bonnet that the light from the jade lamp cast a positively greenish hue upon it. It had a broad, low forehead under masses of thick, blue-black hair, a rouged mouth that would have been passionate had it not now been contorted into a grimace of terror and surprise, and a pair of black-brown eyes. These seemed to have something staring through them from behind like those painted on an Egyptian mummy case. The folds of the dress were in obscurity, and a high furbelow from the bonnet seemed to run up like a plume into the night beyond. Mr. Bonnyfeather's grip on his watch tightened. Several seconds, answered by heart beats which he felt throbbing in his hand, passed slowly before he recognized in the plan of the shadows the familiar lineaments of his housekeeper, Faith Paleologus.

"Creest, woman!" said he, "why do ye creep up like that on a body? It's fearsome." He was glad to hear his own voice and continued to talk as he slipped his watch into his pocket allowing the heavy seals to dangle heedlessly. "Whar hae ye been? It's long past midnight, ye ken. Wha hae ye been doin' wee yoursel' the nicht?" She knew he must be excited to question her thus and to lapse into Scotch, to be so direct and familiar. His voice stiffened her. She resented it.

"I'm not so old yet but that I still like a bit of a fling now and then. It was a carnival, you know, and I danced. Do you really want to know where?"

"Naw . . . no," he replied, recollecting himself. "But if you had been here I should not have had to put him in this room."

"Who is *he* then?" she asked. "I saw the light from this room as I came in. You wonder I made no noise? It's over ten years agone, you know, since . . ."

"Yes, but . . ."

"You opened it then?"

He nodded unwillingly.

"Why?"

He pointed to the boy on the bed.

"John Bonnyfeather," she whispered, "who is it that has come back with her face?"

"Orr-h! You saw it, too?" He went forward and shaded the boy's chin with his hand.

"Saw it! Do you think I need to have you do that? When I looked in here, I thought I was looking at the past again. And I am," she added moving forward so rapidly as to startle him. "Here is a piece of it come back." She snatched the Madonna from the niche and bore it to the light. "It is the same, I know." They bent over it together. "Do you think I could ever mistake that? Look!" Under the candles she showed him the almost invisible fracture in the statue to which the knife of the marquis had once pointed so unerringly.

"I gave it to her years ago, here, in this room, long before she left!" The old man reached out for the Madonna like a child assuring itself of the reality of an object by touch. But his hands trembled so that she kept the statue and looking at him meaningly returned it to its niche. "How did *that* come here?" she again flung at him.

"I dinna ken!" said Mr. Bonnyfeather mopping himself where the edge of his wig met his brow. Trying to explain things to himself, he recounted to her all that he knew of Anthony together with the events of the afternoon. They whispered to each other for half an hour by the boy's bedside.

". . . and that's all I know and the rest is uncanny," he finally ended. A short silence ensued between them.

"An orphan, eh, and from the old place on the hill?" she said. He nodded dubiously.

"I'll have to sleep on it," he sighed rising. "I'm worn out, watching, and waiting for you. You can take your turn now at being a nurse again. For a lad this time."

"He'll be staying on in this room?" she asked, laying her hand on his arm so eagerly that he looked surprised.

"Yes," he said.

"Wait, then. I'll mix some hot milk and wine for you. You'll need it."

He sat down again and waited while she crossed the big hall to the kitchen and returned. As he looked at the boy Mr. Bonnyfeather's satisfaction with his decision increased. His eyes travelled from the figure on the bed to the figure in the niche. He crossed himself and remained for some minutes in prayer.

Faith returned with the posset cup. He drank silently.

"You'll leave this light here?" she asked as he rose again. "I'll get some more candles. He's sleeping soundly enough now."

The old man nodded and left. A few seconds later she heard his door close. The woman took off her bonnet and gathering her wrap closer about her began her vigil.

———————

The candles were still blazing brightly in Mr. Bonnyfeather's room. He looked about him with keen satisfaction. A certain pride and hauteur was visible in his countenance as he did so. If, when he entered the corridor which led to this retreat, he dropped the merchant and became the man; when he finally crossed the threshold of his own chamber and closed the door, a further transformation took place. He then, in his own mind at least, became a nobleman. Nor was this a mere aberration on his part. If Prince Charles Edward Stuart had only been able to pass on from Derby to London and had his father proclaimed at Westminster as well as at Holyrood, Mr. John Bonnyfeather, merchant, would have been the Marquis of Aberfoil. Since George and not James III or his son was now king, all that was left of the hypothetical Marquisate of Aberfoil was a proud memory in an old man's heart, and a room in a mouldering palace in Italy.

Unlike the other chambers in Mr. Bonnyfeather's immediate apartment, his own room had been originally part of the old building. It extended clear across the end of the ancient ballroom and had once been used as a retiring room. At one end there was an immense monumental fireplace where several hundred cupids went swarming through the Carrara helping themselves to several thousand bunches of gilded grapes. The fruit appeared to be dripping like gilded icicles from the mantelpiece itself. Just above this, propped out at a considerable angle to avoid a fat satyr carved on the chimney behind, was a large oil portrait of James II in periwig, sword, and very high-heeled shoes. It had been done at St.-Germain's in the latter days of the monarch when he had become a "healing saint." The lines by the nose were almost cavernous, the corners of the mouth turned down, and the eyes looked puzzled and weary. At the apartment before him, King James squinted with an implacably sullen and gloomy look. Nevertheless, the picture was cherished by Mr. Bonnyfeather. It had been given to his grandfather who had followed his king into exile.

On the mantel itself there was nothing but a handsomely wrought silver casket immediately below the portrait with a heavy candelabrum at either side. In

these were exceptionally large wax candles that burned
with a fine, clear light. In the mind of Mr. Bonnyfeather, here was the family hearth of his castle in
Scotland. It, with the portrait, the casket, and the
candles, had attained in his inherited affections and
loyalties the status of a lay shrine. Nor was the shrine
without its relics. In the casket before the picture reposed his grandfather's useless patent of nobility, a
miniature of his daughter as a little girl, and an ivory
crucifix. When Mr. Bonnyfeather prayed, as he still did
occasionally, he placed the crucifix against the casket
and knelt down on the hearth.

The rest of the room had somehow taken on the
air of that chamber in nowhere that it actually was. It
was furnished with a kind of blurred magnificence. In
one corner there was a painted bed with a canopy over
it. There had at one time even been a railing about it,
but as this had caused amusement to the servants,
Mr. Bonnyfeather had had it removed. Next to the
bed was an immense wardrobe, the panelled doors of
which led upward like a cliff to an urn on the top.

Seen from the door, set off by the gilded parallelo-
gram of the base of the vanished railing, the bed and
the wardrobe resembled nothing so much as a catafalque waiting beside the closed doors of a family
tomb.

Certain lugubrious, and ludicrous, aspects of this
bedroom had in early years impinged themselves even
upon the mind of Mr. Bonnyfeather to whom it was
home. For one thing a heaven full of adipose goddesses
romping with cupids through a rack of plaster clouds
had been ruthlessly scraped from the ceiling, and the
oval, to which for some esoteric reason their sporting
had been confined, had been painted a deep blue. As
a consequence, at night the centre of the room seemed
to rise into a dome. The walls which had once been
the scene of dithyrambic landscapes had also been
painted over. But this coat was now wearing thin and
the original, wild pastoral vistas were faintly visible
in outline and subdued colour as if seen through a light
Scotch mist. The effect was to exaggerate greatly the

size of the apartment. It was like looking in the morning into the vanishing dreams of the night before.

In this mysterious and all but mystical atmosphere, the old merchant nourished his dreams both of the past and of the future. In the daytime with the bright, Tuscan sun streaming through the high, oval windows, not unlike the portholes of some gargantuan ship, the place was warm, dimly green, with half-obliterated forests and cascades slumbering on the wall; glinting with old gilt, and withal cheerful. But with the descent of night all this was changed. The catafalque of the bed seemed to thrust itself forward. The dome rose into the ceiling again. King James glowered. And the family tomb in the corner seemed waiting determinedly for John Bonnyfeather, the last of his race. It was not without a shudder that he could prevail upon himself to hang his breeches there after eight o'clock at night.

To offset the Jacobean melancholy that threatened to engulf the place at dusk, the old man had many years before covered the floor with a bright red, Turkey carpet. He set cheerful brass firedogs to ramping in the fireplace under piles of old ship timbers always ready to blaze merrily, and provided himself with several mirrors and an endless number of silver candlesticks, candelabra of noble proportions, and sconces. Since the death of his daughter he might be said to have developed a passion for light. Mr. Bonnyfeather's weekly consumption of candles would have furnished forth a requiem mass for a grandee of Spain. This room with its nightly illumination together with some fiery old port which produced the same result constituted the chief indulgences of his amiable soul.

Here he retired, laid aside his wig, and put on a velvet dressing gown. Here he pored over his accounts spread out on a huge teakwood desk under a ship's lantern; planned out a profitable voyage for one of his several ships, or answered especially important correspondence. A large globe which he turned often, running his keen Scotch eye with a canny glance over many seas and lands, stood by the desk. There was a

250

drawer for maps and charts. There were compasses and dividers apt to his hand, and down one side of the room a long bookcase was insufficient to hold his tomes. Atlases, almanacs, and port guides of recent dates had begun to accumulate in little towers along the floor.

To stand at the door, as he was doing now, and to run his eyes over the apartment with the candles burning, always had about it the elements of a cheerful surprise. The change from the dimly lit corridor was an abrupt one. A wash of silver light reflected by mirrors, sconces, and other silver objects flooded from the walls of the room. The George flashed on the breast of King James. The comfortable, large, gilt furniture and the books twinkled. Only in the corner the bed remained in mysterious shadow with his slippers beside it like two crouching cats.

The merchant began to undress. He hung his clothes on an old pair of antlers, all that remained of feudal rights in Scotland, put on his wrapper, and drew up a comfortable chair before the fire. He was quite chilled through by his wait in Anthony's room, and the last discovery by Faith Paleologus had shaken him quite as much as his first sight of Anthony's face. He had decided already to keep the boy in the house but upon purely instinctive and emotional grounds. An explanation that would provide him adequate reason for so serious a change in his fixed household habits at first seemed to him an absolute necessity. More important still, the status of the boy was not clear to him. By his actions it seemed as though the old man were trying to extract the answer to these questions by poking hollow places in the fire or by repeated applications to the bottle of port.

But the longer he thought the less likely it seemed that any reasonable and satisfactory explanation could be arrived at. If the marquis had been hiding anything, it was something which he desired to hide. It would be useless, and it would certainly be dangerous even to attempt to follow things up there. That last interview was meant to be a final one. Mr. Bonnyfeather knew that. Mr. Bonnyfeather could not see himself

251

accusing Don Luis of abandoning his own child—even if he had had one that lived—which he had denied. "And if it had not been his child . . . if it had been Maria's!"

The old man's own conscience, his honour, stopped him here. His daughter was dead. The vista opened up for him an instant in a certain direction was one from which he recoiled a second time that night in sheer horror. All the pride, all the intense loyalty and belief in his own blood and family cherished through generations almost to the point of monomania precluded for him further explorations in that direction. With what felt like an actual muscular action in his head, he closed the door against even this suspicion.

He meant to shut it out entirely. But thought is swifter than honour. He had only succeeded in imprisoning the impression, perhaps an intuition, in the cells of his brain.

So he would not inquire any further, at the convent, or at any other place. Whatever was mysterious about this happening might, so far as he was concerned, remain so—far better so. He checked himself again. "Buried in the Alps!" The words came back to him now in the cold accents of Don Luis with a positive comfort. They must be final.

The old man now reproached himself even for his thoughts. How lovely and how innocent that daughter had been! It was a long time since he had looked at the girl in the miniature. He would look at her again tonight. The pain that her likeness never failed to inflict upon him should tonight be his penance. Its beauty and delicacy should also be his comfort and assurance.

He unlocked the casket and took out the locket. He snapped it open. Save for certain subtle feminine contours, there looked up at him from the oval frame the face of the boy on the bed in the next room. Mr. Bonnyfeather grew weak and leaned his head against the mantel. He *felt* now beyond all reasonable doubt what he would never admit to himself he wanted to know.

A small chiming clock on his desk struck four as he climbed into bed. It was answered by the town chimes and echoed by all the ships' bells in the harbour. Mr. Bonnyfeather felt at peace with himself, his Maker, and the past over the decision he had finally made while resting his head against the mantel. Characteristically for him, it was compounded out of an emotional conviction and a reasonable doubt. It took the middle way between the horns of a dilemma. The boy who had come into his house that night should be received and brought up *as if* he were akin, but never acknowledged. The tie between them that he felt to be there but could not understand should remain without a name. That would solve the question by not asking it. It would, it should suffice.

The merchant took a deep breath of relief. From the cellar below the odour of tea and spices permeated his room. He breathed it in with satisfaction. For one who proved himself capable and deserved it, there might be a good inheritance in the vaults of the Casa da Bonnyfeather. "And so we shall see," he thought, "what we shall see."

"God be praised. But you especially, Merciful Virgin, who have had this child in your holy and mysterious keeping, and have brought comfort to an old man's heart."

Outside the last of the ships' bells had just ceased to ring as drowsiness fell upon him.

———————

The same bells which had rung Mr. Bonnyfeather across the borders of sleep had awakened Faith Paleologus in the next room. She had not meant to go to sleep, but she was tired after the carnival. It was only a few minutes after Mr. Bonnyfeather's door had closed before she had forgotten herself entirely. She awoke now with her bonnet at a drunken angle, her clothes disarranged, and her body slumped down in her chair. Her first thought was that she must look a mess. Her second that the boy might see her.

She stole a look at him furtively. He was sleeping soundly. The rosy tinge of healthy slumber had returned to his cheeks. For some time her eyes continued to drink at this fountain of youth. There was no chance of her being seen doing so. Finally one of the candles guttered. She rose silently, straightened her bonnet, and renewed the candles from the pile she had brought from the kitchen earlier. Then she took the candelabrum and tiptoed into her own room. There was a long mirror.

Before this she took off her bonnet and let down her hair. It fell in a dense black mass about her knees. She brushed it and combed it carefully, plaited it in two long, thick coils, and wound them around her head. The ends, after a manner all her own, she pulled up through the loops of the coils and bound them tight with black tape. They stood up over her forehead like two small horns. She next rubbed her face with a soft camel-hair brush dipped in lemon juice, patted her cheeks with a soft towel and noted the effect. She bathed her eyes with cold water. Then she unloosed her clothes about the shoulders and slipped them all, with one simple movement, to the floor. From the middle of this pile, she stepped out of her shoes entirely naked. The carefully demure housekeeper lay behind her heaped on the floor with the toes of her shoes turned in.

The rather splendid moth that had thus emerged from its best silk cocoon now flew across the room to one corner where on the stone floor reposed a ship's water cask that had been sawed in half. It was four feet high and two-thirds full of cold water. Without any change of facial expression the woman stepped into it and crouched down until the liquid met over her shoulders. She remained there for about half a minute as if her head floating free from her body were regarding the room. Then she rose without splashing, dried herself hastily, and began to move quietly but rapidly about. Every trace of fatigue had vanished. There was a certain panther-like sureness, an inevitable grace to her movements that was admirable. At that moment, upon emerging from the cool water which at once soothed her nerves and stimulated her muscles, her brain was like that of a dancer, preoccupied with physical motion but thinking about nothing at all.

Faith Paleologus was tall and appeared to be slender. Her shoulders if one looked carefully were too wide. But so superb was the bosom that rose up to support them that this blemish, if blemish it were, was magnificently disguised. A sculptor of the old school might have seen in her an Artemis to the breasts and above that some relation of the Niké of Samothrace. Perhaps the latter was also suggested by her straight profile that seemed to cleave the element through which it moved as if she were standing on the bow of a ship. Yet there was something too strange about her to name as a guilty one the quality that was uniquely hers. She seemed designed by the inscrutable for a use that was incomplete; for a purpose doomed to defeat by finding an end in itself. It was her hips. They were not those of a woman but of something else. A lemur's perhaps. Exquisitely capable for the relief of lovers they were inadequate for anything more. In their image was implicit an obstruction to life.

Her presence in the house of so honourable, and in the final analysis so religious, a person as Mr. Bonnyfeather was by no means the enigma which this glimpse into the privacy of his housekeeper's room might indicate. The implications of her body were offset and to some extent controlled by a cautious and clever mind.

On the stage of life Faith Paleologus was a consummate actress. Her rôle was a minor one, during the daytime, but it was subtly conceived. When she resumed her clothes in the morning and prepared to move about the precincts of the Casa da Bonnyfeather, her carefully chosen costume, and it was nothing more, her motions, her attitude, and the very tones of her voice proclaimed the staid virgin of uncertain age. In a household predominantly one of male contacts her face afforded no opportunities for amorous speculation. By a stroke which fell little short of genius she had contrived an artfully repulsive bustle to cover her inviting hips. Furthermore, she was never seen outside, even in the courtyard, without her bonnet, a long, perfectly smooth cylinder of black straw. It was worn sufficiently tilted up, and was tied under the chin with a dull bow of such miraculous precision as to cause every honest British seaman she passed to touch his cap with an automatic and nostalgic respect. She had, in short, learned by art the basest note in the cheap scale of respectability. "Never commit an indiscretion at home."

Yet it would be a genuine mistake to suppose that Faith Paleologus was one of the numerous and familiar who regard themselves as a means of gain and find the marketing pleasant. There were several gentlemen in sundry places who congratulated themselves on still being alive to regret having made that error. Her need was as deep as the gulf out of which it arose. It might, if she cared to make it do so, have carried her far. But for her own always immediate purposes, she found Livorno an ideal place.

It was composed, at the time she trod the boards there, of several physical neighbourhoods socially an astronomical distance apart. Along the water front wandered avidly a cosmopolitan flux, keen eyes, ardent souls, and bodies from many shores. During the daytime Faith chose to hide herself from this; to live within the precincts of an orderly mercantile establishment, and to conduct the simple domestic affairs of its owner and his resident clerks. But on some evenings, especially about the full of the moon, she left it, bonneted, and bound ostensibly upon some domestic errand. A few minutes later would find her not only in other precincts but in other purlieus.

There she laid aside her respectable bonnet and received in privacy a male member of the world flux that she had chosen, and summoned as she well knew how, up from the water front. During such interviews her face darkened and took on the rapt expression of some sibyl brooding upon far distant events. The brown iris of her eyes contorted, the black pupils narrowed into an inhuman and almost oblong shape as if she were threading a needle. Then suddenly they widened and grew clearer and calm again. Whether it was some impassioned spirit temporarily appeased or merely a satisfied animal that now looked through them it would be hard to tell.

A young poet, an outcast who had once tarried with her, thought that he had recognized in her face, when the disguise of the bonnet was removed for him, a portrait of that Fate who sits at the gates of first beginnings and tangles the threads of life. He had wondered if this personage could be loose and wandering about the plains of earth. He had returned to Faith again and again, fascinated, trying to read her secret, until she cast him off tired of his impotent curiosity.

But she was respected and even feared at the Casa da Bonnyfeather. Her work was not all "acting." It provided her sufficient scope for the exercise of other abilities. In a town where all save the German and English mercantile establishments were notorious for their clattiness and confusion, she maintained her employer's as a model of order and cleanliness. The private apartments of Mr. Bonnyfeather, into which no guest was ever summoned since the death of his wife, were not only spotless but bordered on the luxurious. Nothing was lacking which at any time Mr. Bonnyfeather or she herself really needed. The one exception to this was the room of Sandy McNab, which was Spartan. He slept there and nothing more.

The master's table, which was always served in the old ballroom exactly under the skeleton of the huge central chandelier immediately opposite the main door, was provided with an abounding plenty. This was more a matter of business acumen than anything else. Mr. Bonnyfeather himself was rather abstemious of both food and drink. Scarcely a day passed, however, without one or two guests, generally ship captains, factors, a brother merchant, or a traveller of note and distinction who bore letters of introduction or of credit to the house. In addition, most men of affairs, bankers, and even priests and artists in Livorno made it a point to drop in occasionally upon Mr. Bonnyfeather both for the good cheer and for the conversation.

From the table talk that went on about his board the merchant gathered not only entertainment but a curious and valuable knowledge of affairs in general, from world politics to how the tides ran in the Bay of Fundy, or why the pilot fees were so high on the River Hoogli. Many a profitable enterprise and many a shrewd deal had its inception or consummation here. There were few rumours adrift on the trade winds of the world which passed him by. The conversation was polyglot. A stray Russian had so far been the only guest who had been forced to discuss nothing but his soup. Even ships with cargoes consigned to his rivals found their captains dining in a garrulous frame of mind with Mr. Bonnyfeather.

This notable table was catered to by Angela, the fat cook, one of the best in town. The dishes proceeded in an orderly manner through a hole in the kitchen wall. Thence they were wheeled steaming on a small wagon with manifold trays by Tony Guessippi, the cook's husband. He was a kind of wizened male spider whose function in life was to convey the dishes which his wife concocted to their ultimate destination and to beget children on her body. A flock of eleven semi-naked youngsters and an equally lavish technique with knife and ladle testified that Destiny had not been mistaken this time in her choice.

On fine days both leaves of the great central door leading into the old ballroom were thrown open. At the top of the wide, low steps which now swept up with a uselessly superb flare, Mr. Bonnyfeather and his guests were to be seen dining under the swathed chandelier. The old merchant enjoyed this. In his secret heart he was the laird of Aberfoil dispensing feudal hospitality to more illustrious guests. Something of that feeling over-flowed into his mien and conversation and served to flavour the meal with both the salt and pepper of an old-world courtesy.

In all this Faith Paleologus was essential to Mr. Bonnyfeather. Not only did she oversee the smooth and profitable abundance of his own board, but the more simple comforts of the rest of the establishment as well. The merchant conducted his business in many languages, and there were no less than nine resident clerks, four Swiss porters, and several messengers and draymen who both ate and slept in rooms that overlooked the courtyard. On one side of this was a kind of small barracks for the "gentlemen writers." A ship's cook and two boys sufficed for them. The scrubwomen, five of whom appeared every morning, also made up the beds. When the master's own ships were in harbour the pursers were provided with their rooms and table, and there were generally transient guests of the establishment who came with some legitimate claim on its hospitality.

Such was the "factory" as it was called of the House of Bonnyfeather in which the housekeeper held unrelenting sway. Over the cellar, the warehouse, the stables, and the office itself hovered the eagle eye of Mr. Sandy (William) McNab.

The one spot in the place exempt from all authority was the purlieus of the kitchen. Here in gargantuan disorder and simian anarchy rioted the clan Guessippi; boys, girls, chickens, cats, and goats. No dogs had been able to survive. It was only when Faith herself appeared there at some crisis of uproar that silence and dismay brought about a specious appearance of order. At such times all the children fled either into or under the family bed. Tony departed to the wine cellar leaving his wife alone with her own bulk. It was well known throughout the neighbourhood that Faith had the evil eye. For that reason no spoons were ever missing, and the scrubwomen invariably reported early. One angry glance, and you might wither away; a stare, and the Virgin herself might not be able to help you.

To a certain degree the authority of Faith had been inherited. Inheritance indeed might account for much else that was peculiar in her. Her father had been a Florentine of Greek extraction. The family tree led back to Constantinople. They were workers in mosaic and had, with the extinction of the Medici, their patrons, fallen upon evil times. The last of them, a boy with a face like a hawk and the mad lusts of a leopard, had fallen in with a Scotchwoman in the house of Mr. Bonnyfeather's father at Livorno. She, Eliza NcNab, was one of several who had followed the fortunes of the Bonnyfeathers into exile. She was a true daughter of the heather. After a while the young Paleologus disappeared to assemble mosaics in parts unknown. He left his wife with a flower-like pattern of bruises, a baby daughter, and the statue of the Madonna. It was this daughter who had become the maid of Mr. Bonnyfeather's only child Maria, and it was she, Faith, who had succeeded in due time to the keys of his house.

At half past four on the morning after Anthony arrived the Casa da Bonnyfeather lay wrapt in the profound quiet which precedes the first stir of dawn. The last of the clerks had returned from the carnival. The only light to be seen in the courtyard was the faint, downward ray cast from the lattice of Faith Paleologus. Presently, it disappeared. She had crossed the corridor and gone into Anthony's room again. She placed the candles on the table and sat down. It was not her intention to remain watching for the rest of the night. The boy was sleeping utterly quietly and could need no further attention. But she, too, desired to study his face again. She had already formed conclusions of her own. In her case there was no point of honour beyond which speculation was taboo. Quite the contrary. The maid of Maria had no doubts about the family resemblance. She concluded that Mr. Bonnyfeather knew more than he cared to tell. Else why had the boy been placed in this room? Then there was the Madonna, of course. To Faith that was simply a confirmation of what she had already surmised. Well, she would find out some day. She had lived long enough to know that one of the best ways to get to the bottom of a mystery is to hold your own tongue. Others invariably wagged theirs sooner or later. Someone's long ears usually wagged at the same time.

She wondered about Don Luis. What was his connection with all this? Of many who came to the Casa da Bonnyfeather he had been the only one who had read her with a glance. "What are *you* doing here?" he had said. But he also could hold his tongue. She had admired him for that, and other things. Their one night together had been memorable. It had been her hope that he would take her away with him along with Maria. For that reason she had urged the marriage on the girl.

So her pretty young charge had given the marquis the slip after all! She would never have given her credit for that. Don Luis was no simpleton. It aroused Faith's reluctant admiration for Maria for whom even when a girl she had felt little else than a well-concealed envy that amounted almost to jealousy. Maria had been beautiful. Faith had been glad to see her leave the house.

So by hook or crook this boy had come back for *her* to look after—with the Paleologus Madonna. She did not like that. She had an impulse to destroy the thing. But she checked herself. No, that would be to give herself away; to cause questions to be asked. She looked up at the statue and glowered. What had been its rôle in all this? Nothing, of course, nothing! It was only a statue, an old one at that. Her eyes sank to the boy's face again.

There was the same unassailable loveliness. How she had envied it once in Maria. It was the opposite with which her nature was ever trying to unite. In this present young masculine mould in which it had been returned to her, it seemed possible that she might yet come to possess it after all, to possess it even for an instant in the only way she knew how, by the only approach to strength and beauty which she had. She was only thirty-two.

Presently her face darkened and her eyes contorted. She rose silently, took the candles, and approached the bed. She listened, and bent over Anthony with an attitude infinitely stealthy. Her breathing deepened. Her hand trembled unexpectedly and a drop of hot wax splashed on his breast. He moved convulsively and opened his eyes. She snatched the candles away and began tucking him in again. But she had not been quite quick enough. In the sudden glare of light as he first wakened the boy had seen her eyes.

"This place is full of them!" he cried out. He remembered where he was now. Then he saw her standing beside him.

"Who are you?" he asked.

"The housekeeper. I'm here to make you comfortable." She smiled at him.

"It was you who covered me up just now?"

"Yes, the sheets had slipped off and you looked cold."

He pondered the information as if it had great importance. "Doubtfully," she thought a little apprehensively. He rubbed his eyes.

"It's funny, but do you know just now I thought I saw that old goat looking down at me again."

"You must have dreamed it," she said. "Can't you see the door's closed? It can't get in here."

"No," he admitted doubtfully. The impression had been a strong one. The door was closed, however. He could see that for himself. He gave it up.

"What's your name?" he finally asked. Then as if in a hurry to make a fair exchange—"mine is Anthony."

"Faith."

"Faith!" He pondered that, too. Then as if to himself, "Father Xavier said faith was the evidence of things unseen."

"And who is Father Xavier?" she asked, an unconscious twinge of contempt creeping into her voice. She loathed priests.

"He is my friend," said Anthony, "and," he added, sensitive to the tone of her voice, "I shall be lonely without him. He is coming here to see me again often."

He flung this as a kind of challenge. Then as if to placate her, "You stay here?"

"I live here. I shall be near you all the time."

"Oh," he said. The conversation paused. He closed his eyes again.

She waited for a long time now as if to pose her new question to what lay so deep within him that it must answer truthfully when spoken to. But she must not let him go to sleep entirely. Time passed. She spoke to him dreamfully.

"Do you remember any other good friend?"

"Yes, I remember," he whispered.

Instinctively she chose now a tone just sufficient to reach him and no more. She leaned nearer carefully.

"Who?"

But the effect was exactly the opposite of what she had hoped for. He suddenly aroused himself, sat up and began to look about in a puzzled way as if he missed someone.

"I thought I saw her here, last night," he said.

"I wonder who *she* was?" thought Faith. "The old man said nothing about her."

The boy's eyes continued to search through the room. He remembered it vaguely from the night before, but he was confused by having been turned around on the bed by the doctor. Presently he twisted himself completely about.

"There!" he said triumphantly, pointing to the Madonna in her niche. "There she is."

"If she had only destroyed that statue last night! That would have been the time," she thought. It was always a mistake not to act on a deep prompting like that, to reason herself out of it. One should listen to one's voices. But it was too late now. The boy evidently set great store by the thing. It, "she," she caught herself saying, was a "close friend." He thought he had seen her here last night! A convent child with visions! Priest-bred, bah! He would have to get over that. Nevertheless, she felt herself balked in some way or other. Her first approach had been frustrated. She cursed herself for having given the statue to Maria. "I might have known it would come back to haunt me. It brought ill luck to my mother." In spite of herself she went cold.

"Well, is there anything you want?" she asked preparing to go.

He shook his head and settled back under the covers. It was a comfortable bed. Like the one at Signora Udney's, he thought. He closed his eyes. Outside a cock began to crow.

Faith slipped back to her own room. She must catch a wink of sleep herself before her day began. Silence wrapped the Casa da Bonnyfeather for another hour. Whatever moved then through its dilapidated corridors stole through them as silently as the dawn that was just breaking.

Chapter Fourteen

Reality Makes a Bid

NEXT morning Mr. Bonnyfeather "communicated" his decision of the night before to Faith. She said nothing, but she approved. Both of them were aware that considerable comment might be expected in and about the Casa da Bonnyfeather. Positions were eagerly sought after there, and the arrival of so young an apprentice and his immediate translation to the sacred apartment of the Capo della Casa would tickle curiosity. Both of them sat at breakfast thinking of this.

"*Hum-um!*" said Mr. Bonnyfeather. "How is he this morning?"

"A little dizzy yet, but quite all right again. Three eggs for breakfast," she replied.

"Keep him by you, in the room for several days," he went on. "Tell them he was badly shaken up. You can stretch a point. It will then be natural enough that you should be taking care of him under the circumstances."

"I had thought of it," she said.

"I knew you *had*," he smiled. "But what after that?"

"You can tell McNab he is too young yet to be in the dormitory with the grown men. They will be glad enough not to have him about carrying tales. It would be miserable for him and them. Also say that no one's position has been filled or is threatened by his coming here. It is just a case of charity for Father Xavier. Most of the trouble here starts over fears or petty jealousies, you know. After a while it will seem perfectly natural for him to keep staying where he is. It will also just have happened. Trust McNab to spread news."

"Exactly," said Mr. Bonnyfeather. He was somewhat surprised by having his own schemes put so eloquently. His housekeeper generally held her tongue. "'But it is natural enough," he thought, "she was Maria's maid." He was relieved and grateful to find that he would not have to try to explain to her what he must never explain to himself. "This is just another orphan to whom we are giving a start. As you say, 'pure charity.'" He looked at her significantly. She nodded and waited. "Do you think anyone else might notice the—his face?"

"McNab, perhaps. He was here before Maria left. He remembers her. All the rest are new."

"Have the barber in and crop the boy's hair close. It will make it easier for me, too, in a way." He sighed. "Also, get him clothes. Out of your household account. I'll not ask you to save there. One good suit. For a gentleman's son."

"Or a merchant's grandson?" she asked suddenly. She saw his cheek bones flush.

"Woman," he said, "dinna propose it in words. I dinna ken mysel'. Let the dead stay buried!" His face worked.

"Peace to you. I'm no gossip. Could you think that after all these years? I'll not whisper it this side of my shroud."

"It's not that," he said, calmer now. "I wouldn't have you think . . ."

"I think nothing," she said, "except that this is a new day and it's time to begin it."

She walked over to a chest, unlocked it, and drew forth two flags which she laid over his arm. "Leave the boy to me now. I'll see to him." He looked relieved and climbed to the roof intent on what amounted to a daily ritual.

Arrived there he hoisted the two flags each on a separate pole. One was that of England and the other his house flag, a red pennant with a black thistle. In addition to this he always addressed a short prayer to some member of the Holy Trinity. He then unlocked the small chest set into the parapet and took out a telescope. From the roof of the house the entire inner and outer harbour and a long vista down the coast was visible. Steadying the glass on a little bronze tripod, it was his custom every morning by this means to study both the molo and the Darsena carefully and to sweep the horizon. In half an hour he would be thoroughly familiar with what was going on at Livorno; what ships were coming and going, and what business they were bound upon. The glass was a good one. He could even recognize faces at a considerable distance. It aided greatly in eliminating from his affairs the disconcerting element of surprise. It would now be seven o'clock.

At precisely that instant Mr. Bonnyfeather could always be seen descending the stair from the roof. At the foot of the stairs Simon, the porter, handed him his gold-headed cane and a freshly filled snuff box. A large ship's bell which hung in the courtyard rang out. The gates were thrown open into the street. The drays began to rumble and the clerks to write. The Casa da Bonnyfeather was open for business.

On the morning after Anthony's arrival, Mr. Bonnyfeather was forced to make one minor change in the ritual. No one else knew it. He took the telescope out and swept the harbours as usual. His thoughts, however, were not upon the various swarming decks which he passed in review but in the room just under his feet. Through the corridor skylight, which was opened every fine morning like a ship's hatch, came the snipping of scissors and clear bursts of laughter. The barber was using his most humorous blandishments while removing Anthony's hair. Faith had lost no time about it.

Mr. Bonnyfeather smiled and turned his glass on the horizon. A cloud of mist seemed to cut off his view on a clear day. "Dampness in the glass!" He unscrewed the eyepiece and wiped it assiduously, likewise the large lens. He looked again. It was still dimmer. Forced to admit the fact in spite of himself, he furtively wiped his own eyes. When he levelled the glass again the horizon stood out startlingly clear.

Into a patch of brilliant sunlight sailed a full-rigged ship. The field of the glass covered her exactly. He could see the figurehead leaning forward and the slow rise and fall of the bows as the waves whitened under the fore-chains. Suddenly the ship hesitated, the sails fluttered, and then filled out on the other tack. All the shadows on them now lay serenely on the other side. In the crystal atmosphere of the glass the ship seemed to be manœuvering with supernatural ease in a better world. It was his own ship, long overdue, that was thus so calmly coming home again. He descended the stairs in the rested mood that often follows tears.

"Tell the draymen," said he, as the porter handed him his cane, "that the *Unicorn* is coming in after all. Be ready at the docks."

"A lucky day, sir," said Simon.

"*Very*," replied Mr. Bonnyfeather. His hand shook a little as he took the cane.

In the corridor under the skylight the last of Anthony's ringlets had just fallen to the floor. Faith led him to Maria's mirror. "I am a man now," said he fiercely. A very tall and slim, and a very young, young gentleman dressed in a pair of plain bow shoes and a decent dark green suit with buckles at the knees was trying to frown back at him from the glass. Even Anthony thought him to be good-looking. It annoyed him vastly to find that the barber was taking all the credit for it as a result of his handiwork. "I grew these all myself," said the boy, turning upon the man angrily and running his hand through his crisply shorn locks. There was a ripple of laughter from the door. "Are you sure of it?" said Faith Paleologus. The barber clashed his shears and departed.

Three mornings later Anthony emerged from his seclusion to take up his duties in the world of men. He was anxious to do so. An overpowering curiosity, and a new, vivid sense of reality, totally submerged any shrinking from the unknown which his temperament might ordinarily have provided. He accompanied Mr. Bonnyfeather to the roof and was there permitted to raise the house flag which he was given to understand was henceforth to be his first daily task. Below him the mules were being hitched to the dray. Big Angela and her progeny were drawing water at the fountain. The clerks were making for the office. Amid the garden-beds wandered his friend the goat. Mr. Bonnyfeather busied himself with the telescope. Presently Sandy McNab beckoned to Anthony. "Come down here, laddie," said he. Leaving the old man on the roof, Anthony descended.

"How are you now?" said McNab in Italian, seeing that the boy had understood only his gestures. He also shook him by the hand with so firm a clasp as to make him wince. "Quite well, sir," replied Anthony bravely. Mr. McNab studied him for a minute. "You'll do now I guess," he said. He looked at the short hair approvingly. "Hold your chin up when you go about, and look out for goats." He grinned. "But not so high as that," he cautioned, shoving the boy's nose down with his thumb. "I mean take your own part and don't be afraid of anybody. You understand? That's what 'hold your chin up' means." Anthony nodded. "Come on now, you're to eat breakfast with the clerks. The other meals you take with the master. And that's lucky for you," he added, taking the boy roughly but not unkindly by the hand. "There is a world of difference in victuals." He led the way across the broad flagstones of the courtyard to the office which they entered together in company with several clerks.

It was the big room where Anthony had first met Mr. Bonnyfeather. But it was now a scene of great animation. Down the aisle between the desks had appeared as if by magic a long table at which were seated a crowd of about twenty men varying in years from youth to middle age. They ate steadily and heartily of dishes strange to Anthony. No time, it appeared, was to be lost. At the extreme end of the apartment Mr. Bonnyfeather's desk rose impressively behind its railing, majestic but lonely.

To the boy's surprise and delight little attention was paid to him when he came in. Those near by looked up and nodded perfunctorily at McNab who sat at the head of the table near the door. He drew a stool up for Anthony next to him and rearranged some plates. "This will be your place now every morning," he said. "Help yourself."

He set the example by pouring himself a large basin of tea and heaping his plate with fish and scrambled eggs. Out of the coagulated mass a mackerel looked up at Anthony with a desperate purple eye. For a moment he could feel again where the goat had hit him. He turned his eyes up to the frescoed ceiling and for some moments allowed them to remain there. Just above him his friend with the winged heels was taking off from a cloud, leaving the banquet of the gods behind. Perhaps he, too, felt dizzy.

"I see you are a man of sensibility," said a pleasant voice in French next to Anthony. Anthony took his eyes from the ceiling and turned to find himself looking into a keen, youngish face with sparkling brown eyes. "I myself," continued the stranger smiling in a friendly way upon him, "have upon several mornings preferred to contemplate the banquet of the gods in the ceiling rather than this breakfast of the English upon the floor." Anthony summoned his small stock of French to mind and replied with immense precision, "Is it that in the ceiling they are not eating fish?"

"Never," cried his new-found friend fiercely, "never a fish!" He waved confirmatively toward a Bacchus

270

just above him. "Have you not noticed," he rattled on, "the terrible Medusa-like stare of the mackerel? It produces in the pit of the stomach the sensation of stone." Anthony agreed. He could not follow it all, but he felt called upon to make a counter-reply.

"But at the breakfast of the English the food is real," he managed to string together. "True," cried his new friend, "your observation does you credit, monsieur, it is a just one. You have named the chief advantage the English have over the gods. But consider, it is only a temporary one. By tonight this breakfast will have become food for an idea. It will have become an idea. That is the end of breakfasts. And think," said he, suddenly whisking about on the bench so that he sat astride of it with his hands on his hips, "think what kind of an idea that mackerel will become which is even now going into the head of Meester McNab."

Mr. McNab's eyes bulged out with indignation. For a moment he seemed doubtful himself as to the destination of the fish and choked. "Hauld your clack," he mumbled, and then turned to Anthony. "Eat your bun, my boy," said he, "and sop it in your tea. Toussaint there is a Frenchman and a philosopher. If you listen to him you'll have naught but an ideal breakfast in your little basket when the bell rings." As if in premonition of famine and as an example to the young, Mr. McNab, after clearing his own plate with a piece of bread in spiral motion, departed for his desk. Anthony, who was embarrassed at thus finding himself the centre of a debate, was relieved to see McNab grinning over his shoulder at Toussaint who laughed back. The latter now continued to regard him with his arms akimbo.

"I can see that we shall get along famously," he said. "You speak French beautifully"—Anthony blushed with delight—"and you dislike mackerel. It is the basis for a firm, philosophic friendship. You look like a northerner. Where have you been civilized? You do not speak English?" Anthony shook his head.

"I would advise you to learn it," his friend rattled

on. "It is the language out of which realities proceed, fish, tea, gold, raiment—and finally power. It will help you here greatly, for that is the kind of thing they are after." The boy nodded as if he knew. "Father Xavier has already said so," he interpolated. "Ah, yes, of course, the Jesuit. He would know. But he has already taught you other things, I suppose?" "Yes, monsieur, Latin, French, and I know Italian. I have read *The Divine Comedy*."

"Excellent," cried the philosopher. "You have begun. I myself will continue your education, in French." He held up a warning finger. "But say nothing about it. Your desk is to be next to mine. Monseigneur McNab has in a way turned you over to me. You see I know where you come from." For some reason the boy felt his cheeks glow.

"Tut, tut, it is a great advantage. You're not handicapped by a mother. It is *they* who make the world civilized and that is what is the matter with it. They want you for themselves. Congratulate yourself. Also we shall circumvent Mr. McNab. I am supposed to teach you about invoices. They are easy. Afterwards we shall put them by in a drawer and converse"—he pointed upwards dramatically—"in the language which is useful up there. You see those nine women dancing about the gentleman with the lyre?" Anthony nodded. "We shall meet them," said he. "Possibly even the gentleman himself. In the meantime, let me recommend to you the conduct of this one, in so far as you see it portrayed there," he added hastily, and pointed to the figure of a boy standing behind the couch of Jove. From the cup which he bore, the page was slyly taking a drink behind the other man's back. "Do you understand, mon ami?" asked Toussaint looking down into Anthony's face.

Anthony nodded, "I think so," he replied. "At least I shall learn French."

"At the very least!" replied Toussaint. "And now I shall prove to you that McNab is wrong." He pulled a fine watch out of his bright yellow waistcoat and looked at it. "You have seven minutes before the bell rings to finish your breakfast. You shall now see what it is to be a natural philosopher."

He assembled some plates rapidly under the fascinated stare of Anthony, placed upon them a fried egg with an unbroken yolk, a piece of thin bacon beside it, a light, white roll and a piece of butter which he cut into a square. Then he poured out some tea carefully straining out the leaves. "It *is* a little cold," said he, "due to my causerie, but you see what makes it inviting is that it is the combination of food and an idea. It is déjeuner and not merely the breaking of a fast. Eat while you still have time." They both broke into a laugh together. The first of many.

"Five minutes till the bell rings," said Mr. McNab with his eyes upon them from the other end of the room. He was already at work. Toussaint made a grimace. Anthony stuffed himself. Presently the bell rang.

Instantly, all those who were still lingering arose. The porters seized the loose planks of which the tables were composed and carried them out bodily with the remains of the breakfast upon them. The stools upon which the planks rested were each claimed by a clerk who carried it to his desk and sat down upon it forthwith, opened his ledger, and began to indite. A man with a broom swept the fragments down the aisle. In a short time a complete silence save for the scratching of divers pens reigned unbroken.

The sun streamed through the windows and only the gods in the ceiling continued to dine. Beneath them the figures of the gentlemen writers bent over the desks, adding up columns or writing letters. Decorum from a niche in the corner smiled. About five minutes later the ferrule of a cane was heard clicking on the mosaics in the vestibule. Mr. McNab left his desk and took his place by the door.

"Good morning, sir," said he as Mr. Bonnyfeather came through the door.

"Good morning, Mr. McNab, good morning, gentle-

273

men," said Mr. Bonnyfeather. A respectful murmur of welcome ensued without interrupting the pens. Mr. Bonnyfeather advanced one more step, took off his hat, and hung it over the face of a dilapidated satyr whose horns were worn giltless by this use. From under the cocked hat it grinned helplessly. Mr. Bonnyfeather, the step, and the simultaneous removal of the hat in the same place at the same time each morning never failed. It had gone on for thirty years. The Frenchman Toussaint Clairveaux was fascinated. He had watched it for seven. The satyr was slowly becoming respectable. There could be no doubt about it. Mr. Bonnyfeather now took a pinch of snuff and advanced to his desk. On this particular morning he made an announcement.

"I shall need all hands at the quay this afternoon to to take stock of cargo. The *Unicorn* has at last been released by the customs." A buzz of excitement followed. All knew that it was a rich Eastern cargo and premiums might follow. Mr. Bonnyfeather believed in prize money in peace as well as in war.

"He is a remarkable man, a gentleman, an honest spirit," said Toussaint to Anthony who was now seated on a high stool near him. The boy looked up to meet an encouraging smile from Mr. Bonnyfeather sitting at the big desk. He felt encouraged. Just then McNab came along and bade him follow. They went over into the corner to the chief clerk's bureau. Mr. McNab took out a heap of papers, spread them out, and looked at Anthony. "These are your indentures," he vouchsafed. "You sign them here." He handed a pen to the boy. At the place which McNab indicated the lad wrote very carefully, *Anthony*.

"Anthony what?" asked McNab peering down at him. The boy looked puzzled. "Your last name?" The boy shook his head slowly. It had never occurred to him that he needed one. Other people had them, of course. Mr. McNab grunted and began to look through the papers.

"A deposition by the Mother Superior of the Convent of Jesus the Child situate in this Our Grand Duchy of

274

Tuscany." McNab grunted. "In the name of the Father the Son and the Holy Ghost, greeting." Grunt. The rest was in Latin.

The chief clerk paused for a minute, gripped the paper more firmly, and gave it a shake. The text, however, remained in the same language. He cleared his throat and looked at Anthony,

"Can *you* read this?" he asked, handing the paper to Anthony. The boy looked at him uneasily.

"Let's see if you can," suggested Mr. McNab in a doubtful tone of voice. "Read it aloud." As if reciting to Father Xavier, Anthony began.

It was a simple recital of the facts of his own arrival at the convent. He had been, it appeared, "but newly born, a perfect man child with a sore navel." Why was that? he thought. The contents of the black bag were then enumerated, himself included. He became intensely interested and pressed on. The corridors of the convent at night with Sister Agatha walking along them carrying a bundle through the shadows leaped out from the bare recital on the page. He knew every turn she would take, the whole scene. The deposition in bad, bare, legal Latin took on for the boy the fascination of a literary masterpiece of which he was the hero. "And on the next day following the said male infant, parents unknown, was baptized Anthony . . ."

"Go on," said McNab.

"According to the rite of the Holy . . ."

"You have no last name," interrupted the man sternly.

"No, sir," said Anthony meekly.

"Also you seem to have entered the world in great adversity," continued his tormentor. He drummed on the desk. "Have you any suggestions?" Anthony shook his head.

"—and to have arrived here under still more adverse circumstances!" Mr. McNab's eyes twinkled. "Well," said he, "why not catch up your past misfortunes into a name and give your good luck a chance? Wait a minute."

He went over to Mr. Bonnyfeather and for some minutes held him in conversation. Anthony could see them looking his way now and then laughing. He felt uncomfortable. Why was it curious not to have a last name? Finally, Mr. Bonnyfeather took up his largest plumed pen and wrote something with a flourish on a small piece of paper. He held it up before him considering it. Then he nodded as if satisfied and handed it still smiling to Mr. McNab. The clerk returned to his bureau and thrust the paper under the boy's nose. On it was written—

Anthony Adverse

"*That*," said Mr. McNab with a Mede and Persian gesture, "is your name." And it was. Mr. McNab pronounced it, "Advarse." It was thus that Anthony always thought of it.

The signing of the papers was now completed and Toussaint called as witness. Anthony watched anxiously to see if his friend would laugh at the new name. He remained perfectly serious. The clerk now drew up a small document of his own. It was a draft on Anthony's pay for nine shillings for a hat, payable to Mr. William McNab. This also the boy signed. Mr. McNab was now satisfied. He stuck the quill pen behind his ear and looked at Anthony.

"There is only one advantage," he said, "in having a name. It prevents you signing other peoples' names to papers. But as in everything else this advantage is outweighed by a corresponding disadvantage." The boy opened his eyes as the man was evidently in earnest. A certain grim kindness now lurked about the folds of McNab's heavy jowl which Anthony had not noticed before. "A corresponding disadvantage," continued

McNab. "You have to sign your own name! Do so as little as possible. And never sign any paper without thinking it over three separate times." The boy blinked. "For example, this paper which you have just signed will cost you two months' pay. No, not quite. Sixty days from now you will receive one shilling. You understand, sixty days! If you had not signed it, you would have received ten shillings. . . . Come with me," said McNab, "and I will show you."

He took Anthony over to a large iron till which he unlocked. From a drawer he drew out ten shillings and placed them in the boy's hand. "All of these would have been yours, *but* you signed a paper, didn't you? Hence," growled McNab, "these are mine." He counted nine shillings out of the boy's palms back into his own. The one remaining seemed to Anthony to have no weight at all. The clerk let the lightness of it sink home. "Sixty days from now," he said, and put the single shilling back in the till with the fatal paper. The other nine pieces he poured into his waistcoat pocket where they seemed to chime. He pointed Anthony to his own desk and walked away.

Pondering over the responsibility of having a name and the enormous difference between one and ten shillings, the boy climbed back on his stool. The tears welled up in his eyes. He was afraid they might drop on the desk so that Toussaint would see them. The latter was writing. Anthony looked up at the ceiling again. Presently his eyes dried leaving them hard and clear. He was soon lost amid the painted clouds.

The young gentleman wth the winecup was also a "perfect man child." His navel, however, was not sore. Anthony noticed that. The other things were all there too. On the lady sitting next to the big man with the beard they were missing. You longed to provide them. His own, for instance. The thought appealed to him as an original one. He cherished it carefully. The group amid the frescoes began to move. A faint glow began to steal up his back. The stool under him grew pleasantly warm. "What if . . .

that woman who had helped dress him and bathe him when he had been ill. How soft her hands had been." It was the same feeling. He trembled. Toussaint was shaking him by the elbow and laughing. All the blood in Anthony's body seemed to rush to his face.

"Come, come," said his new-found friend in a kindly way. "Do you want to turn into one of those?" He pointed to the satyr under Mr. Bonnyfeather's hat. "There are lots of them around here like that."

"I could never be like that!" Anthony flung back indignantly at finding his thoughts so easily read. His face no doubt had betrayed him. He must be careful then in this place where there were so many sharp eyes about. It was not like the convent where you could sit and let the shadows come and go through your eyes with no one to see them. No, no, he must never betray himself by his expression again. His face became so grimly determined that Toussaint laughed again.

"Now, you look like Monsieur McNab," he said.

"Oh, dear," thought Anthony, "that is impossible, too." But he had no time to protest further, for Toussaint was spreading out before him a number of blank forms. On each one of them was engraved a small black ship in full sail with something printed underneath several times over in as many languages.

Take notice: the good ship .... of............
God willing, proposes to sail from ....this........
day of ....17......with the following cargo; to wit, item:

There now unrolled about a foot of paper with ditto marks under "item" and a long line opposite each ditto. On each of these lines Anthony was shown how to copy the list of a ship's cargo from forms already filled out by Toussaint. The forms were duplicates and the work must be accurate. Each line must correspond exactly. It was to be checked later at the customs. At first, no matter how careful he was, he kept making mistakes. Barrels of sugar insisted on inserting themselves upon lines meant exclusively for barrels of pork. Whereupon Toussaint tore up the form. At last Anthony managed to complete a set exactly and felt elated. Another was immediately shoved under his nose. He continued to write all morning. His hands grew cramped and his body tired. Toussaint permitted him to slip down once or twice from his stool and to look on.

"Tell me," said Anthony, pointing to the phrase "God willing" on the form, "what has God got to do with all this?"

"It is a pious word for wind," said Toussaint.

"Oh," said Anthony, "and God makes it blow? Is that it?"

"I suppose so," said Toussaint.

"But he does, of course."

"Perhaps; copy these."

But the boy stopped in the middle of the form. "Who does then?"

"No one," replied Toussaint without allowing his pen to pause.

Anthony had never thought of that. The mistakes multiplied. His world was shivering. Toussaint tore up so many forms that Mr. McNab snorted.

Various visitors came in to see Mr. Bonnyfeather from time to time. You could hear them talking at the desk, but it was better not to look. The room gradually grew hotter. Anthony felt himself getting hungry. Finally, the bell in the courtyard chimed once. A thunder of closing ledgers followed and the clerks rushed out. Anthony and Toussaint were left alone.

From a cubbyhole in the desk, the Frenchman drew forth one of the several small, calf-bound volumes. Here he cherished a microscopic library, shifting, trading, and even buying second-hand books from time to time. In the course of seven years much literature had passed through the cubbyhole but tarried in his head. The Frenchman had a memory for the printed word as though his brain contained an acid which bit the reflection of the page on the surface of a mirror.

"You are hungry now," he said to Anthony, "I know. But it is half an hour yet till dinner and if you will give me that half hour every day, I shall be glad to share it with you. I do not think I shall be wasting my time—or yours. What do you say?"

The man's eyes glowed softly as if within him a banked fire had begun to break through the ashes. He saw the reflection of it in the face of the boy before him. "It is a bargain, then!" he cried. "See, I shall clinch it with this to remind you of it always." He opened up the little book excitedly, crossed out his own name, and wrote Anthony's. Then he handed it to the boy with a noble gesture. "Open it," he said, "let us lose no time." It was a copy of La Fontaine's *Fables* with little engravings.

They turned to "Le Corbeau et le Renard" and began. They translated carefully into Italian, and when this was not precise enough, into Latin. Then Toussaint began to correct Anthony's accent. Again and again he repeated the French. The boy was delighted. Here were more words, and such words! After his flat Jesuit's Latin and soft Tuscan, his tongue seemed at last to have found itself. Finally, Toussaint recited the whole poem. The clean music of it, the caressing stroke of the rhyme, and the charm of the story held Anthony on the stool as if he were looking at a play. He stared up into Toussaint's face with parted lips.

"Anthony," said a kindly voice from the other end of the room. It was Mr. Bonnyfeather. They both rose instinctively.

"We were just having a little French lesson, monsieur," said Toussaint apprehensively.

"Splendid," replied the older man, "but we are waiting dinner."

"I am sorry, indeed . . ." began Toussaint.

"You do not need to be, perhaps later on . . ." Mr. Bonnyfeather drew for a moment with his cane on the ground. "Well, we can let that wait. In the meantime by all means go on here as you have begun." He nodded approvingly. By this time Anthony had joined him and they went out of the door together, the little book in the boy's hand.

Toussaint Clairveaux remained leaning on his desk and dreaming. He saw a small garden running down to the River Loire, a bridge, across the river, a white castle on a hill, and broad steps leading up the steep street of Blois. At a small pond in the garden a man with a scholar's gown thrown over his arm was helping an urchin sail a boat. It drifted out of reach. The man let it go after a few half-hearted efforts to recover it. The wind stranded it amid the reeds. The child began to cry. "Ah, mon cher," said a woman's soft voice behind them, "it has always been like that." The man shifted uncomfortably but said nothing. Presently he took a book out of the pocket of his gown, leaned back, and began to read. The woman picked up the boy and comforted him. He snuggled in her dress. She began to recite "Le Corbeau et le Renard."

Tears ran down the face of Toussaint Clairveaux and splashed upon his desk. How delightful, how dear! Oh how heavenly ravishing were those accents! Would to Christ he could listen to them again if only for another instant now! O fields of asphodel, over which that woman's sad face is now looking, under what sunless rays do you ripple and toss? Are they as beautiful as that glimpse from the garden across the Loire?—the washerwomen along the banks of the river under the willows, the white château in a haze of green buds, a bird singing? He choked.

"Jean-Jacques Rousseau, it was you who tempted me to leave all that, to go vagabonding for Arcadia," he cried aloud, raising his hands dramatically to the ceiling as if appealing to all-seeing Jove feasting away up there. "You make me an exile before the Revolution begins, an émigré to nowhere. And now, I am caught here." He looked about him desperately. He swept the papers off his desk onto the floor.

"I am lost in a prison where a merchant's hat is wearing the horns off a satyr," he shrieked. "I shall never find the country of the beautiful savages!"

By this time the poor man was nervously striding up and down before the rail of Mr. Bonnyfeather's desk, gesticulating at the empty desks below. At every one of them sat a useless regret or vain desire. That was his senate.

"Ah, if I could have reached those wild American forests I should have suffused my soul as a true poet and have blent you all into one." He shook his fist at the nine separate muses who paid no attention. "All into one! I should have charmed the savages. It was that woman with the great eyes who kept me here. Ah, yes! Ah, it was not you, Jean-Jacques, after all. The spirit of man is truly noble as you say, as mine was. Yes, I believe that. This boy I shall lead into your beautiful pages. He shall later cross the sea and find that natural country for himself, unspoiled. He shall see how beautiful are the minds and bodies of men when left to themselves with nature. He shall feast like you up there in the ceiling. I, I cannot go, I am lost, bewitched. And sacred blood of a bitch!" he snorted, returning to what after all was his chief grievance, "ever since I have followed that Paleologus to this place she will not even speak to me."

Mr. McNab looked in and saw a little Frenchman apparently going mad. He grinned. The bell in the court rang twice. "To eat or not to eat, that is the question," the Scot called cupping his hand. Toussaint Clairveaux cursed him, stuffed a copy of *La Nouvelle Héloïse* into his pocket, and raced for his dinner with McNab. The mercurial Frenchman was now laughing, too. Despite the gulf between them, the two men had learned to admire each other. They were both capable of utter concentration on the matter at hand and were completely sincere. Over the desk they ceased to clash.

Anthony and Mr. Bonnyfeather were ascending the steps into the big hall just as the last prolonged resonance of the bell in the courtyard died away. The table under the muffled chandelier was set for four.

The guest for dinner that day was Captain Bittern

282

of the *Unicorn*. He was a very thin man with a hatchet face and a perfectly horizontal, thin-lipped mouth. His hat from being perpetually jammed down on his forehead in a high wind left a permanent red streak in the oily tan of his hide. Deep-set in cavernous sockets, his clear, cold, blue eyes looked out from behind puckered lids past the vertical, bony ridge of a long nose. It was a face which seemed even in the mouldy stillness of the old ballroom to be facing into a high wind. Anthony sat directly opposite it.

He felt instinctively that it would be impossible to disobey or to discount any command or statement that proceeded from those absolutely positive, horizontal lips. During the course of about thirty years several thousand nautical men and "natives" in various parts of the world had agreed with Anthony. One expected to hear a bass voice boom out, but the captain's pitch was a perfectly self-possessed falsetto. The effect of this from such a countenance was startling. The voice piped away steadily, monotonously, unexhausted, like a constant gale keening throught taut rigging. It never rumbled. In the man's ears were two very small gold rings. He had risen from the fo'c'sle to the quarter-deck. The rings remained.

The meal began by Captain Bittern's tilting a plate of soup into his transverse cavern at one fell motion. The lips simply widened toward the ears, and the soup, still on a perfect level, disappeared. The act, if such it could be called, was so irrevocable as to be almost ridiculous. Had it not been for the captain's eyes still looking out over the horizon of the bowl as if in search of distant icebergs, Anthony must have laughed. Mr. Bonnyfeather remembered that he had once seen a shark swallow a child's coffin like that in the China sea. Nothing could be done about it. The captain never laughed. It was impossible to imagine that the corners of those lips should ever be turned either up or down.

Nevertheless, the merchant treated him with great respect. He was the oldest and most dependable of the four captains of the fleet of the house. The single horn of his ship's figurehead pointed into far and dangerous seas, and pointed home again. He was just back from Singapore and the Islands, four months overdue. The account he gave of his cargo made Mr. Bonnyfeather rub his hands. Several long tumblers of raw rum innocent of any water followed the captain's soup. At every return to port Captain Bittern preserved himself in the genial fluid. In transit he abstained. Rum had absolutely no effect upon him except to embalm his body and to heighten the eloquence of his falsetto. He now began, after a series of gastronomic vanishing acts performed with both liquids and solids, to relate the story of his voyage. He took not the slightest notice of Mr. Bonnyfeather, Anthony, or Faith Paleologus. It was exactly as if he were reciting a portion of his memoirs for the benefit of the cosmos while in his cabin at sea.

Anthony longed now to understand English. He resolved to lose no time in learning it. From the tones of the captain's voice and a few words here and there he caught the emotional drift. When the captain was bargaining he did so with his hands. Over one successful deal, he squeaked. He almost broke the spell he cast by that. Anthony started when he felt Faith grip him by the knee. She managed to get him to lean closer to her and began in her low liquid voice to translate what the captain was saying.

The typhoon which had forced Captain Bittern to refit completely at Mauritius was epochal. The low voice of Faith beside him seemed to transmit to Anthony's eyes rather than to his ears the picture of the *Unicorn* dismasted, staggering, with the little beast at the bow waving his horn at the scudding clouds and then plunging for the bottom, while ribbons of split canvas streamed from the futile jury-mast rigged forward. The captain's voice became the constant piping and fluting of the wind. For the first time some conception of the power of the elements was projected into the boy's imagination. Anthony felt a mountain snatched away from under the ship, and gasped as he slid with the vessel into a molten, lead-covered abyss. The effect of wind was intolerable. By a peculiar reversal of effect the storm which the captain seemed to be facing now flowed out along with his words from his elemental face. The voice of the man piped like the wind; the voice of the woman flowed and leaped with excitement like the sea. The two mated in the boy's mind and became one experience.

A large chest and a desk in the captain's cabin started suddenly to slide about and enter into a monstrous combat with each other. The desk burst open and its insides gushed out as the chest leaped upon it. The bilge water and the paper were slowly ground into pulp as the chest continued to celebrate its victory drunkenly. The white paste produced by this milling of water and paper gathered in the panels between the beams. The cabin lamp went out. The stern windows dazzled with blue lightning. The sea rushed in. It went on for days. He went up on deck with the captain and saw an albatross sucked across the sky down into the funnel of the west where the sun plunged drawing the atmosphere after him. Suddenly it was calm again. The crew came on deck like ants out of the earth after rain, and crawled about jagged stumps of masts. Presently Anthony was tasting oranges and drinking from cocoanuts in Mauritius. In memory of the long drought during the six weeks' calm which had followed that storm, Captain Bittern allowed a fourth tumbler of rum to trickle soothingly through his teeth. He smacked his lips. Mr. Bonnyfeather sighed. It was this kind of thing, he thought, that made it profitable for a nobleman to have become a merchant.

That afternoon on the dock Anthony was able to understand why the hull of the *Unicorn* looked so aged and battered while aloft all was new with a varnished spick-and-spanness. He fell in love with the trim ship from the romping little horned-horse that sprang out of her bows to the faded gilt of the taffrail. From the yawning hatches streamed up an endless succession of bales, chests, and long mummy-like packages. The odour of preserved fruit, spices, sandalwood, and tar blent with all the rank smells of Christendom along the docks. He had never thought there could be so many different kinds of things in the world. Toussaint and the clerks kept calling them off to one another hour after hour. The odours and the weight of materials and objects seemed to press inward upon Anthony, to weigh upon his chest. He breathed deeply to free himself of the impression but could not do so. It was there, it was real. It was as real as he was. Even more so, harder and firmer.

What a fine thing it must be to own all of this, actually to possess all of these things. He glanced with a new respect and understanding at Mr. Bonnyfeather who was laughing and talking with some other merchants on the quarter-deck. They were congratulating him; already beginning to chaffer and bargain. Various bales went their way from time to time. The railing of the quarter-deck stretched between Anthony and their world just as it did between him and Mr. Bonnyfeather's desk. There was a difference then between men, which had something to do with all of these things.

He looked about him once more. Nothing belonged to him. He had only his dreams. He was a poor boy, an orphan. He understood that now. In sixty days he would have only one shilling. He had lost nine by the first use of his name. He looked at Mr. McNab standing by the capstan with a pile of papers on it. Toussaint was checking off. Mr. McNab was wearing his new hat. "God willing," thought Anthony, "I shall follow both their advices. I will not write my name on papers, and I shall certainly learn English." He began to listen to the English words for things. His chest expanded. In the days to come he would prove himself.

He went over to the group by the capstan and began to help Toussaint to check the invoices. McNab nodded approvingly. Anthony felt himself suddenly in the main current of real life. The quiet pool of the convent court-yard lay far behind him. "Where was the drift taking him?" he wondered.

"Attention," said Toussaint, "thirty-four bolts of prime Manila hemp." "Thirty-four," said Anthony. "Check," said McNab.

Chapter Fifteen

The Shadows of Faith

ANTHONY was not detained very long by the copying out of invoices and manifests. His first promotion in the world of affairs was to the desk of the correspondents or gentlemen writers. A copperplate hand that had been conferred upon him by Father Xavier, and his proficiency in languages were responsible. The arid years in the convent were now to a certain extent a positive advantage. He could never get enough of the life about him. He absorbed it at a remarkable rate, in gulps.

No thirstier horse had ever been led to water. So avid was he of the words and the experiences, emotions, and facts which he acquired through words that he was scarcely conscious of the barriers between languages. Words were simply the coins minted by the tongues of men with which realization could be purchased. Whether they were English, French, Spanish, or Italian he cared little. All of these, with an infinite variety of dialect, he heard in daily use all about him. The quays, the streets, the counting houses of Livorno, and even the Casa de Bonnyfeather itself were in a state of babel.

For a while language remained for him nothing but the common tongue of mankind. It was not until some months had passed that he began to understand differences. Now, without thinking about it, he instinctively tasted the various savour of words and through them life. He found it good.

Slowly English began to displace in his thought his strange jargon of hill-Tuscan and ecclesiastical Latin. He heard English talked constantly in the office. It was dinned into his ears at the table and in the house. It corresponded to the new and real experiences he was having. It was also an advantage, he found, to use it when employed as a messenger about the docks or to ship's officers. It got you instant attention. He began to realize that his physical appearance corresponded with it. He began to use it when he had some important problem to think out. He spoke it with a slight Scotch tang and a softening of the vowels. The burr had been softened to a purr. The combined effect was musical and rather arresting. It was impossible to tell whence he hailed. His verbal messages seemed to come from some self-cultivated Arcadian nowhere.

Toussaint was a potent force in all this. Mr. Bonnyfeather had been quick to see the advantage of French lessons. They did not long continue to occupy only the half hour before lunch. Before long they were removed to the old ballroom after dinner had been cleared away, and they went on in the afternoon.

Soon Toussaint and Anthony were reading books together. Some writing followed as a matter of course. Later Toussaint put Anthony to copying out correspondence with French firms. In a year he was able to answer letters that required no more than a perfunctory reply. Spanish followed.

At the table Anthony listened carefully. He had learned when in doubt how to resort to a grammar or a dictionary. In the section of correspondence in the office he would pass from stool to stool. Of the several gentlemen writers each was glad to find the boy by his side for the sake of his young and happy presence and for the chance to impress upon him the superlative importance of a particular department. That Anthony was under the special eye of the Capo della Casa all of them knew.

But Mr. Bonnyfeather was most careful about that. He never permitted Anthony to take advantage of it. It was a nice piece of tact. On one or two occasions the merchant had condescended to explain to the boy. There he learned something valuable.

"See and hear everything, but be careful what you do and say," admonished the old man. "Do not tell me that Garcia sleeps at his desk, I know it, I see him nod. If he thought you knew it, he would hate you. Knowledge which threatens anyone's bread and butter should be concealed if you wish to get on."

But there was something more to it than just that. Out of the several occasions when Anthony had been thus admonished he began to understand Mr. Bonnyfeather's careful, masculine sense of honour, the indignity of eavesdropping to all concerned, the pettiness of tattle. In short, that to mind his own business meant he must first possess his own tongue in dignity and peace. A discretion rather beyond his years was thus thrust upon him.

Once he had blurted out something he had heard at the big table while he was walking along the street with McNab. It was about the unexpected arrival of a ship from Smyrna laden with oil consigned to Mr. Bonnyfeather. A smartly dressed young lad standing on the corner had turned immediately and made his way through the crowd into the near-by door of a counting house.

"Did you see yon laddie gang off wi' your tidings?" asked Sandy. "He's Maister Nolte, the nevvy of a German marchant. In ten minutes, they'll be sellin' oot a' their oil at the present prices. If you're no keerfu' you'll be takin' your victuals in the kitchen, laddie." They walked on, Anthony's cheeks burning.

"You'll not say anything to Mr. Bonnyfeather, McNab?" he ventured.

"I always hold my tongue," was the reply. It was a matter-of-fact statement with no scorn in it. But the boy wilted.

"And I'll tell ye this," added McNab. "It's not only statements ye maun be keerfu' aboot, it's questions, too. Ye ask a warld too mony. Watch wi' yer ain eyes and see what happens. Then draw your ain concloosions. Dinna pay attention after ye ken what is gangin' on to what every zany may have to say."

They entered a warehouse and went to the desk of the shipping clerk. Anthony noticed that McNab let the clerk do all the talking, using only an apt prod now and then to his volubility. In five minutes the man had contradicted himself twice and proved himself in the wrong. McNab collected his bill and left.

"Ye see?" said he, peering down at Anthony. The boy never forgot. Mr. McNab blew his nose loudly into a scarlet handkerchief large enough to muffle a horn. That afternoon to the sound of his bugling they collected seventeen bills.

Distance had worked its inevitable negative magic with Father Xavier. For the first six weeks he had come rather regularly two or three times a week. Then for one reason or another his visits became irregular, the instruction desultory. It was finally dropped. The priest had done all he could. He felt that himself. New influences which he could not fully control were impinging upon his pupil's mind. The lives of saints, church history, Latin fables seemed enormously remote to Anthony now. Like the fountain in the convent courtyard they sounded in his ears as something speaking from a dream. Finally he saw Father Xavier only when Mr. Bonnyfeather confessed. This was not often. Then he heard that Father Xavier had gone to Naples. He received a letter and answered it. Another, and he forgot to reply.

Mr. Bonnyfeather's father had changed his religion to suit the Cardinal of York. Something of the old Calvinistic independence remained in the son. Secretly Mr. Bonnyfeather perused some of his grandfather's books on theology. The doctrine of predestination fascinated him. It was with a distinct struggle he persuaded himself that he had laid it aside. Several times he had been on the point of asking Father Xavier about it. Then he thought better of it.

The old man was growing a little rheumatic now. He was often cold and his feet went blue at night. The fireplace which caused so much astonishment to the servants—its like was not in the vicinity—roared constantly on cold, damp nights, which are not unknown at Livorno. Occasionally he would take supper in his room. The warmth and the blaze of the many candles were preferable to the chill and shadows in the great hall. At such times he began to call Anthony in to dine. Over the cover the story of Mr. Bonnyfeather's family began to take shape in the boy's mind. The sudden flight from the old estate by the Scotch laird and his family to King James at St.-Germain's, the long, loyal service at the toy court of the exiles, the hope deferred, the honourable poverty—all this was with Mr. Bonnyfeather a favourite theme.

Then there was the merchant's father, "the second marquis," as the old man loved to call him. He had been invaluable to the Stuarts, a great stirrer-up of Jacobite intrigues. Louis the Great had settled a pension upon him. "Ah, those were great days!" As a very little boy Mr. Bonnyfeather remembered Versailles.

As a lad he had been dragged about the Highlands during the " '45." William McNab had come back with him then. The McNabs were faithful to the old lairds; had always sent the rent. They were family retainers. Mr. Bonnyfeather extolled them. Faith was half Greek, to be sure, but her mother's blood would tell. And then he would tell over again of how his father had fought at Culloden and barely escaped at Prestonpans. His face would light up with the old hope of the victory. Or his eyes would flash as he told how it felt to be the oldest son of a nobleman on his father's estates hunting the stag. At the last, fishermen had rowed them out to a French ship with Cumberland's dragoons sweeping along behind them over the reaches of a misty beach. That was their last glimpse of Scotland. He would sigh and take another glass of port.

"And now," he would say, placing both hands on his breast in agitation, "you see me here, the third marquis—in trade!" He would hasten on as if explanation were essential.

"It came about in this way. When the prince returned again to France my father still followed him. He had become a Catholic in all but name. Then James Third died. We came to Italy to be near the last of the house of Stuart. My father was received into the church with all his family. He held a small place as chamberlain to the Cardinal of York. There he was still called marquis. His title and a small pittance from the cardinal was all that he had. The French pension was no longer paid. I should not forget the crucifix which the pope sent him. I saw how things were going and wrote to some of my Whig relatives in England. One, my mother's brother, smoothed the path for me. I alienated my father, however, by taking advantage of my uncle's offer. I went to England and attended college at Exeter.

"There I met the son of a cloth merchant, Francis Baring, whose friendship has been invaluable and abiding. You will see in this Protestant Bible where he has written a number of things which we then thought profound. And it was he who drew these three clasped hands on the flyleaf. The third hand was for John Henry Nolte, now a merchant at Hamburg. We were inseparable and it is not often that three people get on so well together. Years later, just before my daughter was married"—Mr. Bonnyfeather paused—"the three of us took a long journey together through England and Scotland. I saw then for the last time the estate of which there will be no fourth marquis. But I was nobly entertained by both John and Francis Baring in London. I have since prospered greatly as a merchant myself by remembering as a nobleman what a king once said, 'L'exactitude est la politesse des rois!' You should remember that, too."

Mr. Bonnyfeather invariably ended his oft-repeated

293

story in that way. Something in the intonation of the last phrase, something in the man's attitude and expression as he rehearsed it, looking at the boy over the candles with a supreme earnestness, gradually impressed upon Anthony that for some reason or other here was a tradition he was expected to follow. Further than that Mr. Bonnyfeather dared not permit himself to go. Anthony remained silent. They would get up at last and go over by the fire.

It was at such times over his port that Mr. Bonnyfeather became most genial. He then jumped all doubts and scruples and secretly permitted himself the luxury of feeling that he was talking to his grandson. He had been lonely for years and to have so pleasant and bright a companion as young Anthony sitting before the fire sped their association mightily. He wrapped the boy in a haze of carefully concealed affection, but as time went on gradually opened his heart.

The intimacy and remote ramifications of his business and of the personalities connected with it were discussed as if Anthony had been years older and were the heir of the house. The boy sat and listened gravely. But upon occasion Anthony could also delight with a well-timed question, a smile of understanding, or a surprising reply. The voyages of ships were traced out on the map and globe. Anthony gradually became familiar with most of the great harbours of the world; what was to be had in them, the names and personalities of the merchants, market conditions; what, in a general sense, from politics to planting, was afoot in Europe and America. Nor was it a hardship to listen. With Mr. Bonnyfeather, he became lost in it. The little hectic spots glowed on the old man's cheek bones and the boy talked too, or listened with open lips and glowing eyes. An hour of this after supper, and they would sit down to write the letters resulting from the talk. These were of such a character that Mr. Bonnyfeather did not desire them to go across the desks of the clerks.

Thus Anthony rapidly stepped into being the old man's secretary. As time went on he was able and not afraid to suggest a better phrase here and there or a more trenchant approach. He strove always to see the men to whom the letters were addressed. He learned all he could about them from the captains who had dealt with them, or from the files of correspondence in the vault. There was a roomful. But before he was sixteen he had read nearly all of it. The net which the firm of Bonnyfeather and those that it dealt with cast over the waters of the world was surprisingly well integrated in his mind. Helping always to weave the meshes firmer and closer was the constant talk of the harbour front that daily flooded his ears. But it was not all business by any means which occupied these evenings.

In Mr. Bonnyfeather's room were his books. They were a strange assortment. The intellectual, political, and spiritual adventures of his family might be read in their titles. The Covenanters as well as the Jacobites were represented. The conversion of Mr. Bonnyfeather's father to Catholicism had not prevented his son from bringing back from Exeter a collection at which the *Librorum Prohibitorum* would have shied.

Anthony pored over these. He became lost in the maze of the *Faërie Queene*. The illustrations, and afterwards the text of Fox's *Book of Martyrs* first gave him some conception of the Protestant side of the controversy. He was amazed to discover it at all. Baxter's *Saints' Rest* scared him sick. It required Toussaint to reassure him. Father Xavier might have been amazed, to say the least, to have seen the pastures in which his pupil was not only wandering but feeding. Mr. Bonnyfeather had considerable Shakespeare by heart and was given to a little rodomontade in its recitation, especially of the first part of *Henry IV*, and *The Merchant of Venice*. It served to turn the trick for the boy who would scarcely otherwise have been able to understand at first the nature of the stage. The lonely island in *The Tempest* haunted him. Somehow he thought Mr. Bonnyfeather in his black velvet suit, leaning over the globe and conjuring forth cargoes, was like Prospero.

Before he left Livorno Anthony had whole passages of *Religio Medici* by heart. Milton's Italian poems first attracted him, then the Latin. It seemed perfectly natural to the polyglot nature of the boy that a poet should write in many tongues. As the music of English became more audible to him he went on to *L'Allegro* and *Il Penseroso*. *Paradise Lost* made him drunk. His own experience of visions and dreams at the convent made the scenes and images of the poem rise up for him as if fixed on his retina. The incandescent light, the lambent glooms of the blind poet's dramatic universe peopled by even brighter gods and darker heroes remained for Anthony always the supreme banquet of words in any tongue. There was nothing like the sound of it anywhere else, that great, perfectly controlled, almighty organ vibrating and filling with oceanic and cosmic harmony the cathedral of the mind. It made the Italian operas which he later went to hear at Livorno with Vincent Nolte seem ridiculous. Sometimes the contrast would come across him as he watched a romantic little cockchafer in red tights warbling and strutting melodramatically before his trilling ladybird while brigands supplied harmony. Or he thought of it when the meretricious, saccharine roar of the finale sounded. Then he would laugh, and Vincent, whose syrupy German soul was congealing into sweet crystals and beer, would hiccough with indignation.

Milton and Dante dramatized theology for Anthony. For him it could never be abstract. Even the Holy Ghost had personality. He had a comforting smile.

It was with this life-endowing quality of the mind that Anthony passed on from the poets and vivifiers of language to the necromancers of words. On the middle shelf was a long and daunting array of Catholic and Protestant polemics, theological treatises, works of piety and religion. Anthony had made up his mind to read all the books in the room. So he read these, too; Augustine to Calvin, Athanasius, Chrysostom, Origen, and the Reverend Adonijah Parkhurst. He strained his eyes over Kerson's *Practical Cathechisme*, plunged into Bishop Burton, and heard the remote noise of the sectaries through the years of James I to Charles II arguing somewhere in space. All were totally disconnected in time. They merely occurred on the shelf. All were in words, all were therefore about something.

A universe landscaped with the strange heavens of religious utopiasters; full of maimed souls thrillingly rescued from or delivered to the devil burst on his view. Innocent and inane first parents in delightful, tropical paradises; shining battlements of the City of God on hills clouded by lightning gleamed like oases amid the dark deserts of limbo, where old gentlemen with wigs like Mr. Bonnyfeather's and terrific names gibbered and twittered moral aphorisms and definitions while pouring dust on their own heads. Or they threw worm-eaten tomes at one another. Underneath, always underneath, were the hot, the cold, and the dry, the wet, the noisy, the silent hells. These he could see were logical pictures of indignant devices invented to punish in the other world ghastly extremes of conduct in this. In short, on the middle shelf of Mr. Bonnyfeather's bookcase was a fair cross-section of the Western mind which having lost its own religion was trying to confer Greek order on Semitic nonsense. All of these books were obsessed by one thought. They were perfectly sure that one God controlled everything. Yet Anthony read in one Nicole, "Dieu est la Diable, c'est là toute la religion."

Fortunately for him, most of this curious babble was lost on the boy. Yet his mind retained queer snatches of it, voices that later on would shout advice about his conduct out of limbo. It seemed to him as if a troop of these disembodied theologians followed his earthly experience arguing. Occasionally some louder voice would make itself intelligible, shouting a distinct message to him out of the disputing crowd. In the meantime the gods and demons, the troops of angels, seraphim, and the apocalyptic landscapes were certainly fascinating.

Lowest of all on the shelves, but in big volumes like foundations of the edifice which they in fact supported, were the classics. They were all in Latin for Mr. Bonnyfeather read no Greek. Something in his accurate and precise Scotch mind loved Latin. But he was not scholar enough to carry this to a pedantic extreme. Roman life did not come to an end for him when Cicero ceased to fulminate. It and Mr. Bonnyfeather went on.

In his old age he had come to like Claudian better than Virgil. The hills of Sicily rolling their flowers close down to the sea, but always in a "wildly cultivated" manner, the absurd panegyrics of contemptible tyrants and defeated generals, which yet retained the method of true praise; all this seemed to him as he read Claudian to speak not only of Rome but of his own time. He too could feel the tang of something magnificent coming to an end with confusion to follow. The barbarians were so near.

In the pages of Ammianus Marcellinus the groans and weariness of the great Roman machine rumbling to its end were audible. Yet how great were those heroes and emperors who repaired its disintegrations with the bones of their bodies and the virtue of their souls! How terrible were the selfish tyrants feasting in the midst of catastrophe! Mr. Bonnyfeather would stride up and down reading from the great book, intoning it, while Anthony leaned forward. The story of Julian fascinated them. Ah! how much Europe needed someone like that now, someone to thrust out the sick new things and bring back the strong old gods as they were. Prussian Frederick could not do it, said the merchant. But there was this man Buonaparte. Some people thought . . . at any rate from the roof they had seen the cannon flashing one night over the horizon and ships on fire. The English did not want him. The old man shook his head. Perhaps they are wrong, those islanders. "I, you see, have had my feet on the mainland for some time now," he would say. Then he would end by reading an ancient description of the valley of the Moselle:

Immemorial vines embower the pleasant, white villas. The cup of the valley receives the bounty of the sun god, the gratitude of man rises in pious incense from the hills. The dead are honoured in the households of the living, and the spirits of the distant emperors in the towns. The magistrates punish vice with the approval of the many virtuous. The rich desire no roses in January; they enjoy them with the peasants in the spring. In the amphitheatres the extreme rage of the barbarian provides spectacles for the multitude and laughter for the cultivated; in the fields his chained vigour enhances the crops. The songs of the tenants are heard upon the estates of great landlords. Fortune is seldom invoked, for no change is desired. Through all the valley winds the River Moselle in three reflecting curves.

Anthony understood from the tones of Mr. Bonny-feather's voice that he was yearning for something he had lost, trying to find a country where he could be fully alive and at ease at the same time. The book of Marcellinus and that of Jean-Jacques Rousseau which he and Toussaint were reading both placed that country in the past. It was also there in the Bible and in the theologians—that happy garden! Everybody seemed to have lost it and to be trying to get back to it. He himself at times already regretted the convent garden.

The Madonna had come from there. He had brought her along with him. She was still in his room. He could return to her at night as an orphan wanderer from the old convent courtyard, or like an exile from the garden or the valley of the Moselle—or whatever it was he lost in the daytime—and be at peace again. The Madonna understood. She listened to him. He could tell her of his troubles during the day. Books could not take her away from him, let them say whatever they might. All those crowds of people talking about God stayed outside in the desert. Those who argued could not enter this oasis. He knew! They spent the night howling outside, pouring dust on their own heads. As though from the living boughs of paradise he felt the bright face of the Madonna looking down upon him while he slept.

Faith would invariably be waiting for him when he left Mr. Bonnyfeather's room and crossed the hall to go to his own. It was part of her routine to see that the house was closed and that all were asleep. At night she felt better and more awake than in the daytime. To watch all the others retire, leaving her to darkness, gave her a sense of superiority and freedom in which she revelled. She prowled, silently. She picked over a chicken and sipped a glass of wine in the kitchen. The embers of the dying charcoal looked at her with small red eyes. She sat in corners and contemplated.

Anthony would find her sitting just behind her own door which was opposite his. He did not see her. He became aware of her. The darkness there was slightly disarranged. Its folds seemed to blend, as the jade lamp burnt dimly, with the distorted shadows of the wings and hour-glass carved above the lintel of Mr. Bonnyfeather's door. Whether she watched him or not he did not know.

After he had gone to bed, she would come in, fold up his clothes, rearrange the covers and bid him good night. There was a hint of affection when she touched him, as she did often, which he felt it wrong to repulse but from which he almost shrank. In the balance he remained passive. From the time she had nursed him just after his arrival, she had thus speciously kept the key of his room as it were in her apron pocket. Sometimes she would sit down by the candles on his dresser and talk.

There was a smooth quality in her voice that soothed him. As she talked, always of personalities about the office and yard, he would watch a curious finger-play of shadows that took place at the foot of his bed on the white wall. Perhaps it was the shadow of the curtain or the flow of the candle. He and the Madonna looked at it. Long, black fingers, semi-transparent here and there, kept twitching wantonly at an inflamed point of light. As this went on and her voice accompanied it, he would slowly drift into sleep. Sometimes he would awake a little after she had gone, rise, and close the door to be alone with the Madonna. Another presence interfered. He found it necessary to keep it out. As the months slipped by and all became a matter of habit, he grew less sensitive to such feelings. He began to take the real world to bed with him. Only the lashes when they at last rested on his cheeks finally allowed nothing real to pass.

In the cope over the Madonna's head the little stars twinkled as the great ones did above the house. The Madonna kept looking past the child in her arms into the shadows and darkness of the room as if something were there. Anthony had not noticed that yet. To discover it, her expression must be carefully studied in the light as Don Luis had once done. Don Luis had understood how to use light and shadow only too well.

What was in the darkness bided its time silently.

Chapter Sixteen

Pagan Mornings

EARLY in the morning, long before the flags were flying from the roof of the Casa da Bonnyfeather, Angela, the cook, drove out in her high-wheeled cart to collect fresh delicacies for the merchant's table from all the country around.

The cart was nothing more than a strong, framed platform resting on a high axle with an underslung rack behind it long enough to lie down upon. The rack with its dangling ropes was really for wine kegs. The shafts, which also formed the beams of the wagon platform, ranged straight forward parallel with the ground but pointed toward each other at the ends—as Anthony thought, like parallel lines becoming intimate near infinity. Between them there was just room enough for the lean shoulders and fat rump of a happy little mule.

To the animal's plump sides the padded shafts of the cart were lashed by looped ropes that passed criss-cross over a yellow pack-saddle. The pack-saddle rested in turn upon a broad scarlet pad. A brown leather collar resembling a huge horseshoe engaged bronze rings on the shaft ends with two brass hooks. It seemed to envelop the forward part of the animal hopelessly. Indeed, from this encumbrance the head of the mule projected like a mounted hunting trophy. But its eyes were shielded by beaded straw blinders, it wore a plaited hair bridle, and before its smooth chest dangled an object like a small, brass umbrella shedding strings of parachutes. These were bells.

To meet Angela and her cart in the early morning upon the country roads about Livorno was a spontaneously exhilarating experience. As the cart approached in a light cloud of dust and a swirl of leaves, a mad rhythm shaking its bells, there was something Dionysian about it. One of the small Christian chapels of the neighbouring hill country might, it seemed, have suffered a pagan relapse during the grape harvest and be revelling along on a heathen pilgrimage at a scandalous rate.

The clean, polished heels of the little mule kicked the pebbles out behind him in a lateral hail. The grey, olive-wood spokes were frequently all but invisible. Behind the mule, the car seemed to float horizontally, or to be falling forward downhill in a mist of speed. It looked as if the mule were pursued by it. And on the platform sat Angela, a fat, abundant Earth Mother, leaning back against a wine cask.

Her scarlet slippers, her bright green dress, her flashing smile under her brilliant red hair matched the colour and design of the ribbed canvas hood overhead embroidered with horseshoes, suns, and shooting stars. Her whip cracked merrily, and stung. But no less so than the pungent Tuscan drolleries with which she was given to favour passing travellers and acquaintances on the road. Franciscan fathers would by sheer instinct, and at the very first glimpse of the cart, hitch the rope about their waist a little tighter, and cross themselves as she passed.

"Christ may have died in vain," said Toussaint to himself one morning, as he halted in the courtyard and ran his stick over the spokes which gave out a muted harplike sound, "but here is a perfect pagan thing made by the hand of man and acceptable to God." Of course Anthony was wild to ride in it.

It was not difficult to assume an invitation. He would simply excuse himself from the flag-raising ceremony or deputize Toussaint in his place. Then having risen very early, he would crawl into the wine rack under the cart and wait while Tony hitched the mule and the family Guessippi performed its ablutions in the court.

This early morning cleansing was the only orderly procedure in the riotous routine of their day. Washing had been rigorously decreed by Faith herself. It was therefore enforced by the fear of the evil eye and regarded by the juvenile Guessippis as a malign decree of fate, without reason but inevitable.

As soon the the courtyard was thoroughly light the tribe emerged from the kitchen door in that state in which it had pleased God to deliver them to their parents. They were lined up before the fountain in the order tall to small, the younger ones whimpering in a subdued manner. Angela, the eldest, with an imperturbable expression on her bright, olive face, then soused them each with a bucket of cold water. One muffled whoop apiece was permitted. Just before the water descended Angela called aloud the name of the victim. After each baptism "M" or "N" was permitted to depart immediately for the kitchen to dress.

Thus were daily cleansed and brought to physical grace and the communion of men Arnolfo, Maria, Nicolò, Beatrice, Claudia, Federigo, Pietro, Innocenza, and Jacopo Guessippi. Luigi the infant was mercifully permitted to remain in his cradle stewing comfortably in his own juice near the kitchen fire.

After the last bucketful had descended upon the smallest, young Angela herself would glide behind the clump of snarled tritons composing the central group of the fountain, drop her frock, slip in as deep as her firm, little, pearlike breasts, and wriggle out again. Then after a few moments' mystery with an old towel and snaggled comb she would reappear, climb into the back of the cart on the wine-rack, settle herself comfortably into the straw, and smile at Anthony.

As often as possible especially in the spring and summer, Anthony made it a point to drive out with Angela and to attend this lay baptismal rite of the early morning. The rigmarole of the children's names captivated him. The soft vowels and consonants fell as liquidly from the lips of little Angela as did the water from the bucket which followed them. "Arnolfo—*swish*, Maria—*swish*, Nicolò, Beatrice, Claudia, Federigo—*swish*."

As time went on these names burned themselves upon Anthony's memory. He would mumble over them at his desk like a priest at prayer. In the mornings he began to call them out with Angela. It added a new zest to the occasion. They chanted them together. Years afterwards he had but to repeat the formula and the scene would rise before him.

There was to him something mysterious about it. The early morning shapes of the things about, the characters that composed it, the event itself took on a meaning in another world beside reality. It was like an ancient ritual the function of which had been forgotten. Life was full of things like that for Anthony, happenings that seemed to hide their true significance in a mist of impersonal memory always about to be clear.

If he could only remember what he had forgotten! For a long while he kept trying to do so. Gradually as he grew older the feeling wore away. Then at times it would overcome him as if he were homesick again. Something would remind him of something better somewhere else. Perhaps in this case it was the repetition of the scene in precisely the same terms, its inevitableness, that made it take on an importance which could not be accounted for merely by common sense.

The nine naked children lined up before the little girl—he should have done something to lessen their discomfort, but he could not. Their dismal expectation of the inevitable aroused his pity, and yet it was ludicrous. Gradually he came to understand how he could remain merely a spectator. It was because these children were suffering what was to them mysteriously ordained, what was the common lot of all of them. It was in

305

their different methods of confronting the bucket of cold water that the interest lay.

The stoical Arnolfo thrust out his already faintly hairy chest and allowed fate to run off him as from a roof. Innocenza shivered, the thin-legged Claudia wept, plump Beatrice pleaded, the sullen Pietro dodged. As spectator Anthony was each in turn. He enjoyed where the actors could not, but he also felt with them that fate was unavoidable. When their names were called the water descended from on high. It stifled the howls. It descended upon those forked, naked things, on Nicolò, on Maria, even upon the tiny Jacopo who retired with a pair of cherubic buttocks twinkling under a bucket that engulfed his head and shoulders. From it floated back faintly musical lamentations.

Unknown to himself, before that fountain in the courtyard of the Casa da Bonnyfeather, Anthony lost most of his idle sensations about and tendencies to dream curiously over the human form. His curiosity was surfeited, he saw that humanity was a shape, repeated endlessly with minor variations, and that these minor variations were unimportant in themselves. All one could tell by them was the way that certain kinds of people might act when the cold water descended. Thin people, he saw, acted differently from the fat ones. There was not so much difference between the boys and girls. He learned this from what he saw rather than from what he thought.

Now he saw why the stone children that had danced around the fountain at the convent had all been made the same. They were children of one idea and not each one a variation upon it. They were like the idea from which they sprang, all beautiful and happy. But to sympathize with the Guessippi children he must in turn be Tom, Dick, and Harry. Only part of him was in them at any one time. All of him had danced with the stone children.

How long ago that seemed! How old were the stone children? Oh very old! He did not feel new. He felt older than most people in the world about him. At least he thought so, lying in the cart waiting for little Angela.

So he thought too lying in his room at night looking at the Madonna. She remained. She and he remained as they always had been. All that went on during the day passed in a space between them which they both overlooked at night. Some time he would creep back whence he had come. He would go back and be close to her like that other child in her arms. Other children ran back to their mothers. He longed sometimes to do that, too. It was a need, a desire he did not question.

As for the Guessippi children he made them tolerable to himself by imagining them to be like the stone children in the ring. All alike, beautiful, dancing under the cold water. Now he could be happy with such beautiful things. Their little individual differences had vanished. He did not have to sympathize with each in turn.

As for little Angela she certainly belonged to the children of the stone ring—to that time. She had only stepped out of it into now. He could see how smooth, how delightful and graceful, how self-contained she was. Impersonal. Her being was equivalent to affectionate and caressing sounds, coolness and softness thought of warmly. "Maea," he called her secretly. This word simply bubbled out of the feeling of the fifteen-year-old boy as he lay in the "perfectly pagan" wine cart.

He was envied secretly by Toussaint who passed by with his basin in the early morning with tired eyes to dash cold water upon those windows of his disappointed soul. He too would have liked to ride in that cart back into Arcady with little Angela. He would wink knowingly, conveying by merely assuming it as adults do his own immense experience and prophetic insight to Anthony.

Anthony would wink back, but it was with him only a greeting. He was not thinking about Toussaint. He was waiting for little Angela to finish her bath behind the fountain and to join him in the cart.

There was an assurance, a complete and happy naturalness about "Angela Maea" that he liked from the first. From the vast mass of her mother she had sprouted like an unexpected, delicate bud from a log. The bud had grown into a slim, young branch. When she joined Anthony in the cart, drops from her bath in the fountain would still be glittering in her hair. Her breath was sweet and her face was brown and firm with dark red lips. It seemed as if she had just been passing over a meadow gathering mushrooms before sunrise. Her brown eyes appraised him frankly and liked him. Before the cart would start they would lie and look at each other with quiet delight.

Then Angela the great would ascend the cart. Looking up from the little rack in which they lay at the enormous proportions of the woman before and above them they would both laugh. How different from themselves! "Angela," they would both whisper together as if still calling the roll of those about to be cleansed before the fountain. The vision evoked convulsed them.

Then the whip would crack, then the mule would clatter along through the still deserted streets, through the gate as the morning gun was fired from the Castell' Vecchio—and out onto the long, white road to Pisa. It was that way they nearly always took. Anthony abandoned himself on the hills to the sensation of speed. He was going somewhere. He felt free. The hills of the world were before him. Of them he could never see enough. The pungent smell of burning olive wood, of myrtles, or of a slope of vineyards in blossom seemed to fill his head. It was good. Somehow it was often strangely familiar. There was dew on the new-mown hay. The drops of moisture in Angela's hair drew rainbows. From the farmyards as they passed came the shrill crop of chanticleers that ran over the hills into one far-off, continuous song of morning. They answered the birds in shrill mockery together. Great Angela never looked back. Her back was far too broad even to try to see all that went on behind it.

Big Angela knew the countryside like a cookbook: where the best oil was to be had, who had the fattest ducks, the farm where the freshest cress grew, the most luscious broccoli. As she made stop after stop for bargain and purchase, they drew farther and farther back into the hills.

To the sound of endless chaffer and the clink of small bronze or silver coins the cart took on more and more the aspect of a bit of the hanging market gardens of Babylon on wheels. The small casks behind were filled with wine, the hampers under the fat woman's elbows grew loud with cacklings and quacks. From between the wicker bars thrust forth the snake-like, hissing heads of geese. In his muffled basket a cock hailed a false dawn. Bunches of beets, garlic, onions, heads of lettuce, fruit were suspended from the roof. A small pig twisted on the floor bound by the heels.

On top of all this like a figure of plenty with the harvest about her sat the mountainous woman, a flower thrust into her flaming hair. From behind, the happy faces of Angela and Anthony seemed to mock at famine and the passer-by. Sometimes they drove out far enough to look down into the valley of the Arno with the river twisting through the white villages and grey olive orchards that swept away with it to the sea. They could see the little people tending their vines between the living posts of the mulberry tree. White oxen ploughed and lowed plaintively. Always to the west was the blue flash from tables of sea. Returning, Anthony could look north where the Apennines shouldered away vaguely into the light and haze, growing clearer and greener as the day gained on itself.

Once down a byroad he saw the red roofs of the convent. His pigeons were still circling about the tree. How far off was that, how long ago! At the city gate there was always an argument about the amount of the tax. Then they would be home, cries of hungry acclamation following them along the street. In the noisy drive through the town streets he and little Angela kept close. In the courtyard they slipped away from each other quietly. She to the kitchen, he to the office.

Mr. Bonnyfeather condoned these excursions, enjoyed them secretly. McNab frowned. Toussaint smiled. A small package of cheese was usually his share and a whispered description of the trip. Then the pens would scratch on.

Faith did not approve of these morning adventures, but she said nothing. Anthony, she thought, spent too much time with the Guessippis. She began to find work for little Angela whenever she could. The games of hide-and-seek, the romps with the children in the kitchen wing grew somewhat more difficult and further between. Anthony was fast growing up. Somehow Faith made him feel this. Her effect upon him was something of a paradox. In her presence he felt older, less embarrassed, yet she continued to put him to bed like a child.

Chapter Seventeen

Philosophical Afternoons

TOUSSAINT CLAIRVEAUX, Gentleman Writer,

Monsieur:—It is my desire that you will undertake the instruction of the young clerk, Anthony Adverse, now apprenticed to me, with the end in view of founding him in the following specific things, to wit: *Easy and Legible Penmanship* for both Letters and Accounts (I provide you with models of the letters and figures I wish him to use), *facility in Arithmetic* with particular application to the accounts of this firm, *Geometry* with application to hoisting machinery, tackles, and navigation, *Geography* (he already knows the Globes), let him memorize the entire list of names of places, natural features; in short the principal legend on the set of English great-charts with which I shall provide you, *Natural History* in all branches so that he may have a knowledge of the first origins of various products and the localities from which they come, a *history of trade* sufficient to understand the origin and meaning of commercial regulations, agreements, usages, and the laws of trade and exchange now generally in force, a knowledge of the *different classes and qualities of manufactured and natural goods, products and materials* (for this you will call in the assistance of Mr. William McNab for three hours a week in the storeroom, Monday, Wednesday and Friday. Do not neglect this. Let the boy be able to tell the qualities of cloth by the feel of them in the dark. Let him educate his taste and smell in teas, wines, and spices. It is my desire that you supplement his practice in commercial letter writing in French, English, Spanish and Italian by instruction in the grammar of these tongues, calling in assistance when necessary). I shall myself oversee his Latin. You may draw on the chief clerk for buying what books you deem necessary, first looking upon my own shelves to ascertain that you do not duplicate unnecessarily.

Knowing you to be a man of liberal education and wide reading, albeit somewhat unfortunate in your private financial ventures, I have nevertheless confided A.A. to your charge. Conduct your instruction so far as possible in French. Act (confidentially), on the supposition that you are preparing this boy for the situation in life of a gentleman-merchant. In addition to this I recommended to bring to his attention such works of the Modern Encyclopaedists, Philosophers, and Savants as you can best present yourself, having regard to the tender years of your pupil. I exclude Voltaire.

You are to regard yourself in authority as the boy's tutor. The afternoons are made over to you until further notice. Both you and your pupil will be released from the office from dinner time to five o'clock post meridian. Waste not the time yourself nor permit the boy to do so. Your salary is increased during the time in which you instruct him by twenty-five scudos the month and you will take your noon meal at the big table. Fear nothing in letting me know wherein you cannot fulfil that I may call in aid. I trust you with much, a mind, and perhaps a soul.

May the Holy Trinity guide you,

JOHN BONNYFEATHER.

So day after day and year by year the instruction went on. The maps crinkled on the big table while in imagination Anthony sailed out through all the world. "Pass from Hamburg to Pondicherry," Toussaint would say and the boy would begin. "But you arrive first off the coast of Coromandel," Toussaint would remark afterwards with a slight hint of reproach as if a breach in etiquette had been committed by Anthony's omission. Then the Frenchman would start in to talk of the countries, the towns, the cities, and the rivers; their history, who traded there for what. If there was a classical legend or story about any blur of colour on the map which they passed in these mythical voyages. Toussaint rehearsed it. To many of these places in the course of his hopeless search for Arcadia he had been himself.

"At Malacca are settled many old Chinese merchants who sit smoking opium by their lily ponds or sipping little cups of rice wine. There is good quail hunting in the country behind. In Cochin China they allow fish to rot upon the roofs and from this they make sauce for their dishes. The liquor is brown and put in the centre compartment of the divided dish. Only pretend to dip your bamboo shoots in it when you dine with these merchants. Make a delectable noise when you eat. It is good manners. The charts of the northern coast of New Holland are cartographers' dreams, *Terra Australis Incognita*. Stand off from Bermuda ten miles and burn flares for a pilot. Nothing is to be had there but onions, oranges, yellow fever, and trouble with the admiral. At Malta the drinking water is all brought from Africa and stinks. Since the Reformation most of

313

the knights are French. They choose only old men as grand masters in order to keep things in their own hands and have frequent elections which are profitable. St. Paul himself was wrecked there. The inhabitants are really Phoenicians. There is a bad fever peculiar to the place."

Thus the maps took on reality, and what Toussaint did not know Anthony heard sooner or later at the Big Table or in talking with Mr. Bonnyfeather at night.

For two years the boy kept a set of ships' account books for McNab. It was for the *Unicorn*. At the end of that time Anthony attempted to balance them with the hatched-faced Captain Bittern. In January of the year before he found the captain had made a mistake. The captain himself pointed it out to him. It was serious. After four hours' continuous talk on the subject of Bottomry and agents' commissions Anthony saw what was wrong, but he did not feel sorry.

Bottomry, indeed, was the boy's bête noire. There was a young lawyer in Livorno by the name of Baldasseroni who was an expert in this terrible subject. Assurance in general was his hobby. For several months he came once a week at Mr. Bonnyfeather's request and lectured for hours at a time on the theory and practice of Bottomry. Toussaint finally tried to get rid of him by engaging him in an argument as to the desirability of old age pensions as lately suggested by the republican writer Thomas Paine. In trying to work out a scheme for the Island of Corsica the two quarrelled over the possible number of old people in the island. "Before the French came," said Toussaint, "the feuds prevented anyone from reaching old age." The lawyer became enraged at this insult to Italians and challenged Toussaint to a duel.

There was no way of getting out of it. So one afternoon with McNab as Toussaint's second they rode out to a lonely beach and shot at each other. Anthony was so thrilled as to be delighted. The bullet of Toussaint passed through the haunches of Signore Baldasseroni. McNab plugged him up with his handkerchief, for he threatened to bleed to death. Nevertheless, the laughter

314

of the Scot was Homeric. " 'Twas an aspect of Bottomry the signore had no confarred suffeecint thoct upon you maun say," he remarked to Mr. Bonnyfeather who smiled grimly and dropped the subject from the "curriculum."

Toussaint strutted about like a peacock for days. He felt himself to be a gentleman again. Signore Baldasseroni meditated for some weeks on the bottom he had neglected to insure. Anthony was relieved. Yet the primary facts of marine and other assurance remained in the boy's mind flavoured with a curious reminiscent humour and human connotations.

To a romantic like Toussaint assurance was a road to Utopia, for the selfish and ruthless it was a method of cashing in on old ships and drowned sailors. This was what Mr. Bonnyfeather said about it. To most Latins it was a form of the lottery. Therefore, you assured ships with honest, literal, and unimaginative persons. The British were best. "The kind of people that meet in the little room at Lloyd's, for instance," said the old man. "I once went there with Francis Baring. Those people were able to read figures without lying to themselves or each other about them." "This," thought Anthony, "is the final value of arithmetic. It is why McNab and not Toussaint, who is a much more brilliant mathematician, is chief clerk." Anthony had already begun to see around the Frenchman a little. Against the background of many others he began to stand out in relief. It was possible to see already that behind him were certain shadows.

All that the boy learned, no matter how abstract, remained for him in the terms of men. Even the stars came down out of their spheres to assume human meaning.

John Peel Williams, ex-mate of the ship *Lion*, living on his own scanty savings and the bounty of Mr. Bonnyfeather, came down from his garret in the slums once a week to give practical instruction in the use of the instruments of navigation. He had huge, steady hands and the voice of a hoarse sea lion. While the old house shook to his rumbling and grumbling, the

315

abstract geometry of Toussaint was snatched down out of nowhere and suddenly became the earth and other spheres around it. Outlines of terrestrial and celestial circles, zeniths and nadirs, of small ships crawling through angles and degrees displayed themselves in blue chalk on the floor of the ballroom from Friday to Monday when they were finally washed away. Navigation had been Mr. Williams' only intellectual escape from his own dull soul. His emotional exit was by way of alcohol. The first was his God and the second his demon. A subtle combination of both evoked in him the inspired teacher.

He had read extensively in "navigation" but in nothing else. His admiration for the universe was due solely to his own comment upon it, oft, and eternally repeated, "I tell you the stars cannot lie." Mr. Williams proceeded by the method of the elimination of negatives. He showed Anthony that all other methods than the particular one he proposed were wrong. Thus with immense gusto he orated into limbo the astrolabe. He disposed vigorously of the cross-staff with profound pity for those who had been forced to discover new worlds by its doubtful aid. He frowned upon the half-arc, and he finally with enormous and dramatic emphasis produced his sextant out of a shining leather case, extolled it with infinite explanations, and ascending to the roof, roaring like a bull in springtime, shot the astonished sun. So much for latitude.

As to longitude there was still great difficulty. "Owing," said Mr. Williams, "not to the stars, which cannot lie, but to our own unfortunate position on the earth. The English Admiralty has long offered a prize for the best method of solving it. The log of the day's run and the careful knowledge of drift due to winds, currents, and the ship's habits are the best we can as yet do. But that is guess-work, the rule of thumb. I hear that the comparison of clocks has been suggested, but I myself am at work on a bi-focal mirror, two mirrors and an hemisphere. With mirror '1' you take the sun at sunrise, with mirror '2' you take the moon at moon-rise. You mark the path of their rays as extended upon the hemisphere. The place," said Mr. Williams, leaning forward and lowering his voice to half a gale, "the place where these rays intersect, will, if properly calculated from the data provided by my table, that I am preparing slowly, very slowly, and the degrees marked on the hemisphere, give you your longitude. The chief difficulty is owing to the shifty nature of the moon. However, let me show you this astonishing instrument."

They ascended together the five pairs of stairs of his lodging. At the top floor a door across the hall half opened. An old woman looked out expectantly. Seeing the mate she shoved the door shut again. "She is a decayed gentlewoman," said he in a whisper not audible more than four floors away, "who makes her living by astrology on the fifth floor and keeping girls on the first. She has written a book. In it are all the old lies about the stars." His voice growled with indignation. He picked up a poor, cheaply bound volume and commenced to read like a tremulous cannon.

It is said by savants that the angles of the three great pyramids denote a shifting in the position of the North Star. There will come a time when Polaris will no longer mark the extension of the axis from the northern pole of the earth.

Anthony saw the door across the hall open slightly and the head of the old woman protrude listening. She saw him, and put her finger on her lips.

"Think of it, think of it!" roared the mate. "Here is an old woman who has written a book denying the whole truth of the beautiful and eternal science of navigation. She would have the pole star itself shift. What then would become of all the books and tables founded upon the fact that Polaris remains forever fixed? What would become of them, I say?" His rage was extreme. The door across the hall closed again. The mate bellowed on now like a wounded animal. The book shook in his hand.

317

The stars of the Dipper outline the womb of our universe. Out of the tail of the Great Bear were born the sun and the seven planets that we see. The ancient religions of the earth preserve this essential tradition. The era of Christianity itself can be read in the dial of the stars. We are now entering upon the last phase of an epoch when man has worshipped himself. God is about to become matter. Nature, God and man will be taken for one. All things will then become confused. Words themselves will come to have no meaning. Babel will ensue. When the sun enters upon the region of the Water Carrier a new spiritual man will arrive. The soul will again recognize itself. The cycle is repeating itself. . . .

The mate broke off and hurled the volume into the corner.

"Come up on the roof," said he, "and see my instrument. It is a waste of time to read such words."

They climbed up a ladder to a trap door. On the tiles, resting on a light platform was a half-globe covered with quicksilver and marked with degrees around the edge. Two mirrors on rods shifted about it.

"Now," said the mate, "we are getting back to facts again! But I will tell you something. It is my own discovery. Latitude and longitude are the same thing! With these two mirrors I shall prove it to you." He proceeded to manipulate them. Small suns glittered on the quicksilver globe. He became fascinated. His voice boomed on as he continued for a full half hour to confuse the astonished boy who tried to follow him. Anthony could make nothing of it. The tone of the man's voice reminded him of Toussaint's when he was reading or talking about Rousseau. It was what Mr. Bonnyfeather called "enthusiasm—an emotion without a sufficient cause."

"How can anybody really get excited about quicksilver globes?" thought Anthony.

His own instinct for words came to his rescue. No one could ever get anywhere, he saw, who thought that latitude and longitude were the same thing. He sat for a while apparently listening respectfully, but swinging his feet over the edge of the roof and looking out over Livorno.

The water he saw was exactly separated from the shore. Hills were the opposite of valleys. The sky was not the earth. On the horizon they seemed to meet, but he knew when you got there there was a gulf between.

After a while he crawled back down the ladder without disturbing the mate. Above him the stentorian voice rolled on. As he slipped down the hall the old woman looked out again. She was laughing. As he passed by she thrust her book into his hand. A red card fell out.

Signora Bovino
Explains the Past,
and
Elucidates the Future,
Casts Horoscopes, and Reads Palms.
Her Art is Invulnerable
on the Fifth Floor
Strada Calypso

———

Satisfactory Amatory Entertainment
on the First.

Anthony looked up again but the door had closed noiselessly.

He went home and tried to read the book. A new meaning to religion dawned on him as he turned its pages. But between strange visions of the past which the book suggested, shrieked out a shrill feminine babel of nonsense in print. His head spun. He had had enough of stars.

For a while Anthony had been induced to believe by Mr. Williams that the stars could not lie. It was impossible for him to believe, however, that the art of Signora Bovino was invulnerable, even on the fifth floor. Yet Mr. Bonnyfeather who was now the final appeal in most things confirmed the fact that the North Star actually was shifting. The news caused something to crack in Anthony's head. He blinked. So there *was* something in the old woman after all! Both her art and the art of navigation were partly right. You could not trust anything too far, then. Curious!

He began to wonder about Father Xavier, but that was past now. It was difficult to question what he had heard from him, very difficult. He had accepted it as truth for so long. And then there was Toussaint. Perhaps Rousseau, then, was only Toussaint's enthusiasm. On the days when they walked out into the country and read *La Nouvelle Héloïse* together Anthony began to listen with his own ears rather than those which the eloquence of his tutor would have provided for him.

They used to climb the hills back of the town on hot days and sit down under the trees. There was one place which Toussaint particularly affected. It was a small valley with a nondescript ruin in it which peculiarly moved the soul of the Frenchman. They would lie down by a spring while the grasshoppers chirped in the grass and Toussaint or Anthony read aloud. In his excitement Toussaint would occasionally mount upon a rock and give vent to his feelings at some passage that aroused his enthusiasm. Under the spell of his eloquence the little valley became a charming glade in an antique world.

Toussaint waved his hand. He struck an attitude with his cloak falling from his arm like a toga, and pointed dramatically to the pile of stones covered with vines across the little valley that lay before him.

"Do you see that ruin?" he cried. Anthony could see it plainly. "I shall cause it to rise before your eyes; to become once more the home of simple and happy folk uncontaminated by the vices which a cruel society would now thrust upon them. I am about to show you humanity walking alone, upright, free and noble; the beautiful body and soul of man unfettered by the cruel irons of the fatal social contract. Religion has not been invented. There is only the force of nature reverently and happily worshipped. There is

320

no fear. All is love. There is nothing but the beautiful earth and the most beautiful thing on it, man. The more I think of him the nobler he becomes." With a single and simultaneous gesture of one foot and two hands the philosopher now disposed of the entire Christian era.

"Roll back, you dull ages of slavery, pass three thousand years. I see before me a charming wattled hut. It is near nightfall. In the doorway sits a woman with a distaff. She manipulates the wool, while her naked and beautiful children, while the lambs and kids bound about her threshold. The father returns. Over that hill, out of the beech forest, he appears, huge, noble, but graceful. A slaughtered deer is thrown over his shoulders. A bow is in his hand. The dogs bark. The woman and children run to meet him. Their embraces are unrestrained. The deer is roasted before the fire. Baked roots are raked from the ashes; a simple cake or two. The power of nature is thanked in a simple prayer. The family quenches its thirst at the spring. They leap in the pool and swim in the moonlight. They admire each other. They are unashamed. They lie down to undisturbed rest. There is no care for the morrow. Nature will provide. There are no priests except the father, no taxes, no false manners, no conventions, no neighbours to impose upon them or to be impressed, no books, no lessons except that of husbandry, no, no, no . . ." Toussaint swept away everything with a final gesture.

After these outbursts Anthony was surprised to see that even the ruin remained. It had, he observed, after the mist of oratory cleared away, an obstinate faculty of remaining a heap of stones covered by vines.

Toussaint would then walk about a little. Then he would throw himself down in the grass again and eagerly begin to thumb over the pages of some book which he had brought with him. It was usually one of Rousseau's. He was especially fond of chanting these lines by heart until he found the place he was looking for, whatever it might be:

Emile was filled with love of Sophie. And what were her charms that bound him to her? They were tenderness, virtue, the love of honour. But what most moved the heart of Sophie? Those feelings that were of the very nature of her love: respect for goodness, for moderation, simplicity, for generous disinterestedness, a contempt for splendour and luxury.

Frequently in their walks while admiring the beauties of nature their pure and innocent hearts were exalted to their Creator. But they did not fear His presence, before Him they uncovered themselves to each other. Then they saw their own perfection in all its beauty, then they loved each other most and conversed charmingly on the subjects that the virtuous most appreciated. Often they shed tears that were purer than the dews of heaven.

For some reason or other the recital of these paragraphs nearly always brought tears to the eyes of Toussaint. It brought a scene to his mind as if Watteau had gone sketching in Japan.

It was also during these afternoon walks, readings and "recitations" by Toussaint that the news of the French Revolution had first been brought to Anthony's ears. At first Toussaint had been its prophet, if one could believe him. As the boy listened to him he thought at first his friend was talking about the Kingdom of God which seemed close at hand. Every day now was to be a little better than the day before. Things from now on were to go that way, for some reason. Because that was the way they went. Anthony had read a great deal about the Kingdom in the theological books on Mr. Bonnyfeather's shelves. Toussaint's kingdom was to be a Republic. But it was never clear to Anthony, no matter how much Toussaint explained the "difference," what was the difference between the Republic that the Revolution was to bring and the far-off Kingdom of God, the reign of Christ and all his saints.

"But man will bring about his own perfect state by reason. Can't you see!" Toussaint would cry. "What has God to do with that?"

"Stuff and nonsense," said Mr. Bonnyfeather one night when Anthony questioned him about all this. "You are quite right. The old books were talking about the same thing. Perfection is nothing new. It is just an old dream that had been forgotten for a while. Now they are talking about it again with new words. It is the spirit of just men made perfect. Don't you see if reason is to make just men perfect, then reason must be God? It is only a new word for the Almighty. If not, if it is human reason they are talking about, how can an imperfect thing make a perfect one? Besides," grumbled the old man, "find the just men. Where are they? . . .

"I will tell you something about all this talk of perfection, of constant progress that is going on everywhere now," said the merchant getting up and walking up and down. "It is popular because it is flattering. And there is one great idea under it all that I am convinced from both my own experience and my reading is wrong. It is this man Rousseau that your tutor is always reading to you from, and talking to you about, who is mainly responsible. Listen, this is it. It is the idea that human nature is naturally good; that by pulling on its own bootstraps it can raise itself to God. Do not believe that. If you do you are lost."

The pit seemed to open at Anthony's feet. He looked at his patron amazed, not so much for what he said as for the earnest way he said it. Anthony had never seen him so determined before.

"No, no, the Church is right," cried the old merchant. "I have lived long enough to find that out. Men are not so good as they pretend to be, or like to think they are. They are in fact evil. Besides, I do not know anyone by the name of 'man.' I meet and deal only with men and women. They are evil. They do evil in

323

spite of themselves even when trying to do good. You must be humble in spirit to believe that. That is what humility means. You must not be too proud to ask for help for your evil self from the outside; to pray, to try to commune. It is the people who are always trying to make the world better that are proud. They have no need of God. Those who know they have a fatal lack in themselves will not try to make others perfect. They will only be sorry for themselves and for others; perhaps they will be kind, decent, affable if they can be. They will hope that others will find out how helpless and how liable to do evil they are, too. A thousand citizens like that gathered together in one place would make a good town to live in. You will never find it. Do not look for that town. It is too much to expect on earth. It is the City of God.

"Remember it is only by a miracle that a man can escape from himself. By the power of something more than human. That is what our religion means with all its faults. For it, too, is partly made by man. Can you understand?"

"I can follow what you say," said Anthony.

"You will feel it some time, you will understand it, after you are vile enough, then you will know. Now, good night."

The boy rose to go.

"Am I so evil?" he asked.

The old man stopped suddenly and came over to the door. He put his hands on Anthony's shoulders and drew him toward him. He drew his head back and looked down into his face.

"Not yet," he said. For an instant he held the lad close to him. "God keep you!" he murmured.

During the entire time in which Anthony remained under the roof of the Casa da Bonnyfeather this was the sole positive manifestation of affection which he received from the old merchant. Sometimes he felt restrained in the old man's presence. Of Mr. Bonnyfeather's great affection for him the boy was of course by this time aware. At first he had accepted it with the calm, egoistic assurance of a boy. Naturally, people would like him! But as he grew older he realized that Mr. Bonnyfeather was, as he expressed it to himself, "his earthly father." Between them, though no words had passed on the subject, it was understood that Anthony should some day succeed to the old merchant's place. A hundred little expressions and phrases that the old man used showed it was that of which he was thinking. Then, too, his constant urging of the boy's ambition and the careful preparation and planning of his instruction all pointed that way. Yet there was a reserve in each which the other respected. Mr. Bonnyfeather alluded frequently to his own past. Anthony was finally able to piece most of it together. But the boy's past he never even touched upon.

"It is to save me embarrassment," thought Anthony. Of the lost daughter the merchant said nothing. Faith had once talked of her one night while the shadows danced, but carefully. The boy had no cause to connect himself with her. Rather than ask about something which he knew might give Mr. Bonnyfeather pain, he would have cut off his own hand.

So they sat together in the merchant's room at night talking, reading, going over business affairs. There was in that room as time went on a complete feeling of confidence and ease between them. The dim figures in the wall seemed to Anthony to be in his past, the lost country out of which he had mysteriously come. From that company of dreams he had merely removed as it were into the clearer, into the very clear and precise atmosphere of Mr. Bonnyfeather's room in the bright candlelight. He was now sitting with the man who was a father to him, having the world as it actually is explained and made understandable. Some day he, Anthony, would sit at that desk planning out the voyages of the firm's ships, but not for a long while. No, he would not, could not bear to think of that. But in the room he nevertheless felt himself to be heir apparent. Outside in the court, in the counting house, and in the city there was a subtle difference in their attitude to each other. Mr. Bonnyfeather, he could see, did not care to make plain to everybody what was understood between them when they were alone. And with this tacit arrangement the boy fell in line and acted his part. That was perhaps the crux of the situation. Anthony was sensitive and understanding enough to accept it and not to presume.

Only once or twice in later years had that earlier feeling of restraint fallen upon them. It came at times when Mr. Bonnyfeather seemed about to say something that weighed much on his mind. He would stand looking down into Anthony's face while he was talking. Then a silence would overtake him for a minute as if his tongue had been stopped by an overpowering thought. Anthony felt sure at such times that he was about to hear something of peculiar importance. Then, as if Mr. Bonnyfeather had changed subjects with himself, he would lower his eyes and go on just where he had left off.

Of all these things the boy thought as he went to sleep at night, particularly after Faith had gone. Then he would creep out and draw close enough to the Madonna to be able to see her in the faint light that beat in from the hall. He was thankful that he seemed to have found an earthly father. She herself, the statue, had now become two things in one to him, things gathered up out of all the dreams and experiences of his past. She was that woman who might take a child in her arms and comfort him, even a big lad, when, as he went to bed again, he felt like a child in the dark, helpless and alone; alone as the spirit of every man must be when he attempts to commune with himself. But she had also become that power-beyond of which Mr. Bonnyfeather had spoken, something to which he might appeal, which in his very efforts to talk with it seemed to dictate its own reply within him.

So, creeping close to her by the wall in the warm Italian night, the slim figure of the orphan out of habitude from old times came close to the Virgin to whisper to her of that chaos of thought and feeling that was already burning in his body and mind. For a while, crouched by the wall in the moonlight, he was at home again. He had returned to the heart of that mystery from which he had come.

Chapter Eighteen

Bodies in the Dark

TOUSSAINT had, as Anthony grew tall and took on the promise of an early manhood, begun to talk to him of love. It was always of "love" and seldom of women. Of women Anthony had heard much in a coarse and generally good-natured way about the port.

Sailors who followed girls; clerks related their experiences. These were sometimes strange or drôle enough. Usually they were merely muddled. For a long time they had seemed to Anthony adventures and experiences that could only happen to others, things which could not, and need not, affect him. Indeed, he felt a little superior about it all. He felt that he should pretend an interest, yet secretly glad that he really cared so little.

But the stories of Garcia, the Spanish clerk, were graphic. Indeed, that young correspondent was occasionally given to using the firm's best stationery to draw pictures upon in which the attitudes of human bodies when united with each other were so accurately and intimately portrayed as to leave no room for imagination between them. It was for that very reason that Anthony, who was allowed the privilege of looking at these *graphti* from time to time, was, despite a few natural burning throbs, finally disappointed. There were too many of these pictures for him. It was being too prodigal with something rare. You also saw somewhat the same thing in farmyards when you drove out into the country. No one paid much attention to it there. Why draw pictures about it in town? Big Angela could drive a flinty bargain for sour wine while it was going on in the stables. Only children stared.

Nevertheless, from the Spanish clerk and anatomist the boy learned certain intimate phrases and idioms which even the books of Castilian grammar omitted by pure consent. McNab had given the final quietus to the drawing lessons by leaning over Garcia and Anthony one day during a more than usually erective bit.

"Mon," said McNab suddenly extracting the paper from under the artist's pencil and holding it up, "if you're in that state of mind I'll lend you a hae crown mysel'." Cornering Anthony later he had remarked with a lift to his nostrils, " 'Twas bad enough gazin' at the ceilin' when ye first came. Now you're crawlin' under and lookin' up." The lad wilted. Then he felt sick. After that he confined himself and Garcia to letters in Spanish and nothing more. Behind his desk McNab looked at the pictures, laughed and threw them in the waste bin.

The passage about Emile and Sophie did not move Anthony. He said so. Toussaint was hurt. According to him "love" was allowing the soul to expand. It was important to find someone with the qualities of soul with which one could—expand. Emile and Sophie had been able to expand together, he pointed out. Together their souls had filled the whole world for them and made it beautiful. Yes, they had loved each other's bodies. The human body was beautiful and pure. "Notice," said the philosopher, "when they revealed themselves to each other, when on those charming walks they were naked and lay down in the grass together,—it was then that from the sight of their beautiful bodies their souls most caught fire. Then they had the most beautiful and truly virtuous thoughts. The finest things were said then, their purest tears would flow."

"Why was that?" asked Anthony.

This irritated Toussaint. A Gallic wriggle of his shoulders was really his best answer. To find words to explain it, he was forced again to hunt some place in the pages of Rousseau which was peculiarly "expansive." There it was all clear. One felt that it *must* be so, he insisted. One could weep and be pure with those lovers in the book. In reading the book Toussaint seldom thought about Faith Paleologus. The book and she belonged to two different worlds. He preferred not to confuse them. Yet sometimes . . .

"All those children in the stone ring about the fountain were beautiful," thought Anthony. "Bodies in most books and some pictures are also like that, especially in novels and poems. But real bodies are not all beautiful. Some are disgusting. Not all those Guessippi children are beautiful. Innocenza, she is like a double radish under a smooth little onion. And there is Arnolfo. No, certainly he is not ugly, but he is not beautiful. What could you think about Arnolfo?" There was something about Arnolfo which Anthony would have liked to discuss with Toussaint. But Toussaint was always reading from a book. This was about something that had really happened.

Arnolfo had taken Anthony upstairs one day into the warm, empty room over the kitchen. Then he had closed the door mysteriously and locked it. Then he had let down his clothes. "Look," said Arnolfo, "Look! I can do that." After a few fascinating moments he proved that he could.

"Can *you?*" he asked.

"Could he?"—Anthony wondered. Arnolfo was both triumphant and incredulous. The boy was smaller than Anthony. Anthony felt inclined to lie to him or to boast. He mumbled something, sweating.

330

"I don't think English clerks *can*," sneered Arnolfo. "Straw hair!"

So phrased it was now a dilemma of embarrassments. He must either retire or prove himself. Besides, could he, *could* he? Something must be done. In behalf of himself, his race, and his class Anthony accepted the challenge.

There were a few moments of terrible doubt.

Then he forgot Arnolfo. The walls of the room and the glimmering window retreated to a vast distance. He was left alone, absolutely alone with a new and enchanted self. It seemed as if someone else were touching him; he and himself.

A vision of the fountain in the courtyard at the convent appeared to him. It became clearer and clearer. The water in the pool was bubbling. The bronze boy was capering along the rim like a monkey. The stone children beneath were dancing madly around and around. Suddenly they blurred into a misty ring of speed. The water rose of itself, overflowed, and engulfed the bronze boy. He saw the roots of the great tree entirely exposed. Then it was over. He wilted. The mist cleared.

He was back in the mean, hot little room again. He, Anthony Adverse, awfully naked! Arnolfo was laughing at him!

That little monkey knew it was the first time! He had been with him, peeping at the fountain in the temple. He had seen it! Another great emotion surged over Anthony bringing his strength back to him again. It was anger. His leg shot out by itself. The foot on the end of it kicked Arnolfo soundly. Arnolfo had laughed!

In the face of the elements the Italian boy collapsed and lay white and still. He saw tears of fury in the steely eyes of the boy above him, who, he felt sure, was going to kill him. Arnolfo kept very quiet. His legs and arms relaxed and quivered like the limbs of a sleeping rabbit. His olive skin blanched. Anthony looked down at him.

He understood now the meaning of the form of

Arnolfo. It was like a little animal. What happened to it did not matter. Arnolfo had never found himself. Arnolfo was "lost." What he did to himself was purely physical. It did not concern anyone else nor did it concern anything living in Arnolfo. But to Anthony, ah, to Anthony! He drew his belt tightly about his waist and rushed downstairs out into the cool air and light.

But reminiscent twinges of ecstasy and hot glows of anger continued to flow up and down his spine. For the first time in his life he loathed himself. He ran back through the hallway and peered into Faith's room. She had gone out. The big ship's tub in the corner stood alluringly with its circle of water gleaming. He locked the door, dragged off his clothes, and plunged in.

There, that was better now! It was good to wash yourself, to come out clean and cool. How wonderful water was! He felt that somehow he had been forgiven by it. He went back into his own room and lay down.

Many things suddenly became clear to him in the light of this tremendous experience. Now he knew. By finding out about himself he understood so much more about others. No, it was not all bad, this experience. Not by any means. Love must be something like that. So this was what it was all about. He forgave Arnolfo. He would make up for having kicked him. Yes, it was very pleasant. It was wonderful.

Then an alarming thought occurred to him. Perhaps, after all, he might be like Arnolfo. No, he did not look like Arnolfo—that little beast—and yet how like him, too. After a while he fell into a dreamless sleep. Faith came and looked at him but he did not know it. She saw he had been using her water. The marks of his feet had not yet dried from her floor.

The fascination of this experience did not overwhelm Anthony. That was because in his inmost thoughts he never felt himself entirely alone. It was that with which he spoke intimately, particularly at night. When he called it anything at all it was "the Madonna." God as yet was something remote. He was the spirit which Father Xavier had addressed, the force of nature which Toussaint talked about, the creator of everything ages ago, but hardly present now, hardly something intimate.

But the Madonna was always there in his room. She always had been there. She was a habit. She had a shape and a locality. In addition to her form visible in the statue, which he had long understood to be only a representation, only a statue of her, there was an actual presence of her in his mind which from early time he had been able to evoke in dreams. Lately she had become more of a voice. He would pray to her in the dark. It was not necessary to light a candle before her any more to see her. It was rather helpful not to have a candle. You addressed her first in the regular prayer, Ave Maria. Then you talked to her. When you did wrong she talked to you. When he became like Arnolfo, for instance, when he did that, he lost her. He was left alone with himself. He was afraid. He could not bear to be utterly alone. That was what it meant to be lost. It was like that time long ago before anybody had come to play with him, dark, terrible. He prayed to her to stay with him, to help him. Sometimes she did so. Sometimes he drove her away. Then he could not find her again for days. And on those days he was unhappy, he was miserable. He sulked.

At last he made a discovery. When you did nothing but feel you were left alone. It was only your body you had then. The voice lived only in your mind. "She" was there. To the orphan this voice, which had the form of a woman who cherished a child in her arms, was a necessary comfort. He was completely miserable without her. He instinctively felt that he could not speak to Mr. Bonnyfeather about this trouble that was sometimes stronger than he was himself. As for Arnolfo, he could only feel. He saw that boy was all body, he was like an animal. That was why they said animals did not have a soul. He understood it now. They had no voices in them.

Anthony did not want to be "like an animal." He was afraid too that his own body might come to look like Arnolfo's. Undoubtedly after such times when you looked in the glass your face had changed. Others might not be able to see it, but you could see it yourself. He began to take great trouble with himself. He would disguise that. The clerks noticed that "Mr. Adverse" as they half humorously, half affectionately called him, was getting to be a bit of a dude. They wondered who the girl was and twitted him about her. His pride was aroused. Everybody had a girl or said they had. He believed them. What would they think of him if they really knew! After a long struggle, by the help of the voice and the opinion of the outside world, he was able to remain a man. And he was so proud of it, happy about it. He was master of himself. He longed to tell someone that he was, Toussaint, for instance. But how could he go about that? Yet his triumph became visible.

A new and manly confidence showed in his speech, in the way he carried himself, acted and moved. He felt himself at home now in the world of men. He was almost grateful to Arnolfo. He could be kind to him when he saw him now. He, Anthony, knew, and he had triumphed. "No," he thought, "I am not evil, not as evil as Mr. Bonnyfeather thinks. I am strong. I have proved it." He did not always feel it necessary now to talk with the Madonna as he went to bed. He was so firm in his own new-found strength. No, he did not really need her—any more. Only sometimes. The crisis had passed, he thought.

Besides, he would soon be a full-grown man now. It troubled him a little that at the age of sixteen his soul still seemed to be the same as the one he had always had. Would that never grow up? The child inside of him! His body now was tall, broad in the shoulders, long in the legs. His face was keen. He was proud of that strong, merry yet thoughtful fellow who looked out of his eyes. And it was something to be able to control that body now. It was no longer the soft, fragile, tender thing it had once been. It was swift, eager, warm, strong, and overflowing. He was master of this glorious animal, he, the child inside of him. He was proud of it. Hence the swagger.

Also he knew a thing or two, he thought. Toussaint had a hard time of it in arguments. It seemed doubtful at times if Anthony were going to be an apostle of Rousseau, an Emile to be matched with some glorious Sophie, as the little Frenchman so ardently hoped.

"Ah, if Faith had only had the mind of a Sophie," thought Toussaint, "with that glorious body of hers how happy Toussaint and Faith might have been together!" Even now from the body of this death of his love, from the living tomb of his hope, he could not bear to be parted. He must be near her. It was some comfort to see even the embodiment of his disappointment. His eyes followed her. She never looked at him. Her eyes were elsewhere.

As she sat in Anthony's room now at night her eyes seemed to be resting upon that curious shadow-play at the foot of the boy's bed. If it had not been physically impossible it might have seemed that it was her eyes that somehow caused these shadows to shift and dance. In her deep inexpressive pupils, had you looked closely under the sunbonnet even by daytime, the same mysterious kind of ghostly nothings might be seen at play. Anthony had noticed that.

The eyes of this woman were often upon him, he began to discover. He had been uncomfortable under her scrutiny at first, but now in his new-found strength he felt superior to her. He was a man. Then what she had to say at night gradually grew more and more interesting. She began to tell him revealing little bits of the biographies of those who moved under the same roof as he did. They could laugh together now over certain foibles of others which they discussed. Some of the facts of life were revealed to them in the same way. He would lie watching the shadows and listening to her talk. The tones of her voice, he discovered, thrilled him. They did not send him to sleep any more. It was a new kind of companionship. Physically, she served him in endless ways. She knew his bodily habits uncommonly well and catered to them. She had also been there a long time. She began to recount some stories of the women about the place. It was flattering to know that he as a man could understand. Also it was quite all right to close the door so that Mr. Bonnyfeather need not be disturbed by their voices. Indeed, he never had been. He did not know.

It was now that a series of events occurred for which even long afterwards Anthony was unable to fix the blame. He could not tell whether they were due to Fate, the Virgin, Faith, or what.

"Chance," said Toussaint. "The auld deil," said McNab without hesitation. "Human nature," said Mr. Bonnyfeather. But none of these gentlemen ever knew *all* the story or they might have been as perplexed as Anthony.

Chapter Nineteen

The Numbers of the Virgin

ANTHONY had made up his mind he was in love with little Angela. It was high time, he thought, that he should have a girl. It was not very difficult to persuade yourself that you were in love with Angela, who, heaven knows, was good-looking enough. Anyway, he did not as yet really know any other girl sufficiently well even to pretend to himself that he could be in love with her. "Angela Maea" he still called Angela. It was close enough to Angela *mia* to pass muster when whispering to her without causing him to explain how much deeper than that the name really went.

It was not quite so easy, however, to make Angela understand that you were in love with her; in love, that is, in a really formal way, a situation to be publicly, although very quietly, made apparent to everybody. Angela merely preferred to like you, to be fond of you, and not to be formal about it. In other words, you had such a good time with her, you enjoyed being with her so much, it was difficult to remember to stop to make love to her in the proper way by talking about it as Emile did to Sophie; by letting your soul "expand" as Toussaint had explained.

When you made a speech to her almost as fine as those in the books she would never take you seriously. In fact, she did not seem to know what you were talking about. She laughed. You saw it was funny and you had to laugh, too. That was hardly fair. It stopped your love-making. If you continued, and insisted you were serious about it she finally sulked. Then you had to put your arm around her and explain. After a while she would kiss and make up, but only after a long while. No, it was simply impossible to make love to Angela.

But the kisses of Angela—how cool they were! How happy, and yet how calm! How you forgot yourself when you kissed her! How soft, and friendly, and comfortable were her brown arms about your neck! Oh, how Anthony was to remember them afterwards, those kisses, in thirsty, and hot, and bitter places! Maea's kisses of peace he called them. The cool haze near snowbanks in the spring where the first flowers began to grow—that was to remind him afterwards of the kisses of little Angela.

So if she would not really be his in a way that he could flaunt before the whole clerks' row in the counting house, still it was pleasant, it was delightful, to drive with her back into the hill country in the early morning. Big Angela was glad to let them have the cart now. It was more and more difficult for her to climb into it, for impossible as it might seem, as she grew older she grew even larger. The plump mule was also delighted. These tall, slim youngsters who drove behind him and shook the reins on the hills were nothing to pull. He sped along gayly, shaking the loud bells merrily to the peals of laughter from the cart.

Little Angela remembered all the old places to call and the dainties with which to load the cart. Its advent now in various farmyards was more the signal for gayety than for bargaining. What the two young people

338

who drove it lacked in powers of haggling they made up in the sense of youth and happiness they carried with them. The country gossip they picked up and their talk of the town were vastly appreciated. They learned to retail this gossip with considerable skill and not a little collaboration. The new vintages would be brought out, the new-born lambs exhibited, or they must taste of the most remarkable sausages and cheeses. Boys and girls always gathered around wherever the cart stopped as well as the old people, and Anthony would orate to them of the latest news from the French wars. Then they would drive on to the next place.

Yes, decidedly, even the pleasure of bargaining could be dispensed with for the joy these young people brought, thought the farmers' wives. You could afford to be a little generous in the light of such eyes, the blue ones of the tall, gay, golden-haired English lad who spoke your own language so uncannily well; of the brown-eyed and statuesque girl with the ringing laugh. The hampers that returned to the Casa da Bonnyfeather did not suffer although old Angela pretended to grumble. The geese, she said, were never fat enough and the prices were extortionate, she insisted. Yet secretly in her heart, like all the other wives of the countryside, she blessed the cart and those who now rode upon it.

Then these pagan mornings were suddenly ended. It was when only three of the Guessippi children still remained small enough to be doused in front of the fountain before the cart left. Now it was only, "Innocenza, Jacopo, Luigi." The other names remained, but only as part of the ritual. Just at this particular time it pleased God to make Papa Tony Guessippi, the waiter, rich. As usual Providence moved mysteriously.

In the first place, one morning as Anthony climbed down from the cart on returning from an especially enjoyable drive with Angela, out of sheer braggadocio and exuberance he kissed her. He hoped somebody would see him, and someone did. It was Faith. After that, but not too soon afterward, Faith began to make

339

it her business to look after things in the kitchen herself. They were, so she said, not going to her satisfaction. Big Angela was scarcely to be moved by anything but an earthquake, but little Angela and Tony found it quite difficult to bear her presence. Do what they would, they could not avoid the eyes of Faith. She was there in the kitchen often. They shivered and crossed themselves secretly.

Thus matters stood when, secondly, there was a great thunderstorm and a bolt of lightning fell in the street just behind the Casa da Bonnyfeather. No less than nine copper pans were fused in Angela's kitchen. In Anthony's room the Madonna herself was thrown to the floor.

The consternation produced by these events had hardly died away when, thirdly, Count Spanocchi, the Governor of Livorno, in order to repair the defences of the city, announced by proclamation the establishment of an official lottery with several very large prizes. It was already rumoured that the French were coming. That, however, really did not worry anybody very much except the English merchants. Little else was talked of day after day in the streets except the best numbers to bet upon. Everything, even an event, has numbers. But which were the lucky ones?

Big Angela remembering that nine saucepans had been destroyed by lightning bet 9. Now 10 is the number of lightning. So the good woman squandered nearly all her savings in procuring ten tickets upon each one of which 9 appeared in some combination. Speechless at the cleverness of his wife in reading omens, Tony sat down in the corner of the kitchen and gave vent to his jealous spleen.

"It was not for you to have done that, Angela," said he. "You should have told me and allowed your husband to bet upon those numbers. He is a man and has more money than you will ever have to risk in the lottery."

This was a sore point with Angela. Despite her great bulk and herculean labours, Tony, the insignificant, received more for carrying the dishes to the table than she did for preparing them. He was a man, was he? She determined to dispute that.

"You, a man!" she shouted. "You are a worthless, hot little mouse. Get out!" She descended upon him with the remaining pan. Faith watched without comment, but she followed Tony out. Fixing him with her eyes she said something to him in a low voice that Angela could not overhear. The huge cook was much troubled. Bad luck would follow, she felt sure.

A little later Tony approached Anthony hat in hand. "Is it true, Signore Adverso," he asked in suppressed excitement, "that the Madonna in your room was also struck by lightning?"

"Also?" said Anthony puzzled. "Oh—yes, it is true. That is she was not struck. She was merely thrown to the floor and not even broken."

The man crossed himself. A look of great relief shone on his face. "Ah, then," he said, "I will do it!"

"Do what?" asked Anthony.

"You shall see," he said. "If I win you shall share in my luck."

That evening in the crowd before the counting house of Franchetti adjoining the mayoralty, Tony spent all he had and all he could borrow on the numbers of lightning, saucepans, and the Virgin. The tickets he finally displayed were numbered, 10, 9, 6, 8, 15. In order to obtain these he had to do some costly trading with other ticket holders in the crowd. But he was happy. He had plunged for the cinquina.

He left nothing undone in order to win. He said the Crielleisonne; he said thirteen Ave Marias in as many churches, he invoked Baldassare, Gasper, and Marchionne, the three wise men. Then he went home and quarrelled with his wife. She told him he was "pieno di superba, debiti, e pidocchi." After this he went outside without answering back. This is hard to do, but it is almost bound to bring good luck.

Even little Angela bet. She dreamed her mother was dead. Nevertheless she played that number, 52. The lottery had been heavily subscribed. It was not only popular, but patriotic.

341

Two days of terrible, breathless waiting now followed. Then delirium descended upon the Casa da Bonnyfeather. "Signore Antonio Guessippi" had won 40,000 scudi.

The news came in the morning. Before noon it was necessary to shut the street gates to keep out the acclaiming populace. Poor Tony was beside himself. At luncheon he was drunk. Little Angela had to wait on the table in his place. While she brought the dishes her father's head was thrust through the serving window from time to time alternately bidding Mr. Bonnyfeather a tearful farewell and exulting over him.

"Not once again will I, Tony, bring the soup to thee, thou greyheaded old man. It is I now who am rich. Many persons will henceforth bring soup to me." Just then he was snatched back into the kitchen.

A noise of struggling, the smashing of dishes, and big Angela's remonstrances convulsed those sitting about the table. But it was incredible to Tony that a man so rich as he should any longer be dominated by his wife. His head, somewhat the worse for wear, reappeared through the window. He was weeping now.

"Thou knowest what I have suffered, O best of patrons. It is over now. It is not from thee I would part but from that huge hill, that mountain to which I am married. It is not I who would have had all these children. I could not help myself. I . . ." Here he was pulled into the kitchen again and a pail shoved down over his head. He sat weeping under it, shouting that he was rich. When he attempted to move, his wife held him down. After a while he gave up the struggle and sat quiet.

He seemed to have gone into eclipse under the pail, but it was not so. In its serene darkness bright visions of freedom and affluent grandeur glowed intensely. The money he knew would make him more powerful than his wife. He would leave this scene of his lifelong defeat immediately. Tonight! He would snatch his entire family out of this ignominious kitchen, her field of victory. He would return to Pisa, the scene of his illustrious nativity and the home of his ancestors, in unimaginable triumph. There should be a coach for every single member of his family—except for her. A coach even for Bambino Luigi, who was a prince now. As for fat Angela—that mountain—she should ride with him and watch him throw his money out of the window to the crowd. It would kill her. Not a stick or a dish would they take away of their poverty, nothing but the clothes on their backs. He would bury her in things, choke her with pearls, hire cooks for her—that was a master thought. And he would have a small thin mistress. Never would he be held down on that hill again, never! They would leave tonight, with cavalry! He would ask the governor for an escort.

Seeing him sit so quietly Angela removed the pail and smiled at him. He looked at her with baleful eyes. "Thy home is no more, woman," he said, and spat at her.

She was amazed. It did not seem to be her husband that she had uncovered. Who was this little man who gibbered at her? The day had been too much to bear anyway. She began to cry out and wring her hands. Presently she was surrounded by her brood all weeping hysterically except little Angela. They could feel their world dissolving.

At three o'clock McNab took Tony in hand and went to receive the purse from the governor. Tony could not be trusted alone, of course. A flowery speech of presentation by His Excellency dressed in his gala uniform of a white coat with red vest and breeches, the huzzaing and pandemonium of the crowd completed the nervous devastation of Tony. It was only by the grace of God, McNab, and the hired coach that he got home with the money. It was promptly locked up in the strong room. The rich man's wife did not get a scudo. A few minutes later Tony was gone again, having taken a considerable sum along with him. Big Angela cooked supper as if nothing happened, as if she were not the wife of a rich man. Little Angela served it. Anthony could see she had been weeping.

He managed to press her hand as she took his plate. Faith smiled.

In the middle of the meal a tremendous clamour arose at the gate. An enormous crowd in carnival mood was serenading its lucky hero who was returning in state from the mayoralty. There were shouts, the indecent sounds of wind instruments, the trampling of many horses. The courtyard was invaded by twelve coaches and the guard of honour which had been furnished by the helpless governor. The troopers had some difficulty in keeping the mob back.

In the first coach, the most sumptuous that could be hired in Livorno, sat Tony. A case of fine Florentine wine was opened before him, and he was smoking a tremendous cigar. He was now in a thoroughly truculent state.

"I have come for my wife, my children, and the money," shouted he at Mr. Bonnyfeather who was standing on the steps with Anthony and Faith beside him.

"Scotch woman, with the evil eye, my good fortune will save us from you. Do not envy us at *this* hour." He crossed himself. Then he began to demand his money in an insufferable manner from Mr. Bonnyfeather who stood looking on rather shocked. The corks popped in the coach and Tony raved out of the window.

"You had best let him go, sir, I think," said McNab working his way through the crowd. "He has been to the governor again and got an escort for as far as Pisa. You had better clear the whole family out now. There is a carriage for everyone, you see, even for little Luigi."

The crowd outside which was peering through the gate thought there was some dispute about the money and began to howl. Without waiting for further orders McNab began to carry the bags out of the strong room and to put them in the coach. As each one appeared a roar followed. Presently Angela and her brood were brought out by Faith. The younger children were

344

weeping, carrying a few broken toys. Tony shouted to them to throw them away. Luigi clutched his dirty doll.

"Good-bye, Anthony," said a quiet voice behind him. He turned, startled, from watching the silly scene below. It was little Angela. Angela was going! Maea would not be near him any more. He stood stunned. He could not say anything. Where?—Why? She stood for a moment waiting for him to speak to her but he could not. Then she turned away wearily and marshalled the preposterous brood of her parents down the steps. In the courtyard for the last time she began to call their names.

At this unexpected element of order in the scene of riot and confusion, a sudden silence settled on the crowd and the apprentices and clerks looking on. For the first time, as if by general consent, it seemed to be realized by all present that there was an element of tragedy in the farce.

"Arnolfo, Maria, Nicolò, Beatrice, Claudia, Federigo, Pietro, Innocenza, Jacopo, Luigi," chanted the soft, clear, sane voice. Anthony's lips followed mechanically. But now the water did not descend. As each name was called, that child was bundled into a separate coach. Into the last crept little Angela and burst into tears. Her father and mother were already quarrelling in the first carriage.

"No!" shouted Tony to his wife, "no!"

Suddenly with surprising agility, the huge woman descended again and despite her husband's veto, seized her goat which was innocently looking on. A struggle followed. Cries, screams, acclamations, and the bleatings of the animal rent the air. The goat was dragged into the carriage and the door closed. Then its head appeared at the window looking out beside that of Tony who was now too far gone to object. He mouthed at Mr. Bonnyfeather with a foolish grin.

"Get them gone, Sandy," said the merchant to McNab, "there is something obscene about this."

"Aye," said McNab and signalled violently to the sergeant in charge of the troopers to move on. The

345

procession, long remembered in Livorno, started.

There was, as Mr. Bonnyfeather had said, something obscene about it. A kind of evil grotesqueness, as if the twelve carriages were the happy funeral of an idiot, endeared it to the mob. From the first carriage, where sat the mountainous woman with flaming hair, and from the window of which peered a bleating goat, a madman was flinging out coins. Scrambles, shrieks, fights, and hard-breathing riots, as if society were disintegrating before it, marked the progress of this vehicle of prodigality with its attendant soldiers down the streets. Behind followed a procession of scared gnomes with small, pinched faces against the gaudy upholstery of their grand carriages. The passengers dwindled in size until the now frantic little Jacopo and Luigi passed. In the last vehicle was a young girl sobbing her heart out.

Big Angela did not dare to restrain her husband. The rain of silver continued. Every coin lost filled her with despair. She groaned aloud. It was thus that the procession finally passed through the Porta Pisa and disappeared into the darkness beyond.

In the courtyard of the Casa da Bonnyfeather Anthony sat alone on the dark steps with his head in his hands. He had been sitting there for over an hour. It was very quiet now. The noise of the riot had long died away. Under the shed he could just make out the outline of the cart. Its shaft seemed to be extended up to the stars like empty, beseeching arms. He choked. He could scarcely understand the feeling of tight, dry despair that hindered his breathing. What was it that had happened? Something over which none of them had any control. For the first time an arrow had penetrated his soul. Angela was gone.

He turned and blundered up the steps blindly. There was a light in the kitchen. From old habit his heart leaped out to it. Angela used to be there. He looked. Faith was preparing something hot. The place was in frightful disorder. Amid the broken dishes, cast-off clothes and fragments of food she moved calmly, even a little triumphantly, while the charcoal watched her expectantly with its small, red eyes.

He went in and threw himself down on his bed.

END OF BOOK TWO

BOOK THREE

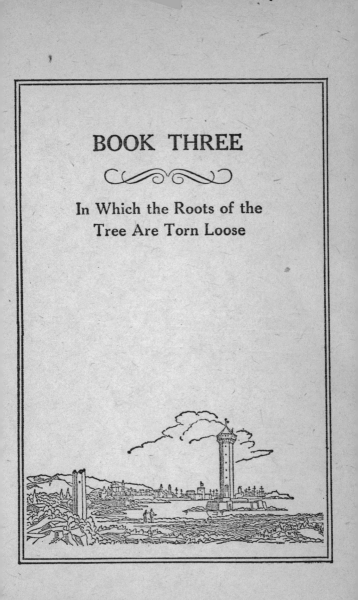

In Which the Roots of the Tree Are Torn Loose

Chapter Twenty

Apples and Ashes

IT WAS a warm night. A faint streak of moonlight
came through Anthony's window and fell across the
foot of his bed, splashing itself against the wall. He
lay with his eyes wide open in the darkness. An occasional shout from passers-by returning from the crowds
that had followed the procession echoed in his vaulted
chamber. These calls grew fewer and finally ceased at
last to have individual significance. They blent themselves with the general, low, musical monotone of the
city's life that murmured now as if mankind were at
last getting what it desired under the full moon while
the trees sighed about it doubtfully. On the wall at
the foot of the bed, as the moon climbed higher, a
faint outline of the shadow-play began. Anthony looked
at it wearily and closed his eyes.

He had never felt so lonely. The realization of all
that Angela meant to him grew upon him. He longed for
her intensely. He wanted to have her now in his arms,
to press her firm little breasts against his chest, to
fondle and comfort her, to be boy and girl together.

That was what "being in love" meant! But he had always kept putting that out of his mind about Angela, —because of Arnolfo, perhaps. But she was different. It would be right with her. He had seen her once when she went behind the fountain. There had seemed to be a light about her. He would like to see her that way again—now! He would make her come back by dreaming her into his room. He opened his eyes to find her. In the full gust of a now manly passion, strangely enough, his strong childhood faculty of evoking vivid visions returned.

For a minute he saw Angela lying beside him in the moonlight. There was a faint, tender smile on her parted lips. Her eyes looked at him wide, and solemnly, as they had sometimes done when she sat on the seat of the cart beside him. She loved him! Why had he not known that before? For an instant her whole form glimmered into a bright, ivory light, glistening. He trembled toward her, the light, quick fire of his youth's desire flowing so that it possessed him. He half sat up and stretched out his hands to touch her. A mist began to curl about her ankles. It seemed to rush up her limbs and vanished with her like smoke into the moonlight.

Suddenly on the other side of the room he saw the table clearly standing against the wall.

He felt as if he were falling and dropped back on the pillow. An agony of grief, disappointment and insufferable sorrow filled him and overflowed from his eyes. And he had not even spoken to her the last time! "Good-bye, Anthony." It rang through his brain. He put his hands over his ears.

What a dolt of a boy he had been to let all that time go by without . . . to let Toussaint persuade him by words out of a book what being in love meant! He tore at his clothes as he thought of that. He shifted uneasily. One thing though, the self, the thing that lived in his body was growing up. After tonight he was not a boy; the life inside him was not childish any more. How fierce and determined it was. How it *would* have its way. He could hardly imagine denying it now. How could you? It owned you. The voice seemed to have gone. He listened. It had nothing to say. Faintly, perhaps. So faintly you could not be sure. But what was it compared to this thing within him that demanded and clamoured and burned? Nothing! Something to be dismissed.

And he had thought he could tell Angela how to make love like Emile and Sophie! To *tell* her that! And so she had laughed at him. She had known. Had she? How did she know? Just as he did now. Now, after it was too late. She had known all along! He understood now why it was that he had been so happy with her when she had looked at him like *that*. *That* was being in love. They had been. They were! And he had thought it had something to do with words.

There was only one kind of words that could give him any satisfaction now—oaths. He had always shrunk from them a little when he heard them along the docks. They had secretly hurt him, the terrible, coarse ones particularly. Now he needed them. A string of them rolled out of his brain through his lips. He whispered them huskily in his throat. He cursed himself. It was a relief. He shifted his head onto his other arm. That cheek was not wet. It felt hot against his muscles. How cool and smooth his arm was.

Then he heard Faith coming down the hall. He forgot everything for a moment but her footsteps. Would she come in? He hoped not. He did not want her to see that he had been in torment, weeping. She would understand. He knew she would. What was it she had whispered to Tony about the Madonna? But how could she know those numbers would win, that Angela would have to go? How could she? But would she come in? He hoped not.

Her footsteps passed down the corridor to Mr. Bonnyfeather's door. He heard her knock and give the merchant his hot, night drink. The door closed. Faith returned to the kitchen again. After all she might have come in. He might have liked to talk to her—in the dark. How hot it was! He was clammy. Even the bedclothes were drenched with perspiration. He

353

began to throw off his clothes now. The thought of the tub of cool water in the room just across the hall occurred to him. Quick! He would run across and cool himself off before Faith returned. On noiseless, bare feet he sped through the door.

The reflection of the full moon from the courtyard turned the walls of Faith's apartment into a dull, silvery grey. The various familiar objects of her furniture seemed to be faintly luminous. What a night it was! He could see the disk of the water in the cask faintly gleaming around the edge. There seemed to be a film of quicksilver on it. He discarded his last garment to step in. At that instant a crisp rustling sound as if someone were drawing a silk drapery over stone, the very faintest of hisses, caused him to turn.

In a patch of moonlight near the door stood a naked woman. He was just in time to see the folds of her dress rustle down from her knees into coils about her feet. She stood poised there for a moment, with her head drawn back, before she stepped out of them. He saw she was beautiful. For some seconds he did not realize that it was Faith. Then he gasped.

In the moonlight she was another person. She continued to look at him. He could feel that and looked down. Then he looked at her again. He stood still, rooted. The faint aroma of her body floated to him. A sudden tide of passion dragged at his legs. He could not help it. He swayed slightly, away from her. Then he felt her arms wind around him in the dark. They were smooth and cool, smoother than his own. Her hand pressed his head onto her breast.

He was half blind, and speechless now. All his senses had merged into one feeling. She seemed to be carrying him somewhere. As he stepped through the moony darkness his legs had lost the sensation of weight. "I shall think it is Angela," he said to himself. But he soon forgot all about Angela. He could remember nothing but himself.

To lie face downward on smooth, soft water with warmth lapping you about, that had always been delightful. How easily your arms and legs moved in such an element. The whole surface of the body felt its soft, exquisite touch. To be supported and yet possessed by an ocean of unknown blue depths below you and to cease to think! Yes, it was something like swimming on a translucent summer night.

Although his eyes were tightly closed, he was looking into dim, moonlit depths where blue and green flashes of light and long silver shafts wavered down to the darker depths below him. On the subliminal floor of this ocean in which he was now submerged, the same shadow-play that had haunted the walls of his room seemed to be going on. Translucent monsters, giant growths dimly opaque, were alive and moving down there.

Now he began to rise and fall with the waves that washed over him and yet lifted and lowered him, carrying with them as they passed a tide of tingling feeling from his neck to his heels. After a while he was just drifting in a continuous, rippling current of ecstasy that penetrated him as if he were part of the current in which he lay. He was completely alone again, but happy, completely happy. "Are you?" something from beyond him seemed to ask. "Yes," he answered, "be quiet . . . not thinking now . . . let me alone."

He drifted on with the current. Wherever it might be going he would go with it. It was moving fast now. He was being borne along more swiftly. Faster yet. The entire ocean was rushing down a slope. He was being whirled around and around, dying with a delicious giddiness that drew on his brain. He was in a whirlpool. He was being drawn into the centre of it.

There began to be something just a little terrifying in the pleasure of the decent. The sensation divided. "Be careful!" He opened his eyes and thrust up his head like one stretched on an exquisite rack. In the blur of moonlight and darkness a vision shaped itself. He saw he was not in the ocean. but swimming in the pool under the tree. He was moving around with the water in it.

The water in the pool was bubbling and whirling at enormous speed. It was shrinking down into a funnel-shape toward the middle. He would be drawn into that. A curious, dim, white animal could be seen at play as the water shoaled toward the floor of the pool. He looked beneath himself. The monster with a pale, smooth belly lay looking up at him. Its eyes were terrible. He began to struggle to avoid it but his limbs were possessed by the lethargy of a dream. He saw that his own movements were reflected in every motion by the bronze boy that stood at the edge of the pool. There was a terrible, mad pleasure that convulsed that boy by more than pain.

There was something in the hollow statue causing that. He must get rid of it; fill up the hollow in the pool and rest again! The bronze boy grew still, trembled. Suddenly from the mouth of the beast below him a flood burst forth and filled up the pool. It overflowed gently now and washed Anthony clear over the brim.

He was lying on his back now looking up at the moonlight filtered through the leaves of the great tree. All was well.

He lay, for how long he did not know, in a timeless trance of relief and release. When he opened his eyes he saw that Faith Paleologus was lying beside him. Her bosom rose and fell softly. Then he remembered Angela.

He was sorry he had forgotten her. As the lethargy passed he made a little mourning within himself for the memory that had been Angela. But he saw that it was for a memory, an ideal, not for Angela herself. Perhaps after a few days that ideal would return. The desire would return and he would dream of it as Angela. He looked at Faith who lay there breathing as if she were asleep. He did not blame her. No feeling of rage overcame him as it had that day in the room with Arnolfo. Yet this was a much more important thing that had happened. It had merely happened to him, there could be no doubt of that. Yet not because of some person, not because of Faith. It was the blind, overpowering feeling that had come upon them both. That was what had done it. A slight noise from the courtyard disturbed his half-dreamful, easy reverie.

He began to become fully conscious of who and where he was. He had better not stay here any longer. He looked at the woman beside him again. She did not open her eyes. There was a blank look of relaxation on her face that the grey moonlight accentuated. Somehow it was a little funny to see a countenance completely the slave of feeling. A mouth should not register mere contentment; be so relaxed. Something inside should make the muscles behave and hold it shut at least. He laughed silently.

Then he was completely aroused. He noticed he did not care whether he had any clothes on or not. What if she did see him now? There was no bravado about it. He simply did not care. It was purely a matter of indifference. Come, this was getting dull. It was over. What he wanted now was a wide bed to himself and a sleep. He stretched himself. He felt completely well and indifferent about things in general. What a relief it was not to be so sensitive about everything. Well, why should he care, or say anything to Faith? She understood.

He got up quietly and walked across the hall into his own bedroom. Then he suddenly remembered he had left his clothes in Faith's room. Some of the possible practical implications of the affair now thrust themselves upon him. It would not always be dark and private as it was now. In the daytime people awoke. They went about seeing and saying things. His shirt was still lying by the water butt in the housekeeper's room. He stopped before his bed. He would like another bath, too, more than before. What should he do about it?

On her bed Faith stirred slightly and put out her arms in the semi-darkness. Her young lover was gone. The shock of the disappointment aroused her. She sat up. Her many experiences with men ashore after a long voyage had destroyed in her a certain subtlety of apprehension which she had once possessed. She now expected the comforting embraces of the aftermath of the first time to verge into the return of warmth of the second. She had forgotten it was not always so. For a moment a sense of loss overwhelmed her. To solace herself she began to think about what had just occurred. From this she derived comfort; over certain details an immense satisfaction.

He had, she felt, belonged to her completely for a few moments. It was the fruit of years of planning. As the boy had grown into a youth, blossomed into first manhood, his presence had obsessed her. He possessed that curious freshness, an aloof beauty that seemed to her to be the essence of innocence in itself, the very tag of it. He was like his mother in that. It was what she had always desired, needed. In Maria it had of course been unapproachable. It was that of which she had been jealous. Now she had possessed it, she felt; crawled within the circle that fenced it off, made it a part of her. She felt she had triumphed over the dead woman, too, the girl who had been carried off by Don Luis.

Ah, *there* would have been a mate for her! There was something hard, unbreakable, unconquerable about that man. She pressed her breasts back upon themselves, her virginal breasts, and trembled. They could bear a great weight. The thought of it possessed her. Her eyes narrowed in the moonlight. Just then a light footfall disturbed her. She looked up. Anthony was coming into the room again.

He passed her bed without a glance, and calmly and methodically, so as to make no noise, stepped into the water cask and immersed himself. Even his head went under. The water overflowed and ran sparkling in patches of moonlight over the floor. He emerged, dried himself, and picked up his clothes.

"Now," she thought, "he will come to me again." As though she did not exist he started for the door.

It was more than she could bear. Before he reached it her arms were about him again. He kept going. She threw herself down and clasped him about the knees. "Stay with me," she begged him, her mouth writhing in a whisper, "I will make you die with pleasure."

He reached down and seizing her by the wrists, unclasped her fingers with a strength that she had not suspected in him. His hands were like a man's. She fell forward on the floor with the palms of her hands on his feet. He withdrew them as if her touch hurt him. She lay there alone for a long time. When she finally looked up the full moon already grey with the opposing dawn was looking in at her. Its mouth seemed to be drawn down like her own.

It was some time before Anthony could orient himself to all that this experience implied. Most of his attitude about it was instinctive. For a long time he did not even care to look at the Madonna. She was still in his room. He felt her there. But there was nothing to be said between them. He had trusted himself too far. He was essentially weak. That was plain. Yet he could not bring himself to ask for help.

Indeed, it was a curious kind of self-balance which he now attained. Mr. Bonnyfeather might be right after all. Perhaps he, Anthony, was essentially sinful, but in the light of that fact he would act with caution. He would not allow himself to be surprised again. With possible pitfalls revealed to him, he walked circumspectly, and yet more confidently and with a new completeness of knowledge. The swagger disappeared, but he stood upright like a man, looking around him, aware and beware. Into the life about him he entered as one initiated.

What indignation he came to feel over the occurrence was gradual rather than of sudden growth and quick ebb. He disliked Faith more and more as time went on. He would not let her come into his room any more, and he resented her eyes which he now felt upon him. That she had long lain in wait for him was plain. He shivered at that. There was something puma-like in her patience, he saw. Yet it was not entirely unpleasant to have been desired. Only he did not want her to desire him any longer. He did not belong to her. That was all. He could not. When he had been with her he had been left alone. He desired someone that he could share himself with. There must be two. The trouble with what Arnolfo had taught him was that when you did that you tore yourself apart. You became two, divided. You were trying to be you and yourself. You touched you. It was a strain, a rending of the person. What you should love, your own dear body, you ended by loathing. That he had found out would never do. You would end by hating yourself, be unhappy, desperate.

Even with Faith it had been better. Not entirely wrong, he thought. But he had still found himself alone. Then there was something too simply avid and sheerly physical about her. What lived inside of her you could not really meet. Was it there at all? With Angela it would have been different. With her he felt he would not have been left alone. He longed for her more now. He continued to miss her as the full significance of his loss became apparent. It was on that account that he finally came to hate Faith. She, he felt in his bones, had arranged the departure of Angela. It was Faith who had put that idea of the numbers of the Madonna into Tony's foolish head.

Even his Madonna, he felt, had something to do with it. He was still unconsciously idolater enough to feel that. It was one of the reasons he delayed returning to her; why the voice was stilled for so long. A hush had fallen upon it. Sometimes at night he was frightened by this. Yes, it was all very complicated. He longed to talk to someone about it. Never could he approach Mr. Bonnyfeather about it all. His solution would be one of action, to dismiss Faith. That would accomplish nothing for Anthony.

And then, added to all this, was the knowledge that in what had happened he had not at all directed himself. He had not willed it. It had merely come upon him. The woman had known that. The male in him rebelled. He should have taken the lead. Yet he did not hold Faith directly responsible. She, he saw, had merely taken advantage of the way the world was arranged. She had merely caught him up in the force which she personified. That was what he must be careful of, the blind force. So he began to avoid her, even to avoid the house. The whole Casa da Bonnyfeather began to become irksome at times, dangerous through familiarity with what lurked there. He began to go out and to be about the town more and more.

For the first time the afternoons with Toussaint, and the lessons with various other people began to pall on him. He struck up a vivid friendship with young Vincent Nolte, the nephew of a Hamburg merchant at Livorno. A rather heedless round of gadding about and tasting life as it offered itself began. It was soon necessary to draw on some small savings from his clerk's salary. They were soon gone. McNab looked serious when he asked for a month's advance. "Gang and ask it o' the maister," he said.

Somewhat diffidently Anthony approached Mr. Bonnyfeather. In a rush of embarrassed confidence he explained the new turn his interests had taken. To Anthony's surprise Mr. Bonnyfeather not only took it as a matter of course but looked pleased. He refused to advance Anthony anything on his "salary." Instead he provided him with a generous allowance from his purse. Of this Anthony was to say nothing. The old man was glad to hear that Anthony was waking up, as he expressed it. He had even thought of hastening the process, it appeared. But he had let well enough alone. Anthony squirmed to think what that "well enough" had been. But he was able to obtain what leisure he desired.

"After the noon bell, then, your time will now be your own," said Mr. Bonnyfeather. "It is harder to spend time and get full value for it than for money," the old merchant continued somewhat sententiously. "You do not believe that now, but you will soon find it true. I shall expect you, however, to go on with your studies, particularly mathematics. You should by this time begin to be interested enough in some subject to begin to pursue it and to plan your work yourself. What would you think of going to England to complete your schooling as I did? To Exeter, say. I still have connections there. It would unify what you

361

already know mighty well. You would also be acquiring the idiom which is your birthright." The old merchant stopped himself suddenly.

Anthony scarcely noticed his expression. He was thinking of the opera that night with Vincent and some companions. He only aroused himself sufficiently from the dream of affluence which his new allowance evoked to promise to consider Exeter.

How often aftewards he wondered with what a different die his life might have been stamped if he had really considered that offer seriously. How different would his path have been? As it was, he considered it only briefly, only with his lips.

Toussaint was hurt to find his pupil straying away. He had regarded him already as a silent convert to Rousseau and the new doctrines. It was especially important to hold him, he felt, now that the Revolution was about to descend upon Italy. Nevertheless, their afternoons together grew fewer although more intimate and intense. For Toussaint realized he was not talking to a boy any longer. He began to open his last reserve. As he looked at Anthony his heart beat with pride, his face glowed with affection. There was an emotion now about their meetings over the table or by the ruin as though each time were to be the last class.

But from Toussaint's intense monologues and exhortations Anthony would now break away with a feeling of relief as soon as he decently could. The little man's great enthusiasm was often funny to him now. Anthony could not share in this intense emotion over abstractions. Above all he disliked having his own feelings probed and made reasonable. The Revolution and the Rights of Man were all well enough, he supposed, but what did Toussaint think about a woman? How would he feel about Faith, for instance? Several times as he listened to some philosophical exhortation it was on the tip of his tongue to say something about Faith, or even about Angela. Toussaint might really know something important after all. At least it would be interesting to find out and to watch his expression.

Yet from embarrassment he still refrained from asking. As time went on, however, the temptation grew.

If Toussaint would only let him say something sometimes! He wanted to explain but he got no chance. The other's voice went on. Anthony would fling out exasperated at last to find amusement and distraction where he could beyond the now irksome walls of the Casa da Bonnyfeather.

He took to fencing after a while with a little Spaniard who kept a place near the Porta Colonella. But he did not care much for it. The polite conventions of the art bored him. Then he and Vincent Nolte with some other youths hired a retired Austrian lieutenant to teach them the pistol. That went well for Anthony. But Vincent was awkward. He could never get over shying at the report. He finally dropped out while Anthony kept on. In six months Anthony developed into a fair shot with several types of handgun. He learned not only their use but how to care for them. Then the bottom fell out of pistol practice, too. Nothing was so pleasant at last as going about town with Vincent. The dandy state was upon them both. They idled magnificently in new clothes along the Corso. They patronized an English tailor and met other young bloods. A pistol, Anthony soon found, was the only thing that Vincent was shy about.

Vincent Nolte, was, as McNab once remarked, "a little too large for his size." He had very light, curly, brown hair that he was conscious of as his chief attraction, and an open, rather sweet countenance. He had light-blue eyes and a firm chin under large, pink, sensual lips. His nose was keen and straight. But it flared out so much at the nostrils as to make the beak of it seem to be just about to recover from a flattening blow. His ears were very small, a little ridiculous, and somewhat porcine. But you seldom saw them. Indeed, if anything, it was their absence you felt.

It was only when Vincent turned his back to you that you saw that his neck and the back of his head formed one and the same plane. It was a racial peculiarity in Vincent accentuated that lent him a fascination. On the pivot of his spine, his head, a little bulging at the brows and crowned with its flaring mass of curls, turned with an unreasonable majesty. His was a pride that could scarcely be allowed in one so young. Still it was impossible to escape the keen, blue darts of his glances.

Yet despite the fact that nature seemed to have tried to make a masterpiece of Vincent Nolte and had then marred it and tweaked it out of proportion at every turn, despite that, the boy had an undeniable charm. There was, for instance, his warm, clear German voice, and there were the bright things and incidents with which he continually managed to surround himself. In their innumerable and unexpected combinations the delight of him lay.

He was the son of a Hamburg merchant, the same with whom Mr. Bonnyfeather and Francis Baring had wandered through Scotland years before. It was for that reason at first, and later on for himself, that the young man in spite of his harum-scarum escapades was constantly welcomed at the table of the Casa da Bonnyfeather. Besides, he was the nephew of Otto Frank, or rather of *Otto Frank & Company*, a most successful German firm in Livorno. At one time they had been a dangerous rival of the House of Bonnyfeather. But since Mr. Bonnyfeather had outdistanced them many years before he could now afford to look upon them complacently enough.

He could even be glad to see, as he secretly told himself, with an eye to possible future advantages and mutual understandings, the heirs of the two houses dining together and a friendship growing up between them. With the French army liable to swoop down at any time on the town it was quite possible that the business of all the English firms at Livorno might be wiped out at one stroke. In that case an intimate connection with the branch of a neutral Hamburg house might be invaluable.

In fact the canny old merchant was already pulling in his financial horns, transferring large credits to his friends the Barings in England and Holland, and trying to collect long outstanding debts. He was simply quietly putting his affairs in order in case the avalanche that had already slipped down into Lombardy should suddenly dam the rivers of trade in Tuscany.

Part of his policy consisted in shifting what business he still carried on overseas into the names of German merchants. Now and then he also began to employ a Yankee ship. The new gridiron ensign had lately began to appear with a surprising frequency in the Mediterranean. He had sometimes even thought of transferring his still reluctant and purely practical allegiance to King George to the Grand Duke Francis and of flying the flag of Tuscany from the roof of his commercial stronghold. But his long connection with the English was notorious. The subterfuge would have been too transparent. There were not wanting in Livorno those who would have been base enough to point it out if the French did come. The presence of the British fleet near by still heartened the old man, and he continued to hoist the English flag every morning as of old, but more thoughtfully and prayerfully as the war clouds thickened about him.

He called in Signore Baldasseroni, by now the best commercial lawyer in Livorno, and made his will. He remitted to the marquis in Spain two years' rent, renewed his lease in advance, and registered it with a notary. Above all he feared being turned out of his beloved rooms in the Casa da Bonnyfeather in his old age. He desired to die there even if it were necessary to close out his business entirely. He kept the *Unicorn* and faithful Captain Bittern close by in case of emergencies, sending the vessel only on short coasting voyages that followed the movements of the British fleet and convoys.

In short, as might have been expected, Mr. Bonnyfeather acted wisely and circumspectly; secretly, and with great forethought. In this scheme an increased allowance conferred upon Anthony to enable him to go about with Vincent Nolte was only one item in his general fiscal policy. It was not, had Anthony only known it, conferred for purely sentimental reasons.

None the less Anthony spent the money merrily. In this way the time went on well enough, it seemed; whole months of it.

For to all outward appearances the placid pool of Anthony's existence continued to reflect unbrokenly the animated but essentially unchanging scenes about him. Of the shifting shadows in its depths the surface at least showed nothing. Only the gentlest of winds seemed so far to have rippled it pleasantly. Perhaps it was this light, animated change playing over deeply troubled waters like breezes and sunlight on the surface of a geyser waiting to erupt that lent the latter days in Livorno all the diversity and fascination which they had. Suddenly, however, the smooth surface of the pool was broken as if by the plunge of a meteor. It was a long time before the rings of so violent a disturbance spread themselves out and calm reflections returned. The meteor was a quarrel with Toussaint. It came, instantly, as if out of the blue.

It all happened because he had overcome his reluctance to speak to Toussaint about Faith. In the little meadow, while they sat together looking down at the ruin one afternoon, the meteor fell.

It had been very warm. They had taken a bottle of light claret along and consumed it. Toussaint had talked for a long time about a perfect state. All Europe was to be included. How heavenly would it be in the halycon future just ahead to withdraw to some earthly paradise with a beloved, with a perfect woman. In words that glowed with a faintly golden, poetic tinge through the soporific mist of their mutual afternoon laziness, and the wine, Toussaint painted the scenes of an ideal, platonic honeymoon on the shores of Lake Léman. No place was quite so beautiful as Lake Léman, he said.

". . . the reflections of snow peaks in water!—but do you hear me?" he asked, looking at Anthony, who was leaning back against the trunk of a tree with his eyes closed.

"Yes," said Anthony. It was not exactly a lie. He *had* heard him over the chirp of the grasshoppers. He had even seen himself going out in a skiff on Toussaint's beautiful lake—with Angela. They would row out together to an island where no one could talk to them —no one! Be alone!

In the mind of Toussaint a woman with the conversational powers of Madame de Staël and the body of Faith Paleologus was gathering flowers with him in a meadow by Lake Léman. The white, cool mountains towered above them. They looked at the lake and talked. "If that Paleologus were only . . . if she only would . . ."

"Yes," said Anthony, "I heard you."

Both their dreams were shattered. They looked at each other and laughed. Somehow they understood what each was thinking.

"Whom would you take with you?" said Toussaint, for the first time dropping completely his rôle of mentor and speaking man to man.

For an instant it was on the tip of Anthony's tongue to say "Angela." Yet he could not. Toussaint was laughing a little. Toussaint evidently enjoyed the embarrassment of the lad before him who sat against the tree blushing. That was obvious. Then it occurred to Anthony that this was his opportunity. He would ask Toussaint about Faith. He would get the advice and comfort of a friend. He wanted that. He wanted to get it off his mind. He began in an awkward and blundering way. It was hard to break down his own reserve. Finally he blurted out the story baldly enough.

It seemed more terrible now that he had put it into sound. Perhaps it was a mistake after all to have let it slip into words. They sounded bad. During the misery of this recital he kept his eyes on the ground. Now he raised them to the face of his friend. There would be sympathy there at least—wouldn't there?

Over his tightly wound stock the face of Toussaint glared at him as if he were being choked by his own neckwear. It was convulsed and livid with fury. He put his fingers up to his neck. Suddenly he leaned forward and without an instant's warning struck

Anthony in the face. A stroke of lightning could not have been more unexpected. For an instant Anthony put his hand to his cheek in a kind of dumb surprise. Then he felt the sharp smart of the insulting fingers. Blinding tears spurted from his eyes. With a roar of rage he threw himself upon the little Frenchman and shook him unmercifully.

Toussaint made no resistance. He seemed paralysed by what he had done. Anthony stopped after a while, frightened by his own strength. What was it that had happened? Why? He leaned back against the tree again, exhausted by rage.

"Mon Dieu!" said Toussaint, reassembling himself painfully on the ground, "vous m'avez tué." He groaned, weeping. Anthony looked at him now in silent misery.

"I love her," shouted Toussaint at him suddenly. "I love her—and it was you! You boy! Meldrun!" He began to get up. "Go away! Leave me!"

Anthony snatched his hat and ran. He got to the Casa da Bonnyfeather breathless. Toussaint came in later much the worse for wear. His coat was tattered. They said nothing. They passed each other and went on as strangers. They both hid it from all the others. They were outwardly polite. But both were heartsick at what had happened. There were no more meetings by the ruin now. In the afternoons Anthony went out. Faith, he saw, had guessed. Damn her! Her eyes smiled. The place was growing unbearable, especially at meal times. It was better at the Franks'.

So Anthony was often at Otto Frank's dining with Vincent Nolte. The counting room and apartments of "Otto Franco," as he was called, were in the great house of the Franchetti on the Piazza della Comunità at the corner of the Piazza d'Arme. From the door of it and from its street windows there was an excellent view of the piazza, where the troops of the garrison occasionally paraded, and of the town hall or mayoralty close by. It was the official centre of both commercial and governmental activities of the town. Something was always going on there. There were sights to be seen, news, and rumours to be picked up. After several years of the life along the docks Anthony was intrigued by the piazza. It was the opposite face of the life of Livorno. To him a new one that he was glad to look upon. He began to go nearly every noon as soon as the work at the office was over to dine with Vincent Nolte.

He would make some purely formal excuse to Toussaint about not being able to spend that afternoon "as usual," hastily change into a new, bottle-green suit, dampen his curls, and dash out of the gate.

To the right of the Casa da Bonnyfeather a long alley led directly from the quays along the Darsena through a maze of high tenements to emerge finally on the wide Strada Ferdinanda. After threading his way over refuse piles, under flapping multi-coloured clothes, past goats, and long strings of spaghetti hung out to dry, Anthony would thus emerge suddenly as if coming out of a shadowed tunnel into the brilliant sunlight of the strada.

By this short cut he had left the world of ships and the sea behind him. By it he seemed to have become at once and at one stride the citizen of a more sophisticated world.

The Strada Ferdinanda ran in a direct line from the Porta Pisa to the Porta Colonella. Alone among the streets of the town at that time it was swept daily. A double line of poplars ran down the middle of it, and it was lined with white marble fronts and bright, stone houses where considerable brasswork twinkled in the sun.

Here the officers of the garrison exercised their horses. Governor Spanocchi was frequently to be glimpsed rolling along in his high-backed equipage of state with gilded harness, outriders, and an escort of cavalry. The landaus and phaetons of the well-to-do dashed back and forth. About noon the gigs of merchants brought them home for the day, the flower vendors from the country made their last desperate effort to dispose of their fast wilting wares, and a golden dust hung in the air from one gate of the city to the other. The flag could then be seen drooping on its staff at the castle. Exactly at a quarter after twelve the diligence from Pisa flashed down the long street with a tooting horn and four horses, to draw up on the piazza before the mayoralty. Here the passports of travellers were examined while a crowd gathered to view the arrivals of the day. The Pisa diligence was probably the only one in Italy that made a point of leaving and arriving on time. So far at least had the influence of English travellers prevailed over the native indifference to the clock. The entire city was nevertheless proud of this daily miracle of punctuality elsewhere unknown.

Anthony always timed himself by the infallible diligence. If it had arrived before he turned into the Strada he could consider himself late for the noon meal. If not, he was sure to find Vincent's uncle, "Otto Franco," at the corner of the Piazza d'Arme strutting up and down before his office entirely bareheaded.

The singular little man would be without a cravat, his linen shirt open so as to allow the breezes to wave the hair on his chest. His morning gown flapped in the breeze. In a pair of huge, red, crescent-shaped, Turkish slippers he slithered along the sidewalks while he gesticulated violently. He was followed by a train of goods and money-brokers and a few clerks from his own establishment ready to grab and carry the luggage of strangers. The reason for this bizarre show was to advertise the importance of the Capo della Casa to the strangers just dismounting from the diligence across the street. There a hired runner announced the merits of his master in several languages and pointed him out to travellers desirous of changing their money or of obtaining passage for themselves or their goods to other lands. And it was seldom that someone was not thus inveigled into his net. Nor did they ever have cause to regret it, for Otto Frank was both able and honest. He differed from his rivals only in not hiding his light under a bushel of dignity. Others who had tried his methods had failed. As he himself explained it, they lacked the courage of Turkish slippers and a naked breast.

When Anthony passed this personage he would invariably receive a loud invitation to dinner. The entire menu was always loudly rehearsed. He would hide his amusement and accept respectfully, going into the counting room where Vincent was usually to be found at his desk looking gloomy enough. For as long as Uncle Otto continued to drum trade in this manner the social aspirations of Signore Vincent Nolte as the representative of a dignified merchant firm were kept in dark eclipse. Vincent's father, Herr Johann Nolte of Hamburg, was, indeed, the head of the house and supplied the capital for Uncle Otto. The uncle's noisy advertising was therefore the more difficult for the son of a long line of Hanseatic merchants to swallow. Nevertheless, there were compensations. Vincent's position in the house gave him considerable freedom. As he grew older more and more of the business of the firm was being concentrated in his hands by Hamburg. Vincent was no fool. Even though his uncle was still consul for Hamburg at Livorno and wore the red coat with one silver epaulette, his nephew was already beginning to rule the roast. In reality it was Vincent's invitation to dine which Anthony accepted.

Vincent would put his hand on his friend's shoulder and tow him upstairs to the long dining-room where the family ate. Although the windows gave onto the Piazza d'Arme the room was in Germany. There was a great Nuremberg stove at one end, a long rack with steins and cannikins against one wall and little, carved hanging-shelves on the other. The table was long and massive, supported by wooden Corinthian columns ending in claws. Set about it were dark, high-backed, Gothic chairs with a wealth of meticulous carving in which a frieze of bears pursued by men in medieval costume armed with crossbows predominated. For some reason or other the pursuit of the bears was not occasionally interrupted by an angel blowing a trumpet out of a wooden cloud.

371

The effect of this room and of the chairs in particular was peculiar. Anthony had never seen anything like it. It was astonishing to see a Corinthian column ending in claws. Evidently things beyond the Rhine rested upon a different pediment. It was somehow like the German language. His Latin, all the past he knew, did not help him much here. Also there was a peculiar cheerfulness and cleanliness about the apartment.

Under the windows, in which a hundred brilliant flowers bloomed in boxes, sat a pale-faced little girl in a kirtle, with straw-coloured hair peeping out under her white, starched cap. She was knitting, although she was only about eleven years old, like any Hausfrau. Beside her a doll sat looking at her with large china eyes. The name of the little Mädchen was Anna. She was Vincent's cousin. When the two young men entered the room she would come forward, curtsy, and put up her cool little cheek to be kissed. Anthony was charmed with her. While the servants were laying the long, white table-cloth he would sit down on the floor beside her and listen to her talk. At first it was all in Italian but as time went on and he began to understand her she lapsed gradually into broad Hamburg Deutsch.

German, indeed, was the chief thing which Anthony acquired from his long intimacy with Vincent and the Franks. That he should pick up another language without thinking about it was merely a continuation of the normal order of his existence. Little else but German was spoken at the table in the Frank establishment and Anthony could soon join in boldly. Occasionally he aroused a good-natured laugh and Anna would correct him. From her he learned most of the German he knew, and he never heard it spoken without recalling the gentle tones of her voice.

While Vincent was donning some gorgeous attire for the afternoon sally, Anthony listened to stories of Hamburg from Anna: to tales of a never-to-be-forgotten visit to Helgoland in the company of one Tante Rachel Rickmers of Bremerhaven. White cliffs were there.

How green the pastures were above them! The sea gnawed at the land like a bone! Vincent had once taken her to the Gymnasium of Professor Carl F. Hipp. She herself had actually sat on his august knee while he "with condescending illustrious eyeshine" talked to so small a girl. Ach, how beautiful were those days! When would they be going back to Germany?

Meanwhile she was feeding her birds, and dressing her doll for dinner. Meanwhile Uncle Otto had appeared at the door, kicked off his Turkish slippers and roared for a stein of beer, which he drank at a gulp to cut the Italian dust out of his throat. "In hot countries the best brew lacks zest," he would exclaim, spit, and dive into his own chamber to change into bright raiment which like his nephew he particularly affected, or, if guests were expected, into his consular uniform of which he was inordinately proud.

After a short Lutheran grace, in which it seemed strange to Anthony that no one crossed himself, the meal began, usually with a buttermilk soup with boiled cherries floating in it of which Uncle Otto was very fond. The smell of beer and sauerkraut would always have penetrated the apartment. There were various pickled meats, Rhine wines, sausages and Pfannkuchen, boiled vegetables with vinegar on them, and, as a slight concession to the locality, always a smoking dish of spaghetti with liver sauce. There was about this German meal a certain acid tang which Anthony had not met elsewhere. At first he disliked it, but it was not long before both its quantity and its bitter-sweet flavours often rendered the food which he had been used to somewhat insipid. Still he could never really like sour things nor control his face when he met them. Anna laughed. For this her mother never failed to reprove her.

It was truly remarkable the quantity of beer which the firm of *Otto Frank & Company*, both uncle and nephew, could stow away. At least a shipload a year, thought Anthony. He looked at them with astonishment.

"The most profound difference between men on the

373

continent of Europe," said Uncle Otto, wiping the foam from his lips, "is between wine drinkers and beer guzzlers. Religion is nothing to be compared to it. Religions change; beer and wine remain. Make up your mind before you are forty where you intend to spend your declining years, whether in a beer or in a wine land. It will make all the difference between a vivacious and a complacent old age."

"What are you going to do with that vivacious wardrobe of yours then, Uncle Otto, if you go back to Germany?" asked Vincent. "It would only be tolerated on an old man in a wine-drinking place. It is, I should say, decidedly a product of the joyous grape; to be conceived of only by an Italian tailor in his cups."

"Ach!" replied his uncle. "Herr Gott! I am not old yet, neither have I gone back to Germany already to beer alone. Besides, when that time comes it will be so distant as to make all these fine costumes out of date."

"Fine costumes, indeed!" continued Vincent who knew that the vainglory of his uncle's raiment was a weak point in his armour. "You should see them, Anthony, the glories of our Capo della Casa; six embroidered and laced coats from azure to sunset-glow, a bottle-green, gold-frogged wedding coat, satin breeches to match, rhinestone buckles in filigree, a sword with a snakeskin hilt and an emerald. Du Lieber! and all of French make, all out of fashion already."

Here his uncle fairly snarled at him.

"I told you so," continued the incorrigible nephew, "I told you that the English cut was coming in. If you had only taken my advice and had your tailor copy the wardrobes of some of the young milords who dine at your own table you would now be in the swim as I am."

Here he leaned back and displayed his London watch fob, his neat but gorgeous vest, the broad, double-breasted coat that was just coming into style. Herr Frank roared at him. All that Vincent had said was true.

It generally took the soft voice of Frau Elisabeth to smooth over these occasions. To her this mere ruffling of the surface of her husband's complacency was a stirring of her own depths. Her voice was like oil. Presently Uncle Otto would tell his one and only joke. Something about a Dutchman who swallowed peaches whole and complained that the stones hurt his throat. They would all laugh at him, and pleased at the success of his joke he would rise smiling.

A bell was struck, the servants cleared the remains of the meal rapidly. Another cover was laid. Frau Frank again took her place at the head of the table for the "second cover," and as Uncle Otto, Vincent, and Anthony walked out the paying guests of the establishment trooped in. Anthony would look back. The face of the German woman would be solemn with a silent grace, the heads of the travellers, mostly English, bowed, and little Anna would be sitting in her chair again knitting, with the birds hopping about above her.

Uncle Otto would lead the way to his desk. "Do, my good nephew, have a look at this correspondence," he would say. "I need your advice about it—and thine too, Herr Adverso, the Spanish is difficult." Then he would go away leaving Vincent to settle all the pressing problems of the day.

The two young men would work together over the letters. Vincent's trust in Anthony was absolute. There was no question here of the old rivalry of the two commercial houses. Knotty problems were discussed on their merits, as if confidences could never be betrayed, and in the process both of them learned respect for each other's experience and powers of decision. After the replies to the piles of correspondence had been written and various directions noted, they would look up at each other and laugh to think how helpless and pompous Uncle Otto was in the face of the simplest difficulties—and how able they were themselves. How pitiable was the vain old man! Vincent would shoot the ledgers back into their racks. Then they would both take up their hats and gloves, give each other a whisking, take a last reassuring glimpse into a small bit of mirror, and sally forth into the Strada Ferdinanda canes in hand.

Chapter Twenty-One

Adventures of a Shepherdess

I T WAS fashionable to walk in the strada from half
past three to five o'clock. But you must appear to
be going somewhere, about to make a call, or at
least prepared to meet up with friends to make supper
engagements and rendezvous for the evening. All the
world made it a point to know just exactly where it
was bound for while walking on the Strada Ferdinanda between half past three and five. Hence, if you
did not have an engagement you assumed one.

At first Anthony would have had to assume one had
it not been for Vincent. But with that popular young
gentleman's arm linked in his own he was always sure
of a supper engagement before the castle clock struck
five. For there was no one more certain of getting a
promising party of young bloods together for the
evening than Vincent Nolte. At worst you could always
turn up at the galleries of Signore Terrini, the painter,
now grown prosperous and fat, surrounded by the
phlegmatic portraits of the purse-proud or the originals
of them eating cakes and sipping wine. Signore Terrini

was now the only painter in Italy who could still make his nudes look absolutely naked. "True to life" in every particular. For that he was admired by the foreign merchants who composed his clientele, and his studio, which contrived to hint of naughtiness, with some canvases turned to the wall, yet remained at the hour of cake and claret, or gooseberry wine, "elegant." In Livorno it was even taken for a salon.

Here on any afternoon two well dressed young men introduced by "the master" were sure of not being permitted to look forward to a lonely evening. This was an unfailing resource. But after a while it was unnecessary. Social prestige like any other ponderous body when once set in motion acquires momentum. Attracted into the orbit of Vincent, sometimes an eccentric one, Anthony was soon whirling by his own proper motion. It was pleasant, he found, thus to glide along.

Several of the impressive doorways along the strada were in a few months' time quite familiar. It was soon evident to both Vincent and Anthony that the daughters of bankers provided not only the most substantial collations but the most luxurious transportation to the opera. To call on anyone whose father did not at least keep a coach was soon, unless other attractions were unusual, voted beneath their mutual dignity. Theatre nights particularly were those upon which they chose to shine.

When there was a company at the opera or a band of actors in town, *that* afternoon they would only walk the length of the street once merely to be in good form. Then they would turn back to the piazza. There one of them would stand in line for a few minutes chatting with other young dandies while waiting for the half-blind clerk at the little booth like a sentry box to make out their opera tickets.

The old clerk wrote a beautiful hand but naturally very slowly. It was also necessary to mark down every assignment to the boxes in a book and to call out the name of the purchaser. Thus it was possible to take exception to anyone who was not qualified. There had at one time been duels over certain seats. But times were changing now. The old clerk merely carried out a ritual. A great many people now were vulgar and rich enough merely to send a footman for the pink slip. Knowing and ardent young gentlemen, however, still saw to it that they got a box due their rank.

"The Stall of the Angels, tonight, Signore Adverso." How it thrilled Anthony to be unexceptionable as he folded the long, pink slip three times precisely, counted his change into his tasselled purse, and stepped aside with a slight bow and flourish. Provided, of course, that the next in line was a gentleman. If it was a footman you held your place and permitted a gentleman to step up. Of late there had been a good deal of grumbling about that from the lackeys. Like a first rumbling of revolution among the lower orders there seemed to be some tendency among these fellows to combine. The gentlemen, of course, became even more punctilious. Buying a ticket was now like attending a Spanish levée. At last one afternoon a burly Swiss footman was positively insolent and required a touch of Vincent's cane to settle the matter while Anthony held his place. There was to be a double bill that night and the queue was a long one.

"The Revolution has not yet arrived here, my fine fellow," said Vincent.

"But soon," muttered the Swiss rubbing his arm. His fellow servants seemed about to make the prophecy come true. The young bucks gathered about Vincent. He laughed and stood the man off while Anthony coolly bought the tickets and handed his place over to Luigi Pontrovo, the bishop's secretary. After that there was no more trouble. But class feeling was already beginning to run high. The story of even so trivial an incident spread. That day the names of Anthony and Vincent were passed about from lip to lip on the Corso.

That evening they were pointed out in the Stall of the Angels sitting with Maddalena Strozzi, the daughter of a Florentine banker, and her friend Mlle. de Rhan visiting her from Nantes. In the sconces at the side of the stall, and in the two high candelabra provided extra, burned the best French beeswax candles which the Casa da Bonnyfeather imported. It was considered by all present to be an extravagant and nice little attention to the young ladies. The tallow dips provided by the management in the other stalls guttered in drafts and dripped sadly. One had to be careful how one used one's fan with only a tallow dip just above. In the Stall of the Angels the fans fluttered merrily and carelessly as fans should, and from the front of the box shimmered a peculiarly clear, yellow light. Farther back in the shadows sat Donna Anna Montefeltro, the duenna of the banker's daughter. Her fat, powdered face like a white mask had a huge laced and ribboned coiffure above it that disappeared into the darkness of the box curtain. Her eyes, which never seemed to take time off even to wink, glittered like brown, polished wood.

The bill that night was a double one, *La Veillée et la Matinée Villageoise* out of compliment to the large number of French émigrés in the audience, followed by Schröder's comedy of *Die Unglückliche Ehe aus Delicatessen*. The latter was given at the request of a number of German merchants who had not often in Livorno the opportunity of hearing a play in their own tongue.

Vincent was forced to translate the German for the two girls and Donna Montefeltro. "From too much refinement come unhappy matches," he whispered, touching Maddalena on the arm when he thought no one was watching, and looking wise. She looked at him with mock surprise over her fan. The powder creases in Montefeltro's face assumed a conventional, shocked design.

"There is no chorus I hope to this German play with the revolting title, Signore Nolte," she said. "Maddalena is not permitted to view the ballet as yet. You promised me, you know." Vincent hastened to reassure her.

"There will be little or no dancing, signora. You know this is not the local staff on the stage this evening but the company which has been thrust out of Brussels and is on its travels. They will go by way of Vienna to Hamburg, avoiding Buonaparte. Nothing could be more genteel than that. In addition all the chief figures in the plays tonight are men. You see I have even been too careful. But Mees and Bergamis are both famous actors. The main event, indeed, is the fact that Debrülle who acts Count Klingsberg in the German comedy has borrowed my uncle's uniform coat for the part and it will undoubtedly be recognized. My uncle and his wife are sitting just across from us there. Watch the fun." Vincent bowed to his uncle who somewhat pompously replied.

Uncle Otto was not aware that his coat had been "borrowed." He sat bored enough beside his frau through the rather short performance in French which came first. He looked somewhat puzzled at the polite applause which followed and from which he refrained. Not having been able to find his consul's uniform that evening had made him a bit glum. He sat waiting for the German play to begin, sullenly, dressed in his most gorgeous, pink, French costume.

Already he was conscious that what his nephew had said about his clothes was true. In the long, frogged paletot and knee-breeches he already felt somehow a little out-of-age. Secretly it was as if he were going about in a dressing gown and drawers. He looked over the audience for consolation. About half of it was still in wigs and velvets, the more distinguished half, of course! What was coming over the world? All these young men in their own hair, wide-breasted coats, and breeches half-way down their calves! And the women with those thin, Greek night-gowns, a tight ribbon under their breasts! Uncle Otto snorted.

A vague feeling of uneasiness, of unexpected and undesired change in all the ways of life and the familiar habiliments of things sent him suddenly cold. He wished he were back in Hamburg; that he had on his consul's uniform, the long, red coat with the gold buttons and the silver epaulette on one shoulder. In that he looked like a British general. The feeling of authority and position which it gave him would have warmed his heart. Where was it? He turned again to his wife, who was breathing heavily in her stays, to renew his reproaches. At least she might keep his wardrobe in order! The dispute grew loud enough to amuse those sitting near by. Across the theatre Uncle Otto could see young Vincent whispering into the ear of the banker's daughter. What did that young dog care in his high choker and loud, English watch fob. The thing flashed in your eyes clear across the pit. Wax candles for the mädchens, moonstone cufflinks! He leaned back and fanned his purple cheeks. The curtain went up for the entr'acte.

For Anthony this proved to be the event of the evening. It was one of those little plotless pieces in which poetry, moonlight, sentiment, and music waked the old court tradition of shepherdesses and the sylvan village in the background to a brief charming life. Something just a little old-fashioned about it now gave it a hint of yearning. This was announced by the low, full-throated overture of the fiddles and the baritone singer Debrülle. He, dressed as a shepherd, warbled a melodious reveille to his love still asleep in a village wrapped—behind a gauze curtain—in the mists of morning.

A low, happy reply of girls' voices, the high, feminine note of the violins, and the clever imitation of a cock's crowing brought a ripple of pleasure and amusement from the audience. Anthony had managed to secure Mlle. de Rhan's hand and an electric thrill from the returned pressure of his fingers caused him to breathe deeply. The gauze curtain was withdrawn. A few more candles in rose-coloured lanterns contrived to throw on the painted, rustic village, now plainly revealed backstage, the illusion of sunrise. The music quickened into dance-time with the theme of a song emerging. Anthony leaned forward.

The great apron of the stage swept out into the semi-darkness of the audience, ringed round by its half-mystic, mellow candle footlights. The little hood for the head of the leader of the orchestra cast a wide fan-like shadow across it. Down there you could dimly see the white, upturned faces of the audience, wigs, and the flutter of a fan, the twinkle of women's jewels. Debrülle was standing in the middle of the stage with outstretched arms, pleading in a rich baritone for his love to

> "Come forth, come forth,
> Into the morning light,
> The dew is on the rose,
> The rose, the birds begin . . ."

when from the preposterously bucolic houses on each side of the grass-painted street emerged a troop of milkmaids in green stockings and red bodices. Half of them carried milking stools and the others bright, silver buckets. They advanced now, clicking their heels, and performing various evolutions with the stools and buckets in that kind of dance which it is well known that all milkmaids indulge in just at sunrise.

> "The dew is on the rose,
> The birds begin, begin,
> The milkmaids rise . . ."

Insisted the now impatiently impassioned voice of the baritone—

> "But where is she, the charm—
> The charming shepherdess
> My morning love . . ."

It seemed as if the music had reached the crest of yearning.

"Ah, where indeed?" thought Anthony. He had forgotten her for a moment. Where had she gone, his dear, little girl? The very word "girl" sent a thrill through him. He lingered over it as if it tasted sweet. Would there never be any answer to all his useless inquiries? She had driven through the Porta Pisa—and disappeared into the great world beyond. Would he never see Angela, Angela, Angela again? The trembling fibres of his fresh, boyish body stretched to the last, high, pathetic fall of the shop-worn chords.

How much greater his sorrow for her loss, his need of her, had been than he had ever known before! The music opened new depths in him. It was all dark and lonely there. The strange, pallid memory of Faith moved slipperily about there in the shadow-play. He shuddered. "Angela!" Angela could save him.

In a little village like that they might have had a house together; be happy forever. Why not? He could forget everything there, even the Madonna. He would have Angela. Have her! He choked. Unknown to him the poetry of his own longing had transposed the cheap little scene before him into the most exquisite art. How beautiful it was! "The dew is on the rose." He could smell it; feel it on his own bare feet as on the grass those lost, lovely mornings out on the road. In love with Angela! "Gone, gone, lost, *lala, lala la-a*," the fiddles wailed. "O God, even a poor convent child can pray to you! Listen to me." There were tears in his eyes for himself. He could not see Uncle Otto over there any more. He dropped Mlle. de Rhan's hand to dash them away furtively. Her lips curled in surprise.

Then the violins, as violins do, surpassed themselves. What had seemed the summit of ecstasy proved only an overture after all. They went up and up into a madrigal of pure happiness. The baritone paused.

The boy was beside himself now. The warm air and perfumes from the stalls below poured up and intoxicated him. Someone just underneath must be crushing lime leaves in her hand. His temples and wrists throbbed to the music. From behind the wings came a girl's voice, fresh, but rich and full-throated as a song from the orange groves of Sicily heard far up on the slopes in the early morning.

A little shepherdess with her crook, in red, high-heeled shoes and a short apron-skirt, now advanced down-stage answering with high thrilling notes the amative welcome of her swain. Their mutual warblings moved the audience to applause. But Anthony could only *see* that. In his own ears the blood was crackling. That voice, the way she pointed her toes, the movements of her limbs were deliciously familiar. Could it be . . .? He felt the sweat running down his back under his coat.

She was wearing an absurd little straw hat, wide-brimmed at one side, curved up archly at the other. As yet he could not see under it. Then she turned her face upward into the light. It was Angela.

He was afraid it was a dream. It would escape him. His knees fell apart and he leaned farther forward clear over the front of the box. He would have called out to her but his voice failed. Then he remembered where he was. Surely she would see him. She was looking directly at him now. He made his arm move. Someone else's hand on the end of it seemed to take out his handkerchief and shake it. Presently in the middle of the dream he became aware that Angela was lifting up her arms toward him and singing at the box. Oh, yes, he and Vincent—and the other girls were in it. It was real! He smiled and moved his lips in their old formula. He knew she would hear what he was saying. He laughed aloud.

Some of the faces in the audience now began to be turned toward the Stall of the Angels. It was plain that between the young shepherdess on the stage and the young man hanging over the railing with a trembling handkerchief in his hand there was an understanding. The baritone gladly took up the local lead and the song was finished off obviously addressed to the good-looking young folks in the box with the clear wax candles.

Anthony sat back dizzy with happiness and lax with relief. She had come back to him out of the country where she had been for a while. In that delightful little village . . . Of course! How could he have ever doubted it? He had found her again. Angela had come back! Far down on the stage he saw two white hands toss him a kiss. The handkerchief replied. The curtain fell on a round of laughter and applause. People kept looking up. Now for the first time Anthony felt terribly embarrassed.

Across the pit Mrs. Udney raised her glasses to examine the box which had been receiving so much attention. She was sitting with her husband the English consul, her daughter Florence, and a young Scotch merchant, David Parish, the scion of a rising commercial house at Antwerp. David, she hoped, was the young man to be. Mrs. Udney smiled as she watched the obviously fluttered party opposite and started somewhat as her focus finally fixed upon Anthony. She thought she had never seen a face so completely happy. And yet where had she seen it before? Just then Anthony happened to look up, a streak of light gilding his hair. Mrs. Udney suddenly remembered him looking up at her from under a priest's hat while she stood at her library window years before.

"My dear," she exclaimed giggling with excitement, "look who is in the box there!" She handed her glasses to Florence. "Do you recognize your prince of the church? An old sweetheart of Florence's," she continued, smiling on David Parish and touching him on the arm with her fan. It suited her plans quite well to claim a fashionably dressed young man in a box with two bankers' daughters as her own daughter's first conquest. Florence looked. Her small chin took on a serious angle for a minute under the binoculars. She blushed.

"Yes, I remember." She might have said more, her mother thought. Mr. Parish and Mr. Udney had each had his turn. The former smiled complacently.

"My word!" exclaimed Mr. Udney, "Father Xavier and I made no mistake. Mr. Bonnyfeather has certainly done well by his appren—"a tight squeeze from his wife stopped him—"ahem, by his ward."

"Decidedly," chimed in Mrs. Udney. "We must have him in to tea again," she looked sidewise at Parish. "What do you think, Florence?"

"Certainly, mother. Will he sleep in the spare bedroom this time?" asked Florence, seemingly out of a reverie. Her mother could have pinched her. The consul chuckled. Mr. Parish looked at him a little uncomfortably. The curtains went up on *Too Much Refinement Makes Unhappy Matches*—in German.

Anthony sat in a trance through the comedy. He had

even forgotten that Mlle. de Rhan had a hand, that she existed. Mademoiselle felt her throat tighten a little with jealous chagrin. She would scarcely have credited the young creature in mouse-grey who sat next to her with having known an actress. He was deeper than she had supposed. Donna Montefeltro was outwardly scandalized and inwardly pleased. The box of her charges had been pleasantly prominent that night. It might pay to cultivate this young Englishman. How innocent he looked. She grinned over her fan, remembering.

With Vincent, Anthony's stock had soared. The young dog! and never to say a word about it! He pawed his friend excitedly but was only shaken off. Presently he and Signorina Strozzi were leaning forward breathlessly waiting for the cue when Uncle Otto's coat should appear. Presently "Count Klingsberg" strutted out. For a few minutes nothing happened. Then someone giggled. A whisper began to run about. "The coat of El Signore Consolino di Amburgo, ah!" Then Uncle Otto became aware of it. He snorted and shook his stick. His nephew bowed back. Even those who could not understand German could understand this. Gusts of applause shook the house. The actor played up to it. The curtain went down on a great hit—and the audience filed out laughing and talking.

Vincent's friends waved at him. The boy's little ears tingled with excitement. He and Anthony had contrived to be the most popular young men in Livorno that night. The girls fluttered their fans in the gay light of public approval and looked pleased and excited, even a little impressed.

As they filed out Anthony looked down on the crowd surging toward the door below. A long poke bonnet with a prim, black bow was for a second turned up toward him. At the bottom of it, as if at the end of a shadowed tunnel, he saw the face of Faith. It was pale, he noticed. Always she seemed to be looking out from shadows. He went cold for an instant. Too bad *she* had to spoil an otherwise perfect evening! But how wonderful it had been. Angela!

On the way out he forgot Faith. The Udneys stopped him. He saw Florence standing behind her mother. How lovely and fragile she had grown! Only the brown, golden hair and the deep grey eyes of the plump little girl remained. "Anthony, mother is asking you to tea." She laughed as she withdrew her hand. It was true. And she had called him by his first name. He drew himself together to reply in almost too perfect English. Vincent was now included in the invitation. "This is Mr. David Parish," said Florence.

"How do you, *Mr.* David Parish?" said Anthony. Everybody laughed except Parish. "Yes, indeed, they would both come."

"Delighted," added Vincent, telling the literal truth and looking with rapturous approval at Anthony. His friend seemed to know everybody. The English consul's daughter! Vincent whistled under his breath as he drew on his gloves.

They went out and bowed Maddalena and Mlle. de Rhan into their carriage. Donna Anna was by this time completely persuaded of the eligibility of the two young men. The English consul's wife was impeccable. Yes, they might call on the two signorinas tomorrow. The carriage rolled away.

Anthony and Vincent turned to join the crowd of young men standing behind them. There was considerable chaffing to be endured. "Who was she?" "How did Anthony know her?" After some minutes of hearty German backslapping and heavy jokes, they managed to put them off. The two were left alone at last standing on the curb.

Anthony clutched Vincent's sleeve. "How can I speak to her—now?" he cried. Vincent laughed. After all there were some things this English friend of his did not know.

"That's easy enough," he exclaimed, "follow me." He led the way toward the dim lantern over the stage door. Moonlight pricked out the pictures and messages scrawled upon the bricks of the old theatre. It was a warm, calm night. The noise of carriage wheels died away through the streets. By this time everybody would be taking the air on the Corso.

Vincent would have liked to be walking there, too. By this time the news of the doings of the theatre would be noised about and it would be pleasant to be greeted knowingly by acquaintances. But this adventure of Anthony's was also alluring, worth following up just to see what would happen. Anthony was proving to be somewhat mysterious he felt. Nevertheless, one would like to walk on the Corso, be in two places at the same time. Besides it would never do to go home till Uncle Otto had cooled down about the coat. No, he would have to make a night of it.

They gave a small coin to the man at the door and went in. Behind the curtain the theatre seemed vast and dark. A few lanterns hung here and there in the wings lighting up bits of stacked scenery like autumnal glimpses of a valley seen through the clouds. The wreck of the little village lay strewn about. They stumbled over a pile of the milkmaids' buckets, making a ferocious din. Finally someone emerged from the wings shouting, "This way, this way, messieurs," and led the way down narrow, brick stairs in the wall to the cell-like dressing rooms. A door opened letting out a wash of light and revealing a man standing there stripped to the waist and washing the grease paint off his face with a coarse towel. It was Debrülle himself.

"Come in," he half shouted, "I thought you would come for it." He handed Vincent his uncle's coat with the silver epaulette. "I am a thousand times obliged to you, my dear fellow," he hurried on, "it was the hit of the evening. Ah, your friend! The young man in the box." The actor murmured his pleasure. "We are also greatly indebted to you, signore,—I suppose," he added seemingly not so enthusiastic over Anthony's part as he was over the coat. He continued to address himself to Vincent. A flat, stale smell of old cigars, sloe gin, and damp cellar permeated everything.

"Can you tell me, sir, where I can find Angela?" said Anthony after a while, unable to refrain any longer.

"Angela! Ah! the little shepherdess, I suppose?" said Debrülle. "No," he continued dubiously, "she has gone to her lodgings by this time. We are a very genteel company, *very* strict, you know." He winked at Vincent. Anthony could not hide his disappointment. So she had not left him any message and it would not do to inquire. "They were very strict." Presently Vincent rose to leave. Debrülle shook hands with Anthony with an amused gleam in his eyes.

"It was a great pleasure, sir, to hear you sing tonight," the young man gasped. He was sincere enough in this and he had to say something.

The face of the actor lit up radiantly. "I am glad to hear you say so, my dear boy," said he. "It is not often we receive a compliment so genuine, after teasing our admirers—and so well deserved," he added laughing again. "Of course, she left something for you. Unless the girls go home early, you know, they are bothered to death. Here it is." He rustled about among his paint pots and cigar stubs and produced a small red card. Anthony grasped it blushing.

They stumbled up the brick steps together, Uncle Otto's coat on Vincent's arm. There was a ripping sound. "Heavens!" said Debrülle striking a spark, "you have tramped off the epaulette." It was true. Vincent turned a little pale. "Gott! I shall be sued by your uncle, the consul, now. I do not envy you either." Debrülle went on up, laughing, his voice rumbling through the wings. At the door he stopped under the smoking lantern and scribbled something on a card.

"There," he said, handing it to Vincent, "come to the matinée tomorrow. Thanks again! I wish you both luck. You with your uncle and the coat, and you, monsieur, with—a happy pastoral night!" He flourished his gold-headed stick and went clicking down the sidewalk toward the Corso. A stave of the song to the shepherdess drifted back through the moonlight. The gin made him place his feet carefully. He stopped to look back once and raised his hand. It looked like a blessing. They both laughed.

"But what *am* I going to do about it?" asked Vincent, anxiously examining the coat from the shoulder of which the epaulette drooped disconsolately. To Anthony the predicament of his friend seemed trivial. He went close to the lantern and by its smoky light examined the little red card.

Signora Bovino
Explains the Past
and
Elucidates the Future,
Casts Horoscopes, and Reads Palms.
Her Art is Invulnerable
on the Fifth Floor
Strada Calypso

Satisfactory Amatory Entertainment
on the First.

Underneath was a dainty sketch of a small shepherdess with angel's wings and a ribboned crook. Anthony laughed. He thought of the longitude machine on the roof at Signora Bovino's. Well, he would take care not to waken Mr. Williams. Doubtless he would be taking the moon. Let him. His pupil would have a different use for it tonight "on the first floor." A recklessness and warmth intoxicated the boy as he stood looking at the card. It was his first adventure—all his own. A faint haze came between the card and his eyes. He felt suddenly competent, by "the art of Madame Bovino," to foretell the immediate future. He grasped Vincent by the arm.

"Come on," he said. "Forget that small trouble." Vincent kept fingering the rent in the coat. "I'll tell you what we'll do. Tomorrow we will take it to a tailor and have *two* epaulettes sewed on it. You can tell your uncle it is a compliment from his friend the actor who knows what the uniform of a consul ought to be." He linked his arm in Vincent's sweeping him along by his own recklessness. In the moonlight it was as if they were both a little drunk. Anything seemed possible. Vincent felt his friend to be inspired. Recklessness was always the mood most contagious for Vincent.

"I think there might be someone waiting for you, too," whispered Anthony excitedly as they swept along. "I know it!" He had completely taken the lead now. Vincent gave a low whistle. He felt the warmth and tenseness of his friend's arm. The two hastened even faster.

As they turned into the street, of high, narrow houses with flat roofs where Anthony had so often come by day to work out his problems with the stertorous ex-mate, he looked upward by habit. Sure enough, on the house of Signorina Bovino the outline of the old sailor could be seen against the skyline "shooting the moon." Anthony cautioned Vincent and they began to walk softly. It would never do to have that enormous voice hail them from the roof. They crossed the street quietly, and keeping close to the wall arrived safely at the door. A few lights glimmered from the lower shutters, but the door was barred and the house was silent. It would not do to arouse the mate by using the bell pull. He would be peering over the parapet instantly. Vincent tapped at the lowest shutter. He was beginning to take the lead again. After another tap it was opened. A white hand came forth. Vincent slipped something into it. "The signora," he said.

"Have you been here before?" asked Anthony feeling indignant.

"No, no, it is always the way, you know," answered his friend offhand while tossing the consul's uniform over his shoulder nonchalantly. "When you see a hand, put something in it." A mischievous smile pre-empted Vincent's lips. "I have a notion to put Uncle Otto's coat on."

"Oh, don't, Vincent, you are in trouble enough with your uncle," whispered Anthony.

Just then the door swung back noiselessly, revealing Signora Bovino in a loose, linen wrapper. She started to laugh, but Anthony put his finger on his lips, and pointed upward. She nodded and beckoned them in.

"So you have come for a lesson in navigation, Meester Adverso. No! What can it be then?"

Anthony looked so confused that she laid her hand on his arm. A senile giggle escaped her. "Come, I know. She has told me. Madre Maria! I do not blame you. She is a dear piece, and in the best front chamber. Clean linen! And she will let no one else come up now these two nights since she came. A lady! But your friend here. Is he with you?"

"Yes, oh, *no!*" said Anthony seeing what she meant. "I thought perhaps you could . . . at least . . ."

"But yes! The whole troupe is staying here. You know, signore, I do not keep a regular house, though." A look of fierce respectability stiffened her. "Only transients. They usually have their own gentlemen." She held up the candle inspecting Vincent. The epaulette caught her eye. She looked pleased. "Ah, of the military, I see." Vincent swaggered. "You do not need to be afraid, sir, and hide it. Everything here is of the greatest discretion. I merely tell fortunes." She winked. They went upstairs very quietly. A smell of garlic and perfume permeated the passage. Presently the old woman swung her candle up.

"Her room," she said to Anthony. "Good night, Meester—" she laid her finger on her lips and laughed. In the dying candlelight as she led Vincent down the corridor Anthony could see there was no paint on the panels. Could this be the door to happiness? It was dark now in the hall, but there was moonlight flowing under the threshold. He leaned against the door-post, a lump in his throat. How long it had been! He took a deep breath.

"Angela!"

There was the sound of someone stirring but no answer. Silence. He tapped lightly on the door. The sound of padding feet.

"Who is it?—you?"

He leaned close to the panel whispering, "Arnolfo, Maria, Nicolò, Beatrice, Claudia—Angela Maea."

393

Someone caught her breath. The door opened suddenly. He stumbled forward into the moonlight and found himself in her arms.

"Oh, I thought I had lost you, Angela Maea!"

"Then you *did* care, you never forgot me," she cried low, clinging to him. "Anthony, how you are trembling! Let me see you." She led him to the window. "Oh, yes, it is you, *you*. I thought I might never see you again." She looked up at him in the moonlight with a half-doubt and trouble in her face.

"What is it?" he whispered. "Aren't you really glad to see me?"

"I am only half as happy as I expected to be," she said, hiding her face against his shoulder. "I cannot see you for the tears." Her thin night-gown fluttered about her and he wrapped her closer.

They went over to the bed and sat down. She lay back, breathing dreamfully and contentedly with her hands under her head, looking up at him. In the moony twilight of the room it was like a dream to both of them.

"Let me come behind the fountain to you, Angela. I saw you that way once. Did you know? Both of us that way now! There is no one else but you and me now."

"No one," she sighed. "You are all that is left of those days. They are all gone but you, did you know that?" He felt her tears again. "Only 'Anthony' and 'Angela.' There is no use saying the other names any more. No one will answer."

"Angela!"

He felt himself overcome by an access of pity for her. It merged into passive tenderness, then into a kind of wild weeping passion for what he did not know, something he felt through her. Presently they were utterly quiet. A deep, pagan peace slowly and surely enveloped them. He closed his eyes.

Down an immense vista as if a poke bonnet had been elongated into a straw telescope he saw the gloomy face of Faith Paleologus looking at him hungrily out

394

of the shadows. It was an immense shock, the reverberations of which echoed through Angela.

"Tell me, tell me! Anthony, what is it?"

He raised his head from her breast. "That woman, Faith! She is here in the room. The night after you left. Angela!" He was crying to her for help. She soothed him, smoothing the disturbing vision away with her soft hands, putting her mouth to his. Her breath permeated him. It was well again. Only Angela could do that, he knew, only Angela. With her he could forget everything. And she was his now, forever. His strength flooded back at the thought. An undisturbed and perfect pleasure of both the inner life and the body perfectly shared, all else forgotten, rest, and comfort as of a divine blessing freely imparted and necessarily given engulfed them both. Outside the moonlight died from the street and slowly paled into day. On the bed the youth and the young girl slept as one in being, their curls and legs tangled together as if they lay on an island beach washed by the ocean of Nirvana. Towards morning he began to dream.

He saw a wave run up a beach, leaving a faint, lacy trace on the sand. Then another, and other. Each destroyed the trace of the one preceding and left its own. All the outlines they left on the sand were different. Yet they were all the same, all pictures of the wave of waves. It went on forever.

Then the noise of the waves merged slowly into the murmur of the leaves on the great plane tree in the court of the convent. He was lying in the pool of that place, looking up into the moonlit branches of the tree. The pigeons were faintly awake. Like the blood murmuring in his ears he could hear their sleepy love-making. He lay and floated, happy in an ecstasy of calm. The waters were troubled no more.

Then in the shadows he saw that both the bronze boy and his lost brother were there. The lost twin had come back! Their limbs seemed to melt into the roots of the tree in a quiescent embrace. The Madonna was there, too. She emerged slowly out of the light of the tree. It was the woman of the statue he knew so well, her features and her grace, but much younger, naked. Her hair seemed caught in the net of leaves and of the stars behind them, and the smile on her lips was without sorrow. There was no child in her arms. Slowly she merged herself in the pool. The water rose and he felt himself washed over the brink. But he could still see himself there. He looked down upon himself over the brim as he had when a child. His own utterly happy face came up to meet him as it used to do—the eyes wide with a dream, the hair burning and golden, laughing, dazzling.

He opened his eyes to see the vision better. The sun was streaming in through a chink in the shutter. Angela lay beside him brown and rosy, covered with little glints of the dawn as if the sun were shining on her through the leaves of the great tree. He drew her even more closely to him. She looked at him out of innumerable centuries with his own completely happy smile. For an hour they lay so. Then the noise in the street began.

Someone in the room below them began to stir. They could hear the mumble of talk, movings around, slaps, small outcries, and laughter. Presently the door banged and a man with heavy boots departed. A bed creaked once again and all was silent. Then there were funny little snores.

They laughed themselves, and began to talk in low voices. How easy it was to talk to Angela, like having thoughts with another self. Half of the things you said were already answered. She asked eagerly about the Casa da Bonnyfeather. He told her all that had happened, also about Faith.

"I knew last night," she said.

The quarrel with Toussaint, Mr. Bonnyfeather, the new friend Vincent, the life about town—how clear and meaningful it all seemed now as he told it to her.

"But you, Angela, where have *you* been? Here I have been telling you all about myself." She tossed her curls at him.

"Even you, Anthony. They always do."

"They, who are *they?*" he asked.

"Men," she said whimsically, "all of them."

It was the first shock of disillusion after the dream. So she had known others before him then! His mouth went hard . . .

"But you had Faith," she said.

"No," he replied indignantly, "she had me. I . . ." he stopped, colouring and ashamed. It was true. She drew him down to her again.

"Listen, I will tell you," she whispered. "Do not blame me. I loved you. But I thought I would never see you again when we drove through the Porta Pisa that night. You remember! We had not gone five miles before the carriages stopped in a lonely place. It was dark by then. One of the soldiers came back and took all of us children up to the front carriage. They had dragged father out on the grass and he was lying there shivering and singing. Then they began to take out the money bags and divide them up. Mother tried to fight them but they tied her hands behind her back, and a rag around her face. We were too frightened to say anything. She sat by father, rolling her eyes. Some of the soldiers and drivers started to quarrel over the money but the sergeant drew his pistol and made them take what he gave them.

" 'If you come back to Livorno,' the sergeant said, 'you will get this.' He gave Arnolfo a terrible kick and pointed his pistol at mother's head! 'The guards at the gate understand. Do you see!' He threw one small purse in mother's lap. Then he herded us all into one carriage and made that man drive off with us toward Pisa, swearing he would cut our throats if we made a noise.

"After about an hour the new coachman stopped and made us all get out again. He took the small purse from mother that the sergeant had given her. She begged and held up Luigi, but he only laughed. 'Pisa is there, not far,' he said, and whipped up his horses back to Livorno. Father was dead drunk.

"We got mother's hands untied and waited till morning. We started toward Pisa. Arnolfo and I tried to carry father. He became violent. We could see he was not drunk now but out of his mind. He cursed mother for hours. Finally some men with hay carts came along and took us into the market at Pisa. They had to tie father. We arrived at the door of my grandparents weeping, hungry, and without a scudo. They are very poor. My father who still thought he was rich had to be locked in the cellar. A few days later some men with staves and irons came for him. He shrieked and called out. We did not see him again. He is always going to be mad.

"My grandmother went to her priest about it. After a while he told us that word had come back from Livorno that our story wasn't true. It was the governor, I guess. He and the sergeant. We could do nothing and we were very hungry."

Angela put her hands over her face as if to shut out the memory. He saw tears trickle through her fingers.

"There is more yet. Shall I go on?" He nodded. She waited a while before she could begin.

"At Pisa the smallpox came. Luigi, all the younger ones, died. They would not let us leave the house and there was nothing to eat. One goat. After a while we ate her. Big Angela—her loose skin hung around her like rags! Arnolfo got out one night and ran away.

"At last no one but my grandmother and two of the girls were there. One day the old woman took a broom and beat me with it! 'Go out, big girl, and bring us some money,' she said. 'We starve!' I could not give myself to the soldiers. I was afraid. I begged only enough to keep us alive. My grandmother continued to give me many blows. At last one day I was sitting on the steps of the Duomo when Debrülle, the singer, came along. I went with him. Do you see how it was?"

Anthony lay stretched out, going hot and cold. He was dry-eyed now. So it *had* been that big German with the baritone voice. "I hate him," he said simply.

"Do not. He has been very kind to me. He took me to Milan with him, bought me some clothes, put me on the stage with his company as a flower girl. He taught me to sing. Anthony, I have a lovely voice, they

398

say. I am the shepherdess now. I shall be a great actress some day. The lights, the people! I shall have beautiful clothes, jewels, and see the world. No, he is very good to me, Debrülle, he has been like a father."

"Do you love him?" he asked.

She shook her head. "Not like that, you know. He, he is not with me often," she whispered. "I bear him."

"Then you will not marry me, Angela?" he said. He looked at her with a terrified determination and drew her to him.

"Once," she said, "but not now. It is too late."

"But what are you going to do?" he cried.

"I am going on," she said. "Now I have had you, I am going on." A smile of triumph and tenderness lit her face.

He pleaded with her, but she merely turned her head away and closed her eyes. "Come," she said after a while, "lie on my breast again." Thus they strove to forget together.

Later in the morning the signora knocked at their door. She finally put her head inside the room. "Pardon, last night I forgot to bring you the napkins of pleasure. Here they are now. When you dress yourselves come up to my room. There is a charming breakfast there. Your friend, the man with the great voice, has had it brought in. And you are to come, too, Meester Adverso. Ah! how generous is the noble singer to his shepherdess! Yes, I have heard about you both from his lips. It is true love then. You will bring luck to my house. Come, I will tell your fortunes for nothing. Jesù! how beautiful you are." Her eyes rested on them burning with admiration and regret. "Do not be ashamed," she said. "I was young once. Now there is nothing left but the pleasure of the eyes." She closed the door reluctantly and went upstairs sighing.

They lingered for a while but presently from upstairs the full-chested tones of Debrülle rolled down to them:

> "The dew is on the rose,
> The birds begin, begin,
> The milkmaids rise,

But where is she, the charm—
The charming shepherdess,
My morning love?"

And there was something so whole-hearted and good-natured about those tones that they hastened in spite of themselves to rise and dress.

"You will like him, you see if you don't!" said Angela. Anthony shook his head.

"Yes, yes, you will. For my sake anyway, promise!" She pouted and kissed him. They moved toward the door and opened it. A great pencil of sunlight washed down the stairs. The smell of German coffee and frying sausages rolled down to them. They heard a gay laugh and a cork popped loudly in the apartment of Signora Bovino. The colour heightened in her cheeks. They stood for a minute at the threshold. He caught her to him madly.

"Good-bye, Angela, my own Angela Maea. Oh, you do not know how I love you!"

"But where is she, the charm—
The charming . . . my morning love?"

trolled from upstairs. It was from that voice that he would hold her fast forever.

"You do not know."

"But I do, Anthony, dear, I know. I have found out. I love you. I thank the Virgin I found you again. And now we shall always be like this." She flung her arms around him choking, giving him a long kiss. "Boy, mine, dearest always, some time you will know, too."

"But where is she . . ." began the voice again upstairs.

"Coming, coming, papa mio," she cried; dashed the tears out of her eyes and dragged Anthony over the threshold. The wind banged the door behind them. She ran laughing up the stairs to Debrülle.

She had thanked the Virgin. Well, so would he, the beautiful young Virgin without the child who had come to him last night in the dream. To her then! He stretched out his hands to her. A great peace and calm of completion was on him. He could have, or be, no more than that no matter how long he lived. With or without Angela then! He blew a kiss back at the closed door. Then he went up the stairs.

The apartment of Signora Bovino was a great surprise. It was awash with sunlight that fell through a skylight now wide open. Bright, blooming plants waved in the windows and a far door led out onto the roof where there were tubbed flowers. A great yellow cat lay spread-eagled in the sun out there. And there was a table set with a snowy cloth that flapped lazily. In one corner the signora busied herself over a small charcoal stove. In the other sat Vincent looking happy and foolish with a large German girl on his knees. Debrülle was doing some dance steps and humming to Angela as she copied him, one foot after the other, daintily. The whole room hailed Anthony with a shout. It was impossible not to accept such a welcome. The last bit of ice left for Debrülle thawed under his ardent captivating humour. He clapped Anthony on the back with an undeniable affection.

"You, my prince charming, and your shepherdess have nearly starved us. Didn't you hear me singing to you? In another moment the sausages would have been in flames. Come now, not a minute longer. Herr Nolte, Fräulein . . .? ahem."

"Anthony, Anthony, it is to be *our* breakfast," cried Angela, dancing up. "You and I are to sit at the head of the table." Her eyes were still shining like skies after a rain. She led them all out and they sat down. The old woman beaming and grinning, rapidly set the dishes.

"When you have finished, signora, be pleased to sit down with us," Debrülle said. "Thou, too, wast once a lady I see." From somewhere in the past she summoned a grand curtsy. They all applauded.

"Ladies and gentlemen," said Debrülle, pausing and looking around for anybody who might dare to contradict him, "*Ladies and gentlemen*—This is a kind of impromptu and unofficial wedding breakfast for the

401

charming couple at the head of the table. It is the best under the circumstances," he continued, looking at Anthony significantly, "that we can do. May they always be as happy as they were last night. Always," he added as if by an afterthought—"wherever they are."

They drank with a shout. Over his steaming bowl of coffee Debrülle broke into a German love song that clutched them all by the heart. At the second chorus Vincent chimed in, carried away by the sheer, rank sentiment of it.

"One night at least a wandering knight may have,
    Though disinherited from all the past,
And bear the memory of that burning love—
    And bear that memory with him to the last."

The high, clear voice of Angela trilled in. The boy next to her felt his breath pause as if that moment were too poignant and clear to require an earthly atmosphere to live it.

"And bear that memory with him to the last."

All their voices blent in a long, sentimental, drawn out, dying chord that left them sitting astonished with their own harmony. Indeed, it seemed as if they had not made it themselves. It had been drawn upon an unexpectedly rich account of pleasure, a draft that left happiness undiminished.

Debrülle now opened small brown jugs of Asti Spumante that foamed like Normandy cider. It was clearer and lighter than champagne, a noble morning drink, bringing a glow of joy without heat or thirst. Anthony could see by the way he looked at Angela that Debrülle loved her; loved her with a kind of fatherly pity as if care of her happiness had been conferred on him as his part in life. Anthony understood now the expression on the actor's face the night before in the dressing-room. It was his greater knowledge and his pity, a wise generosity beyond a purely possessive male instinct that had allowed Debrülle to let Angela have her young lover. And this gayety now? It was partly to drown regret, regret that Debrülle was not the same age, was not Anthony. And yet there was wine and music and happiness this morning! It was as if Debrülle had shared in the joy of the night before by some occult transference. Angela and Anthony would have to take him in. He was there. How strange! How could he have ever imagined an association like this?

Anthony shook his head. He had possessed her completely, and she him, yet somehow he was going to lose her again. He looked at her now beside him putting a little flower into her hair, joyous and cool. He thought of the young Madonna in the dream who had slowly blent herself with the cool water. Perhaps Angela was like that—something that overflowed, that ran away like cool, clear water, a natural thing that one could not possess by clutching with hands. One could only be in it a while and be washed over the brink when it overflowed—and look back upon one's own happy face, glorious like the sun beating across the parapet through the green cool leaves of Signora Bovino's plants. He walked over to them a minute to be alone.

The calm and deep joy of the night before leaving his blood cool and his limbs relaxed in well-being, the present gayety and sunny happiness, the harmony of dear voices searching his soul, the strange premonitory loneliness of the days to come without Angela,—all blent and existed simultaneously within him in a mood so far beyond thought that he stood for a minute like a god among the leaves lost in an indescribable flood of bright, imageless feeling. Then they called him back.

The instinct of aloofness on his part made the occasion become even a little gayer if possible. It was as if the others in order to confirm their own mood became more abandoned so as to take him along. Not the least element of a spectator could be tolerated. Nor was it now hard for them to prevail. Now that he understood it all; had thrust it down past words and argument anl resolved it into pure feeling, he let himself go. The wine helped.

Presently he was singing too, whenever he could, with a better voice than he ever had thought he had. After even the professional repertoire of Debrülle was exhausted, Vincent's girl proved to be able to make convulsing faces. All the past was forgotten now. Only the present existed. Then Signora Bovino began to tell fortunes.

She cast their horoscopes and they bent breathless over her books and queer charts where zodiacal animals swarmed amid the stars.

"You have an immense fortune in diamonds coming to you," she promised Angela. Debrülle would never have any children. He clapped his hand tragically to his forehead. Vincent would be rich but would die poor. A long life but a merry one! A hard dark man with a huge beard was to be the lot of the Fräulein. " 'Küche, kochen, und Kinder.' Ach!" The Fräulein sulked. For some reason the signora had left Anthony to the last. She now turned her piercing eyes upon him and began her formula again.

"What day and hour were you born?"

He had sat suddenly frozen when she began to ask the others that. The mood of the morning passed. The wine died in him. A look of embarrassed misery now crept into his features.

"I do not know, signora, I—you see . . ."

He coloured to the brows. In the name of God, who was he?

There was a moment of silence. Then the kindly Debrülle stepped in. He sneezed and made them laugh. "Doubtless the illustrious signora," he went on with the tears of the sneeze still in his eyes, "has other methods of foretelling the future."

"Oh, yes, holy saints and angels!" There were other ways. "Yes indeed!"

How much did Debrülle know? Anthony wondered. How much had Angela told him?

The signora opened an old, black box and took out the ancient shoulder blades of sheep, and a black veil embroidered with faded stars. She sat down at the table and throwing the veil over her head began to click the sheep bones mysteriously behind it. An ancient Tuscan chant with gibberish come down from the days of Etruria mumbled from her gums. They looked at her, awed in spite of themselves. The dark veiled head now had the outlines of a sibyl and the power to stir something in them, they knew not what. *Click, click,* went the bones. A voice began.

"You were born at midnight between a lucky and an unlucky day. I see many ships. A crucifix is speaking. You will see the King of the World and serve him. There is a great fire by night. I cannot make this out. There is a veiled woman, a mountain very far away, a great tree, stars." She threw off the veil and looked at Anthony with interest and surprise. "I am only sure of two things," she said, "you will travel far, the earth turned under you; and you must beware of cold steel. You will not always be very happy, my son." She looked at his palm and nodded confirmingly. "Now," she said, "put something in mine."

It occurred to Anthony, as he felt in his pocket, that Signora Bovino might be performing a function which the world could not do without and yet would never acknowledge. One should pay well for that. He would owe her a great memory.

"And bear that memory with him to the last."

The stave seemed to sing itself for him. He gave her his best gold coin. Debrülle and Vincent pressed forward. The old woman soon had cause to be pleased and showed it. Seeing her auspicious expression the Fräulein thrust her palm under the signora's nose.

"Have you nothing better to tell me?" she asked wistfully.

A long line extended right across the girl's hand like the hinge of a leather box. Her fingers closed on her wrist like a lid. There were no vertical lines from the wrist. The old woman looked at it.

"Go along with you," she said, throwing the girl's

hand aside like an object. "You are not one of us. Your grandfather must have been a Chinaman."

It was true, the whole room burst into laughter. They had not noticed it before, but there was something Mongolian about this girl; an almond creep to her eyes.

Debrülle rose and took his cape. Angela hurriedly got her things together. "The matinée, you know," he said, and held out his hand. Anthony took it and paused. He owed the man much. "Thank you, I know, now. Thank you! Take care of Angela," he whispered. The man caught both his hands and squeezed them hard. "By God, I will." He went out first.

With a low cry Angela ran across the room and flung her arms about Anthony. For one instant he felt her warm cheek beating against his. He crushed her lips with a cry. Then she had gone.

He was left standing in a universe deserted, alone beyond all sounds, undone. He could see nothing. "Madonna, sweet Mother of God, come to me now!"

As if his inner life were a plant that flourished in the soil of his body he felt it sicken down to the most remote and delicate roots. The nerve tips which are always in motion bathed by the rich liquor of the blood upon which they draw for nourishment and warmth ceased for a moment to move and became numb. He felt them dimly loosen. He grew cold. Then the heart throbbed again overcoming the shock as if by sheer energy. But living was for a little a great misery.

Another aspect of life had confronted Anthony. Existence might be painful! For the first time the thought flashed upon him that escape from it might be a relief. There was a gate out of this. How dark the garden of the world could suddenly become, how scentless the flowers. The clear, sheer joyous morning light was over. What would hot noon be like? Thus the man's soul was first torn loose within him. He stood leaning on the table with one hand. He tottered a little. The figures of things had become confused. A cool sweat burst out just above his eyebrows. He looked ill.

The old woman, mumbling something kindly, thrust

him into a chair and gave him a fiery drink. When he could see clearly again the German girl was projected before him just across the table, sitting there with tears in her eyes still looking hopelessly at her palm. Poor soul! Life was sad for her, too! Something had happened to her before she was born. A pity overflowed the boy, warming him again. For the first time he understood what it was to be a simple child, a lost angel caught in a body without hope. A look of understanding passed between them. There was comfort in it.

"Come, come," said Vincent, who did not understand exactly what had happened, but could see that his friend looked white. "If you are ill, I will go home with you. It is time to leave anyway, I guess." He picked up his uncle's torn coat. They went out onto the landing. A door opened across the hall.

"Ahoy there," said a voice in a tone that was just now to Anthony ghastly with heartiness. "Do you think you can get away from me like that? I have been listening to you all morning." It was the navigating Mr. Williams. They both stopped helplessly. He came down to them with his sextant in a bag. "I'll go over to the casa with you now," he roared. "We can work out that new way of plotting the longitude this afternoon." He followed them like fate.

"Oh, my God!" said Vincent, "he's coming!"

Anthony felt too far-off to resist. They turned up the street together. The immense voice boomed on, causing cart drivers to stare. It was warm and sticky outside after the cool breezes of the roof.

"I tell you the stars cannot lie. . . they . . ."

Yes, it was true. That was the worst of it. If you could only decide these things for yourself. Then . . . then Debrülle would not go off with Angela, for instance. But there was something else, something beyond your own will and desire, that did the deciding. All your plans were as nothing to that. He, Anthony, had felt it at work this morning, fate, something beyond appeal. Things had happened. The little cottage with the garden around it would never rise from Toussaint's old ruin as he had pictured to himself. Never! It would remain a heap of stones.

Toussaint was a fool, a fool! Mentally Anthony took out his grief that now lapsed into anger on that little man. It was foolish and sentimental, he knew. But he had been hurt, sickened. Someone must be at fault. Would that great ass of an ex-mate never stop roaring at him? He was sick of them all. Of every one of them. Of the casa, of Mr. Bonnyfeather, of Faith. Damn her! He couldn't stand her any more. To take his boy's body that night!

"The admiralty is right after all. They will have to agree on a line of longitude and keep one clock to that time. Then you will have another clock that . . ."

"Christ deliver us!"

They turned into the vaulted archway of the Casa da Bonnyfeather. The three pairs of feet echoed hollowly. The bell rang releasing the clerks for luncheon. They streamed across the yard, glad to escape. So would he be, he thought. He was tired of it all, the whole familiar scene. There was no one by the fountain either. Angela! After a while as though at a distance he saw they were all sitting down to lunch. Vincent was trying to be merry as usual. Toussaint was still looking sorry. Mr. Williams rumbled. The old merchant sat more quietly than usual as if there was something troubling him. It all went on. How hot the day was. Suddenly he felt someone's hand under the table laid on his knee. Even through silk it felt cool, but it trembled slightly. With her other hand Faith was fingering a spoon.

"Let me alone," he cried leaping up so that they all stared at him.

"What is it?" said Faith.

"You . . ." He turned and ran to his room.

"Anthony is a bit ill today," said Vincent after an awkward pause. "We had . . . *er*, a rather—somewhat of a go last night."

"Does he need a leech, do you think?" asked Mr. Bonnyfeather.

"I'm thinkin' ye can spare yoursel' the expanse,"

408

said McNab, looking at Faith. So was Toussaint. For the first time she turned slightly pale.

Once in his room Anthony locked himself in. He paid no attention when Vincent came to the door later. He was dry-eyed now. He wished only to be left alone. He walked up and down. Then at last he cast himself down on the bed before the Madonna. Of what good was the outside world? It intruded upon your own only to give pain. It had taken years, but now, now at last he could open his heart up to the Madonna again. She and he were left alone as they had been when he first came there.

Chapter Twenty-Two

Icons and Iconoclasts

IN TIMES of great change it is a question whether the restlessness of the human heart is due more to individual dissatisfaction with experience than to the drag and flux of the age. The two play upon each other, reverberate, and are inextricably intermingled. In this interplay there is no rest to be found anywhere. No adjustment suffices. Few can attain equilibrium. The pendulum of the time is felt trembling at one extreme, high above all heads, and threatening them. Men dash about underneath it like disturbed ants.

Yet every rational being desires a "home" of some kind for body and mind. Men cannot act spasmodically for ever. They finally gather together about some standard bearer and press in some definite direction always labelled "Forward." No matter what the vista ahead may be they must come to some decision at some place, be it a battlefield marked by graves. Here at least is a rest, an end. Perhaps, who knows, a beginning. The normal symptom of such times is the feeling of the approach of war. Usual things, moods, modes, interests, and passions, even lusts, lose their zest. The familiar becomes unreal. Foundations hitherto taken as eternal begin to crumble.

In the last few days which Anthony spent in Livorno he was intensely possessed by, if not wholly conscious of, the sensation of something new impending. Remembering it afterwards, his attitudes and actions— which then and for some time later seemed inexplicable —became plainer to him. He could see that along with the vast majority he had unconsciously temporarily suspended his own will in order to drift with a new tide in the affairs of men. Whither he did not seem to care. It was a relief; easier just to watch and see what would happen to him. Who could expect to direct, control, or even understand so titanic a thing as the European current? The frantic outbreak of gambling in society everywhere, which overflowed into the very streets of the town and obstructed the gutters with card players and dicers, was one expression of this, "Let fate decide." The universe was thrown back to its original state. The Guessippis had been merely some of the first lambs to be shorn. The crowds roared now every night before the lottery. The governor became ridiculously rich and the government bankrupt.

Against this background the patient habits of mercantile industry as a gainful occupation began to appear silly and to disintegrate. Minor firms began to close their doors as if by premonition.

Almost alone, in a scene that was already trembling toward chaos, the sedate Mr. Bonnyfeather continued calmly to hang his hat on the horns of the satyr every morning. The counting house hummed. To some plan, to which he and McNab alone were privy, the storerooms began to empty themselves. At Nantes, Hamburg, Rotterdam, and London the accounts of "*John Bonnyfeather, merchant*," began to show snug balances. The grim Captain Bittern came and went with the *Unicorn* upon mysterious errands under the protecting guns of Nelson's fleet.

Anthony worked over a flood of papers, which seemed to him to have lost all vital interest. He made his eyes and hands do things. He answered and filed mechanically only to escape at noon with Vincent Nolte. Sometimes he looked at Toussaint working beside him. They no longer exchanged anything but necessary words. He too was feeling the electric weather of the time.

The face of Toussaint Clairveaux had become a military and political barometer. As the news of the successes of the French continued to arrive, as he felt the "glorious revolution" approaching, his countenance became more and more radiant. He seemed to have secret sources of information. At the thought of seeing the personification of all his hopes and ideals, the invincible Buonaparte in the streets of Livorno, he glowed with an almost ethereal enthusiasm. Even Faith was temporarily forgotten. He thought he did not care what might become of himself or her when Mr. Bonnyfeather should no longer hang his hat on the horns of the satyr. The new age would have arrived before it was too late.

He looked at the satyr. A small remnant of gilding still glimmered on its horns. It might not be too late after all. Anthony he now regarded as lost. Rousseau, Toussaint now saw, was merely a John the Baptist. The messiah of the age was about to enter Jerusalem in the person of Buonaparte, on a war horse. Anthony had been worshipping Venus. He would not be among the elect. His one favourite pupil! How he yearned over him. "Ah, he had failed there—that woman again!" He sighed. He longed to talk with Anthony. He was utterly alone.

The French émigrés who had settled at Milan and Florence now began to troop through Livorno, lingering a little before going elsewhere. English families came and embarked. Otto Franco did a roaring business. Some of the beaten Austrian battalions hustled onto transports with the grand duke's treasure. The town throbbed with drums. In the night the garrison departed. License revelled by moonlight while the watch tactfully proclaimed that all was well. Provided with letters of marque from Mr. Udney, the *Unicorn* departed from the now empty quay before the Casa da Bonnyfeather, "bound for Gibraltar." The dray mules were sold at public auction. On the old courtyard a strange silence had fallen. The clerks soon wondered what they were going to do.

It was now that Mr. Bonnyfeather began to employ Anthony on constant trips to Mr. Udney for the execution of various documents. Among these was a copy of his will which had been carefully drawn just before the final departure of the *Unicorn*. It was witnessed by McNab and Captain Bittern. It was the old merchant's care to register it with both the local and British authorities.

Had Anthony known the contents of the document the sudden renewed cordiality of the British consul might not have caused him so much personal satisfaction as it did. Mr. Udney was a practical man. The prospect of property in a young man's future by no means darkened it for the Englishman. After the will was filed a slight shade of deference crept into his attitude toward Anthony, which, if inexplicable to that young gentleman, was none the less flattering.

He and Vincent had of course long ago availed themselves of the invitation to come to tea at the Udneys'. It was not at the old villa but at the consul's rooms over his *case*. The flag of England on a staff and the gilded royal arms over the door gave it a certain "dash." Upstairs, due to the participation of the consul in the recent satisfactory condemnations of certain prizes, the apartment was furnished in the latest Parisian style. Amid the heavy travesties of Greece and Rome, shining brass wreaths and republican fasces, Mrs. Udney's old English spinet remained with both the voice and the appearance of a charming ghost. Here, seated on a great "X"-shaped chair that might have supported the bulk of Tully, from a huge urn surmounted by a Roman eagle she poured tea.

It was the first almost English tea that Anthony had seen, or drunk. David Parish, who still remained constant and took Miss Florence driving every day with her mother, passed the gingerbread, Mrs. Udney's

413

specialty after a youthful sojourn in Jamaica. She talked of the island often. It and Nevis were the nicest places in the world. Florence argued for the country about Totnes in Devin while Mr. Udney, consuming bowls of hyson from the bottom of the urn, nodded his approval.

He loved his moors. Please God, he would soon see them again! He was fifty-three and all his teeth were out. It was time Florence was marrying. This chap Parish was attentive enough, good prospects, too. Yet there was something about Anthony that attracted him. Evidently the boy had crept into old Bonnyfeather's heart. To a good tune at that! Unknown origin, of course. But good stuff, look at him. Well, well, things would have to take their own way, he supposed—or his wife's. Unconsciously she and fate had become for him, in his domestic affairs at least, synonymous.

They had never had a son. He had given it up. It made him too tired now. He remembered that day at the villa years ago when Florence had brought Anthony. How the boy had moved his heart—and that priest's, poor fellow! They had both done well by the boy. It was those secret impulses that counted. They shaped the world; made plans. He looked at Florence talking to Anthony with a mixture of pride and happiness. Oh, well, let *her* have a son. He turned to his wife. "My dear, another cup of tea, from the lees, strong."

"Why, Mr. Udney, since when did you start to take it off the lees?"

"A long time since," he replied firmly with the immense capacity for self-pity of the older male in his voice.

Florence was all of girlhood that Anthony had missed. The kind of person from the kind of family that he felt somehow he belonged to and had been robbed of. How easy it was to talk to her. It was something like talking that night to Angela but less intense, more assured, more casually satisfactory. Her frocks were so fashionable—neat and clean, *not* like Angela's

—softly unusual he thought. She was wearing a white, high-waisted gown of the new Greek cut with a cross-ribbon binding in her waist under her breasts. There were little ribboned puffs on the sleeves which covered her arms, just halfway to the elbow. She was not too plump any more. Long, and slim, and cool with firm legs. Those white sandals! One could see her pink toes through the thin net stockings and straps.

Florence was "Miss Udney," too. Someone to be proud of knowing. One's equal—or more? A new, a right, and a nice experience, safe from the dark magic of Faith. His kind!

In addition, unbelievable as it might seem, Miss Udney had eyes, nose, and lips. And it was probable that she continued under her dress. But he did not care to think of that just now. She used a faint violet perfume. From her emanated a fragrant coolness as of a lush spot about a thawing spring in early April. It was that which caused him to lean near her and to talk in a hushed way. And it was difficult, he felt, for both of them not to keep on looking at each other's eyes. Parish evidently did not care much for this. He kept passing the gingerbread a little too frequently.

They talked of England, mostly. Florence had been home to school for several years since she had seen Anthony. Her description of Devon made him "home-sick." He felt the same way about Florence's country as Mr. Bonnyfeather felt about the valley of the Moselle. It was dreamland and Utopia, only real. England was on the map. He and Florence were often there together, alone. It was a comfort to know that Angela could not come there. No one could disturb them as they played under the huge stones of the bridge at Post Bridge, or looked for white heather where the moor ponies fed above Widdecombe and watched the rabbits playing about the tors. Florence was more graphic than she knew. He could see it all. Together they lingered over it in conversational dreams. Florence found it pleasant and effortless to talk with such a listener. With Anthony she talked about what interested her; with Parish about what was supposed to be interesting. She sighed. Yet

415

she had come to make herself like Parish. He was touchingly attentive, generous, and in love. Her mother liked him too, she felt.

Mrs. Udney was secretly a little alarmed now over the arrival of Anthony. She almost wished she had not brought him around. Parish was getting too restive. She had merely meant to spur him on. He might shy off. She wished Anthony would join in the talk more generally. Finally she would go to the spinet and looking back at them both, touch the chords of "Malbrouk s'en va-t-en guerre." That tune always brought the colour to Anthony's face. He felt a boy again and awkward. Yet it touched a chord of sympathy. Florence remembered, too. So for a good many afternoons it went on.

Vincent had dropped out entirely. The plump, Florentine banker's daughter was more to his mind. She had surrendered to him furtively. Taking tea to Vincent now seemed a waste of time. Anthony had gone to the Strozzi's once or twice, too. He found Mlle. de Rhan quite intriguing. But she had soon gone back to Nantes. He had promised to write and he did so once. Vincent's intimate details about Maddalena began to revolt him. One did not care to think of Vincent that way. There was something between the pig and the rabbit about the German. He was kin to Arnolfo, Anthony thought. Smooth! He remembered the big blonde at Signora Bovino's crying. So they saw less of each other. Vincent was troubled about this separation. What had happened? —he wondered. He intended to speak to Anthony about it.

But upon all this stirring about of tea leaves in cups, and drifting of rose petals in casual breezes blew the strong wind of war.

One afternoon Florence had seemed particularly gay and attractive. Her face shone from some inner excitement. Mrs. Udney had been careful to thump the spinet more than usual. She gathered them all around her and made them sing. As Anthony left Mr. Udney entered suddenly and beckoned to him.

"Give this to your guardian," he said. It was a

416

sealed letter. "Be *sure* not to forget," he called. "It is urgently important, hurry home!"

That was the last Saturday of June 1796 when Mr. Udney's letter apparently began to act as a solvent on the world which Anthony had known as "Livorno" and the "Casa da Bonnyfeather."

Mr. Bonnyfeather opened the letter with his carving knife when Anthony came in late to supper. "As I expected," he muttered. He sent the waiter out and leaned forward a little pale. McNab, Toussaint, Faith, and Anthony sat waiting.

"The French are at Florence, the consul informs me," he finally said. "Buonaparte will certainly be here by Tuesday if not sooner. That gives us about forty-eight hours to close this factory." He paused painfully. The happy excitement on the face of Toussaint died out. They were all looking at the old merchant with pity now. A slight flush tinged his high cheek bones as he went on.

"Not a word of this to anyone. I shall want you, Mr. McNab, Toussaint, and Anthony, with me in my own quarters tonight. The clerks must all be gone by Monday. Everyone—but those present," said Mr. Bonnyfeather. "Keep the cook and one porter. Make your arrangements accordingly, Faith, and no delay."

They ate hurriedly.

"May I tell Vincent and the Franks?" asked Anthony as they rose.

"That is well thought of. They should know," said Mr. Bonnyfeather. "But hurry back." The Franks were enormously grateful for the tip.

By the time Anthony returned the lights were burning in the old merchant's room. Files of papers and cash bags were on the table with McNab and Toussaint hard at work. They made out a discharge and a letter of recommendation for each employee, counted out the total due each clerk plus a quarter's pay, and made a pile of the coin. Mr. Bonnyfeather answered any queries while he burned correspondence steadily. They worked all night.

Early next morning rioting broke out in the piazza.

The lottery was closed and the money gone. Rumours of the French advance flew about. The town throbbed. At noon the British fleet anchored off the molo under Commodore Nelson. Save for the now frantic activity of English departure along the docks of the Darsena the town lay quiet under the British guns. In the court of the Casa da Bonnyfeather all hands gathered after lunch looking rather glum. Mr. Bonnyfeather appeared on the steps. The little crowd below him uncovered. He began haltingly but then went on gallantly enough.

"Gentlemen, Buonaparte will be in this town in a few hours. Although England and France have quarrelled for purely spiritual reasons, all British property will undoubtedly be confiscated. Trade is at an end. The gates of this establishment will never be opened again in my time for business. The Casa da Bonnyfeather has ceased to exist. I have retired." He paused with all eyes upon him.

"I have not forgot any of you. You will receive immediately from Mr. McNab your full pay plus a quarter's salary gratis, also letters of recommendation to other merchantile firms, and your passports. Those of you who are British subjects had best go aboard the fleet tonight. Do not on any pretext delay. There are many things I would say now but cannot. This sudden decision is due to the act of a tyrant who comes proclaiming liberty. I have done all I can for you who have served me faithfully. Receive my thanks, and may God be with you!"

There was a moment's dead silence. Then the English gave a cheer. There was a rush to pack belongings. In a few hours the place was as quiet as the courtyard of a ruined castle. Outside only the slap of a brush on the front of the establishment as a sailor white-washed carefully over the legend "Casa da Bonnyfeather" disturbed the silence of its now deserted quay. Mr. Bonnyfeather beckoned to Anthony. They went up on the roof and hauled down both the flags together.

"My son," said he with emotion as they locked them

in the chest, "if anyone ever raises them again it must be you." He snapped the lock. Anthony stood by feeling a lump in his throat.

"And what shall we do now?" he asked.

"I shall talk about that with you later," the old man replied. "Just now—" He broke off and went to his room.

For some moments Anthony stood there. The past seemed locked in the chest. Then he remembered the present and hastened over to the Udneys'. The consulate downstairs was in an uproar but Mrs. Udney, Florence, and Parish were upstairs.

"Oh, I am so glad *you* came," Florence cried. "We are leaving tomorrow with the fleet." She checked herself suddenly colouring to the eyes. "I did want to say good-bye, you know."

Of course, *they* would be going! He knew that, and yet until the last moment he had hoped not. How much he had hoped he was aware of only now as he looked at her standing so near him. So Florence was going away, too.

"All the world is going away!" he blurted out looking miserable and depressed before he could recollect himself. "I wish you were staying. Is it England?"

Her eyes suffused with tears. "No," she said, "Rotterdam!"

"Rotterdam!" he mumbled.

"I think you had better tell Mr. Adverse, my dear," broke in her mother. "Florence, don't turn your back on us that way. It isn't polite."

"Good-bye," said the lips of Florence to Anthony though no sound was heard. When she turned to her mother and Parish she was gay again with bright colour in her cheeks.

"Isn't she a little goose about it, David?" said Mrs. Udney. "Florence wants to tell you, Anthony, that she and Mr. Parish are engaged. It will be announced shortly." She looked at him keenly. But his face did not change now.

"Rather wooden," thought Mrs. Udney.

"I hope you will like Rotterdam as well as Totnes, Miss Florence," he managed to say.

"Believe me, she will," said Parish sitting down beside her with the air of a proprietor. "It is a fine town with lots of English and Scotch merchants."

Anthony nodded. He sat on his chair with his knees straight out before him and drank his tea alone. For the life of him he could not think of anything to say. He felt unaccountably sad. Parish talked on confidently. As soon as he could Anthony bade them all good-bye. On the way down he met Mr. Udney coming up. Anthony was surprised by the heartiness of his good-bye. "Good luck, my boy, write us. I want to hear from you!" He caught him by the arm as if to keep him.

"Mr. Udney, I have a great deal to thank you for. I . . . I shall miss you sadly. It will be very lonely . . . with all the English gone . . . very . . . I——"

"Cheer up, my boy, we English always come back, you know. You are staying on with your guardian I suppose?"

"No, I am leaving!" said Anthony, and looked shocked. It seemed as if someone else had made the decision. But he was sure of it, sure!

"Hadn't you better consider your . . ." began the consul.

"No, sir, *I am leaving Livorno!*" He flung out of the door

"Humph!" said Mr. Udney and went upstairs to his wife, who was alone now.

"Our young friend seems to be bady cut up over the recent trend of events here."

"Does he?" she said doubtfully.

"Yes, he is going to leave. I should think he would stay on and look after Mr. Bonnyfeather's interests—and his own."

"His *own?*" She put down the teacup.

"Yes, didn't you know he is Bonnyfeather's heir?"

"Henry!" she cried. "Why didn't you tell me? Oh, you . . . you old fool!"

She turned and began to play violently on the spinet.

"Well, I'll be damned!" muttered Mr. Udney.

Just as Anthony turned the corner of the street the strains of "Malbrouk s'en va-t-en guerre" reached him faintly like an echo from a past life. He winced and clenched his fist. Mrs. Udney might have spared him that. *That* settled it. He *was* going.

With a heave of his shoulders as if he had cast off a load, he raced to Otto Frank's. They had a merry supper there. That night they watched the post-chaises and carriages dashing away southward. Everybody, everybody was going.

About one o'clock there was a ringing bugle call at the Porta Pisa. A few minutes later the high, clear, thrilling strain burst out at the end of the long street. Down the Strada Ferdinanda with a clicking of sabres, sparks streaming from under their horses' hoofs, and the wind whipping in their pennons streamed a squadron of French cavalry. The old days were done. Only the English finished loading goods under the guns of the fleet.

In the great hall of the mayoralty the French major swore. Cavalry was no good on the sea. That had not occurred to the major before. He was a cavalryman. He could do nothing to stop the British. But he began to arrest people right and left as a relief to his own feelings and as a proof of his zeal

Uncle Otto was led off protesting, in his uniform coat despite the two epaulettes now sewed on it. Thus was the neutrality of Hamburg wantonly outraged. With many other important merchants of Livorno Uncle Otto spent a miserable night locked up in an old banquet hall at the mayoralty. But on the lists of merchants taxable, which the French officer conveniently used for arrests, the name of John Bonnyfeather no longer appeared. He had retired and was now listed as "widower tenant of the Marquis da Vincitata, age 76, one female housekeeper, and four servants." The French were not arresting "widower tenants." Mr. Bonnyfeather slept at home.

He and Anthony lingered long over their breakfast next morning. It was pleasant in the cool of the summer morning with the great door wide open, with the long shadows in the court and the murmur of the fountain now plainly audible in the strange quiet. Everyone but he and Anthony had left earlier to watch for the arrival of the main body of the French.

Mr. Bonnyfeather was pleased to find himself contented and relieved at having "retired." He would never have been able to do so himself without the aid of circumstances. He would have died in harness. Now he would have the beds in the court planted with flowers, keep a carriage and pair and drive out when the French departed. He would rest his soul and die in peace here. He had plenty, well secured. He would have in a few old friends to very, very special little dinners and play chess. Ah, he had never permitted himself the time for that. He must get out his notes on combinations again. McNab and Toussaint could stay on a little and look after the few loose ends of things that remained, discreetly of course. The faintest premonitions of physical and spiritual lethargy were pleasant this first, lovely summer morning of his retirement. He relaxed, stretching, with his feet under the table and musing. A rooster in the old mule stables crowed dreamfully. Mr. Bonnyfeather looked at Anthony.

The lad was musing, too, but with a troubled face. "What a strong, lithe, young blade he had grown to be," thought the old man. "And how much, how much he still looked like Maria! Ah, he would forget that now, it was long ago. Let the dead bury their dead." He started. With his business gone this youth was the only vital concern he still had. Well, he would not have to conceal that any longer, now that he was alone. He put his hand gently on Anthony's.

"You look troubled, my son."

"Yes," said Anthony looking up with the expression of frank affection and confidence that had long been customary between them in privacy, "I am greatly troubled. I do not seem to be able to find any comfort anywhere."

"At your age I was restless, too. It is in the blood."

"No, it is not exactly that. I hardly know how to begin to tell you. I have been thinking . . . I have been troubled by things that have been happening to me. I do not know just what I should do, where I should go. You see . . ."

"If it is about the future you need not be greatly troubled about that. I have made sure provision for you there, and in the meanwhile. This has been your home since . . ."

"Do you know anything before that?" Anthony asked by an impulse he could no longer restrain. "Who am I, where did I come from? I do not even know my birthday! My father!"

The old man withdrew his hand suddenly.

"Oh, do not think me ungrateful, please, sir, do not think it. It can never be told you in words what I feel. I know I was a miserable orphan, a— You have been my father. I have read those convent records, the day I got my last name, you remember. But is that all? Don't you know—anything?" His voice trailed off. Mr. Bonnyfeather sat looking into the distance.

"I have been thinking about it a great deal lately," Anthony plunged on. "I didn't used to, but now lately. I will tell you why."

Before he knew it he had plunged into the story of the horoscope at Signora Bovino's, the whole story of Angela, the loss of Florence, his decision to leave Livorno, even the quarrel with Toussaint. The world seemed crumbling about him. If he did not know who he was he must go out and become somebody. He even spoke of his comfort in the Madonna that seemed to link him with a past. "To give me some roots as if I had not just happened, been an original creation. I have never told anybody all this. No one, only you. I needed to tell you. Don't you see? That is all. There is nobody else who would understand me, man or woman." He then remembered Faith and stopped.

How did he instinctively know that she would understand? He had not thought of that before. The thought reminded him that he not only disliked her but feared her. She knew, evilly! No, he could not speak to her, or of her. No one should ever know about that, only himself and the Madonna. Toussaint! Too many knew already. He looked at the old man anxiously. What they saw in each other's faces now made them both pale.

Mr. Bonnyfeather leaned forward, pondering long. At last he spoke.

"I will show you something," said he. Then after another long pause—"but you must promise me on the honour of your soul, as a gentleman—you must know what I mean by that now—never to ask me any more questions or to try to inquire further. Nay, I *must* ask you something more, for my own sake. If you are grateful to me and love my honour, do not, even if in the future you should accidentally find out more than I can tell you, permit your discovery to be known. Keep it close. Die with it safe." An expression of fiery pride, that for a few seconds made Mr. Bonnyfeather look years younger, quickened him.

"Will honour be equal to the fundamental curiosity I have aroused? Do you understand what you promise, Anthony? Give me your hand." They looked at each other steadily.

"I promise you," said Anthony.

"Come," said the old merchant, and rising from the table he gravely led the way to his room.

Under the picture of the exiled James he opened the little casket with some difficulty. It was years now since he had looked there, he reflected. In fact not since that night when Anthony had been brought to him. He took out the miniature of his daughter and holding it cupped in his hands looked at it again. It was almost like having her come back from the dead. A tremor shook him.

Whatever might come now, he reflected, he had protected her memory. Even her son, if son of hers he was, should never know, should never try to find out. Perhaps it was a cruel promise to exact from the boy, but he had exacted it of himself, and kept his promise even in secret thought. The Bonnyfeathers had preferred ruin

424

to disloyalty, always. This boy— The boy owed him much. This should be the price, the test of loyal gratitude. And he had tried to teach him what "honour" was —the honour of a Bonnyfeather.

He gazed with avid eyes on the face of his child and bowed to kiss the picture as sometimes in the night, when he knelt by the dying ashes of his fire, he kissed the crucifix. And by the rigid code of his feudal soul he had no doubt but that he was doing right, now, and to the past. The name of Bonnyfeather was going out. Let it die in honour—and rest. He turned with his icon in his hand.

"My son," he said, "come here. I am putting our honour in your hands."

He laid the picture in Anthony's palms.

"I believe," said he, "that she was your mother. I am not certain, but I think so. That is all I can say."

Looking up at him from the locket Anthony beheld the same face that he had seen reflected from the fountain of his dreams. It seemed to him as if he were peering down again as a child upon his other self. It was the same face that had gazed back at him that night with Angela when the young Madonna came to bathe in the pool, his own face, and yet more lovely, tender and hazily radiant. That was the way his soul thought of itself, if the world would only let it be. As if a shadow had fallen on the water the image glimmered away from him still laughing innocently through his tears.

"Mother, beautiful mother. I know what I am like now. Let me not forget."

It was for that reason that he did not turn with an inevitable and instinctive, "Who was she?" on his lips, despite his promise. It seemed to him that he already knew her as he knew himself.

He gave the picture back again, silently.

"Wait for me outside," said Mr. Bonnyfeather. "I wish to be alone for a little."

From the ashes he began to rake together a few bits of unconsumed branches to make a small fire. Presently by the aid of the bellows the coals became white hot. He did not look at the picture again. "Farewell, Maria, may it be soon." He stooped low and half closed his eyes. The bellows sighed; the gold melted.

When Mr. Bonnyfeather returned to the old ballroom the only material likeness of Maria which existed was that which was still traceable to a knowing eye in Anthony's face. The eyes which could best trace it there were already growing dim.

"So much for the past," said the old gentleman gallantly. "Have I answered your question?"

"You have given me your best gift, I know it," said Anthony. Mr. Bonnyfeather felt his old blood warm him again.

"That was understandingly said, I think," he replied. "I am repaid. We are even! In the future you will remember that whatever you may do for me will be in your own interest as well. Do you understand me?"

"It has always been so before, sir!"

"It is a little more certain now." Yet some shreds of his long reticence were so firmly rooted in precaution that Mr. Bonnyfeather could not bring himself to mention his will. He preferred to delegate the bald mention of it to another.

"Ahem . . . if I were you I would not let these youthful love affairs make me melancholy," he went on. "It is very seldom that one finds happiness that way. Our loves are both our joy and our undoing. Remember, it is that way life is evoked, and life is both happy and full of sorrow. In youth we think only of the pleasure. I did. I was undeceived. Do not think that these first light shades can darken your soul. You are restless, too. The times are disturbed. I have thought of that. You need to change this place for another, to go out and prove yourself on the world."

"I should not care to go to England, to college, just now," said Anthony—thinking that Florence would not be there.

"No, I have thought of a better school than that for you. I mean the age itself. Also I need you now. It so happens that you are the only one left who may be able to carry out a certain plan of mine successfully. Neither McNab nor Toussaint will do. It is the collection of a large sum of money long due me, about nine thousand pounds. It will take you to Cuba. What do you think?"

Anthony leaned forward too eagerly to permit his interest to be doubted.

"It is like this," continued the merchant, "you may have noticed from our Spanish correspondence that with the firm of *Don Carlos Gallego & Son* in Havana we have long had extensive dealings. Owing to the nature of our transactions, which was somewhat peculiar, their payments have been in kind as well as in cash. We would ship them, for instance, cargoes of brass wire, calicoes, toys, millinery, Brummagem muskets, chain shot and handcuffs, together with horsebeans, German beads, Manchester cottons, gewgaws, and kegs of Austrian thalers coined under Maria Theresa. It is that last item in particular which has been costly. Such things, you are aware, are eventually destined for trade in Africa, and there can be no doubt but that the firm of Gallego conducts slave operations, both hunting and selling, on a large scale. They in turn send us cargoes of palm oil, ivory, various fine woods, and so forth. They also remit at various times bills to our credit. Thus, although we were forced to extend a large credit to these people and to carry them for long terms, the profits in the end were so high as to warrant even the risk of the loss of an entire cargo by pirates or guarda costas.

"As matters now stand it so happens that we have in the last three years shipped them three cargoes and received only one in return. A debt of an unusual amount is therefore due us, the largest remaining on our books. With the disturbed conditions now existing on the high seas, and this port in the hands of the French, it will be impossible for the Gallegos to ship us any more ivory. We must collect from them in cash or by bills on France or Spain, or not at all.

"Furthermore, for over a year we have had no answer to our correspondence, although I know our letters were delivered at Havana. The old Señor Gallego is honest by long proof. He is very old, and it is possible that he may have lately died. Of his son I know nothing, nor of the present condition of the firm. There is no way at present in Havana to collect this large debt legally. Spain forbids all direct trade with her colonies. Everything, therefore, depends on the attitude of the colonial officials, frankly upon our finesse in bribery, if we are to realize even our own outlay. You will therefore have to act as a private diplomat on a ticklish mission rather than as an aggrieved creditor. But you speak and write Spanish, you have been instructed carefully in the ways of trade according to my own plans, and I think I do not flatter myself in having confidence in your intelligence, ability, and eventual success. A reasonable accommodation would do. I should expect to dispatch you with funds, and letters to my agent in Havana. He is an Italian, one Carlos Cibo, amply capable of instructing you in all the villainous indirections necessary to conduct honest business in a Spanish colonial capital. The temptations of the place are said to be curious—" Mr. Bonnyfeather then added as if by afterthought, raising his eyebrows and twinkling—"something like Livorno it would seem. Do you care to hazard yourself in the enterprise?"

"It will be a dream coming true, sir. I could not imagine anything more to my mind."

"Perhaps?" said the old man. "Well, well, prepare yourself for the journey. Consult McNab about what you will take. He knows Havana from old times. We shall take the first opportunity of getting you off. A neutral ship would be best now if one happens along. The neutrals will profit by these troubles. But we shall see. Here comes your friend Vincent bubbling with news."

Vincent was indeed afire with excitement. The French were entering the town in full force now.

"They expect Buonaparte directly. I thought you might both like to come over and watch from our windows when he arrived. Uncle Otto has been released but he has been badly scared and is in bed."

Mr. Bonnyfeather would not go, however.

428

"I shall not go so far as to imitate your uncle but it will be wisest for me to stay here. You go, Anthony." He waved them out and remained sitting in his chair while Vincent and Anthony hastened to Otto Franco's. The streets and the piazza were thronged.

Mr. Bonnyfeather took a book from the sleeve of his wadded dressing gown and began to read.

Britannia Rediviva
A Poem on the Birth of the Prince, Born on the tenth of June, 1688.

How different it would have been for John Bonnyfeather, for instance, if that prince had reigned. The old Jacobite, a compound of feudal sentimentality and commercial acumen, read on, allowing his dreams of what might have been to warm his heart with ghostly comfort in the silence of the deserted house. Suddenly the pomp of the courtly verse seemed to take on for him a peculiarly personal meaning. A good omen for Anthony's voyage, he thought, a light on the past. He lingered over the lines:

> Departing spring could only stay to shed
> Her blooming beauties on her genial bed,
> But left the manly Summer in her stead,
> With timely fruit the longing land to cheer,
> And to fulfil the promise of the year.
> Betwixt the seasons came the auspicious heir,
> This age to blossom, and the next to bear.

Well, he had seen the blossom. And he would not have to bear the next age. Thanks to the Virgin that would rest on other, younger shoulders! "Anthony, my son, my son."

The thunder of the cannon of the departing British fleet saluting the Tuscan flag still flying on the castle startled him and made him drop *Dryden* to the floor. So they were going! All safe. The pulse of the French drums could be heard answering coming through the Porta Pisa.

Half an hour later there was a roar from the crowd. The tricolour had taken the place of the grand duke's ensign. But John Bonnyfeather had not heard that. He was sleeping peacefully an old man's nap in the afternoon sun. Only the echoes of the outside world whispered in the Casa da Bonnyfeather. On the shadowed wall behind the merchant a faded Sisyphus was trying to roll a huge rock up an impossible hill while various imps were laughing at him. About two o'clock the gate clicked and Faith came stealthily across the court in her bonnet. She looked down at the old merchant sardonically, smiled, and passed on to her room noiselessly.

Meanwhile from the upper windows of the Casa da Franco Anthony, Vincent, Toussaint, and the Franks, with the exception of Uncle Otto, were watching the arrival of the French. When the castle was seized Governor Spanocchi had been found there and was now brought to the mayority at his own urgent request under guard. The crowd howled at him for its lottery money, which he was shrewdly enough thought to have shipped off with the town treasure chests. About two o'clock the cannon from the castle were heard firing vainly at a few English ships just steering out of the roads.

Shortly afterwards a column of French cavalry came galloping down the Strada Ferdinanda with a magnificent horseman at their head. He was at first taken for General Buonaparte and was cheered by a radical mob. It was Murat. He dismounted and began to arrange a fitting reception for the conqueror.

The governor and his staff were forced to get into gala uniform. The various foreign consuls were assembled. Uncle Otto was made to get out of bed and put on his official coat. His pallor was extreme. It took a great deal of beer and the reassurances of both Vincent and Anthony to get him across the narrow street. Amid the crestfallen group of city officials and important merchants dragged out for the occasion and standing uneasily on the steps of the mayority just opposite, his shoulders sloped most disconsolately. His nephew waved to him from the window, but in vain.

As usual with all military occasions an interminable delay now took place. The crowd grew restive, insolent, and was squeezed against the walls by the French horses for its trouble. Cries and curses arose, the screams of a child. Presently a little girl was carried away gasping and moaning. She had been trampled by a horse. Toussaint looked down pale and shocked. He could not bear the noise the child had made. Just then the police knocked at the door ordering every house to illuminate that night. "Liberty" had officially arrived. One must rejoice now or go to prison.

Anthony laughed and began to quote Rousseau at Toussaint. Then he was ashamed of himself for his thoughtless cruelty. The face of his old tutor was haggard with disappointment. For the first time in months Anthony took him by the hand and with quiet remorse begged his pardon. He could see that it was a real crisis for the idealistic little Frenchman.

"Toussaint, mon maître, you who were so sweet to me when I was a little boy—how could I be so cruel! Do you not know I love you? What has just happened, do not think of it. The child! It was a cruel accident. The hero is yet to arrive. Be yourself, a philosopher as always."

The little man looked up at him with so great a thankfulness in his face as to touch Anthony infinitely. He could never forget that bland, sweet look. How foolish their misunderstanding had been. About what? About Faith!

"You forgive me that blow, then, mon vieux?" Toussaint asked.

Anthony reached over and rumpled the short curls on the little man's head.

"There," he said, "an insult for an insult! Now we are even." They walked back to the window again arm in arm.

The drums in the piazza had begun to roll. A sharp command could be heard. As they looked out together a thousand sabres flashed out as one. In the late afternoon sunlight it seemed as if the arrival of Jove were being announced by a steel lightning and thunder. A noise of galloping horses and wheels was heard in the distance. The world craned its neck.

Down the Strada Ferdinanda a plain carriage drawn by grey horses and followed by a few mud-slashed guards careened into sight. It was moving at great speed. A small, hatless, pale man with his lank hair blowing in the wind was leaning back in the middle of the rear seat reading a book. He paid no attention whatever to the roars of the crowd. As the carriage turned into the piazza the heavy, rear artillery wheels with which it had been fitted described a quarter circle on the cobbles, grating hideously. The man in the carriage sat up at the same instant and tossed his book out into the street. Some urchins scrambled for a treatise on ballistics which fluttered and fell among them like a hurt butterfly. Another flash of lightning, the sabres came to salute. The carriage stopped with a jerk before the mayoralty.

The pale young man, who now seemed as he sat bolt upright to occupy not only the entire carriage but the piazza as well, put on his hat and saluted. Flash, flash, and the sabres grated back in their scabbards. The men sat at attention like ragged, equestrian statues with bronze faces. Murat came down the steps to meet Buonaparte.

"Well, general," said a high clear voice which would have been feminine had it not been so crisp and accusatory. "So you were too late!"

"The ships had already gone, mon général . . ." began Murat when he was cut short.

From the carriage an accusatory finger pointed at the group on the steps. It was fixed on Uncle Otto.

"Is that an English uniform I see?"

"No, padrone," moaned the terrified little German. "No! Questa è l'uniforma di Amburgo!"

Even the troopers grinned with their general. "*Padrone!*"

"*Hamburg!*" said Buonaparte as if he had already abolished the place, and got out of the carriage. He

432

ran up the steps and took the governor's sword which was held out to him like a bodkin.

"I shall expect you to provide my troops with ration, fodder, clothing and shoes, especially shoes," shouted the little man looking at Spanocchi like a small eagle. "That is what you exist for now. See to it that the requisitions are filled."

"The dearth is extreme, Highness," faltered the poor man used only to addressing Austrian superiors. "The prices . . ."

"Tut, tut! Omelettes are inflated due to the extreme scarcity of eggs. You talk like a merchant, now *go!* Hullin," said he turning to a tall major of grenadiers, "I appoint you city major. Comb out the place. Do not be such a simpleton as you were at Pisa. If they have let the English go, make them pay. Money! Take the shoes off their feet. Court-martial the governor. Act as if you were taking the Bastille again."

He swept his eyes about the piazza as though noting who was there to see and hear. For ten seconds or more he seemed to be looking directly into the Franks' window at Anthony and at Toussaint whose face worked with emotion. He whispered something to Hullin, who glanced up and shook his head.

"A fine welcome you give me here," he continued turning now on the quaking merchants. From the window across the narrow street Anthony and Vincent could see him clearly and hear every word. His voice rose to a high pitch.

"Do not doubt it. I shall give the English a final lesson. I march on Vienna and then northwards. Hamburg, every hiding place of these water rats shall be ferreted out, swept clean. Then their island next." He beat his left leg with his gauntlets. The leg trembled. Livorno was a bitter disappointment. He had seen the sails of Nelson glimmering away as he entered. Beckoning to an adjutant he reseated himself in the carriage.

To Toussaint it seemed as if Buonaparte had turned on the crowd the unseeing glance of a mummy. There was no speculation in those eyes Only dull flashes as from the fires of Stromboli over the horizon at night.

He was pallid, yellow. His long, sleek, jet-black hair dangled around his face like the locks of a Seminole Indian threading the swamp. He sat there diminutive, youthful, in a worn simple uniform with gloom on his brow.

"No light," thought Toussaint. "Bon Dieu! no light!"

The sabres flashed only lightning once more. Hullin stood on the carriage steps in an attitude of profound respect listening to some last muttered admonitions. Then as suddenly as he had come, and with the same ominous rumble of wheels, Buonaparte was gone.

To Anthony looking down from the window, watching all this, there had come that inexplicable feeling that his own fate had somehow been laid in the hands of the little man whom he had watched getting in and out of his carriage. How and why? Out of what immense ramifications of events had the threads of his own existence been laid in those hands? One thin thread to be sure, but it was bound up and woven into that thick rope of Europe, those millions of other gossamers tangled into a strong strand by which the world was to be towed along for a while; towed out of stagnant waters into new.

It was a curious thing, but of all the thousands of eyes that had looked on Buonaparte that day in Livorno there was scarcely a pair but took this for granted. For a few moments Anthony had actually watched a section of that strand running through those nervous, white hands. It was a relief to have them gone. He felt as if he had to recapture the skein of his own life again. He did not know where it might lead, but at least he could follow it now himself, even if blindly. "To Havana," Mr. Bonnyfeather said. Anywhere, as long as it led away from Livorno.

For months past all the threads in the town had been warped out of the normal blocks and pulleys through which they ran. All the world now seemed out of gear. His own thread had slipped clear off the familiar pulley where it had been running in what might have become a ceaseless round. Now it flapped free, was hurtling off into the unknown. He was glad of that. It would not be his hands only that would rig it to the tackle of life again. No, there was a strong mysterious drag on it, he felt. He would see the world now. Never could he see enough of it. The void of his first ten years was still deep as a well. One lifetime was not sufficient to fill it. He turned from the window with an unconscious gesture of hail and farewell to find himself in the Franks' room with Toussaint sitting on the sill beside him. The little man sighed.

"It was the gloomy face of a tyrant, Anthony," he said.

Uncle Otto came in trying to recover face and exclaiming "Birbante!" His wife and the little girl and Vincent did their best to soothe him. The small ego of Uncle Otto had met something so cosmic he looked shattered.

Anthony and Toussaint walked home together, the latter gloomy. But that night at supper Faith began to talk with Toussaint and actually smiled at him. Sunlight burst in upon the little man and shone again from his face. To Anthony there was something sinister about it all. Yet he was surprised to find that much as he disliked Faith he did not care to have her kind to Toussaint. He was enraged with himself at this. What strange unknown depths were in him? Actually he could not tell himself what kind of person he was. What would he do under new circumstances in other worlds? Who and what was he?

He sat half-undressed on the edge of his bed pondering. Now he knew why Mr. Bonnyfeather had said, "God keep you." You did not even know why you were yourself. The face in the miniature came back to him now with comfort. That was what he wanted to be like. Only this morning he had felt he was like that, his mother! Part of him. Who and what was the other part? He wondered. But he could never ask now. His father!

"*Father, mother, father, mother,*" he kept saying the words over again trying to give them some reality, shape, and memory. He was somebody's son. He would some day be a father. Angela might have a child! He had not thought of that. What did it all mean? These human words had always had a sound of prayer about them, still had.

"Mother, son, father—Holy mother," he turned to the Madonna on the wall. The old formulas sprang to his lips full of new meanings. It was a relief to be able to pray that way again! He had not been able to do so for so long. Not until the other day. Whatever he might do he was not to be left alone. The misery, restlessness, and youthful despairs of the past hectic months rushed from his lips in a whispered confession to the Virgin. All doubt had vanished with the blessed relief. Was she not there, on the wall, in heaven, as always! Had she not come to him in his dream with Angela, young and beautiful? He and the Virgin were very old, very old together. He had seen her that night as his soul remembered her, looking back through ancient doors of birth and death made transparent by the light of eternal passion breaking through them. Before, now, and forever, he had seen her merging with the waters at the root of the great tree as he remembered her in the springtime of the world.

"Ah, they called her mother, mother of sorrows. But she was mother of joy as well. Yes, he believed that. She was sitting there now, as always, with the child in her arms. But in the dream there were two of them. The other heavenly twin had come back. Who was he, that lost one? Was he like Anthony lost for a while on earth? Was he Anthony? Anthony who could return to her knees, in dreams? Ah God! if he could only lay his head on her breast! Be rocked to sleep there as he never had been, forget and forget, already he would forget."

He drew near to her in a dreamful mood in which the life within him seemed to leave his body sitting breathing, while he drew closer to her against the wall. He laid his head there and kneeled looking at her head lost among the stars. Silence and peace and silence. To be and not to think, only to know and feel. Ecstasy.

At last he opened his eyes again and found that he really was kneeling against the wall. By the dim light that burned before her, very dim, except about the little shrine, he seemed to see her now more clearly than ever before. His eyes were wide awake and rested. They were made to peer into far spaces. It was not necessary even to wink. He looked steadily and easily at the statue.

It seemed to him that he saw her there now as the Madonna of his dreams, but older, sweeter, with something more tender, more human, the mystic woman of the fountain touched and wafted by some ineffable experience into a being far more beautiful, sympathetic, and divine. And it seemed now to him, too, that for the first time he saw she was holding the child out to him as if he should draw near and touch it. He had been like that once. Was he now? Partly perhaps. The child was her son. Father Xavier had told him the story. Born in the rocky stable amid the oxen under the stars. And there had been more to that story. It was about the babe after he became a man. He had thought very little about that. Perhaps he should think more. Why did she hold him out that way? Should he really draw near and touch him? He put out his hand. Then he saw that the child was still sleeping on her breast. He dared not awaken him. Not yet. "After a while," he thought. It was as though his lips went on speaking another's words. "After a while when you find him again."

Late in the night he awakened cold. He was still leaning against the wall, but the light had gone out. It was dark now. He slipped, half-dressed as he was, under the covers and slept exhausted. Next morning the room for the first time for months seemed washed with a happy light as he woke.

"There will not be many more mornings here," he thought. How quiet and how home-like it was. He pressed his cheek against the pillow, enjoying it and whistling softly. How wonderful, and after all how happy his days had been here! A light tap sounded on his door.

"Anthony, are you awake yet, my boy?" said the kindly voice of Mr. Bonnyfeather. "Get up and dress yourself. I have news for you."

437

Anthony smoothed out the dent on the pillow where his head had been and put on his clothes. In the big room they were already at breakfast. The court lay quiet and serene in the morning sun with the shadows withdrawing from it as if by magic.

Chapter Twenty-Three

Farewells and Epitaphs

"Y OUR ship has come in, Anthony," said Mr.
Bonnyfeather. "At least I hope it has," he
added hastily, smiling at the involuntarily
prophetic nature of the remark.

"Nolte sent word this morning. It is an American
brig and he and his precious uncle will be taking advantage of this neutral to get rid of some of their
anxious fellow travellers. Frau Frank must have had
her hands full feeding a dozen or more at once. You
and McNab, go down and look her over. If it is
necessary you might ask her captain to supper tonight.
I might persuade him to make your voyage direct. But
be careful, arrange everything if you can, yourselves.
We do not want to attract notice here just now. So far
the French have ignored us. You will have to avoid
all clearance papers."

The old man turned to his latest London newspaper
which he scanned anxiously. A month ago victory was
inevitable, he noted ironically—over his chop.

Anthony and McNab hurried through breakfast and

went down to the quay at the lower end of the Darsena. A trim little brig was warped in close to the dock but not into the slip. She had springs on her cables, and running his eye aloft McNab noted that, while to an unprofessional glance the canvas might seem snugly furled, it was stowed so as to be let go if necessary with a run.

Anthony liked the ship. He had never met anything quite like her. She appeared a little more frail and bird-like than any other craft he had seen. From her sharp bows blew back the carved eagle feathers of an Indian chief's head-dress. His hooked nose seemed to snuff the surges. The masts raked aft at a sharp angle and were stayed so tautly that the standing rigging hummed in the morning breeze. Her deck was spotless. Between the two masts was a "long tom" carefully covered with canvas. Aft, the box over the captain's cabin rose above the quarter-deck. Even in port her hatches were battened down. Except for these, and her polished wheel and hooded binnacle, there seemed nothing else on deck.

"All a-tanto and not a soul aboard?" grunted McNab. They walked down past the brig a little farther, giving their eyes a sailor's treat. The wind whipped the ensign out over the water. It flowed out into the breeze, curling with long tiger streaks. On a blue field a circle of stars seemed whirling about nothing. It was the first time Anthony had seen the Stars and Stripes. Then, just around the corner of the galley, they saw whatever afterwards he thought of as the spirit of the ship.

Seated in a sea-chair lashed to two large wooden half-moons sat rocking contentedly, and with an air of self-possession that only she herself could convey, a prim, bony woman with extraordinarily pointed lips. She was knitting a positively gigantic stocking with the heaviest yarn imaginable, and for every stitch and click of her needles she twisted the extreme tips of her lips. It looked as if she silently whistled. At the distance of a few yards they stood looking at her over the water as at an apparition. On McNab and Anthony she did not

440

bestow a glance. For a while they watched time being destroyed while the stocking grew.

"Ahoy, the brig there," said McNab at last tentatively.

"*Ee*-lisha," said the woman without missing a stitch and continuing to rock, "Ee-*lisha!*"

"Comin' on deck," said a deep voice from the cabin with a restraint so abject as to make McNab grin. A red-faced man with an iron-grey beard and cold blue eyes stuck his head through the aft sliding hatch and looked at them.

"Ahoy, the brig," said McNab again.

"Ahoy, the dock there," said the man and glowered. The woman continued to knit. It seemed to Anthony as if they had reached an impasse. McNab cleared his throat.

"If you'll waft us a wee bit o' a skiff, captain," said he, "I'll put that in your lug will belike warm your pocket."

"*Aye?*" said the man. "Philly!"

A darky stuck his head out of the galley.

"Fetch the gentlemen."

"The crew are ashore," he bawled. "Ye won't mind having the cook get ye, I hope," he continued, evidently to Anthony, who was dressed like a merchant's clerk.

"Not at all," said Anthony, "if he's a good cook."

"Best 'tween here and Boston," replied the captain.

"He ain't," said the woman.

The little boat sculled by the negro danced to them over the few yards of harbour.

"It's na miracle the French hae no seized yon brig," said McNab as they were ferried across. "Yon carline wi' her knittin' needles would stand off Buonaparte I'm thinkin'."

WAMPANOAG
Providence, R. I.

gleamed across the duck-like stern as they passed. They climbed up the dangling ladder and found themselves

441

on deck in the tremendous white light that beat about the rocking chair.

"Good morning, ma'm," said McNab touching his hat, despite himself a little sneakily.

The woman missed one stitch. "Ee-*lisha*," she said.

"Come below," roared the captain.

At the foot of the ladder they found themselves standing in the most peculiar captain's cabin imaginable. It was neither a ship's cabin nor a New England parlour. It was both. There were four bunks built into the ribs of the ship. Two of these like Dutch beds were provided with folding shutters. The two, round stern windows were curtained with an effeminate lace. Under each of these eyes was a chest painted pure white, labelled respectively "Jane" and "Elisha." Between the two chests the great keel beam of the ship curved out like a nose and widened toward the floor as if it were trying to expand its bolted nostrils.

The effect of all this was to give the aft end of the cabin with its half-curtained eyes the appearance of a peculiarly bestial face trying to be coquettish in a lace night-cap. As he looked at the two chests standing out like white, bared tusks from the cheeks of this sinister countenance, Anthony felt as Red Riding-hood must have when she first began to realize that her grandmother was a wolf.

But if the cabin was sinister toward the stern it made up for it by being safely domestic forward. Lashed to the ship's ribs by a perverse puzzle of beautifully intricate knots was a mahogany sideboard of undoubtedly genteel lineage. Its gracefully curved limbs seemed straining outward. The lady was plainly being held there against her will—facing the wolf. A sturdy, manly sea-desk near by watched this perpetual crisis indifferently. It was stuffed with ship's papers to the point of self-importance and it wore a plume pen in its inkstand hat with an air of "business or nothing."

Anthony and McNab sat down upon two chairs spiked to the deck while the captain seemed to preside from the chest labelled "Elisha."

"Captain Ee-lisha Adonijah Jorham of Providence Plantations, New England," said the red-faced man looking at them with level eyes. "Gentlemen, at yer service. She," he continued jabbing upward with one thumb, "is my wife, Mrs. Jorham. She was a Putnam— *once*." He lowered his voice slightly.

Having no means of controverting this McNab and Anthony introduced themselves. It was not long before the captain and McNab had taken each other's measure. Yankee had met Scot. Both were interested in each other and fenced carefully. Ten minutes went by and neither had learned anything.

"I'm thinkin'," said McNab, "that the deil will soon be dizzy gangin' aroond the bush. Let's talk till the point."

Captain Elisha opened his chest and took out a bottle of rum. As he did so, as if by prearrangement, his wife came down the ladder and stood knitting. She would not sit down. The captain sighed. Nevertheless, the discussion went on.

After an hour it appeared that the captain would be glad to consider a voyage to Havana on charter terms, provided he was allowed to make certain ports of call on the way. Yes, he knew of course of Mr. Bonnyfeather, and of the conditions at Livorno. On their mutual dislike of the French he and McNab almost clinched the bargain. Then the captain sheered off. He would prefer to sign with Mr. Bonnyfeather himself.

But there were to be no papers, reminded McNab. It would not do now. Mr. Bonnyfeather was no longer in business. It might compromise him. This was to be a purely private affair. Merely to take the young gentleman to Havana. It could all be arranged verbally.

All the more reason then for seeing the merchant personally, said the captain. It was McNab's turn to sigh. Mr. Bonnyfeather, he knew, would not drive so close a bargain as might be. Nevertheless, he was forced to play his last card and invite the captain that night to dinner. In the presence of the lady Anthony thoughtfully added her to the invitation.

"What do you say, Mrs. Jorham?" asked the captain. All realized it was a final appeal.

"I won't mind some shore fixin's—if they're turned out right," she added non-committally. "Ye might send Philadelphy along with that Bank tartle to help out. I'm plum worn out watchin' the critter tryin' to get away."

"Like the sideboard, ma'm?" said Anthony unable to restrain himself. The captain laughed.

"Young man," said she icily, "where might *ye* be expectin' to spend etarnity?" Her mouth pointed.

"Wall, wall," cried the captain trying to move them out before the threatened gale could break. "At eight then, after dark. I'll mind the patrols. So long now." He looked with an approving but anxious eye at Anthony. The knitting had stopped and his wife was watching.

"I don't care if I do," said McNab pouring himself a drink from the square bottle and tossing it off. "A wee doch-an-dorris, noo . . ."

But no sooner had his hand left the bottle the first time than it was seized by Mrs. Jorham and deposited in the chest marked "Jane." It was the first drop that had passed, and the last for any of them. A parched twinge wrinkled the lips of Captain Elisha, but he waved them out as his wife locked the chest. They went.

"A watched bottle never gurgles," said McNab as they went down the ship's side. In the cabin the typhoon had burst.

"'Twas an ill jest o' yours, laddie. If you sail in yon ship you're no like to hae heard the last o' it. Losh!"

The captain, his face more fiery than before, was hailing them.

"I'll send the nigger with the tartle," he shouted at the dock. Then he must have heard the voice of his mate calling him, for he dived below.

The dinner for the Jorhams was to be an unusual

444

feast; one not for business alone. Indeed, McNab had been instructed to return to the brig and to arrange for Anthony's passage on the captain's terms. He had done so. He and Philadelphia had returned with the turtle which was killed in the courtyard amidst immense curiosity. Dinner was to be a memorable, final feast.

Mr. Bonnyfeather had planned it with a double motive. As a farewell to Anthony it was to be a merry one. He would spare Anthony the sadness of a sorrowful parting and he would also spare himself the lonely, private agony of a good-bye that he scarce dared to face. "The last, the dear last of us all," he thought looking at the boy's golden head. They sat in his room together talking, making last arrangements, pausing, and reverting to familiar topics as one goes back to look at something for the last time.

Faith was very busy outside packing Anthony's chests. They could hear her moving about in the hall.

"I suppose you will be taking the Madonna with you, Mr. Anthony," she said coming in suddenly.

"Oh," said he getting up. He had almost forgotten her. "*Yes*, wrap her up carefully. Put her in the big chest."

Faith nodded. So she would see the last of *that*, she thought. She turned the thing face downward and closed the lid. "Farewell to the bad luck of a Paleologus!"

In the room Anthony and Mr. Bonnyfeather sounded very merry. But it seemed to both of them at times that the misty landscapes on the wall were hazier than usual. The old man lighted his candles. He wiped his spectacles and put them on again several times. Thus they both talked through the long twilight as if they would always be able to do so till evenings were no more. At eight o'clock the guests arrived.

It fell to Anthony that evening to do the honours. He found Captain Elisha and Mrs. Jorham, the latter assisted gingerly by Philadelphia, climbing down in the court from a high-wheeled cab. The captain was dressed in a homsespun suit so tight that it gave him the cherubic outlines of an overgrown cupid. Mrs. Jorham trailed behind her a long sea-green skirt of a mid-century, colonial vintage. Into this ocean of faded velvet a pointed bodice thrust violently like the bow of a ship. Above it her head rose like a teak figurehead. She carried a canvas umbrella with whalebone ribs and what appeared to be a spar for a handle. On the end of the spar was a yellow ivory ball like a doll's head. The whole affair, which had a belligerent air about it, flapped about the point, bulged in the middle, where its hips might have been, and was tied about the waist with a rope. As Mrs. Jorham stood in the court holding it maternally close to the folds of her skirt it appeared to be her bashful replica in miniature and might have been her female child.

"Philly," said she, "take my umbreller." The captain laid his peajacket over the darky's other arm. Holding these objects majestically before him, Philadelphia ushered them up the steps.

The Americans seemed to have learned from the Indians the savage custom of shaking hands. They shook hands with Mr. Bonnyfeather, with Anthony, with McNab, with Faith, solemnly and with malice of forethought. It looked as if Captain Elisha would shake hands with himself when his eye fell upon the dinnertable already set with many glasses. He and Mr. Bonnyfeather disappeared to talk business while Anthony was left alone with Mrs. Jorham and the umbrella.

They sat facing each other on two heavy gilt chairs. Seemingly at a vast distance from them in the great apartment the white round of the table, much enlarged for the occasion, lay in a cheerful glow. But by contrast all the rest of the room was in darkness. The folds of the angular woman's skirt swept around her and into the shadows. Above them in the twilight gleamed the bony ribs and the pale ivory knob of the umbrella. She seemed to emanate a kind of masterful, yet maternally-virtuous disapproval of everything, whose only softening influence was a touch of lugubrious woe. Having said "how" to this chieftainess in whalebone, Anthony was now at a loss. He could not shake hands again. At the very thought he started to smile. The woman's lips pointed indignantly.

"I trust," said she, "that ye haven't spent the arternoon jokin'. Ye seemed in an idle mood this mornin'. It was not that I object to what ye said about my sideboard! It was yer levity in comparin' it to a woman."

"I have been getting ready to leave home all afternoon, Mrs. Jorham. I can assure you there was not much levity in that, and I was not idle."

Mrs. Jorham looked somewhat mollified but nevertheless shook her head doubtfully. "Mere earthly consarns are not sufficient. You should cast your eyes above." Anthony looked surprised. "Unless you have devoted some time during the day to prayer you may consider it wasted, you know." She laid her umbrella across her knees and folded her hands in her lap.

Embarked thus on the pursuit of her favourite quarry, the soul, she began to feel more congenial. In the semi-darkness her outline lost much of its rigidity. She cuddled the umbrella. It no longer seemed likely that she might open it in the twilight and flit off on the wings of a bat. There might even be shelter under it for two. Anthony wondered about the captain.

"Whenever I'm fixin' to make a v'y'ge," snapped Mrs. Jorham, "I go in for extensive prayer. V'y'ges are solemn things. Ye can never tell. I pack my duds in the mornin', all but the scriptures, and I usually goes to the ta-own churchyards in the arternoon and takes the good book along for reference. There's nothing like a few chice epitaphs and a little solemn scripture to put you in a frame of mind fit to go to sea. It makes your petitions gin-uine, the kind that goes straight through to the marcy seat. I tell ye I know it. Have ye any clever graveyards here?" she inquired suggestively.

"Several," said Anthony, "but most of the clever epitaphs are in Latin."

"That's the way in heathen parts," she went on. "I am glad to tell that it's dyin' out at home. I must say Latin's Greek to me, although I was a Putnam."

"Do the Putnams speak Latin like the Jesuits?" asked Anthony. He wondered if they were tonsured, too.

447

"Nope, they don't need it to git along in Bosting, and most of my family round Nuburyport went in for rum and ile. But all of 'em got fine epitaphs. Granite stones, too. Not a soapstone in the lot. No, siree." The lady paused triumphantly.

"Ye ever been to my pa-arts?"

Anthony shook his head regretfully.

"Well, sir, there's a fine parcel o' ta-owns in New England. A feast for Christian eyes with white churches and neat houses. The snow comes regular and kills off the roaches. We don't have critters except what comes in ships from Jamaiky and other foreign pa-arts. But the best thing about the ta-owns is the clever grave-yards. I've seen a sight of 'em all up and da-own the cyoast. But they Southern planters sleeps too proud o' their own private plots! You'd think Gabriel was goin' to call ra-ound and give some souls a separate toot. No, sir, there'll be just one long, common blast, and them that sleeps late'll fry. One o' the slickest church-yards I ever see was at Bridgewater, Mass. I spent a hull week there. Visitin'! I got them inscriptions pat. Some of 'em was poetry. Here's one: 'Here lies buried Mrs. Martha Alden, the wife of Mr. Eleazer Alden, who died 6 January, 1769, aged 69 years." Mrs. Jor-ham broke into song.

> "The resurrection day will come,
>   And Christ's strong voice will burst the tume;
>   The sleeping dead, we trust, will rise
>   With joy and pleasure in her eyes,
>   And ever shine among the wise.
>
>   A-men."

The nasal tune twanged its way about the moulder-ing frescoes. It seemed to curl up among the clouds that had once been rosy with a false dawn but were now like rolling billows of blue and grey smoke through which the chariots of the gods plunged in a growing twilight.

"It'll do the heathens good," said Mrs. Jorham roll-ing her eyes aloft and askance. "And that naked man

lling his barrel in hell. Well, I cala-late their clothes
would singe off, but it don't seem right. I wouldn't
low even the damned to expose themselves."

Anthony sat silent in sheer amazement. The woman
as evidently having a good time. He remembered
ving read about persons like this in Mr. Bonny-
ather's Protestant books. There was, for instance,
The female Saint of Wimbledon." What was it, that
rase the old author used, a classical scholar, he was,
, yes, "That chaste Diana of endangered souls,"—
mething, something, rolls—

"The heat of pious ardour lit her face
As through the wood of error roared the chase,
Acteon-like the heretic was torn
While scornfully she wound her Christian horn."

nd so on ad infinitum.

O lord! he wished Vincent would come. He could
ar the snatch of harmony at Signora Bovino's ringing
ut now as if his mind were defending itself auto-
atically. Undoubtedly he was being chased.

"In memory of Capt. Seth Alden—
The corpse in silent darkness lies
Our friend is gone, the captain dies . . ."

"Thar she spa-outs, and thar she bla-ows," roared
e voice of Captain Elisha who emerged just then from
e corridor with Mr. Bonnyfeather. They had clinched
eir bargain over a bottle of rum, at least the captain
ad, and he was not what might be termed his better
lf.

"Has that old cachalot been spa-outin' dirges to ye,
oung man? I'm sorry for ye, plum sorry!" He clapped
nthony on the back. "A little sea-vility, a little sea-
ility is what you Putnams need to larn, Jane. I allers
aid so. I'm the man to larn yer. The idear. I kin smell
em tumes right through the tartle soup."

"Ee-lisha, ye've been drinkin'," said his wife sniffing
omething else than turtle soup.

"I hev. And what's more I'm goin' right on for th
rest of the evenin' and ye can belay yer temperanc
drip and *mo*-lasses." He looked approvingly at th
table. "Philly, is that potage perfected?"

"It air, suh!"

The captain made a gesture which in its generou
expansiveness included the more remote members o
the solar system. "Come on," said he, and led M
Bonnyfeather by the arm to his own table.

"Mr. Adverse," said Mrs. Jorham in a voice nov
so subdued that Anthony felt sorry for her, "don'
forget what I have been tellin' ye. Do a graveyar
or two, before . . ."

"Belay them sepelchrees, Jane," called her husband

But Anthony promised and saw that he had made
friend. Slipping her arm in his they advanced to th
table.

"Madame," said Mr. Bonnyfeather escaping, "yo
will also permit *me* to do some of the honours." H
seated her on his right. All the gentlemen now tool
their chairs, and with this display of manners Mrs
Jorham was obviously touched. She permitted hersel
a dab at her eyes.

"Ye make me feel at home," she said to Mr. Bonny
feather.

"I regard that," said he, "as a touching compliment.'

Mrs. Jorham began to rally and to remember wh
she had once been. "I do miss the fixin's sometimes,'
she sighed running her eyes over the glass and silve
and fingering the table-cloth. "And land's sake th
napkins! We do live like Injuns on the *Wampanoag!*
often says to Elisha, says I . . ." but the captain wa
looking at her. "Anyway it's nice to be settin' witl
gentlemen and a respectable female again!"

"I'll say it is," slipped in the captain, also lookin;
with approval at Faith.

Suddenly an electric thrill ran through him. He ha
seen Faith flutter her eye at him. There could be n
doubt of it. It hadn't happened to him for years.

"Woman," said he, tossing off a glass of wine to he
with a loud smack, "it's a tarnation wonder someon

idn't marry ye years ago. Years ago! I say." He
anged his fist on the table so that the soup jumped.

Mrs. Jorham's eyes narrowed. The landscape did
ot seem so respectable as she had thought a moment
efore.

"There's some things a woman can wait too long
o change her mind about," she said dryly. Faith's
hroat rippled. There was an awkward pause. Toussaint
umped into the breach gallantly.

"Madame, I can assure you it has not been for lack
f opportunities, or want of a philosopher to persuade
nademoiselle that she remains a . . . er, single. Mon-
ieur," said he catching Mr. Bonnyfeather's eye, "may
be the first to propose a toast—*To the Ladies*."

"Gaud bless 'em," added McNab with a sardonic
wist looking at the two women glaring at each other.
'What would we do without them?" The crisis might
ave continued but just then Vincent dashed in late
haking the rain off his curls.

"Well! Elisha, I told ye it would rain," said Mrs.
orham.

"Aye, ye're a clever barometer, I'll give ye that,"
aid the captain.

"Vera sansitive to dampness in any form," muttered
McNab to Faith. But Faith was proposing the return
oast.

"I propose something we can all drink to," she said
miling at Mrs. Jorham, "and I with as much hope
s any of you, perhaps more, who knows? 'The
uture.' "

"But not without faith," amended Mr. Bonnyfeather
vho could not avoid the obvious.

Mrs. Jorham hesitated. She had been trapped.

"Come on, Jane," said Captain Elisha appreciating
he housekeeper's finesse.

"I'm a temperance woman," she snapped.

"Madame," said Mr. Bonnyfeather, "allow me. A
ery light wine, a remedy for the climate, never intoxi-
ating, in small doses. The custom of the country." He
owed, his eyes twinkling, and from a decanter filled

451

Mrs. Jorham's glass with a fiery burgundy. He stood waiting.

Mrs. Jorham arose with a stiff yet coy reluctance. She hesitated but finally clinked her glass against Mr Bonnyfeather's as if she had already been seduced and nothing could be done about it.

"The future," she murmured, her cheeks tingling at her inconceivable abandon. Then she swallowed the burgundy with a gulp.

"The auld deil," whispered McNab to Anthony.

She sat down slowly. Her hands remained spread out on the table as if placed on a faintly pleasant electric contact.

"Well, darn my mother's socks!" said the captain.

Everybody laughed and broke out talking at once. The ice had been broken.

Anthony glanced at Mr. Bonnyfeather. He was sitting with a look of great satisfaction at the success of his ruse. As for Mrs. Jorham there was no doubt that she was wrapt in a deep spiritual experience. The end of her nose was slowly beginning to glow.

Vincent was as full of news and as merry as ever. "Have you heard the new song the gamins are singing? It throws the French out of step when they pass." He broke out with his full tenor.

"Io cledevo di veder fla pochino,
Che se n'andasser via questi blicconi:
Dia Saglata! ne vien ogni tantino
Quasi, quasi dilei, Dio mi peldoni!
O che anche Clisto polta il palticcino,
O che i Soplani son tanti minchioni!"

The happy, careless voice transported Anthony again to the molten hours they had wasted delightfully together along the Corso. In the gay mocking lilt was concentrated the life of the streets of Livorno. How he loved it all. Now that he was going, how homesick for it he was already. Could it, could it be possible that so much happiness, and dear sorrow, could pass? "The future?" What was it? Let them always sit listening about a table like this. The voice ceased. The silence seemed unbearable.

"Sing again, Vincent, sing again. The song we sang that morning together, do you remember?"

Vincent burst out with it. Anthony joined in. On the surge of his own notes he recovered himself. His voice rang out clearly. He could blend it with Vincent's beautifully. For another moment he was gayly happy. But this time with a new poignance.

He looked at Mr. Bonnyfeather. With the music and the words he poured out his boundless gratitude and at the end reached over and filled his glass to the old man. They all understood and drank with a shout. The table rose, Captain Jorham grunting.

The bright red flush appeared on the merchant's cheek bones. He was much moved. The young voices had gone home. He rose slowly and held out his glass with an air that the world had already forgotten.

"Anthony, my dear boy, God bless you."

They drank it silently. Anthony caught Faith's eye. He was aware that behind her serious expression she was amused at all this. A minute ago he could almost have forgiven her. But not now, not ever. It would be war between them to the last. Poor Toussaint! He wished Faith would make up her mind to leave Leghorn. They were sitting down now. He would have to reply.

Heavens, what was that strange noise?

Captain Jorham had also been moved by the occasion, and his potations, to the point of song. His face glowed like a bonfire. A husky roar proceeded from his chest.

> "Yanke skipper comin' down the river
> Yankee skipper, *HO . . .*"

He had forgotten the rest of the words. He hummed the tune, rumbling like a cart going downhill. Then a look of inspiration came into his eyes. He had remembered the last line just in time.

"Yankee skipper comin' down the river."

He ended triumphantly, gurgling. Then he filled his glass till it spilled and slopped over as he raised it.

"To the v'y'ge!"

The success of the toast was disturbed by a sound as of dry sticks crackling. It proceeded from Mrs. Jorham. Mr. Bonnyfeather was about to pat her on the back when it became evident that she was laughing.

"Why, Jane," said her husband, "ye ain't gorn off that way since ye was a Putnam."

"Ain't I?" she spat back. "How do ye know?"

For some reason, perhaps because a small bright bead seemed about to leave the fiery tip of Mrs. Jorham's nose but miraculously did not, they all laughed. She joined in heartily. A whole brush-fire seemed to be alight, crackling and snapping. Suddenly in the middle of it a hen was disturbed and went off cackling. Wine is a marvellous playfellow. They all lay back and roared. McNab nearly split his tight waistcoat. At this he suddenly looked serious and they went off again. Captain Jorham was still standing like a nonplussed colossus with his glass poised questioningly. He glanced at his buttons uneasily. They were all right.

"Whar's the joke?" he rumbled.

Then they all wondered. Something, something that nobody could quite remember now had been so funny. Anthony still wheezed but it was purely physical. His stomach seemed to have collapsed with the joke. A cold voice stilled them all.

"Elisha, be ye fixin' to go to Havaner?" demanded Mrs. Jorham. She seemed to have accused him of a crime. They all looked at him. How would he defend himself? He put his glass down defiantly.

"I be," he said.

"Then," said she, "who's goin' to do the navigatin'? That's what I want to know."

She looked at them all appealingly.

"The last time we come over we started for London. Do ye know where we fetched up at? Lisbon!" she shouted. "Lisbon!"

"Woman," he said sitting down heavily, "I forbid e."

She had touched him to the quick. For the past wo years something terribly wrong had overtaken he navigation of Captain Elisha Jorham. He could not fathom it. Secretly he had taken to coasting from ort to port picking up what he called "cargoes of otions." He had turned many a lucky penny. But he cargoes of the *Wampanoag* had become as eccentric as her course when she took to the high seas. He had hoped to conceal his difficulties. Only Mr. Bonnyfeather's exceptional offer of an hour before had finally screwed his resolution to the point of heading for deep blue water again. That Lisbon landfall had shaken him terribly, and now his wife had betrayed him.

He sat looking crushed, shaking his head at her.

"Ye've taken the bread out of yer own mouth," he muttered, "I *know* the way back."

"I'm sure you do, captain," said Mr. Bonnyfeather, "besides Mr. Adverse here is by now an excellent navigator in theory. All he needs is some actual practice. You and he can work your reckoning together. You can give him his final polish in the art. Just what he needs."

Captain Jorham looked much mollified and relieved.

"When do you plan to get under way?" continued the merchant.

"Thar's a strong land breeze usually picks up about dawn on these coasts," said the captain in his own element again. "If Mr. Adverse can come aboard at about two bells we'll leave first thing in the mornin'. Better not delay and risk trouble with the authorities."

Mr. Bonnyfeather looked at Anthony. A glance of understanding passed between them.

"Get your chests down while it's dark and then keep below till you are out of the Darsena. Your passports might be an awkward question now with Mr. Udney's visa.

"Vincent," he added, "I regret to interfere with any of your uncle's plans, but I'm afraid your aunt will have to entertain some of her refugees a few days longer. I have engaged Captain Jorham to take Anthony to Havana. He goes north to Genoa first to pick up cargo. There is nothing for him here, as you know. If Genoa suits any of your travellers' plans, they will have to be aboard tonight."

"I'm only sorry for one thing, sir," said Vincent.

He put his arm around Anthony.

"Aye," said the old man, "we're a grieten sair o'er that! And noo let's hae a stirrup cup tigether for the last time, and no more good-byes, for I canna bide them."

All their cups touched. Anthony felt very proud and tall and straight. Excitement he knew would now lend him wings to clear the threshold. He thought of his old friend Mercury taking off from the cloud with the banquet behind him.

They broke away from the table. Anthony looked up just in time to see Mr. Bonnyfeather vanish into the door of his corridor. He did not look back. The door closed.

"Faith," said Anthony, "will you do me a favour?"

"Yes, Signore Adverso," she said trying to look through him it seemed. He met her glance. "Certainly."

"Fetch my hat and cape and the small bag on the table from my room. I do not care to go back there any more."

"I'll take care o' the chests," said McNab.

"Good night, Captain Jorham, I'll see you directly," he called after him. It helped thus to be doing ordinary things. Vincent still sat at the table turning a glass about in his hand. Their eyes met affectionately.

"Good night," bellowed the captain from the court. "Two bells, mind ye. The tide won't wait. A clever evenin' it was, fine and dandy. Philly."

"Yes, suh."

"*On* them chests!"

"I'll swan if it ain't rainin'!" said Mrs. Jorham. She

raised the immense umbrella over them. They disappeared under it.

"Yankee skipper comin' down the river," trilled the captain. The echoes awoke in the old court in a kind of jargon.

"Land's sake, 'Lisha, ye'll wake the dead," they heard his wife say.

"Anthony," said Vincent turning to him. "Is it all right between us? Lately I have thought, sometimes, you know . . . I didn't want you to leave without being sure. I . . ." he choked.

All that was best in his nature shone in his face. Anthony grasped his hands.

"Yes, yes, all right for always, Vincent."

"Let's swear it," said the German looking dramatic and sentimental but earnest as ever.

"The same old Vincent," said Anthony laughing. Then he grew silent. "But we'll call it an oath." They exchanged grips again.

Just then Faith returned. She also smiled. The little bag was very heavy and as she gave it to Anthony she said, "I see you are leaving with more than you brought."

"Are you sorry?" he asked.

"No," she said. She brought her hands up halfway to her breast tensely and then let them fall.

"No, I'll tell you something. It belongs to you!" Then she turned and began to gather the silver together on the table. It bore the Bonnyfeather mark.

He saw his chests go out. "Did you put the Madonna in, Faith?" he asked just to be sure. She had always looked after his things. His voice suddenly sounded boyish again.

"In the big one with the books."

For an instant he caught her eyes burning at him over the table like wells of night. Then she blew out the candles.

He and Vincent stumbled down the steps together. The rain was over but clouds were still scudding across the moon. The courtyard was awash with writhing shadows. He stood looking at it for the last time.

The fountain dripped musically like a faint bell. As he and Vincent turned into the street the only light in all the harbour was on the *Wampanoag*. It moved very quietly. They were bringing her up to her anchor.

Anthony remembered the Darsena that day that he and Father Xavier had first come to the Casa da Bonnyfeather. All the busy life of the place, the bells, the voices, and the ships had departed. Something had dragged them away as if upon an invisible tide. The tide was ebbing from these shores. He, too, felt it tonight. It clutched him strongly. He was going out with it. He would not remain here looking at the past. It and Mr. Bonnyfeather would remain closed up together in the room with the misty walls.

Here just on this corner he had stood as a little boy first looking at the bright, new world. Right here Father Xavier had caught the orange that he had shared with him. How sweet it had tasted then. Now he would catch the whole orange for himself, the whole round world of it, press it to his lips and drain it dry. It was only the rind of it that was bitter. "Golden fruit of the Hesperides growing in the west, I shall find the bough." On the quay he parted with Vincent.

Two bearded Yankee sailors rowed him out to the *Wampanoag*. They looked at him curiously, sitting in the stern sheets with a coat-of-many-capes falling over his shoulders. He had bought a knitted cap for the voyage and under this his hair, now just beginning to turn brown, struggled out about his cheeks. His eyes looked widely into the darkness and his lips were parted with happy expectation. He had seemed very tall and straight as he stood for a moment on the thwart. There was something pleasant and strong about him. Something of the sweetness that had been Maria and the passionate strength of Denis Moore, a wide, clear, Scotch forehead and a provoking Irish smile. The man at the stroke oar winked at him as they shoved off.

"Be you the young gentleman we're takin' to Havaner?" he asked.

"Yes, do you want to go there?"

The man laughed and spat over the side.

"Not that we're ever axed. But westward bound *is* homeward bound, and that suits *me*." He brought the boat around with a long sweep under the stern.

"Ho, it does, does it?" said Captain Jorham looking over the taffrail and lowering a lantern so that it cast a smudge of light on the black water. "Wall then, lay forward with ye, and bring the anchor to the peak. Stand by to cast loose on the jibs. Did ye slush them blocks like I told ye? Belay your jam tackle now, and no stampin' and caterwaulin' round the capstan. Pipe down and a quiet getaway. Pass the word for that again. Mind *ye*, Collins."

"Aye, aye, muttered the sailor, and went forward.

"Ye'd best go below now for a while," said the captain to Anthony. "Yer dunnage hez been stowed in the cabin and Jane's made the starboard bunk up for ye. Ye'll be snug enough. Don't mind her. She do snore."

Anthony went below. A lantern was burning and cast a dim radiance over the place. His chests were already neatly lashed to the stanchions. He started to hang up some things. Just then over the chest marked "Jane" one panel of the closed bunk opened and the head of Mrs. Jorham in a night-cap looked out. She pointed her lips.

"That's right," she said, "that's yours. Elisha sleeps over there behind tother shutters. This is mine. But don't mind me. I'm used to it. I'm glad to have you with us." She beamed on him, pointed her lips, and closed the panel.

He sat down and laughed silently. She reminded him of a picture of a toucan he had once seen, "extraordinary female bird walled in." What a beak it was! The thought of Elisha and Jane billing and cooing through that panel sent him off again. He lay back and enjoyed himself thoroughly. He felt the anchor thump gently. Ropes dragged on deck. Then through the side of the ship came mysteriously the low laughter of ripples as she began to glide. He laid his ear to the planks rejoicing in that hushed, half-merry and semi-sad chantey of farewell. "Good-bye, Livorno." Feet stamped over his head.

Half an hour later his now sleepy reverie was disturbed by Captain Jorham's lighting a rank pipe at the lantern.

"Ye can come on deck now. We're out o' the Darsena and passin' the molo. Now's the rub." He stumped on deck with Anthony. The brig was slipping along very quietly in a following wind with nothing but her jibs set.

"They don't stand out like a squaresail against the sky," said the captain, eyeing the molo with its row of cannon and the flagstaff still bare before sunrise. "In ten minutes we'll be by. The tide's with us."

Suddenly Philadelphia emerged from the galley beating a pan. "Breakfus is re-ady!"

"God *dang* ye!" howled the captain plunging at him and smothering the pan. They watched the shore breathlessly. There was a spurt of fire on the sea wall by the molo . . .

"*One, two, three, four, five, six,*" counted the captain.

Bang, drifted to them the report of the sentry's musket.

"Make sail," he ordered. "Over two thousand yards. We'll make it, Mr. Adverse."

The *Wampanoag* surged forward. Both her masts were now blossoming out sail after sail. As yet there was nothing more from the fort. Then they saw some lanterns glimmer behind the embrasures in the morning twilight. The captain gave the ship a sudden wide yaw to port.

Flash, flash, flash. Along the molo smoke and thunder. The round shot smacked just to starboard and astern. Captain Elisha whistled as he twisted the spokes of the big wheel again and brought the *Wampanoag* back on her course.

"The trick is not to spill more'n half your wind," said he calmly.

"They are old Spanish pieces, captain," said Anthony.

"Aye, aye," said he, "and sleepy gunners behind 'em."

Flash, bang, smack.

"Kind o' vicious about it, be'n't they? But the stern of a ship ain't much to hit at nigh a mile in the glimmerin' dawn. Tide hasn't half ebbed yet and we'll keep our backside pinted at 'em clear over the bar."

"Lay aloft and douse them sails down, all hands. Philly, God dang *ye*, buckets, buckets!"

"The canvas is still wet from the rain last night, sir, isn't it?" asked Anthony.

"Yep," said the captain looking not too pleased. Then he laughed. "By God, ye're right, young man, ye're a cool one! . . . Belay that," he bellowed. "Collins, h'ist the grand old gridiron, let 'em see what they're shootin' at."

Well out from the lee of the land, the ship gathered way rapidly as she flashed down the roads with a bone in her teeth and the morning light tingeing her topsails. It was a long and lucky shot that would catch her now! But the French were evidently annoyed and continued to burn powder.

Thus with the fort thundering behind her and the Stars and Stripes snapping at her peak the *Wampanoag* rushed forward into the open sea.

END OF PART ONE

THE BEST OF THE BESTSELLERS
FROM WARNER BOOKS!

BLUE SKIES, NO CANDY by Gael Greene   (81-368, $2.50)
"How in the world were they able to print **Blue Skies, No Candy** without some special paper that resists Fahrenheit 451? (That's the burning point of paper!) This sizzling sexual oddyssey elevates Ms. Greene from her place at the head of the food-writing list into the Erica Jong pantheon of sexually liberated fictionalists."—**Liz Smith, New York Daily News**

DARE TO LOVE by Jennifer Wilde   (82-258, $2.25)
Who dared to love Elena Lopez? Who was willing to risk reputation and wealth to win the Spanish dancer who was the scandal of Europe? Kings, princes, great composers and writers . . . the famous and wealthy men of the 19th century vied for her affection, fought duels for her.

THIS LOVING TORMENT by Valerie Sherwood   (82-649, $2.25)
Perhaps she was too beautiful! Perhaps the brawling colonies would have been safer for a plainer girl, one more demure and less accomplished in language and manner. But Charity Woodstock was gloriously beautiful with pale gold hair and topaz eyes—and she was headed for trouble.

BLOOD OF THE BONDMASTER   (82-385, $2.25)
by Richard Tresillian
Bolder and bigger than **The Bondmaster, Blood of the Bondmaster** continues the tempestuous epic of Roxborough plantation, where slaves are the prime crop and the harvest is passion and rage.